NO ONE'S GOING TO FRIGHTEN MISS MUFFET AWAY

"You did good, doll," he said finally. "Made my job one helluva lot easier."

I felt my cheeks going warm at the praise. "Thanks."

His eyes narrowed, crinkling a little behind his ski mask and giving me the impression that he was grinning. "But you know, you shouldn't be out here alone at night, even if you *can* kick ass," he admonished. Then he reached up and twisted one of my ringlets around his gloved index finger and pulled gently before letting it spring back into place. "I'd hate to see harm come to a girl as pretty as you."

My eyes went wide. *Holy shit.* "Nicky Blue?" I gasped. "*You're* the Spider?" He jumped to his feet and took a few quick steps before I found my voice to cry out, "Wait! Nicky! It's okay—I know you!"

He halted midstride, and shook his head. "No, you don't," he said over his shoulder. "No one does. Not anymore."

The Transplanted Tales Series by Kate SeRine

RED

THE BETTER TO SEE YOU

ALONG CAME A SPIDER

Published by Kensington Publishing Corporation

Along CAME A Spider

A TRANSPLANTED TALES NOVEL

KATE SERINE

KENSINGTON BOOKS
Kensington Publishing Corp.
http://www.kensingtonbooks.com

KENSINGTON BOOKS are published by

Kensington Publishing Corp.
119 West 40th Street
New York, NY 10018

eISBN-13: 978-1-60183-121-7
eISBN-10: 1-60183-121-8
First Electronic Edition: August 2013

ISBN-13: 978-1-60183-130-9
ISBN-10: 1-60183-130-7
First Print Edition: August 2013

Printed in the United States of America

For R. A. S.
My ray of sunshine...

ACKNOWLEDGMENTS

As always, many thanks to my friends, family, and fans. Your love for the Transplanted Tales inspires me! And a big high five to the amazing group at Kensington. It is an honor to work with every single one of you!

Special thanks to my unbelievable agent, Nicole Resciniti. You keep me sane with your friendship, guidance, and encouragement. I don't know where I'd be without you, Nic! I also need to thank my agency "siblings," all very talented and supportive authors who have been there for me every step of the way.

And speaking of being there, loads of hugs and kisses to Cecy Robson and Kait Ballenger—two incredibly talented authors whom I have the privilege to call my friends. Thanks for all the laughter on the good days and the encouraging hugs on the bad ones. Love you gals!

Lastly, I have to take a moment to thank my dear friend Paul Parnell, who suggested the character of Rumpelstiltskin to me. Paul, I hope I did him justice! And special thanks to Kathryn Merkel for giving Rumpelstiltskin his "true" name.

Prologue

I remember darkness—deep, impenetrable. Not even a hint of ambient light in the void that had consumed me. And falling. I was tumbling through space and time in a nauseating spiral that forced the blood to my feet and sent another sort of blackness rushing toward me. Clinging desperately to consciousness, I curled into myself, wrapping my arms around my abdomen in an attempt to stop that sickening rush that made me want to vomit and sob at the same time.

A scream of terror surged up from the center of my chest, but I bit it back, forcing myself to remain in control. I had to keep it together, could not let the fear consume me. That's what my father had drilled into my head time and time again.

You must control your fear, Beatrice, or your fear will control you. Never let your mind slip into the abyss where chaos reigns....

I'd been there once before and had clawed my way out of the chasm one agonizingly pitiful inch at a time. And now I was falling again—but this time the abyss was not of my own making.

One moment I'd been playing on the floor of our cottage with my niece Mariella, and the next, my body had been snatched away from all I'd known and loved. I'd heard my family's cries of surprise, caught the look of horror and panic in my father's eyes as his arm shot out to grab my hand, but his fingertips had just barely brushed mine before I'd been jerked into the void.

And then I was falling. In darkness.

Suddenly there was light. A blinding flash that made me wince even though my eyes were already squeezed shut. Then a sudden impact jolted the breath from my lungs. I had to blink several times before I realized I was lying on my back in a field, staring up at a sky that was not familiar, at stars that didn't shine nearly as brightly as they should have.

Slowly, I sat up and looked around, seeing others nearby—just as dazed and disoriented as I was. They were Tales, some of whom I recognized from my little village. But we were no longer in Make Believe. That was clear. Gone was the scent of dew-kissed roses and sunshine on daisies. The air that now filled my lungs was stale, thick, heavy. The wind that whispered through the trees did not bring with it the laughter of fairies or the secrets of the pixies flitting about in the night. And the grass beneath me was no longer the velvety soft bed I'd lain upon as a child, watching the clouds drift lazily into fluffy white knights on pudgy steeds as they leisurely made their way to battle. Coarse and savage, *these* blades poked through my muslin dress, stabbing my skin like a thousand Lilliputian swords.

"Are you hurt?"

My gaze darted toward the sound of the voice. The man standing over me was devilishly handsome, his chiseled features stark and sharp, giving him an air of danger, but his dark amber eyes were kind as he gazed down at me.

"Are you all right?" he asked, phrasing the question differently in response to my blank stare.

This time I nodded and took the hand he extended, letting him pull me to my feet. "I think so."

"Good," he said, the corner of his mouth hitching up in a mischievous grin that completely altered his countenance. He lifted his hand and wrapped one of my buttercup yellow ringlets around his index finger. "Hate to see harm come to a girl as pretty as you."

I felt my cheeks growing warm at the intensity of his gaze and quickly looked away, not wanting to peer too deeply into those amber eyes for fear of what I might see. "What has happened?" I asked, glancing around the crowd as confusion and panic began to make them uneasy, their frightened voices growing louder. "Where are we?"

The man at my side shrugged and shoved his hands deep into his pockets. "Not in Make Believe, that's for damned sure."

I let my gaze drift over his shoulder and saw a tall Tale I recognized from the story of Aladdin trying to take control of the rapidly deteriorating situation, his deep voice booming over the din of sorrow. "My friends—please! You must remain calm!"

A woman with long black hair and eyes as blue as robins' eggs hurried past me, glancing my way and giving me a terse nod before joining Aladdin as he tried to herd the crowd toward a series of carriages drawn by black horses. "That was Tess Little," I breathed.

"Little Red Riding Hood?" my companion asked, his brows arching with interest.

I nodded. "Yes, but . . . Well, it can't be! She disappeared almost a hundred years ago with the others." My heart began to pound. "Have we been transplanted, too?"

He shook his head. "No idea, but I'll tell you one thing—I'm not letting them haul me in like a criminal just so I can find out. If I've broken out of Make Believe, I'm making the most of it."

At this, his eyes met and held mine. I felt the connection beginning and started to look away, but his gaze was so unguarded, so unapologetic, I let it come. And in that glimpse, I saw a soul so steadfast, so dauntless and true, that I gasped at the beauty of it.

It was rare that a Tale let me past his defenses, rarer still that I was so taken with what I saw. But here was an intensely intelligent and quietly courageous man who could command respect from his friends and instill fear in the hearts of those who weren't. He was also capable of genuine kindness and the deepest and most profound love. But I was shocked to see that he had absolutely no idea what a remarkable man he could be.

"Want to come with me?" he asked, grasping my hand in his and severing the connection between my soul and his.

I blinked at him, hardly daring to believe what he was saying. But more surprising was that I *did* want to go with him even though logic and reason warned me that such a thing was reckless and foolish. I swallowed hard, hating what I was about to say. "I cannot," I told him, wishing I had the courage to flout propriety and take my chances with a man whose name I didn't even know. "It wouldn't be proper."

He chuckled and pressed a kiss to the back of my hand. "Well, maybe some other time." He backed away, grinning a little sadly as he released my hand, his fingertips touching mine for just a moment before he gave me a wink and turned away.

"Wait!" I called, hurrying a few steps after him as he sauntered toward the tree line. "What's your name?"

He turned and offered me a rakishly charming grin that held more than a hint of mischief. "Nicky Blue."

"You there—with the curls!" I started at the voice behind me and whirled around to see Tess Little striding toward me, her long black duster flapping around her dark skirt and cherry red high-button boots. "Time to go."

I obediently moved toward the carriages with her. "Is it true?" I asked. "Have we been transplanted?"

"Afraid so," she replied. "But don't worry—we have people with the FMA who will help you settle in."

"The FMA?"

"Fairytale Management Authority," she explained. "I'll tell you everything on the way to headquarters. By the way—I'm Tess Little. But everyone calls me Red."

"Beatrice Muffet," I replied, attempting a smile. "Everyone pretty much just calls me Beatrice. Or Ms. Muffet." I chuckled a little. "Except my niece Mariella—she has trouble pronouncing my name." My voice caught in my throat, the words lodging around the lump of sorrow that had rapidly developed at the thought of never seeing little Mari again. I coughed, forcing my emotions away, and blinked rapidly to clear the tears that pricked the corner of my eyes. "She calls me Trish."

Tess motioned me toward the last remaining carriage. "Well, welcome to the Here and Now, Trish."

I placed my foot on the step, but paused and turned to search for Nicky Blue, hoping that perhaps he had changed his mind and had decided to come with the rest of us after all. My heart sank when I didn't see him. I sighed, a part of me already regretting that I hadn't gone with him. But it was too late to change my mind. Nicky Blue had vanished, having faded deep into the shadows like a spider in the night.

Chapter One

I pulled on a pair of latex gloves, the no-nonsense snap as comforting as always. As the head of Forensics for the Fairytale Management Authority, I never quite knew what I might find at a crime scene, but as I strode toward the shadowy figure standing at the mouth of the narrow alley on Chicago's South Side, I took a deep breath and let it out slowly, mentally preparing myself for what always came next.

"What do we have, Grimm?"

Nate Grimm, the FMA's lead detective and part-time Reaper, doffed his fedora and ran a hand through his dark hair, stirring the shadows that surrounded him. "It's not good, Trish."

I raised my brows, perplexed by the fact that he seemed a little distressed. The guy had been a Reaper for centuries. Seeing him rattled by death was enough to drop a cold stone of dread smack-dab in the middle of my stomach. "Is that why you called me personally instead of going through headquarters?"

He nodded. "I didn't want Red to show up here."

That stone of dread got a little heavier. If he was keeping something from his fiancée, who was six months pregnant with his child, this was going to be even worse than I'd thought. "She'll be here eventually," I told him. "I was in the lab when you called. My assistant knows I went out. Tess is probably already on her way, and she's going to be seriously pissed when she finds out you were trying to keep this from her."

Nate placed his fedora back on his head, pulling it down a little over his eyes. "Come take a look and you'll know why."

I followed him into the alley and felt the hair on my arms begin to rise even though I was bundled up against Chicago's bone-numbing February winds. I'd been working for the FMA as a coroner and forensics investigator for going on a century, but that initial hit of negative energy surrounding a violent death still had the power to bring me to my knees if I let it get to me. And this one was particularly nasty, sending a chill of apprehension up and down my spine. I swallowed hard against the bile rising in my throat and focused on the details of the crime scene, making note of everything I saw and cataloging it in my head to include in the report I'd write later that night.

I glanced up as I walked, searching the network of fire escapes for anyone who might be lingering to watch as his deeds were discovered by the authorities, but the rusting ladders were deserted. And no one peeked out from behind the curtains of the dilapidated apartment building. Apparently, whatever had occurred had gone down quietly, not drawing the attention of any of the people living in the low-rent apartments.

Dumpsters heavy with trash that wouldn't be picked up until morning lined the length of the alley in evenly spaced groups of two. It was just beyond one of these groupings in the darkest part of the alley that Nate paused and jerked his chin toward the shadows. "There."

I peered into the darkness and gasped, my arm coming up reflexively so I could bury my nose in the sleeve of my FMA standard-issue wool pea coat. "Shit."

I shook my head slightly, clearing away my emotional response, and ran the facts in my head. White male, medium build, sandy blond hair. Deceased. But the manner of his death was what got me. His throat had been ripped open. No, that wasn't exactly true. It had been *gnawed* open. And his blood had been drained from his body so quickly, his skin had shriveled and sunken in upon itself.

Frowning, I pulled my small flashlight from my pocket, shining it on the ground, the wall, the dumpsters, but there were no blood splatters that I could see in the immediate area. He'd either been killed elsewhere and dumped here, or drained so swiftly no blood had even dripped from the wounds. Either way, not good. I'd seen wounds like this before and knew the kind of creature behind it.

"Vampire," I announced, a wave of apprehension washing over me again as I uttered the word aloud. I heard Nate curse roundly under his breath. There was no shortage of vampires that had crossed over from the folklore of Make Believe—and even some who'd already been hanging out in the Here and Now long before we ever showed up—but their attacks rarely resulted in death. We made damned sure that our bloodsuckers were rehabilitated and taught how to control their cravings to keep them from showing up in the Ordinaries' tabloid newspapers and blowing our cover among the humans.

Every once in a while one would lose it and we'd need to call in FMA's Damage Control agents to spin some ridiculous story that was promptly debunked and then forgotten. But this particular attack—so savage and brutal—wasn't like anything I'd seen in decades. Not since—

"Dracula," Nate growled. "He's back, isn't he?"

I glanced over my shoulder at the Reaper, understanding the deadly edge in his voice. It'd been almost two years since the infamous vampire had gone to ground after being involved in a series of killings perpetrated by an enchantress named Sebille Fenwick. Nate had killed Sebille when she'd tried to add Red to her list of victims, but a radical group of Tales had tried to raise her from the dead a few months ago, believing she would lead them to a new day where Tales ruled supreme in our adopted world. I'd been around to witness that incident first-hand, having nearly become one of Sebille's victims myself. But Lavender Seelie, Cinderella's former fairy godmother and the reason why we'd been transplanted in the first place, had killed Sebille for good, making it impossible for her to ever return.

Knowing that Sebille and Dracula had been in league once before, I'd done a full investigation of the events at The Refuge, but had found no connection between Vlad Dracula and the plot to resurrect Sebille Fenwick. The findings were comforting in that he hadn't been behind the plan, but had also left me with more questions.

Like what the hell Dracula *had* been up to since he'd disappeared.

There'd been murmurings of sightings now and then—but they always turned out to be unsubstantiated, Tales who'd been spooked and just blamed the ultimate villain at large. What *was* indisputable, however, were accounts of Ordinary women found dazed and confused with two puncture wounds in their skin. Unfortunately, even then we couldn't confirm anything beyond that a Tale was to blame.

I had my suspicions that Vlad was responsible, taunting us, leaving a trail of blood-soaked bread crumbs as part of his game to draw Red out so he could make his move and finally claim her for his own. I couldn't prove it, but my findings would've been enough to send Tess after him. She had a score to settle and was determined to bring him down at any cost—even if it put her in serious danger of getting herself killed.

Which was why I'd been doctoring my reports and burying any evidence that could've been even remotely connected to the bloodsucker of legend.

I'd promised Nate I'd do whatever I could to keep Tess safe, and I was going to keep that promise no matter what. Not just because I'd struck a deal with Death or because Tess Little was my closest friend and more like a sister to me than my own back in Make Believe. The fact was, we Tales needed her. She was one of the only reasons we had it as good as we did in the Here and Now, and I'd protect that safety and security with my life if I had to.

"Shit," Nate muttered. "Looks like we've got company."

I turned toward the mouth of the alley and saw Red's brand-new Range Rover screeching to a halt, a black FMA van right behind her. "I'll get what I can from the victim," I told Nate. "Then you can take his soul."

Nate gave me a tight nod, then headed toward Red, starting his apology before he'd even reached her. I grinned for a moment, imagining the kind of hell Nate was catching, then turned back to the victim. The dead man was a Tale—the auralike impression Tales could sense in one another still hovered around him, although it was growing faint. I analyzed the blurring edges. He'd been dead only about an hour.

Damn, Nate was fast.

I squatted down in front of the victim and carefully lifted his suit jacket, looking for a wallet or some other form of identification, but he'd been stripped of anything that could make my job easy.

Figures.

I braced my elbows on my thighs and took a deep breath, preparing for what came next. The man's eyes were wide open, glazed over with that faraway gaze that was unique to the dead. Swallowing my nerves and pushing my fear aside, I locked onto his gaze and felt the connection taking hold.

Now for the fun part.

In seconds, I was drifting into the dead man's psyche, latching on to the last impressions seared into his memory before his light had been snuffed out.

The images came fast and furious: *Tingling on his tongue as the Cristal slipped past his lips. Euphoria and arousal. Blurred faces of two women—grotesque and surreal, like reflections in fun house mirrors—pawing at his clothing, pushing him down onto the bed, bright red fingernails clawing at his chest, then slipping past his waistband to roughly caress. Animalistic sounds of lovemaking and release. Then—just as he was collapsing into postcoital exhaustion— fangs plunging deep into his jugular, drawing out his blood with a snarl that reverberated through him, a persistent buzz vibrating just below his skin. He wanted to scratch, tear it out, but his limbs were paralyzed. He couldn't move. The terror pumped adrenaline into his system in a fervid rush, making his heart pound furiously against his breast.*

Panic rose up from the depth of his gut and he tried to scream, but no sound came. More fangs sank into his skin, drawing away his life one great pull at a time. He was drifting now, the images growing dark as death edged closer. He was cold, could no longer feel his toes, his fingertips, his legs. . . . As the shadows drew closer, an image came to him of a beautiful woman who moved with feline grace, and regret brought tears to his eyes. He felt a single warm tear slip from the corner of his eye and marked its path as it trickled across his temple and toward his ear. And then—

"Hey, Trish."

I started so violently, I toppled over, ass-planting on the pavement. "Damn it, McCain!" I snapped, casting an irritated glance toward the Enforcer who'd interrupted my connection and stolen the dead man's final image from me. "You can't interrupt me when I'm reading the dead."

"Ah, hell—I'm sorry," he said, having the good grace to look contrite. "Go ahead and do what you need to do. I won't say a word."

"Won't work," I grumbled, pushing up to my feet and waving away his offer of help. "I only get one shot." I brushed the dirty snow from the back of my coat and looked over at McCain, taking him in at a glance. Black male. Close-cropped hair. Brown eyes. Athletic build. Six feet two inches, two hundred twenty pounds of lean muscle. After nearly two years with the FMA, he was still considered the new guy. The kid was doing everything he possibly could to try to impress the higher-ups but hadn't quite made the marks yet.

"Was there something you needed, McCain?" I asked, trying to be patient as he stood there, rocking a little on his heels.

He shoved his hands deep into his coat pockets. "Red sent me. She thought maybe you'd like—"

I held up my hand, cutting him off. "Let me stop you right there, sparky, before you embarrass yourself," I said, my tone a little pitying. "I'm not going out with you."

He blinked at me. "What?"

I sighed. "Listen, I know Tess totally busts your balls and makes you nervous as hell, but *I* think you're doing a pretty amazing job. And, I'll admit, you're seriously good-looking and seem to be a great guy—you know, once you get past the constant ass-kissing."

His brows came together. "Um, thanks."

"So, really, it's nothing personal," I explained. "You're the tenth guy she's tried to set me up with in the last few months, but I'm married to the job. I don't have time for a personal life. So, you can tell Red thanks, but I don't need her to play matchmaker just because she's happy and wants all of her friends to be happy, too."

He nodded. "Okay. I can do that. But she only sent me down here to see if you wanted some coffee. She's sending me on a Starbucks run since it looks like we'll be here awhile."

I felt the heat rising in my face. "Oh."

Alex jabbed his thumb over his shoulder. "So . . . you, uh, need anything then?"

I stripped off my latex gloves and wiped my wrist against my forehead. "Yeah. Thanks. That'd be great. Cream, no sugar."

He looked a little uncomfortable for a moment as if trying to figure out how to gracefully make his exit. "So, I guess I'll just . . ."

"Yeah, yeah. Thanks."

As soon as he turned away, I let my head fall back and closed my eyes for a moment. "Nice, Trish," I murmured. "Way to make an ass of yourself."

When I opened my eyes again, I glanced down toward the opening of the alley where Nate stood with Red, his body half wrapped around hers, a protective posture they often shared. Her arms were crossed over her chest, her chin tilted up and away from him in anger, but it was mostly for show at this point. She just wasn't quite ready to let him off the hook yet. Then, as I watched, Nate bent and pressed a tender kiss to Red's brow and rested his hand on her belly. In response, she turned and gave him a pert look but accepted his brief kiss, letting him know she'd forgive him, but he'd be making it up to her as soon as they got home. I looked away again before envy could take hold, and turned back to the dead man, wondering who the beautiful woman was who'd invaded his thoughts before dying.

Was she his lover? Wife? Unrequited love?

With a twinge of sadness I wondered what beloved face would bring me comfort in my dying moments. Whose eyes would I picture and long to see just once more? It was a question I'd asked myself over and over again since coming over, but the answer never changed. I'd had a few lovers over the years, both Tale and Ordinary, but no matter who I'd let into my life, there was no one else who'd ever come to mind.

I drew from my pocket a handkerchief with the initials *NB* lovingly stitched in black silk thread. Nicky Blue. I couldn't even guess how many times I'd thought of him since the day we'd come over. I'd often wondered if he ever thought of me, too, but when I'd finally come face to face with him again two years ago, the answer to that question had been made crystal clear. After all, how could he think of me when he didn't even remember me?

He'd walked into my lab when I was analyzing evidence from the Sebille Fenwick case—not to see *me* but to bring additional evidence to Red and Nate. And then he'd greeted me, not like an old friend but as a new acquaintance, and had handed me the handkerchief to wipe a smudge of blood from my cheek.

I didn't really expect to see him again after that. But after his wife, Juliet, had been tragically killed and Nicky grievously wounded in a confrontation with Sebille Fenwick, I'd been one of the first on the scene. I'd had to witness the pain and torment in the eyes of the man I loved as I tried to stabilize him enough to get him to the Tale hospital. He'd gripped my hand, silently pleading, his gaze holding mine. He hadn't needed to speak—I knew he was asking me to take care of his lovely bride, to make sure she was treated well. I'd nodded, letting him know he could count on me. And I'd made good on that promise.

I just hoped I'd never have to tell him what I saw when I'd looked into *her* eyes just before I let Nate take her soul to its final rest. With a sigh, I tucked the handkerchief back into my pocket. Seeing as how Nicky had gone off the grid after Juliet's death, the odds of me ever having to face that dilemma were pretty slim.

I made my way to the mouth of the alley and jerked my chin at Nate. "All yours."

"So, what did you see?" Red asked. "Anything to help you identify the killer?"

"Killers," I corrected. "Plural. They were women, but I didn't get much else."

Her eyes narrowed at me. "Really? That's all?"

I squirmed a little. "Vampires," I admitted, knowing she'd see through me in a heartbeat if I strayed too far from the truth. "But not Vlad. I didn't sense him at all." I frowned. "There was something weird about these women. They had a Tale aura to them but . . . I don't know. It felt wrong."

Her brows shot up. "Do we need to have a chat with some of our contacts, let them know there could be a problem?"

I barely held back a groan. I knew exactly what she meant by "contacts." We didn't out ourselves to many, but there were a select few Ordinaries who'd been brought into our confidence—sometimes whether we liked it or not. So far they hadn't divulged any of our secrets, but there was always the possibility that one of them could let something slip, which made me nervous as hell about sharing any intel.

"I'd rather hold off getting in touch for a while longer," I told her, pulling on my winter gloves to keep my fingertips from going numb. "No sense dealing with them any more than we have to."

Red gave me a tight nod. "Works for me. I'll just—" She winced, sucking in air through her teeth, and bent forward a little, her hand going reflexively to her belly.

I closed the gap in an instant and put my arm around her. "Tess, you okay?"

She nodded quickly, but her eyes were a little confused. "Yeah, I'm good."

I gave her a disapproving look as she straightened. "When did this start?"

"Earlier today," she told me, her voice just above a whisper. "It's nothing, though. I'm sure everything's fine."

I glanced around us to make sure none of the other agents on the scene were listening too closely. "We have no idea what your pregnancy will be like," I reminded her. "Considering Nate's not really a Tale, there could be complications we can only guess at. The minute he gets back, Nate's taking you to the hospital to get checked out. Understood?"

When she met my gaze I saw fear there—something I'd never seen in her eyes before. Even so, Tess Little wasn't the kind of person to admit she needed help. She opened her mouth to protest, but I cut her off. "Just go! I got this." I laughed a little. "I mean, seriously— the guy's already dead. What could possibly go wrong?"

Chapter Two

I sipped at my coffee and cranked up the heater in the van as I watched the Investigators pack up their equipment. They'd finished photographing the entire crime scene and were loading the body into the van to send back to the lab for further examination. Nothing to do now but pack it in and call it a night.

"I'm surprised *he* hasn't showed up," Alex McCain mumbled, pulling his gloves back on as he prepared to leave the warmth of my van. Why he'd felt the need to keep me company was beyond me. He hadn't really said a word the entire two hours we'd sat there together.

"Sorry?" I asked, not really needing further explanation. I knew who he was talking about.

"The Spider," Alex said. "He's been popping up all over the place lately, coming in, kicking some ass, and disappearing before the Ordinary cops arrive. The New Orleans office said he took out a couple of Tales down their way, though, so he appears to be an equal opportunity ass kicker. It's like something out of a comic book."

I grunted. "Comic book heroes don't get themselves killed by butting in where they don't belong," I mumbled. "The guy's a vigilante and he's breaking the law just as much as the criminals he's taking down. Don't romanticize it."

Alex shrugged, then hopped out of the van and made his way to the unmarked sedan he'd driven to the scene. He lifted a hand and offered me a cautious smile. I forced a smile in return, still feeling the sting of humiliation from my earlier tirade. As soon as he drove around the corner, I blew out a relieved breath and put the van into gear.

Thank God that was over.

I was just pulling away from the curb when I caught a sudden movement out of the corner of my eye. I slammed on the brakes and threw the van into park, then squinted into the darkness where the light of the street lamps didn't quite reach. As I watched, the shadows shifted, darting to the left and slithering along the bricks before vanishing into the alleyway.

"What the hell?" I muttered. Without stopping to think, I hopped out of the van and hurried down the alley, my eyes searching for the false shadows. Only as my hair began to rise on the back of my neck and a heavy feeling of being watched descended upon me did I stop to consider what I might be walking into. "Oh, shit."

I whirled around to race back to my van, but slid to a halt. Blocking my path was a woman with long blond hair who was clothed only in a cocktail dress and stiletto heels, the cold obviously not bothering her in the least. As I stared at the woman, her lips curled in a mirthless smile, revealing the tips of her fangs. I immediately recognized that bloodthirsty snarl from the dead man's thoughts. Not waiting around to be a midnight snack, I spun and sprinted toward the other end of the alley. It was blocked by a chain-link fence, but I scaled it in a matter of seconds and dropped down on the other side. Only to find her companion waiting for me.

The brunette hissed at me like a cat, baring her fangs. She lunged, her hand outstretched to take hold of my throat. At the last instant, I sidestepped her attack and swung my fist, catching her hard on the side of the head and using her own momentum to take her down. Then I dropped, driving my knee into the back of her neck. I heard an ominous crack and she screeched with rage, flailing around, her limbs no longer under her control. I scrambled back to my feet, but a sudden impact knocked me to the ground, sending me sliding across the snow-slick pavement. Before I could scramble to my feet, someone grabbed my arm and twisted. I cried out as the bones snapped and white-hot pain shot through my wrist.

The blonde launched herself up, dragging me with her as if I weighed nothing, and hurled me toward the side of the building. I grunted as I crashed into the bricks and dropped, a pile of cardboard boxes breaking my fall.

I cradled my broken wrist against my chest as I rolled up to my knees, but the blonde was already on me, grabbing me by the hair and jerking my head up. She crouched down next to me and hissed in my ear, baring her fangs, preparing to plunge them into my neck and drain me dry. I whimpered and cringed away, forcing her to lean with me. Feeling her balance shift, I brought my good arm up behind her neck and flipped her over my shoulder. The second she hit the ground, I drove the heel of my palm into her nose. She howled in pain, but I didn't wait around to go at her again—there was no way I could take down a vampire on my own. The best I could hope for was a little time to escape to someplace with lots of people around, where it was less likely she'd attack.

I glanced over my shoulder as I ran, discouraged to see she was already on her feet and prowling toward me. There was no need for her to sprint after me—if she wanted to catch up to me, all she had to do was pour on her vampire speed and I was a goner. Worse yet, the brunette had recovered from her partial paralysis and was joining in. They stalked forward slowly, their heads lowered between their shoulders, their eyes blazing red with feral light, obviously done screwing around.

"Shit," I spat, hugging my arm closer and running faster. My snow boots slipped on the ice and snow, but I kept my footing and made a break for the opening of the alley. Then suddenly the brunette was in front of me, looking righteously pissed off.

I spun around to dart back in the other direction, but the blonde was right behind me. She grinned, knowing our little game of cat and mouse was officially over.

Son of a bitch.

I glanced around, searching frantically for some escape, but it was useless. Unless I suddenly discovered some latent ability to leap tall buildings in a single bound, I was well and truly hosed. I pressed my lips together and squared off. If I was going down, I wasn't going to make it easy. They'd have to earn my blood.

"Come on, you bitch!" I growled at the blonde. "You want a piece of me? Bring it on!"

She leaped forward like she was on a spring. My eyes went wide, my courageous last stand suddenly not such a brilliant idea. But a split second later, she jerked back with a screech, her hand clawing at a small black arrow lodged in her shoulder. I heard an answering screech from the brunette and swung around in time to see her head snap back as an arrow pierced her eye.

What the hell?

There was a scuffling noise behind me that brought my head around in time to see the blonde struggling with a figure dressed in black fatigues and wearing a black ski mask. As I watched, he swung his fist, catching her jaw with a right hook, then slamming her chin with a left uppercut that knocked her on her ass. In the next instant, he had a knee on her chest and snatched from his ammo belt something that looked like a railroad stake. The blonde didn't even have time to react as he drove it down into the center of her chest.

I hadn't realized I was holding my breath until it burst from me with a gasp. But my relief was short-lived. An arm came around my throat, cutting off my air. I drove my elbow into my attacker's ribs, but it barely fazed her. I grabbed her arm and tucked my chin down to take some of the pressure from my esophagus, then drove the edge of my snow boot down along her exposed shin, making her howl in pain.

"Get down!"

My eyes darted toward the sound of the man's voice. He stood over the body of the blonde, a small crossbow aimed at the brunette. I bit down on the vampire's arm as hard as I could, drawing her tainted blood. When she roared with rage, her grip loosening for a fraction of a second, I dropped, rolling out of the way as the man in black fired the crossbow. The arrow struck the center of the woman's chest. Her eyes went wide for a fraction of a second before she crumpled into a permanently dead heap.

So this was the infamous Spider . . .

I totally took back everything I'd said about the guy being no better than the criminals he brought down. He was my new BFF. I was tempted to see if he was a bit parched after the ass kicking he'd just doled out and maybe wanted to join me for a super stiff drink at Ever Afters, but then the mind-numbing pain in my wrist reminded me I probably had other business to tend to first.

Out of breath, I scooted myself back with my good arm until I could lean against one of the dumpsters. My adrenaline left me in a rush, and I was suddenly completely exhausted. I closed my eyes and let my head fall back.

"Are you hurt?"

My eyes snapped open, my stomach clenching painfully. There was something so familiar about that voice. . . . "What?"

My rescuer squatted down in front of me. "Are you all right?"

I blinked at him, suddenly experiencing a serious case of déjà vu. The man's tone was rough, clipped, and there was no hint of mischief or roguish charm. *Still* . . .

"My wrist is broken," I said a little breathlessly. "But it's already healing. I'll be fine by tomorrow."

He gave me a tight nod and started to rise, but then seemed to reconsider and resumed his crouch before me. He studied me for a long moment, giving me a good glimpse of his eyes, but they were in shadow, obscuring the color, and he was completely on his guard. There was no way I was getting in.

"You did good, doll," he said finally. "Made my job one helluva lot easier."

I felt my cheeks going warm at the praise. "Thanks."

His eyes narrowed, crinkling a little behind his ski mask and giving me the impression that he was grinning. "But you know, you shouldn't be out here alone at night, even if you *can* kick ass," he admonished. Then he reached up and twisted one of my ringlets around his gloved index finger and pulled gently before letting it spring back into place. "I'd hate to see harm come to a girl as pretty as you."

My eyes went wide. *Holy shit.* "Nicky Blue?" I gasped. "*You're* the Spider?" He jumped to his feet and took a few quick steps before I found my voice to cry out, "Wait! Nicky! It's okay—I know you!"

He halted midstride and shook his head. "No, you don't," he said over his shoulder. "No one does. Not anymore."

I scrambled awkwardly to my feet, my knees still shaky from my encounter with the vampires, but when I looked up again he was gone. I turned a full circle, searching for him in the shadows, but he had slipped away as silently and mysteriously as he'd come. I let out a disappointed sigh.

"You're wrong, Nicky Blue," I announced to the darkness. "Nobody knows you better than I do."

Chapter Three

"How's Red?" I asked Nate from my seat in the back of the ambulance as the FMA medic wrapped my wrist to help it finish healing properly.

"False alarm," Nate told me, his relief easy to read in his voice in spite of his usual calm tone. "But they're keeping her overnight for observation, just to be sure."

I wiggled my fingers a little for the medic to show him I could still move them. "Sorry to drag you out again tonight, Nate. I know you'd rather be at her side."

"Gran's with her," he said, neither confirming nor denying my supposition. "I'll head back as soon as we're finished here."

I nodded, watching the FMA cleanup crew doing their thing for the second time tonight. Alex was running the show in Red's absence, and doing a damned good job of it from what I could tell. He was just directing the photographers to pack it in and let the team bag the bodies when the sound of an approaching vehicle brought all of our heads around.

"What the hell is *he* doing here?" Nate mumbled.

I groaned, then offered my medic a tight smile and nod. "Thanks, Barry. That should do it." Then, steeling myself, I hopped down from the back of the ambulance to go greet our visitor.

"There's nothing for you here, Spalding," I spat, my lack of enthusiasm at seeing the Ordinary punctuated by the throbbing in my wrist.

Ian Spalding offered me a patronizing grin as he slammed the door of his black Lincoln. "Well, if it isn't Trish Muffet," he drawled. "It's been a long time."

"Not long enough," I snapped. "I thought we had an agreement."

He gave me another smile, this one the style of smirk unique to those so completely confident of victory, it costs them nothing to be cordial. "The Agency stands by that agreement," he assured me, inclining his head a little. "However, I'm afraid *you're* the one overstepping bounds this time."

I traded a glance with Nate. "What do you mean? These vampires are Tales, not Ordinaries."

Ian raised his dark brows. "You sure about that?"

Well, no, actually I *wasn't*. I'd told Red I sensed something strange about them when I'd read the dead man, and then seeing the vamps in person had confirmed my suspicions that something was decidedly *off*. In fact, the last time I'd seen a Tale signature like theirs, it had belonged to a little Ordinary boy who'd been raised from the dead by Sebille Fenwick's flunkies. But there was no way in hell I was going to tell Ian Spalding that.

Ian was a member of a shadowy US government organization that helped police the unexplained of the Ordinary world. When tales of alien encounters really picked up in the fifties, these guys became known in modern folklore as Men in Black. But they referred to themselves simply as the Agency. And they'd existed well before any aliens—real or Tale—had entered the scene.

From what I understood, we'd had our first encounter with the Agency about five years before I came over, but thanks to Al Addin's powers of persuasion—and a deal to keep them informed of anything we came across that wasn't ours—they eventually agreed to leave us alone as long as we stayed out of trouble. Unfortunately, the werewolf murders perpetrated by Sebille Fenwick two years earlier had spilled out into their jurisdiction when an Ordinary named Molly O'Grady had become one of the victims. Al had had to do a lot of smooth talking to set things to rights again.

"As soon as I'm finished with the bodies, I'll be happy to turn them over to you to experiment on," I told Ian, not bothering to hide the disgust in my voice. "You guys are good at that from what I understand."

His mouth quirked up in one corner, but there was a hint of barely disguised anger this time. "Oh, I don't know.... I think we've managed to exhibit an admirable amount of self-control, especially where a few potential specimens are concerned."

"Self-control?" I hissed, getting up in his grill. "Seducing me to try to get a peek at my ability was your definition of self-control?"

He shrugged. "Hey, we could've just thrown you into a lab, hooked you up to a bunch of machines, done a little slice-and-dice number on your brain. But instead we opted for a more *entertaining* approach."

"You arrogant, self-righteous—" I lunged forward, my uninjured hand balled into a fist, ready to knock that smug expression from his face.

Nate snatched me up around the waist and swung me away before I could get in a good swing, and plopped me back down on my feet at a safe distance from Ian. "He's not worth the paperwork, Trish."

Ian held up his hand in truce. "I didn't come here to rehash what happened between us, Muffet. I just want the vampires."

"You can shove them up your ass," I hissed. "You're not getting them."

"I'm afraid you don't have a choice," Ian said with an indifferent shrug. "They're part of an open investigation."

"What investigation?" Nate asked, the shadows around his face growing darker.

Ian glanced at Nate, noticeably uncomfortable with the Reaper questioning him directly. "Seems there's a vigilante going around knocking off vamps. Shows up out of nowhere, takes them out, then disappears before we can arrive at the scene. We've nicknamed him the Spider." Here Ian turned his attention back to me, pegging me with a pointed look, which I pretended to ignore. "You know a thing or two about spiders, don't you, Trish? Care to tell me what you know about our guy?"

My blood went cold, sending a chill through me, but I just lifted my chin a notch. "Piss off, Ian. I'm not telling you jack shit. If it's your investigation, get approval from Al, and then you can have the bodies. Until then, you can go fu—"

"Oh, would you look at that!" Ian interrupted, producing a folded document from his pocket. "What is *this*?" He made a show of looking it over. "Could it be an acquisition form signed by the Director of the FMA?"

Nate snatched it from Ian's hand and opened it up so I could read it with him. "It looks legit," he muttered. "We're going to have to hand them over."

I shook my head. "I'm calling Al." I stomped a few paces away and dialed Al's emergency number. He picked up on the second ring. Before he could even speak, I barked, "What the hell are you thinking?"

"Hello to you, too," he drawled.

"I'm not handing them over," I said, speaking low into the phone. "I need to get a look at these vampires, Al. There's something odd about them."

"Apparently, you're not the only one who has noticed that fact," he pointed out. "I'm sorry, Trish. There's nothing I could do this time. They've got us by the balls right now. If they expose us—"

"Who'd believe them?" I practically shrieked. I took a deep breath and let it out slowly, then said in a calmer tone, "We're fictional characters made real, Al. Let them tell whoever they want—no one would believe them."

"People believe anything if they hear it often enough," Al replied. "And the Agency has the power to make it really bad for us if we don't cooperate, Trish. You still have the victim. Give them the other bodies."

I huffed, not believing that the man I'd looked up to and admired for his fearless self-sacrifice and unwavering principles was giving in so easily. "Al—"

"That's an order, Trish."

I hung up without another word and pocketed my phone, then paced a few furious steps one direction and then another before getting it together. I strode over to Alex and said through clenched teeth, "Tell the team to pack it in."

His brows shot up. "What?"

"Just do it," I snapped. "Right now. Tell everyone to drop what they're doing and get in the vans."

He frowned at me in confusion, but said, "You got it."

I marched back over to where Nate and Ian still waited. "Go ahead and take off, Nate," I told him. "Go be with Tess."

Then I cast an acerbic glance toward Ian, biting back the furious words racing through my head as I brushed by him, knocking into his shoulder as I passed.

"So does this mean we're squared away?" Ian called after me.

I merely lifted my good hand and offered him a very pointed reply.

Chapter Four

I flipped on the light in the foyer of my apartment and tossed my keys onto the credenza as I locked and bolted the door behind me. The familiar sounds of homecoming were answered by the nearly silent padding of paws. Within seconds, I felt the comforting bump of a feline head rubbing against my calf and heard the low buzzing purr of greeting.

I bent and picked up the armful of gray fluff and nuzzled against her for a moment. "Hi, baby," I whispered. "Did you miss me?"

Sasha nuzzled under my chin, assuring me she had. I grinned and let her hop to the floor to lead me into the kitchen for her dinner. Or was it breakfast? The poor thing's schedule was as screwed up as mine these days. I filled her bowl, then set out some fresh water and gave her a good scratch behind the ears before leaving her to her meal. I was just exiting the kitchen when Sasha suddenly began to growl, her fur standing on end, her head low between her shoulders as she peered around me.

I whipped around, fully expecting to see someone standing there, but the room was empty. "What's the matter, Sasha?" I asked, frowning at her. Her growl faded a bit but she was still on alert, her eyes never leaving the doorway even as she resumed eating.

A little unnerved by her unusual behavior, I did a quick walk-through, turning on all the lights in my living room and dining area as I went. Finding nothing out of the ordinary was almost as unsettling as if I'd come upon a burglar trying to abscond with my meager possessions. Just to be on the safe side, I walked the perimeter of the apartment, double-checking the locks on the doors and windows and the sliding door that opened onto my balcony.

Satisfied that all was still secure, I headed for the bathroom, slipping out of my button-down as I went and tossing it into the hamper. My khakis were pretty much ruined, the knee of one leg ripped out from my altercation with the vampires, but I tossed them into the hamper anyway. Standing before my bathroom mirror in nothing but my pale blue tank and panties, I met my own gaze, noticing that lack of sleep was already bringing out dark circles under my eyes. I pulled my hands through the curls that came down to just below my chin, then watched them with a sigh as they sprung back into place.

God, no wonder Nicky had called me "doll." What grown woman had ultrablond freaking ringlets? And there wasn't a damned thing I could do about them. I'd tried cutting them, coloring them, straightening them. . . . Nothing worked. No matter what I tried, my curls would be back to their ol' springy selves by morning.

Of course, if my ringlets made me look younger than I was, my eyes made up for it. After all I'd seen over the years, there was an ancientness to them that was sometimes a little disconcerting even to *me*. I leaned closer to the mirror, peering deep into the dark green gaze that stared back at me, wondering for probably the trillionth time what I'd see in *that* person's soul if I could get a glimpse.

Would it be memories of Make Believe, of family and friends that I'd left behind, or would the horrors I'd witnessed since coming to the Here and Now override those happier images? I'd tried to purge my mind of all the terrifying sights—the memories of the criminally insane, distorted and surreal; the murderous and depraved thoughts of those who were evil at their very core; the innocent driven mad with terror before their final seconds—but I had a feeling they were all there somewhere, haunting the shadowy corners of my brain.

The sudden and completely foreign sound of giggling brought me around with a startled gasp.

What the hell?

My heart pounding, I snatched back the shower curtain, shivering when I found the bathtub empty. Frowning, I opened the bathroom door and poked my head out, taking in the rest of the apartment in a glance. With a shrug, I closed the door again and started the water for a shower. "Just your imagination, Trish," I muttered. "You've been working *way* too hard."

A moment later, I stepped into the shower and let the steaming hot water wash over me again. My entire body was beginning to ache from the beating I'd taken from the vampires, and my wrist was still throbbing. I awkwardly managed to wash my hair with one hand while trying to keep the wrapping around my wrist dry, and had just finished rinsing off when I felt an icy blast of wind. I shivered violently at the sudden change in temperature and poked my head out from behind the shower curtain. The door to the bathroom stood wide open.

Huh. I could've sworn . . .

"Sasha?" I called, expecting to see the cat tucked into some secret hiding place in the bathroom, but she padded in from the other room at the sound of my voice and offered me a cautious *meow* as if she was as puzzled as I was by the open door. I shivered again, but shrugged off the creepiness with a forced laugh. "Jeez, Trish, get a grip! You get jumped by a couple of vampires and you suddenly go all paranoid?"

I quickly finished my shower and pulled on my favorite blue and black plaid flannel pajama pants and a black T-shirt with a skull and crossbones blazoned across the chest, then headed back out to the living room to my desk and booted up my computer. Even though I was seriously freaking tired, I wanted to capture the events of the evening along with my impressions of the victim as well as his vampire assailants before I turned in.

Sasha padded over and twisted around my ankles and the legs of the chair in which I sat, the soft drone of her purring so warm and comforting, I felt my lids growing heavy as I typed. I'd only managed to get through my thoughts on the victim when my head dropped suddenly, startling me awake. I glanced around guiltily, my face going warm, embarrassed to be caught dozing. But then I chuckled at my reaction. Why be embarrassed? Who the hell was going to see me? Sasha? Hell, I could drop dead in my apartment and no one would even notice until I didn't show up for work the next day. And even then they'd probably just think I was out on a case.

My shoulders sagged. God, how depressing was that?

The same feminine giggle brought my head around with a gasp.

"Who's there?" I demanded.

I scanned the corners of my apartment, looking for signs of a pixie or some other sprite who'd sneaked in to wreak a little havoc on the poor, overworked FMA agent, but even as I glanced around, I heard the floorboards creak near my bedroom. I leaped to my feet, trying to swallow the lump of fear firmly lodged in my throat. My gaze narrowed as I watched the dark doorway to my room, waiting for the shadows to part and reveal my intruder, but although I could hear the footsteps coming closer, I couldn't see anything—not even a ripple of movement to betray where she was.

"Show yourself," I ordered, trying to keep my voice from shaking. And failing. "What do you want?"

I heard the footsteps walking the perimeter of the room and slowly turned, tracking their movement and trying to keep my breathing under control, my fear in check. Then the footsteps suddenly stopped. I held my breath, listening intently, my skin prickling with apprehension. I swallowed, waiting. The *tick, tick, tick* of the clock hanging on the wall seemed amplified in the unnatural silence, becoming a pounding rhythm in my head.

Suddenly, there was a loud *thump* above my head and a giggle and then the *bam, bam, bam* of my upstairs neighbor's headboard banging against the wall. I let out my breath in a gasp and laughed, the sound coming out as a thin, shaky chuckle.

What a dork.

I should've known it was all just Tracy the Tramp entertaining her boy-toy du jour. I laughed again, a little louder this time, but my relief was cut short when a horrible coppery taste filled my mouth, jolting me a little. Frowning, I touched my tongue and looked at my fingers, startled to see blood there.

"What the hell?" I hurried into my bathroom and leaned close to the mirror, opening my mouth to get a look, but there was nothing there. No blood. No evidence of injury. Nothing. "Weird . . ."

Behind me, the door slammed shut, startling a scream from me. I whirled around and grabbed the knob to pull the door open, but it wouldn't budge. I gripped it harder, my knuckles turning white as I strained to turn the knob, but it was like someone was on the other side, holding it shut. I rattled the door, trying to jerk it open. *No go.* My chest heaved with panicked breaths as the walls in the tiny bathroom seemed to be closing in, slowly squeezing the air out of the room.

Great—perfect time to become claustrophobic.

"Let me out, damn it!" I yelled, pounding on the door with my fist, trying desperately to keep it together, rein in the fear and not let it take over. I had to keep calm, use my head. I let go of the door and took a deep breath, exhaling slowly. "Okay, okay, okay," I muttered. "There's a logical explanation for all of this, Trish. There's nothing in here with you."

In response, the lights began to flicker, creating a strobe effect against the bright white tile. I spun around and pressed my back to the door, my eyes searching the intermittent darkness. *Well, shit, there went that theory. . . .*

"Knock it the hell off!" I screamed. "Leave me alone!"

The giggle came again, bouncing off the walls, the sound distorted and disorienting. The sink faucet splurted to life, spraying out water with such force it overflowed the sink to splatter the mirror and rain down over the lip of the vanity and onto the floor. Then the shower came on, the water so hot, steam began to fill the air almost immediately. I turned back toward the door, fear making me pound on the door so hard, I thought my hand would break. But I didn't care—I just wanted *out.*

"Help me!" I shouted over the roaring water, my feet now damp from the overflowing sink. "Someone help me! Please!"

As if on cue, the bathroom door exploded inward, smacking me in the forehead and knocking me on my ass. I slid with the force, nailing the back of my head on the toilet. For one terrifying, dizzying moment, the world went black, but I forced myself to keep it together and shakily managed to drag myself toward the open door. My apartment tilted precariously, and my stomach lurched, but I forced down the rush of vomit and grabbed the doorjamb, pulling myself to my feet.

The moment I was upright, the faucets abruptly shut off and the strobe light ceased, plunging the bathroom into darkness. I stumbled through the open doorway, shaking so violently I was barely able to control my legs beneath me. As soon as I was through the door, I pressed my back to the wall, my chest heaving. I gulped down the bile rising to my mouth and was glad for the distraction of the burning sensation as it went back down. I shook my head. *Screw this!* I was taking my cat and getting the hell out.

I pushed away from the wall and all the lights I'd left on throughout the apartment blinked out at once, sending a fresh shot of fear-infused adrenaline through my veins. "Oh, God," I moaned, dropping back against the wall. I squeezed my eyes shut for a few seconds, steeling my nerves, praying like hell that I wouldn't see someone standing in front of me when I opened them again. I blew out a couple of quick breaths, then forced my lids open, scanning the room at a glance as my eyes adjusted to the darkness.

"Sasha," I called, my voice little more than a strained whisper as I continued to watch for any movement. "*Sasha!*" I heard her answering mew coming from my bedroom and nearly wept.

I edged along the wall, creeping toward my room, and heard a soft thud as Sasha jumped down from her usual perch on the window seat, but she didn't emerge as I expected. Then I heard her low growl and glanced around frantically, wondering what she saw that I didn't. A single bead of sweat trickled down between my shoulder blades as if in slow motion, ratcheting up the persistent niggling of dread creeping under my skin. "Sasha, come here, baby!"

With a trembling hand, I pushed open the bedroom door, wishing like hell that I had a gun or a baseball bat. Of course, even as I wished it, I had a feeling neither weapon would've been much use against the invisible creature who had invaded my home.

As the door swung open, I darted inside and flipped on the light. Startled by my sudden movement, Sasha yowled and bolted from the room, nearly scaring the shit out of me in the process. "Damn it!" I cried as I stumbled backward, crashing into the door, the doorknob jabbing me painfully in the kidney. "Shit!"

I winced at the pain and rushed back through the doorway, only to stop dead in my tracks. The man standing in my living room reached out and pulled the chain of my desk lamp, turning on the light. I gasped at the sight of him. He'd ditched his fatigues and was now dressed in a black turtleneck sweater and black slacks that hugged his athletic physique in all the right places. For a split second I thought he might be a figment of my imagination, but then he pegged me with that intense amber gaze of his, and I knew he was real.

I was so shocked and relieved to see Nicky, I didn't even care why he was there. Without stopping to think, I rushed to him, throwing my arms around his neck in a fierce hug, squeezing my eyes shut to hold back the tears. After a brief hesitation, his arms came around me, hugging me back, holding me as I clung to him.

"Hello, doll," he whispered in my ear, his voice so soft and soothing, I wanted to melt into him, but then I reminded myself that he didn't know me—no matter how well I felt I knew *him*.

Embarrassed by my impulsiveness, I abruptly released him and pushed away. "I'm so sorry," I stammered, hastily wiping my eyes. "I just—"

"Forget about it," he interrupted, tilting his head a little to one side, his lips curving into a bemused smile. "I never turn down an embrace from a beautiful woman." His grin grew and he spread his arms wide. "In fact, anytime you want to throw yourself into my arms again, doll, you go right ahead."

As tempting as his offer was, Sasha's low growl started up again, and I glanced down at her, seeing her peering out from under my desk, her yellow gaze trained on the bathroom door. As fear twisted my stomach into knots, I scooped up my cat and grabbed Nicky's hand. "We need to get out of here," I announced, dragging him with me as I hurried toward the apartment door.

"You're soaking wet," he pointed out, pulling me to a stop. "You can't go outside like that."

I jerked out of his hold. "There's no way in hell I'm staying here." I hastily shoved my feet into my snow boots, my heart hammering. Sasha bared her teeth, hissing at some unseen menace. Her back claws dug into my stomach and tore at my T-shirt while her front claws did a number on my shoulder as she fought to get out of my arms, but I wasn't about to leave her in my apartment with whatever was haunting it. I bit through the pain with a groan and grabbed my keys from the credenza just as the bathroom door slammed shut. Then my bedroom door. My desk chair tipped over with a crash. Then the coffee table upended, sending magazines and remote controls flying. I heard the cabinet doors in my kitchen burst open and then the sound of shattering glass.

"What the fuck?" Nicky mumbled, his brows drawing together in a confused frown as he instinctively moved to shield me.

"Go!" I shouted, throwing open the apartment door. "Go, now!"

As I grabbed the doorknob and slammed it shut behind me, I

caught a horrifying glimpse of a ghostly face swooping toward me, its furious expression twisted with hatred and rage. I cried out as the door rattled in the frame as if someone was trying to wrench it open from the other side.

Not needing to be urged again, Nicky grabbed my hand and raced with me to the elevator. I punched the Down button over and over again, glancing over my shoulder several times during those long, agonizing seconds it took the elevator to arrive, fully expecting to be attacked again. Nicky was tense, alert, his gaze trained like a laser on my apartment door down the hall. His right hand was behind his back, tucked up under the hem of his sweater where I guessed his gun was concealed. Just as the elevator doors slid open, my apartment door burst inward and spewed a roiling mist into the hallway.

Nicky shoved me into the elevator, backing me into the corner, putting himself between me and the open doors, his gun now drawn as the doors creaked shut. There was a deafening crash against the closed doors just as the elevator hopped and began its descent.

My legs too weak to hold me any longer, I crumpled against the wall and would've ended up on the floor but for Nicky's arm going around my waist. He stowed his gun, then wrestled Sasha away from me. "Turn her loose, doll," he urged. "It's all right. I got her." It was only then I realized the cat was yowling with rage at being nearly squeezed to death in my panicked grip. With a gasp, I relinquished her to Nicky.

The next thing I knew, Nicky was half carrying me from my apartment building and shoving me into the front seat of a black Escalade. When we'd managed to put a few miles behind us, he slowed down a little and glanced over at me, his face drawn. Seeing me shivering in the passenger seat, my teeth chattering, he cranked up the heat. But it didn't matter what temperature it was in the car. The chill in my bones had nothing to do with the cold.

Chapter Five

"You doin' okay over there?"

I started at the sudden sound of Nicky's voice, sending Sasha scrambling over my shoulder and into the backseat with a yowl of protest. I swallowed hard, considering his question, then nodded. "I think so."

He glanced over at me and gave me his patented half grin. "That sounded convincing."

I attempted a smile. "I'm a bad liar, I guess."

"Yeah, well, I guess there are worse things to be bad at." He waited a beat, then asked, "So, you got anywhere you want me to take you?"

I thought for a moment. Any other time I would've had him take me to Red's, but she and Nate were at the hospital for the night. Besides, the last thing I wanted was for her to find out about this latest development before I knew what was going on. She had enough to worry about without adding my safety to the list. And a hotel was out of the question—I'd left in such haste, I hadn't even grabbed my coat, which had my credit cards in the inside pocket. So I shook my head. "No, I don't have anywhere to go," I told him. "And I'm not going back to my apartment without Nate Grimm. Or maybe a priest."

Nicky chuckled a little. "Got it. Well, forget about it—I got somewhere you can stay."

We sat in silence for a few moments longer before I had to ask the question that had been burning in the back of my mind since the moment I saw him standing there in my living room like some dark knight in shining armor. "How did you know?"

He cast a quick glance my way, his brows drawn together. "Know what?"

"That I was in trouble."

He shook his head a little. "I didn't."

Now it was my turn to frown. "Then why were you there?"

He shifted a little in his seat and adjusted his grip on the steering wheel. "I need your help."

My brows shot up. "So you figured breaking in to my apartment was the way to go about asking me?"

"The lights were off," he said by way of explanation. "I thought you were asleep."

"So . . ." I said, drawing out the word as I tried to follow his logic. "What? You thought I'd talk in my sleep or something?"

His lips twitched, but I couldn't tell if it was from amusement or annoyance. "You *do* talk in your sleep—"

I jerked back a little, my eyes going wide. "How the hell do you know that?"

"—but I never get much intel that way. I just needed a look at your report from tonight."

"My report?"

"Yeah, I needed a recap of everything that happened. I gotta give you credit, doll—you're the best." He sent a grin my way. "You don't miss a thing."

I felt a little flutter in the center of my chest at the compliment but quickly shoved it aside. "Thanks," I said, my tone cautious, "but how do you know about my reports? Or my sleeping habits, for that matter."

"Anytime I lose the trail of that motherfucking bloodsucker, drop in to see what you've got on him," he said with a shrug. breaking into and entering my apartment while I was asleep, into my computer, and reading confidential reports was a work. Of course, considering I was riding in the car w the Tales' most powerful crime syndicate, it probab

"You've been tracking Dracula," I guessed. *motherfucking bloodsucker* he was referrin been doing for the past two years?"

At this, his chiseled jaw tightene

first," he said, his terse tone contradicting his shrug. "I went looking for Sebille Fenwick's body first. My gut told me things weren't over yet with that bitch."

"You were right," I told him, the image of Sebille's fetid, maggot-ridden face flashing through my mind.

"Yeah, I heard about that." He gave me a nod. "I owe you one."

I shook my head. "It wasn't me. It was Lavender Seelie. All I did was stick my nose in where it didn't belong and nearly get myself killed."

"Yeah, well, no offense, doll, but I'm getting the impression that's your MO."

There was no judgment or censure in his voice, but still I felt the heat rising in my cheeks. He was obviously referring to my colossally stupid decision to go chasing after strangely undulating shadows earlier that night. Nothing says *dumb-ass* quite like walking straight into a vampire ambush. "If I waited to call in for backup all the time, I'd lose my lead."

He laughed full-out this time, the sound a deep rumble so velvety and soothing it brought goose bumps to my skin. "I think you've been hangin' out with Red too much. She's rubbin' off on you."

"So, why don't we get back to the part about you breaking into my apartment on a regular basis," I snapped, not entirely sure why his comment about Red had made me angry. She *was* rubbing off on me. Over the last couple of years I'd become more reckless, more head-strong, and much less willing to take anyone's shit. Plus, I'd become

mouth, casting aside my milder curses for the

lorful versions she used and finding it com-

ng.

asked.

ed what you've been doing and ask to

eason you're doctoring your reports

la's been a very busy boy."

ouple of times before adding,

v're calling you the Spider,

ow."

u saved my life tonight,

so I figure I owe you. But the Agency has your number. It's only a matter of time before they make the connection and track you down."

He grunted again, but this time there was no mirth in it. "Those fuckin' guys couldn't find their asses with both hands and a compass. I'm not worried about them."

"You should be," I protested. "They've been chomping at the bit to get their hands on a Tale to carve up and study. Al's been able to protect us all so far, but if they find out one of us is a criminal—"

He sent a dark look my way.

"—who's interfering with their investigations, I don't know that Al will be able to do a whole lot."

His jaw went tight again, the muscle twitching ominously. "Don't worry about me, doll. I can handle myself."

Well, I couldn't really argue too much with that after what I'd seen tonight, but I had a feeling Nicky's skill would only take him so far. Statistically, at some point he'd slip up. And the Agency was good at waiting.

"You know, you can't keep doing this alone," I told him, trying a different tactic. "It's not safe. You should've come to me sooner."

He grinned. "I did."

"You broke into my *apartment*," I pointed out. When he glanced over at me expectantly, I added, "While I was *sleeping*."

He shrugged. "Yeah. So?"

"So that's not the same thing as asking for my help! Listening to me talk in my sleep . . . well, that's just *creepy*."

He immediately stiffened, casting a dark look my way. "You got a small apartment, doll," he said as if that was a completely valid defense. "Can't help it if I overheard everything you had to say."

I shifted a little, trying to fight the heat I felt rising in my face. "So . . . uh, what kinds of things did I say?"

His full lips curled up at the corners. "Why? You worried?"

Hell, yes, I was worried! I'd been dreaming about that stupid grin on his face nearly every night since we came over. And some of those dreams were a little . . . *speculative*. But I forced a laugh, trying to shrug off the question. "No, no, of course not," I lied. "I was just curious."

He chuckled. "I'm just messin' with you, doll. I never heard you say much of anything that made sense. Mostly just nonsense about spiders."

A shiver passed through me, knowing well which dreams he had overheard.

"So, that whole 'along came a spider' thing is true then?" he asked.

I nodded, my fingers gripping the leather seat as the fear came rushing in on me. I pushed back and took a deep breath and then another, shoving the images away. Dreaming about them was bad enough. I sure as hell didn't need them intruding upon me while I was awake.

"You don't really strike me as the kind of dame who'd be afraid of a little spider," Nicky continued.

I gave him a wry look. "You ever get a peek at what's going through a spider's head?"

He sent a perplexed frown my way. "No. Can't say that I have."

I shuddered again. "Yeah, well, it isn't pretty. If you had seen what I had, you would've been frightened, too."

We sat in silence for a long moment before he said, "Sorry. I didn't know about that."

I glanced over at him, pegging him with a pointed look. "Well, I'm sure there's a lot you don't know about me."

"I probably know more than you think."

Part of me wanted to test that theory, but I wasn't quite ready to break into a rousing rendition of "Getting to Know You"—especially where I was concerned. Before he could ask any potentially uncomfortable questions, I said, "Thank you, by the way. For saving me tonight. Twice."

"What the hell was goin' on at your apartment anyway?" he asked, turning off the main street and driving through a set of electrified gates that opened onto a long, winding driveway lined with trees.

I hugged myself, remembering that horrible face. "I don't know."

"Was it one of the vampires from earlier?" Nicky probed. "Was one of them coming after you?"

I shook my head. "No, it wasn't one of those women. Nate took their souls."

"Did you recognize the ghost at all?" he pressed, his voice taking on a harsh edge of urgency.

"No."

"Maybe a dame you busted who wants to take you down?"

"No."

"Are you sure? I mean—"

"I don't know, okay?" I yelled. "I have no freaking clue *who* that woman was or *why* she was trying to scare the shit out of me! What part of that do you not understand, for chrissake?"

Nicky let out a long sigh as he came around the final bend in the drive and pulled up in front of a sprawling two-story mansion with a beige stone facade. I blinked in disbelief.

"This is your house," I murmured. There was no way I could mistake the place, not after what I'd seen there.

He put the Escalade in park and sat staring at the front door for a long moment, a far-off expression on his face. I studied his angular profile, watching his attempt to control the emotions that played across his face. When he finally spoke, his voice was tense with barely restrained rage. "Yeah, well, as it turns out I got plenty of room."

Instinctively, I reached out and touched his arm, feeling the tension in his muscles through his sweater. "Nicky . . ." My voice trailed off.

I wasn't sure what I'd intended to say. There wasn't anything I *could* say to take away the horrors of the night Juliet died. I didn't have to imagine how it had happened. I'd seen it all in Nicky's eyes when he'd thought he was dying: *They'd fought earlier that night— Juliet hadn't been happy to see Red at the party—and was even less thrilled to find out Nicky had brought his former flame to stay at their home. But he'd charmed his wife back into good spirits on the car ride home, and when they opened the door they were chatting about the party they'd just come from, complaining that the music had been too loud, the conversation too dull.*

But then it all happened so fast. . . . Red screaming, Nicky shooting at the beast coming at him, Juliet getting knocked to the floor so hard by the beast that her skull shattered, splattering her gray matter all over the foyer floor. . . .

Nicky's arm trembled ever so slightly beneath my fingertips, but when he turned to me, he forced a cockeyed grin and winked. "Come on, doll, let's get you inside."

I coaxed Sasha out of the backseat and into my arms before following Nicky into the house. As soon as I stepped into the foyer, my own images of walking in that night and seeing Nicky lying on the floor, bleeding out quicker than his almost indestructible Tale body could heal itself, made me shiver. Sasha yowled in protest and hopped from my arms to go explore her new surroundings.

"Sorry!" I called over my shoulder as I took off after her. "I'll catch her before she gets into anything!"

I heard Nicky calling my name, telling me not to worry about it, but the last thing I needed was my cat peeing on Nicky's carpet or clawing up his curtains. I was already imposing enough as it was.

Sasha shot up the stairs like a bat out of hell. I tried to follow, but my clunky snow boots were making pursuit difficult and I quickly fell behind. "Damn it, Sasha! Come back here!"

I finally made the landing and pulled off my boots, tossing them aside. I caught a glimpse of her shooting into one of the bedrooms and ran down the hall after her. When I reached the room, I flipped on the light and gasped, wondering if I'd just stepped back in time. The room was the size of my entire apartment and decked out with heavy wooden furniture and opulent crimson and gold brocade. In the center of the ceiling hung an intricately designed gilded chandelier that looked like it belonged in an Italian palace, not a mansion along Chicago's North Shore.

I saw movement out of the corner of my eye and turned my head just in time to catch a glimpse of a woman hurrying into an adjacent room. Thinking Nicky must've already started replacing his staff since returning to town, I hurried after her. "Excuse me!" I called. "I'm looking for my cat. Have you seen—"

I was surprised to find myself standing in a massive closet nearly the size of the bedroom. Alone. I turned in a slow circle, looking for another door where the maid might've exited before I came in, but there was only the one way in or out. The closet was filled with beautiful—and expensive—clothes, some with the tags from Saks and Burberry still attached. Blouses, jackets, skirts . . . and enough shoes to make Kim Kardashian green with envy. Oddly, though, everything in the closet belonged to a woman. There wasn't even the slightest indication of a male presence. This had been Juliet's room, I guessed—and Juliet's room alone.

"Trish?"

I gave a little yelp, nearly jumping out of my skin. I whirled around, grasping my chest, where my heart felt like it was about to burst out, and let loose a vivid tirade of curse words that was positively inspired.

Nicky held his arms out, crouching a little as if he expected me to attack him. "Whoa, whoa—it's just me."

"I saw a woman come in here," I barked at him. "Where the hell did she go?"

He shook his head. "There's no one else here, honey. It's just you and me."

I glanced around the closet again, searching the racks of clothing still hanging in neatly color-coordinated sections, fully expecting to see someone peeking out from between cocktail dresses or silk blouses. "B-but . . . I *swear* I saw someone. . . ."

Nicky came to me and took hold of my shoulders. "There's no one here," he assured me, enunciating each word as his gaze locked with mine. "Just you. And me."

I felt a little tug between us, that initial hitch that told me a connection was starting. But it was different from anything I'd felt before. Instead of originating deep inside my psyche, this one started in the center of my chest, pulling me closer to Nicky. Perplexed by the new sensation, I tried to resist, but it jerked me back with a sharp tug, making me stumble forward and right into his arms.

"Oh, God," I mumbled, clumsily trying to extricate myself from his hold. "I'm so sorry."

He chuckled. "Forget about it," he said with a shrug. "I thought maybe you were just taking me up on my offer."

I frowned up at him. "Your offer?"

He hit me with that grin of his and spread his arms wide, gesturing toward himself with his hands. "Throwing yourself into my arms?"

I rolled my eyes, trying my damnedest not to blush to the roots of my hair but probably failing miserably. "Oh, *that* offer."

He chuckled, bringing a sleepy smile to my lips as I tried to stifle a yawn. "I think it's time you got some sleep," he said, putting an arm around my shoulders and leading me out to the bedroom. "It's been one hell of a night."

The presence of his arm around my shoulders and the warmth of his body so close to mine was making it hard to concentrate—and breathe—so the best I could manage in response was a slight nod.

"Feel free to help yourself to some of Juliet's clothes," he said, gesturing absently toward the heavy dresser against the wall. "You're about the same size she was, so you should be able to find something. You've got to be freezing in those wet pajamas."

Oh, not as much as you might think. . . .

I snuggled into his hold ever so slightly, and to my surprise his arm tightened, curling me into him for a brief hug before he released me. "As soon as you change, I'll show you to one of the guest rooms. I never liked this room much."

I glanced up at him, wondering what about this room he disliked, but his expression had gone dark. Asking any questions was clearly not an option.

After watching him leave the room and close the door, I set about finding something warm and dry to put on. I had to shake my head at Nicky's proclamation that I was pretty much the same size as Juliet. She'd been five foot eight and all legs. And I was . . . well . . . *not.* I managed to find a pair of yoga pants that had probably been capris on Juliet and so luckily didn't drag the ground when I pulled them on. Finding a shirt, on the other hand, proved to be more of a challenge. I pulled out several cotton baby-doll shirts that were so tiny I quickly tossed them aside.

"Good lord," I grumbled, "didn't this woman have any boobs? Criminy! What grown woman wears an extra small *anything?*"

I finally found a plain pink T-shirt that had probably been Juliet's kicking around shirt for those days when she was feeling a little bloaty and didn't want to wear her clothing as a second skin. It fit me well enough, accentuating my hourglass curves without looking like it'd been painted on.

I took a look at myself in the mirror. The outfit didn't scream *Do me now, Nicky,* but at least I wasn't soaking wet anymore. But, dear God, my hair was a train wreck. I quickly ran my hands through my ringlets a few times, trying to smooth them a little, but it didn't do a lot of good. I finally huffed and threw my hands up in despair. Oh, well. What the hell did it matter? He'd already seen me at my most disheveled and hadn't run away screaming in horror.

Nicky was leaning against the wall when I came out of the room, and when he looked up and met my gaze I felt that odd little tug again and gasped. His intense amber eyes took me in at a glance, and an emotion I couldn't quite place passed across his face.

Great.

Seeing me in Juliet's clothes had to be stirring up all kinds of emotions he'd been trying to bury down deep these last couple of years. Awesome.

"Feel better?" he asked, his smile strained.

"Just exhausted," I admitted.

"How's the arm?"

I glanced down at it, surprised to find it wasn't throbbing any longer. "Uh . . . fine, actually." I quickly unwrapped it and rotated my wrist, testing the joint. It was completely healed without even a lingering ache. "Weird. There's no way it should've healed that fast."

"Of all the crazy shit that's gone down tonight," Nicky drawled, "I'd say your wrist healing faster than usual rates pretty low."

I stifled another yawn. "Point taken."

He jerked his head toward the end of the hall. "Come on, it looks like you're ready to drop. Let's get you all tucked in."

Was he serious? He was actually going to tuck me in?

I didn't even bother taking a look around the room Nicky led me to. I was so freaking tired I wouldn't have cared if the bed was made of nails as long as I had a place to catch a few hours of sleep.

As soon as I climbed in, he pulled the sheet and duvet up over my chest. "There's a bathroom across the way," he said. "And I'm down the hall if you need me. Third door on the left."

I had a million questions I wanted to ask Nicky—not the least of which was what he'd found out about Dracula's whereabouts and what he planned to do to take him out. But work would have to wait. The only question I could form coherently suddenly seemed much more imperative. "Why didn't you share a room with Juliet?" I asked around a yawn, sleep deprivation affecting my ability to keep my curiosity in check.

"She needed her own space." He made a noise that was something between a grunt and a laugh. "Can you imagine? In a house this size?"

"I can't imagine ever wanting to spend the night away from you," I muttered, sleep descending quickly.

I closed my eyes and curled onto my side, reaching blindly to pull the duvet up under my chin and finding Nicky's hand instead. My heart gave a little hitch at the contact and I knew I probably should've pulled my hand away, but my eyelids were too heavy to open, my limbs too heavy to move.

To my surprise, Nicky's fingers curled around mine. I felt him smooth my hair with his free hand, then twist one of my ringlets around his finger, letting the hair slide across his skin as he released the curl. And just as sleep rose to claim me, he pressed a chaste kiss to my temple and whispered, "Only *sweet* dreams tonight, doll."

Chapter Six

The dream always started the same. I was sitting on the little stone bench in my parents' garden, my black patent leather shoes gleaming, my pale blue pinafore pristine and crisp. I was swinging my feet and humming cheerily while eating my breakfast—porridge, not the curds and whey mentioned in my nursery rhyme—when a particularly intricate and beautiful spiderweb nestled among the rosebushes caught my eye. I set aside my bowl and hopped down to go investigate. The dew from the cool spring morning still clung to the gossamer threads, glistening in the sunshine. I was grinning, delighted with my find, as I leaned closer.

I didn't even see the spider until it was right before my eyes. It was an enormous, fat, furry black spider the size of my fist. I'd heard of these monstrous arachnids, the kind witches in Make Believe used in their potions, but I'd never seen one. My childish curiosity urged me to take a closer look, so I bent forward until my nose nearly touched the web.

And then it happened. My eyes locked with the spider's—hollow and black, infinitely deep, impossibly dark—and I felt a little tug in the center of my brain, a quick jerk deep inside my head. And then I saw. A barrage of graphic and gory images assaulted my mind, filling it until it overflowed, engulfing me, dragging me down, down, down into the darkness. . . .

I jolted awake, shivering violently, my clothes soaked with sweat.

I threw back the covers and lunged from the bed, but my limbs were weak with terror and wouldn't hold me, and I crumpled to the floor. On my hands and knees, I scurried to the corner of the room and pressed myself into it, my chest heaving with hysterical sobs. I squeezed my eyes shut and put a hand over my mouth, muffling the sound.

Control the fear, Beatrice. . . .

I nodded quickly. *Yes. Yes. Control the fear.* Had to control the fear. I couldn't let it take me again. Not like before. I'd never go to that place again.

I took several slow, shaky breaths and muttered aloud the Fibonacci sequence to force my mind away from the remembrance of the horrors I'd experienced that day and focus it on something else. I don't know how long I sat there, trying to bring my shattered psyche back together, but eventually my pulse slowed to an almost normal rate and my shivering began to subside.

"It's okay, Trish," I whispered. "It's okay. Everything's okay. You're fine now."

And a few moments later, I slid up the wall until I was standing and tested my legs to make sure they would carry me back to the bed, but once I was there, I couldn't bring myself to climb back in. There was really no point. I knew from experience that there was no possibility of getting any sleep once the dream had come.

As quietly as possible, I slipped from the room, glancing down the hall to where Nicky had said his bedroom was. The door was wide open, the room completely dark. The house was still, but I heard no sounds of sleep coming from his room. Curious, I crept down the hall and peeked in. The bed was still made, obviously not having been slept in. I frowned a little, wondering where he might have gone.

Shivering again now, but this time from the sweat-soaked clothes I wore and not from sheer terror, I made my way back to Juliet's room and managed to locate a luxurious pink bathrobe hanging on the inside of the closet door. I stripped out of the workout clothes down to my panties, then pulled the bathrobe on, tying it loosely around my waist before making my way downstairs. I had to wander down a few halls and recover from a couple of wrong turns that led me to a laundry room and then what appeared to be a game room before I finally managed to find Nicky's kitchen.

The kitchen was much easier to navigate. I had no trouble locating a saucepan and the supplies I needed to make some hot chocolate—the final step in my recovery ritual on the nights the dream came. I was just turning off the burner and setting the pan aside to find a coffee mug when a soft shuffle behind me brought me around with a gasp.

My shoulders sagged with relief when I saw that the noise was not from a ghost intent on terrorizing me or a massive spider whose horrifying memories of murdering her victims were going to send me spiraling once more toward insanity. "There you are!" I said with a chuckle. "Where the hell have you been?"

Sasha padded toward me, her answering meow carrying a hint of admonishment.

"Hey," I shot back, "I'm not the one who ran off. You should've stuck around." She sat down directly in front of me, her tail twitching back and forth lazily, then gave me an expectant look.

With a sigh, I rummaged through the cupboards until I found a small bowl, then poured a little milk into it. "There you go, you spoiled brat," I muttered with an affectionate grin, squatting down to set it on the floor in front of her. I scratched her ears for a moment while she lapped at the milk, glad to see that she seemed unaffected by our ordeal at the apartment. I was still grinning when I rose to my feet.

"Can't sleep?"

This time I started with a ridiculously girlie yelp that sent Sasha racing out of the room again. "Damn it!"

"Sorry," Nicky said from where he leaned nonchalantly against the frame of the kitchen doorway. "Didn't mean to scare your cat off again."

"I didn't even hear you come in," I said, still breathless. "How long have you been standing there?"

He shrugged and pushed off the door frame. "I came in when I heard pans clattering around in here."

My brows came together. "Why didn't you say anything?"

He shrugged again as he came forward, looking a little unsteady on his feet. It was then I noticed he held the neck of a bottle of Legavulin in his hand. A mostly *empty* bottle of Legavulin. "Didn't want to interrupt." He plunked the bottle down on the counter of the kitchen island. "It's been a long time since anyone has used this kitchen—kinda nice to see someone here."

"It doesn't look like it's gone unused." I shook my head a little, frowning in confusion. "The pantry's fully stocked."

He lifted a shoulder and let it drop. "Habit. Juliet loved to cook, so I always made sure she had everything she needed. First thing I did when I got back to town."

"Was she a good cook?" I asked, noting the shadow of sadness that had passed over his face when he mentioned his dead wife.

He laughed that deep rumble that brought goose bumps to my skin. "No—everything she made tasted like shit." He lifted the bottle and took a long pull of the amber liquid. "But it was her outlet, especially when she was pissed at me. So I felt I owed it to her to eat it."

"Well," I said, "I don't know that I'm much of a cook either, but I'd be willing to share my hot chocolate with you, if you'd like some."

His mouth lifted at one corner. "Thanks, doll."

When I set his mug in front of him, he jerked his chin at it. "So, what's doin' with you? You're practically dead on your feet. Why are you awake already?"

"Nightmare," I said with a tight smile. "How about you? Why are you awake?"

His answering chuckle was filled with bitterness. "Haven't been to sleep yet. I have a few nightmares of my own."

I blew over the edge of my mug and took a tentative sip, then said, "I'll tell you mine if you tell me yours."

This managed to produce a true laugh, dissipating the shadow of sadness in his eyes. "Fair enough." He jerked his head toward the kitchen door. "Come on."

He led me into a sunken living room where a fire blazed in the massive hearth, filling the room with soothing warmth and casting it in shadow. I curled up in one corner of the leather sofa, adjusting the edges of Juliet's robe to cover my knees.

Nicky set his hot chocolate on the coffee table, then dropped down in the opposite corner, the bottle of Scotch propped on his knee. His face wore a dark scowl made darker by the shadows cast by the fire. We sat in silence for several long moments, Nicky lost in his own brooding thoughts as I watched him out of the corner of my eye, wondering if he really had wanted to talk or just needed someone else in the room with him.

I'd polished off the last of the hot chocolate and was just rising to my feet, intent on excusing myself to leave Nicky to his thoughts, when he suddenly said, "So, what's with all the nightmares? They because of what you saw in that spider's head?"

I sat back down, curling into myself even more at the mention of those horrifying dreams. "Partly," I admitted, my mouth going dry. "What I saw there . . . it traumatized me. I mean, I was just a little girl—and a very sheltered, pampered one at that. I didn't realize any creature could even *have* such murderous thoughts."

Nicky grunted, obviously not having any such delusions.

"Well, back then Tales didn't do such a great job dealing with people suffering from trauma." I sighed, thinking of the cases I'd worked over the years. "I don't know that we do a whole lot better now. Anyway, my father thought the best treatment was to make me face my fears. We had a deserted little root cellar on our property— no one had used it in decades. My sister swore it was haunted, and to look at it, you'd certainly believe her. All the village children were terrified of the cellar, of what might be lurking inside, waiting to gobble us up."

Nicky turned his head, his full attention on me now as I told my story.

"One morning, my father carried me out to the root cellar, kissed me on the cheek and gave me a big hug, then locked me inside." I shuddered, remembering the terror that had consumed me when I realized what was happening. "It was so dark . . . so close. And crawling with thousands of spiders. I pounded on the door until my little fists bled as the spiders crawled all over me, screamed until my voice was little more than a whisper."

"Jesus," Nicky breathed. "How could a father do something like that to his own kid?"

"He thought he was helping me," I told him. "It was a different time; we had no knowledge of psychology back then. He thought it was the only way to bring me back from the edge of madness, to cure me of the effects of what I'd seen."

"How long were you in there?"

I shook my head. "I have no idea. My father stayed with me most of the time, trying to talk me through the fear, reminding me that I could control it. When he finally opened the door, it was dark. I think he mistook my silence for triumph over my fears, but I was really just too exhausted to fight it anymore."

"God, I'm sorry," he said softly. "What happened after that?"

I took a deep, shaky breath and let it out slowly. "I vowed I'd never go back to that dark place, not ever. No matter what, I'd control my fear. I'd never let it rule me again."

He gazed at me for a long moment, an emotion I couldn't quite place in his eyes. Then he nodded. "I figured you were one hell of a woman, Trish," he said. "But I don't think I knew the half of it."

Feeling my cheeks go warm at his unexpected praise, I looked away, studying the room to hide my pleasure at his words. "You have a gorgeous house," I told him, desperate to change the subject and feeling totally lame the moment I said it.

Apparently, though, he didn't mind. A slight smile curved his lips. "This is my favorite room."

I nodded. "I can see that. It has your personality."

He gave me a curious look. "Yeah? And what do you think you know about my personality?"

I wrapped my arms around my legs and rested my chin on my knees. "You sometimes come off as a bit hard around the edges, but you're actually a softy and have a way of making people feel comfortable and safe without even trying. You intentionally present the impression of ease and charm with a vibe of underlying danger, but when I look closer, I can see there's much more than what's on the surface. You have a sturdiness and steadfastness of spirit that's rare these days."

He took another swig of his Scotch, then grunted. "And you got all that from my furniture?"

I shook my head. "No. I got that from how you've looked after your friends all these years, the respect and loyalty you command from the people who know you, the fear you inspire in the people who don't. I got that from how you fought those vampires and how you didn't even think twice about helping me when I was in danger from that ghost. How you could've dumped me at FMA headquarters or on any one of my colleagues, but you brought me to your home."

He grunted again. "Well, I'm sure there are some people who'd disagree with your assessment."

"People like Juliet?" I said, hazarding a guess. Based on the way his jaw tightened, I knew I'd hit the mark.

"She hated this house," he said, gesturing with the bottle. "Didn't think it was grand enough for a Capulet. She wanted something more befitting her rank among the Willies. She was a *Lit* after all. I was just the kid who'd fallen asleep on the job once and had turned into a petty thief when no one else would hire me. I had to fight to get where I am in the Here and Now, to make my fortune. You'd think that would've been enough. But she never let me forget that I was just a Rhyme and that she'd married beneath her."

I shook my head. "But I thought . . . I mean, you loved her."

He nodded. "Yeah. I thought she was what I needed—classy, smart, sexy as hell. She was a good dame. And I think she loved me, too. For a while anyway. Things had gone pretty cold between us there before—well, before that night."

"Because of how you felt about Red?" I asked gently.

He shrugged. "Red and I had one helluva time once upon a time, but we were a lot better off as friends, and eventually we both realized it."

"But Juliet worried there were still feelings between you?"

He pulled his hand down his face, scrubbing at the stubble growing in at his jaw. "She was convinced I was still sleeping with Red—which was total bullshit. That's not my style. Anyway, things were getting better with me and Jules there at the end."

My heart broke a little as I sat there listening to him proclaim his tentative optimism about his relationship with his wife. I'd never in my life wished more vehemently that I could unknow what I'd seen in a dying person's thoughts than I did at that moment.

"I'm sure they were," I managed to force out.

He cocked his head to one side. "Did you see her thoughts that night?" he asked. "Did you—what do you call it in your reports?—*read* her that night?"

I felt my skin prickle with panic at being put on the spot. "Of course," I told him. "I read the dead at every crime scene."

"What was she thinking?" he asked. "You never put anything about her thoughts in your report from that night."

God, this was my worst-case scenario. Part of me wanted to tell him what I'd seen, what I'd discovered, but part of me didn't feel that dropping that bombshell was really my place. "She knew you loved her," I said, forcing a sympathetic smile. It was about all I could manage.

He nodded, then leaned his head against the back of the couch and closed his eyes. He sat there for so long I thought he'd fallen asleep. My own eyelids were finally beginning to grow heavy again when he suddenly said, "Thanks, Trish. For everything you did to help Juliet. To help *me*."

"I'm sorry I couldn't do more," I told him sincerely. "Juliet died when her head hit the floor. You know that, right? She didn't suffer at all."

He nodded. "Yeah, I know. But . . ." He heaved a heavy sigh and his voice was strained with emotion when he continued. "*I* should've done more. I wasn't quick enough. I wasn't strong enough. I couldn't protect Jules. I couldn't protect Red. Hell, I couldn't even protect myself. It was just sheer dumb luck that Sebille didn't kill me, too."

I shook my head. "No, Nicky—"

"That's what keeps me up at night," he interrupted. "Hating myself for my helplessness. Sometimes the dreams are just replaying what happened, reminding me how I totally fucked up. Other times they're worse—Sebille tearing out my guts and eating them over me while I scream, or tearing Jules apart before my eyes and devouring her heart. Sometimes it's Red that bitch is ripping open. And lately—" Here he paused and turned his head back to me, his eyes tortured. There was something there on the tip of his booze-loosened tongue, something more he wanted to say, but even in his inebriation he couldn't bring himself to put it into words. He opened his mouth to speak again, but then his jaw snapped shut and he turned away, adding only, "Anyway, no matter who's in the dream, I can't do shit."

There wasn't anything I could say to help him. I knew that from experience. There were times when no words could negate the feelings of helplessness, complete lack of control over one's own fate— or the fate of others. I felt it every single time I looked into the eyes of the dead and dying, witnessing their fear and pain and knowing there wasn't a damn thing I could do. But I knew what had helped Nicky the night he'd been slipping away with his guts held in only by his dead wife's cashmere shawl.

Without a word, I slid across the space between us. He didn't even seem to notice I was beside him until I pried the bottle of Scotch from his fingers and leaned forward to set it down on the coffee table. His eyes followed my movements, and as I came back toward him, he took my hand and pulled me onto his lap, wrapping his arms loosely around my waist.

I swallowed hard, trying to keep my heart from racing. It meant nothing, I knew. He merely needed a warm body to hold, another person to share in his sorrow. And I was there. That was all it was. I knew that. And yet sitting there on his lap with his arms around me, looking into his eyes, I felt that little tug in the center of my chest and thought—just for a split second—that Nicky felt it, too.

"You know," he said, his tone a little dazed as if surprised to find me on his lap, "I wasn't lying when I said it was a long time since I'd had a woman in my arms. Jules and I—"

"Nicky," I interrupted, squeezing my eyes shut, not giving a damn about him and Juliet, or anything else for that matter. "It's okay. I need this, too."

"I think I'm shit-faced."

I laughed a little. "I *know* you're shit-faced."

He chuckled in response. "Well, as long as we're both clear on that, come here." He pulled me close then, tucking me under his chin, his hands smoothing along the fluffy pink chenille of the bathrobe. Then his arms tightened around me, pressing me closer. And when I slipped my arms around his neck, he buried his face in my shoulder, clinging to me in what I guessed was a rare moment of vulnerability.

I held him close, smoothing his hair. "It's all right," I whispered, the words of reassurance as much for me as they were for him. "Everything will be okay now. I've got you. . . ."

At some point, we fell asleep together there on his sofa, arms around one another, finding in that embrace the solace we both needed. And at least for the rest of that night the nightmares were kept at bay.

"Just humor me."

Nicky was dressed now in black jeans and a black T-shirt that showed off a little too clearly the bulge of his biceps as he sat on the edge of Juliet's bed, forearms resting on his thighs, hands clasped, while he watched me rummage through Juliet's things looking for something to wear besides workout clothes.

"There's nothing to tell," I called over my shoulder, digging through the dresser drawers and finding lots of shorty-shorts that were *so* not going to cut it. I wasn't about to go traipsing around Chicago in the middle of February with my ass hanging out. Check that. I wasn't going to go traipsing around Chicago at *any* time of year with my ass hanging out.

"I wake up and find you curled up in my arms," Nicky drawled, "and you mean to tell me *nothing* happened? I didn't even kiss you or anything?"

"Nope," I said, somehow managing it without adding a disappointed sigh. I could feel his pointed stare at my back and turned around to face him, leaning against the dresser and crossing my arms. "All we did was talk. I swear."

"I remember the talking part, doll. I just want to make sure I didn't drink so much that I missed anything else. It's bad enough I missed out on the hours when I was sleeping."

Flushing, and wishing like hell that I had more to report, I turned back to my search, jerking open another drawer and quickly rifling through it.

"I can't believe I didn't even try to *kiss* you," he mused.

I clamped down on my back teeth to keep from screaming. "Try."

Obviously not picking up on my irritation, he continued to mull it over aloud. "I mean, you were sitting there in that little pink bathrobe looking so adorable—"

Adorable? Perfect.

"—what with the cute little curls . . ."

Cute? Cute?!? Fucking curls.

"I really didn't even *try* to put the moves on you?"

"Okay," I said, *so* beyond tired of talking about how he *hadn't* kissed me, "this isn't going to work. I'm going to need to go back to my apartment and find something to wear before we do anything else."

He frowned. "You sure that's a good idea? What about dragging Nate or a priest along?"

"Going to have to risk it," I insisted. "I'm just not going to find what I need here." *And at this point I'd rather face off against a hundred angry phantoms than continue this particular line of conversation. . . .*

"There's gotta be something you can wear."

"Let's face it, Nicky," I said, "I'm five foot four and have cleavage. I'm not exactly the supermodel material your wife was."

His even gaze met mine. "You are to me."

My breath caught in my chest as I blinked at him, wondering if he was joking, but there was no sign of humor lurking in his eyes. "Thanks," I finally managed softly.

He gave me a tight nod, then stood and put his hands on his hips. He dropped his eyes to the carpet for a moment, then finally looked back up at me from under those long dark lashes of his, devastating me all over again. "Listen, I really am sorry about last night," he said, running his hand through his hair. "I don't usually drink like that. Seriously, if I made a total ass of myself—"

"You didn't," I interrupted with a laugh. "You were a perfect gentleman." *Damn it all. . . .*

For a split second he looked as disappointed as I felt, but then he gave a nod. "All right, then. So, whaddaya say we get outta here? I'll buy you something to eat on the way to your apartment."

I narrowed my eyes. "And coffee? My coffee habit's almost as bad as Red's, you know."

He inclined his head in agreement. "Coffee it is."

I gave him a terse, satisfied nod and started for the door, but he grabbed my arm as I passed. "Trish . . ." he began, his expression oddly tortured. Then his face cleared and he winked at me, giving one of my curls a playful tug, but the smile that came next was a little sad. "You know, it'll be strange not having to sneak into your apartment anymore now that the jig is up."

I laughed, appreciating his attempt to lighten the mood a little. "Yeah, well, *Spider,* I'm sure you can find some other unsuspecting gal's apartment to break into. I hear Sleeping Beauty just moved into a new high-rise—might be a challenge."

"Ah, but you've got it all wrong," he said, casually draping his arm around my shoulders as if it was the most natural thing in the world, and leading me from the room. "The challenge was never the *building* but the gal *inside.*"

I sent a sidelong glance his way, a tentative little spark of hope springing to life in the center of my chest.

Chapter Seven

Nicky never left my side the entire time I was in my apartment, his eyes constantly darting around, watching for even a ripple of movement in the air that might signal an attack. I quickly changed clothes and threw together a bag to take with me, then gathered up Sasha's food and bowl. Last was my laptop and what I could salvage of the various notebooks strewn all over the living room.

"Are you sure you don't mind me staying at your house?" I asked as we loaded everything into the back of his Escalade.

"Are you kiddin' me?" he asked. "Forget about it. Like I'm going to let you come back to *this* place?"

I shoved my hands into my coat pockets and let out a sigh, watching my breath freeze in the air and thinking about the attack on me the night before. "We really should talk to Nate and Red about this."

Nicky cast a guarded look my way as he slammed the hatch shut.

I cocked my head to one side and narrowed my eyes at him. "You haven't told Red that you're back in town, have you?"

"Let's get going," he muttered, ignoring my question.

I followed him around to the driver's side and stood in front of the door, my arms crossed over my chest. "Why not tell her you're back? Why keep it a secret?"

He zipped his leather jacket, apparently realizing I wasn't going to be deterred until he answered my question. "It's complicated."

I knew Nicky still cared about Red; that'd been clear in the images

I'd seen in his thoughts while he was dying. And to see her so happy with Nate—his best friend, by all accounts—must've felt awkward at times. Hell, I could relate to that probably better than anyone. *Complicated* was an understatement.

"Fine," I sighed. "Just drop me a couple of blocks from headquarters then. I have to check in before someone notices I haven't made it to work yet. Besides, I need to see what I can find out about our victim from last night, get an ID on the guy."

Nicky shrugged. "Don't bother. I know who it is."

My brows shot up. "How could you possibly—" I didn't even finish the question. "Who is it?"

"Tim Halloran."

I blinked at him in disbelief. "The Sandman?"

Nicky's head bobbed impatiently. "Yeah, now can we get in the car? I'm freezing my nuts off out here."

Once we were in the Escalade and on our way again, I asked, "Why the Sandman?"

"Not sure," Nicky admitted. "I got a tip something was getting ready to go down here in Chicago, so I headed back."

"A tip?" I echoed. "How'd you get a tip on something like that?"

Nicky shrugged. "I know a guy."

Of course he did. . . .

"And you didn't do anything to stop the vampires from killing him?"

"There was nothing I could do by the time I found them," he said, his words clipped.

Tim "the Sandman" Halloran had been Nicky's biggest rival and one of the most ruthless crime bosses among us. Unlike Nicky's Outfit, which operated on a system of friendship and loyalty in exchange for protection and the occasional favor now and then, Halloran's tastes ran to trafficking in fairy dust and financing Tale businesses in exchange for more than his fair share of the returns. And there was certainly no love lost between the two men. During the fifties, they'd had a full-out war going on between them, with Nicky's Outfit coming out the victor thanks in no small part to the loyalty of those who were lucky enough to call him a friend. In spite of their history, I found it hard to believe Nicky would've just left Tim Halloran to die. Even so, I could tell he was hiding something, holding back on me.

"I still want to take a look," I insisted.

"I'd skip Halloran and take a look at those vampire dames if I were you," he said. "Those bloodsuckin' broads had a Tale signature, Trish, but they weren't from any idiom I recognized. What the hell is that all about?"

"Wish I knew," I admitted. "Unfortunately, I'm not going to find out any time soon. The Agency took them."

"Sons of *bitches!*" Nicky growled, something dark passing over his features.

I blinked at him, startled by his sudden rage. "Nicky, I know it sucks, but—"

"*Sucks* doesn't even begin to cover it," he snapped. He glared at the road in silence for a long, tense moment, then suddenly slammed his palm against the steering wheel. "Shit! I'm *this close,* Trish. I can feel it. I'm this *fucking* close to bringing down that bastard Dracula and making him pay."

"We'll figure it out," I assured him. "Right now, let's focus on Halloran. When I was reading him I saw an image of a woman—stunningly beautiful with white hair and bright green eyes. Do you know who she is?"

Nicky shrugged begrudgingly. "Sure. That's Sophia—Halloran's girl. She's a shape-shifter from folklore."

I nodded. "Okay, good. Well, someone should probably let her know what's happened, right? I'll make the death notification and see what she can tell us."

"You can't just go barging in to Halloran's compound alone and tell his were-tiger girlfriend he bit the big one—or, more to the point, that a couple of vampire whores bit *his* big one before bumping him off."

"You're right," I readily agreed. "Guess you're going to have to come with me."

Nicky's grip tightened on the steering wheel. I could tell that making a death notification to the dead crime lord's girlfriend wasn't the kind of action he was used to taking. But he nodded. "Fine. Have it your way. But, you're right—if I'm gonna start poking around out in the open I should probably talk to Red first."

"Where the hell have you been, you son of a bitch?"

Nicky glanced at me, the look he sent my way conveying "I told you so" loud and clear. "Good to see you, too, kid," he said, offering

Red a grin. Then he nodded toward her belly. "You and Nate have been busy. Congratulations."

"Don't try to turn on the charm with me, Nicky Blue," Red hissed. "You couldn't take five minutes to send me a fucking e-mail?"

"So you could show up on my doorstep when you had no business—"

"No *business*?" Red's eyes went wide. "Are you shitting me? After all we've been through together? After I saw you lying there on the floor with your guts hanging out, you have the nerve to tell me I have no business caring what happens to you? Fuck you, Nicky! Get him the hell out of my office, Nate."

"Tess," Nate admonished mildly before taking up what had become his usual perch on the corner of Red's desk and turning his dark gaze on his old friend. "It's good to see you again, Nicky, but I can't say I totally disagree with her on this one. You want to tell us what the hell you've been doing for the last two years?"

Nicky shifted a little uneasily, casting a furtive glance my way. "I've been here and there. You know."

"No, I *don't* know." Red leaned across her desk as much as her pregnant belly would allow, her blue eyes now bright with angry tears. "Do you have any idea how worried I've been, you unbelievable jackass?" She snatched a tissue from the box next to her and swiped irritably at the tears spilling onto her cheeks. "Shit! Seriously? Now I'm *crying*? God, pregnancy has made me lose my fucking mind!"

Nicky cleared his throat a couple of times, growing increasingly uncomfortable at the sight of Red's tears. "I'm sorry, kid," he said, his voice taking on a gentleness that made me bristle. "I never meant to worry you. I just had to get my head together. And, well, I've been doing a little moonlighting since I left town that's been keeping me busy."

She eyed him warily. "What kind of *moonlighting*?"

"You know"—he shrugged—"some cleanup work like back in the day."

Red flopped back in her chair, her face going slack. "Like back in the New York days, Nicky?"

"Somethin' like that," he admitted.

I heard Nate curse under his breath before pegging Nicky with a look of warning. "Are you sitting here confessing to a crime, Nicky? You know we'd have to arrest you if you are."

Nicky spread his hands and leaned back in his chair. "I'm not confessing to anything. I'm just stating a fact. I had some things to deal with, so I've been doing a little work to clear my head."

"You promised me you'd never do another hit, Nicky," Red reminded him, her voice barely above a whisper. She glanced at her closed office door before adding, "After you got shot, you said you'd stick to making a point in other ways."

"I have," he insisted. "This had nothing to do with my own business."

Nate crossed his arms over his chest, his face going dark. "Seeing as how I never got any calls for a hit on a Tale, I'm assuming these were Ordinaries?"

Red cursed a blue streak. "Perfect. That's *exactly* the kind of headache we need right now."

"Trust me," Nicky said, "all these guys had it comin'. Nobody's gonna miss 'em."

Red ran a hand through her thick black hair, letting it fall around her shoulders. "So what does any of this have to do with Trish?" She jabbed her finger at his chest. "So help me God, Nicky, if you drag her into your bullshit . . ."

We'd agreed on the way to headquarters that we were going to steer clear of Nicky's vigilante alter-ego and the connection to Dracula, but we had to have some reasonable explanation as to why he would be helping me on an open investigation or Red would put the smack-down on both of us in a fairytale minute. "Trish needed my expertise on a case," he said with a shrug.

I glanced over at Nate, not surprised to find his bottomless black eyes on me, narrowed with a silent question.

Red wasn't nearly so subtle. "What kind of expertise?"

Nicky glanced around as if expecting the authorities to come barging into the room at any moment. He leaned forward a little in his chair and hissed, "Insight into my business ventures."

"Tim Halloran's dead," I blurted, impatient with the euphemisms and innuendo.

Red's brows shot up. "How? When?" She then turned an accusing glare on Nate. "And how did *you* not know this?"

Nate shook his head, clearly as baffled as Red. "Got me."

"He was the victim in the alley," I explained. "Nicky got a tip about his identity from one of his associates and passed it along to me."

Nate nodded. "That guy's soul was so traumatized by his death it was unrecognizable. I couldn't tell who it was. Damn. Hell of a way to go."

Red seemed unmoved as she pegged Nicky and me with that look of hers that tells you to stow the bullshit. "And you two teamed up how?"

"Nicky and I bumped into each other sometime back. And, well . . ." I paused, my heart suddenly in my throat as I thought about what Nicky and I had agreed to say. It was just a little too surreal to utter the words aloud. Fortunately, I didn't have to.

"And we've been hooking up for a while," Nicky supplied. "I came by Trish's apartment last night after I heard about the vampire attack." He took my hand in his and raised it to his lips, his gaze locking with mine. My face was instantly aflame, no doubt confirming his insinuation, which was most likely his intention. *Oh, man, he was good. . . .*

Red gaped. "Say *what* now?"

"Trish was pretty shaken up, so she spent the night at my place." Nicky smoothed the back of my hand with his thumb, setting my heart racing when that wickedly handsome grin curved his lips. And for a brief, blissful moment, I actually believed him, too. "Hell of a night, right, doll?"

I swallowed hard and my voice was a little thready when I said, "To put it mildly."

Red cocked her head to one side, regarding me closely. Then she said, "Guys, I think you need to give me the room." We all immediately got to our feet, but she added, "I meant *guys* as in *gents.* Take a seat, Trish."

I plopped back down in the chair, sitting on the edge with my back board straight. It hadn't occurred to me until just then, when I'd heard the edge in her voice, saw the stern look in her eyes, that even though Tess Little was one of my closest friends, she was also my boss. And she was *seriously* unhappy.

Nate and Nicky both glanced toward me as they sauntered from the room, Nicky looking a little apologetic. I gave him a smile that I hoped didn't look as lame as it felt.

As soon as the guys shut the door behind them, Red crossed her arms over her chest. "So, you wanna tell me what's really going on?"

"I have no idea what you're talking about," I demurred.

She gave me a knowing look. "You're a horrible liar, Trish. And I know you've been lying to me for a while. I just didn't know why. Now spill it."

"Really, Red—"

"How long has this been going on anyway?" she cut in. "How long have you been sneaking around behind my back, trying to hide all the evidence?"

Oh, shit. . . .

She was totally on to me. Somehow she'd found out about the doctored reports, about my agreement with Nate. . . . Now I just had to try to keep her from taking off, half cocked, to go after Dracula.

"Tess, it was for your own good," I said, my tone as gentle as I could manage. "I was trying to protect you."

"Protect me?" she echoed, her eyes going wide. "Last time I checked I was a big girl, Trish. I think I can take it."

I sighed. "I know. I'm sorry. It's only because we love you that we didn't want you to get hurt—"

"Damn it!" She shoved back from her desk, her face taut with fury as she got to her feet and began to pace the room.

I snapped my jaws shut and pressed my lips together. There was really nothing I could say to dig myself out of this hole. I'd known all along that Red hated being treated like she was a delicate little waif incapable of taking care of herself. She'd struggled for almost two hundred years to break away from the story that had haunted her. About the only thing she hated more than being underestimated was being lied to. And I'd committed both sins by hiding the intel on Dracula.

"Please forgive me," I said softly. "I never should've deceived you."

She waved away my apology, then sat down in the seat Nicky had vacated and let out a long, mournful sigh. "Do you love him?"

My brows came together in a frown. "Huh?"

She leaned back in the chair, scooting down a little so she could rest her head on the back. "Just be straight with me," she said. "Are you in love with Nicky?"

"Oh!" I gasped, a nervous little twitter of laughter coming out before I could stop it. "You're talking about *Nicky!*"

She turned her head to frown at me. "Yeah . . . Who were *you* talking about?"

"Nobody," I said in a rush, relief washing over me like a tidal wave. "No one. I mean, Nicky, of course."

Her expression became one of wary concern. "You feelin' all right?" When I nodded and forced a smile, she went on. "Trish, I love Nate Grimm more than the air I breathe—and I'd probably suffer less without air than without him. The man is everything to me. But Nicky . . . Well, he means a lot to me and always will."

I nodded. "I know. He means a lot to me, too." At least that part was the God's honest truth. And it must've been enough because she suddenly laughed in a burst of mirth not unlike Nate's.

"At least this explains why you kept turning down all the insanely hot guys I've been trying to set you up with," she said with a grin. "I mean, seriously? You said no to *Achilles*. Who *does* that? Most women would fight to the death for one night with that guy."

"And he knows it," I drawled, rolling my eyes. "No one will ever love Achilles as much as *he* does."

She chuckled, then smiled a little sadly. "Just be careful, okay? Nicky's been through a lot. He's not . . . Well, he's not quite the same, you know? I can see it in his eyes. There's a darkness inside that wasn't there before—not even during the New York days."

There was a light rap on the door that brought our heads around. Nate poked his head in. "Everything okay in here, sweetheart?"

Red pushed awkwardly to her feet and put her hands on her hips. "Other than the fact I'm so hungry I could gnaw my arm off, everything's good."

"Well then"—Nate grinned as he sauntered in—"I guess I'd better take you home for lunch." He pulled her into his arms and pressed a kiss to the side of her neck before murmuring, "But eating might have to wait. You're looking damned sexy right now."

Red winked at me. "See what I mean? *Love* this man." Then she leaned around Nate and called, "Nicky!"

Nicky stuck his head in the office, looking uncharacteristically sheepish. "Yeah?"

"I love ya, you son of a bitch," she told him. "So I'm glad you're back in town. But you break Trish's heart, and I don't care how off the grid you go, I'll make it my personal mission in life to hunt you down and kick your ass. Are we clear on that?"

"Crystal clear, kid."

"Good." She jerked her chin toward the door. "Now get the hell outta here and go with Trish to pay a visit to Halloran's girlfriend so she doesn't end up as tiger bait. And let me know if you find out why those vamps were craving a Sandman sandwich."

I hurried from the room with Nicky, shutting Red's office door behind me, but not before catching a glimpse of her and Nate in a passionate kiss. I sighed and glanced over at Nicky out of the corner of my eye.

"Well, that went better than expected," he mumbled once we were safely down the hall. "What did Red say after she booted me and Nate?"

I shrugged. "You know. Girl stuff."

"No, really," he said, punching the button for the elevator.

Luckily, the elevator doors slid open at that moment, letting out a handful of men in black suits gruffly leading a powerfully built man wearing sunglasses and an impeccably tailored suit, his red gold curls pulled back in a ponytail at the nape of his neck.

"Gideon?" I gasped as the agents shouldered between Nicky and me. I'd only met him once, when Lavender's mom had demanded Red's and my presence at her country club for tea so she could inspect her daughter's bridesmaids. Although the entire experience had been so unbelievably uncomfortable I wanted nothing more than to wipe it from my memory, Gideon was impossible to forget.

Gideon shrugged easily out of the grasp of the man holding him, letting them all know he'd only been coming along for show anyway, and turned toward me, giving me a sharp nod. "Ms. Muffet. Pleasure to see you again."

"Nicky Blue," I introduced, "this is Gideon Montrose—he's a dear friend of Lavender Seelie and bodyguard to the fairy king and queen."

Nicky instinctively reached out a hand in greeting, but the handshake was awkward with Gideon's massive wrists in magic-dampening manacles.

"Pleased to meet you, Mr. Blue," Gideon said with a nod. "I've heard a great deal about you."

Nicky grunted but offered the man a grin. "Can't say I've heard of you—but I imagine that's by design."

"What's going on?" I asked Gideon. "Why are you being brought in?"

"It's not your concern," a pinch-faced agent interjected, grabbing Gideon's arm.

Gideon jerked away and shoved the guy. Before the man could react, I stepped between them and put a hand against the guy's chest, holding him off.

"Who the hell are you, Tale?" I demanded. "I haven't seen you before." *Because I would've recognized your rat face and beady little eyes.*

"Norman Fredericks," he replied, looking down his long nose at me. "I've been working on special assignment with the Agency as the Tale liaison."

I heard Nicky snort. "Freddy the Ferret."

Ferret? Well, I wasn't far off. . . .

"Haven't seen you in a good twenty years," Nicky said, his tone cordial, but a coldness coming into his eyes. "Not since you got pinched by the feds for money laundering for the Ordinaries."

Freddy's beady eyes narrowed on Nicky. "My talents were underappreciated by the Tales back then. I get the respect I deserve now."

"I'm sure you do," Nicky drawled.

"What does the Agency have to do with Gideon?" I cut in, bringing us back to the point before they could get into a full-blown pissing match.

"We caught him trafficking fairy dust to Ordinaries," one of the other agents explained. I didn't like the look of him much better than I did Freddy the Ferret.

When I glanced at Gideon, his face was impassive, completely unreadable. But I could smell a rat both literally and figuratively. The Seelies were the only authorized fairy dust distributors among the Tales; and having the corner on the market raked in millions of dollars every year. I seriously doubted Papa Seelie would jeopardize his empire by selling to Ordinaries. And even if he was expanding their market, Gideon didn't strike me as the kind of guy to get caught doing it.

"I'm sure there's been some kind of mistake," I said, forcing a smile. "Turn Gideon over to me and I'll get to the bottom of things."

"I don't take orders from little girls," Freddy scoffed.

Nicky was up in his grill in a heartbeat, his expression deadly. "You'd better watch your mouth, Ferret."

Freddy laughed. "Right. And what are *you* going to do about it?" He shook his head. "Word is you've gone soft, Nicky. Your wife buys it and you go running off to hide?"

I grabbed Nicky's arm and pulled him back a few feet, pressing my hand against his chest. "It's all right, Nicky. I'll handle this."

"Yeah, Nicky," Freddy taunted. "Listen to your little girlfriend. *She'll* handle it. You sure as shit can't, you pussy."

Nicky moved so fast I didn't even see it coming. In one swift motion he grabbed Freddy's hand and twisted his arm at such an unnatural angle, the guy dropped to the floor with a howl of pain. "Who's the pussy now, Freddy?" Nicky spat. "Huh? Who's the pussy *now*, you rat-faced little *fuck*?"

Next thing I knew, all hell was breaking loose. The other agents went for Nicky, but Gideon busted the manacles apart with a quick jerk of his wrists and stepped in. His fist connected with the nose of one man, dropping him, and then had the other one on the ground so fast I didn't even see how.

"What *the hell* is going on?"

Nicky immediately let go of Freddy at the sound of Red's voice and took a step back.

"I asked a question," Red snapped. "Somebody better give me a goddamn answer!"

Freddy got to his feet and straightened his suit. "Assistant Director Little, we were bringing in this suspect when we were assaulted by your associates. You'd better believe I'll be filing a complaint with Director Addin."

Red grunted. "Get in line, Rat-boy. Next time you want to bring someone in, you Agency sellouts might want to call first. Now get outta my building."

"Assistant Director—"

Red batted her eyes at Freddy, daring him to go there. "I'm hungry, you little shit, and you're in my way. Are you seriously gonna push me on this?"

Freddy cast a furious glare at Nicky, knocking into him as he passed, then motioned for his cronies to follow him. As soon as the elevator doors had closed on them, Red jerked her chin at Gideon. "So are you guilty?"

Gideon's lips curled up on one side in an amused smirk. "Of many things. But not of the things of which they were accusing me."

"And what would those things be?" Red demanded.

He quickly repeated what he'd already told us. "The king is decidedly unhappy with someone selling D on the black market to Ordinaries and trying to make it look as if it's his people doing it. He sent me out tonight to gather intelligence."

"And?" I asked. "What did you find?"

He shrugged a powerful shoulder. "Nothing conclusive."

"What do you say you share the *in*conclusive, then?" I suggested. "Let us take it from here."

Gideon's expression grew somber once more. "No offense to the FMA," he said, "but the king prefers to handle this matter himself."

"Bullshit," Red snapped. "We have enough vigilantes running around right now."

I cast a nervous glance at Nicky, but he seemed unperturbed.

"You can tell his Royal Pain in the Ass that I'm not going to let him start a war with the Agency and blow our cover among the Ordinaries. The FMA will handle it."

Gideon's already hard face seemed to grow even harder. "I don't think he'll take very kindly to that directive."

"Not my problem," Red shot back.

"We Tales number in the thousands in the Here and Now," Gideon pointed out. "Perhaps you don't understand that there are those who believe we now have sufficient numbers to declare our presence."

Red took a menacing step forward, hands on her hips, ready to rip into the man towering over her, but Nate deftly swept in between her and Gideon with a placating smile. "Of course, the king is not among those who believe this, right?" Nate said.

Gideon inclined his head. "Of course not. My words were merely a statement of fact—not a warning."

"If your king knows something, he needs to tell us," I insisted. "We need to find out who's behind these factions."

Gideon shook his head. "My king would never discuss such matters with the FMA. He does not care to have his business matters scrutinized too closely."

"Then he can talk to me," Nicky interjected. "We have associates in common."

Gideon inclined his head. "I will put forward your request for a meeting."

"Fine," Red said with a huff as Nate unlocked the remnants of the manacles around Gideon's wrists. "I'm gonna grant some leeway on this one, but Trish goes with Nicky. Now, get outta here, Gideon, before I change my mind. Oh, and be sure to tell Lavender's mom I said hi."

Gideon actually chuckled at this. "I'm sure she'll be delighted." In the next moment the fairy was gone, having slipped through the fabric of time and space.

"What the hell was that all about?" Nate asked no one in particular as the four of us got into the elevator together.

"This is total bullshit, Red," I said. "The Agency's up to something."

She nodded. "Damned straight. I don't like this. First Spalding was butting in and demanding the bodies of those vampires, and now Freddy and his stooges are hauling in suspects like they run the place?"

"Why is the Agency getting so involved in our business all of a sudden?" I asked. "They've been content with our arrangement up until now."

Red didn't respond, but she was frowning, mulling it over. And she was still frowning when we parted from her and Nate and started for Nicky's Escalade.

"So, you and Freddy go back a ways?" I asked after we pulled out of the underground parking lot and into traffic.

"He came over from folklore in the nineteen-fifties and took up with the Sandman," Nicky told me, his voice dripping with disdain. "He liked being a button man for Halloran. Enjoyed doing all the dirty work his boss didn't want on his own hands."

"And now he's working for the Agency," I muttered. "Fantastic. This just keeps getting better and better."

Beatrice . . .

I straightened with a start at the sound of my name and glanced into the backseat, fully expecting to see someone sitting behind me.

Beatrice, come to me. . . .

"What's doin'?" Nicky asked, glancing over at me with a frown. "You okay?"

I twisted in my seat, craning to look into the back of the Escalade.

"Did you . . ." I didn't bother finishing my question. Of course Nicky hadn't heard anything. That was clear from the puzzled look on his face. I did one last check of the backseat, reassuring myself that no one was there. "Yeah. I'm fine," I lied, wrapping my arms around myself to hold in the shudder of apprehension threatening to break. "Let's just get this visit over with."

Chapter Eight

We waited a full forty-five minutes in the foyer of Halloran's mansion with his doormen glaring daggers at us before a stocky man with a barrel chest and biceps so large he couldn't lower his arms strode toward us, his face as hard as his abs. In spite of the fact that he wasn't particularly tall, his presence was menacing. There was no doubt in my mind that he was a force to be reckoned with.

"What the hell are you doing here, Blue?" the man demanded. "You got a lotta nerve showing your face around this place."

"I'm not here to start anything with you, Aloysius," Nicky shot back. "In fact, I'm not here on business at all. I'm just escorting Ms. Muffet. She needs to talk to Sophia."

Aloysius narrowed his eyes at us, his glare for Nicky particularly hostile. Finally, he nodded. "Follow me. She can see you in the study."

Calling the room where Nicky and I were taken a *study* was a gross understatement. Tim Halloran, crooked businessman and smarmy crime lord, had never struck me as being particularly erudite, but the room was filled with books on such topics as economics, finance, logistics, and accounting. Apparently, someone had been doing his homework. Or, the cynical side of me countered, he more likely wanted people to *think* he'd been doing his homework.

Unlike our wait in the foyer, our sojourn in the study was relatively short. We'd barely been alone for two minutes when the door opened again and a white Bengal tiger slunk in, prowling toward us warily.

Nicky reached for my hand and pulled me behind him, putting himself between me and the tigress. "Hello, Sophia," he said cautiously. "It's good to see you again. This is Trish Muffet from the FMA."

She slowly circled, sizing us up. Nicky shuffled with her, keeping me behind him, facing her at all times. Finally, there was a shimmer in the air and where the tiger had been now stood a beautiful—and completely naked—woman with long white hair and striking emerald eyes. I glanced at Nicky to gauge his reaction, but he seemed completely unmoved by the vision of loveliness before us.

"Hello yourself, Nicky Blue," Sophia purred, her voice a little husky, bringing to mind Eartha Kitt's portrayal of Catwoman in the old Batman TV series. She prowled toward him, a seductive smile curving her lips, then pressed into him, nuzzling up under his chin with a provocative noise that was something between a mew and a moan. "It's been a long, long time. And it was so good of you to bring a little kitten for me to play with. . . . I promise to be gentle with her."

I choked a little at what she was implying. "I'm sorry—*what?*"

Nicky cleared his throat and drew back a little, casting a slightly uncomfortable glance my way. "I'm afraid this isn't a social call, Sophia."

"Too bad," she purred, letting her long nails skim down his throat and along his chest. "There's nothing a cat enjoys more than batting around a couple of balls." She twisted away with a sigh, rubbing her backside against his crotch before sauntering a few steps and stretching out on the sofa, not bothering to hide any of her breathtakingly gorgeous body. "So, if you and your lovely friend didn't come to play with me, why are you here?"

Nicky led me to the closest chair, then took the one next to it and leaned forward, placing his forearms on his knees and clasping his hands together. "I'm really sorry, honey, but we have some bad news. Halloran's dead."

Sophia blinked her eyes languidly, her expression not altering in the slightest. Finally, she took a deep breath and let it out slowly before saying, "Good."

Now it was my turn to blink in astonishment. "You aren't distraught?" I blurted before I could stop myself.

She lifted a slender shoulder and let it drop again. "Perhaps once I would've been. But he has been very . . . *occupied* lately. I do not mind sharing, but he would not let me come along and did not bring his lovers here."

"Do you know anything about who they were?" I asked, trying to swallow my disgust at her lack of emotion over her dead lover. "What were their names? How did he meet them?"

Sophia turned her slightly feral gaze upon me. "You ask a lot of questions, Ms. Muffet."

"It's my job to ask a lot of questions," I reminded her. "Now, is there anything you can tell us that would help us determine who these women were? It's possible that his new lovers are the same two women who murdered him. One was a blonde, the other brunette."

She ran her hand along the edge of her body and over her hip in a seductive motion, and I saw Nicky perk up a little out of the corner of my eye. "No idea," she demurred. "All I know is that he was introduced to these women by an associate—as a celebration of their new partnership. This associate's name was not told to me. I know only that the deal was not quite finalized."

"Do you know if there was anything . . . *peculiar* about his new lovers?" I prompted.

Sophia batted her eyes at me. "Peculiar? I am a *tigress,* my dear. There is little I find peculiar."

"Were they vampires?" Nicky interjected, getting to the point.

Sophia shrugged again, lifting her chin haughtily. "I do not know. I do not care."

Beatrice. . . . Come to me. . . .

I jumped at the sound of the voice from the car and instinctively glanced around to look for the speaker, but once more I saw no one there. "Um," I stammered, feeling Nicky's curious gaze upon me and trying to recover. "Is there . . . uh . . . that is, would anyone else know who these women were?"

Sophia shrugged. "Perhaps Aloysius," she suggested. "The Sandman had grown very paranoid lately and would not let anyone else around him but Ally. However, they recently had a falling out because Ally was planning to leave and go into business with his lover at the whorehouse." Sophia's lips curled into a lascivious smile as she brought her leg forward and ran her hand down her thigh. "Now, if you're finished pumping me for information, there are other activities the three of us would no doubt find *much* more enjoyable. . . ."

Time to go.

I jumped to my feet, ready to be away from the hot little feline tramp before she started flashing her little kitty at us. I grabbed Nicky's hand and pulled him to his feet. "Let's go talk to Aloysius."

I dragged Nicky from the room with me and halfway down the hall before he pulled me to a halt. "Hey, hey—slow down. Where's the fire?"

"In her vagina, apparently," I muttered.

Nicky chuckled. "Sophia's always like that. You get used to it."

I grunted, doubting that very much.

Not having any clue where to start looking for Aloysius in the enormous mansion, we checked with the doormen to request an audience, only to find that the bodyguard had taken off as soon as Sophia was on her way to the study.

"Why would he leave so suddenly?" I asked Nicky once we were back in his Escalade and driving down the lane toward the main road. The afternoon sky was already growing dark, heavy clouds in the sky threatening to dump another round of snow on us. "We weren't even planning to question him."

Nicky shrugged. "Got me. But if I was going to lay odds—" He suddenly broke off, frowning as he squinted through the trees.

I followed the direction of his gaze and saw headlights in the distance, coming up quickly. Nicky switched off his own lights and pulled off the road, parking the Escalade in the shadows. A moment later, two black Lincolns drove past, and at the end of the caravan was a black box truck. "You've got to be kidding me," I muttered. "What the hell is the Agency doing here?"

Nicky flipped on the lights. "How about we go find out?"

The Agency goons had only about a thirty second lead on us, but by the time we reached Halloran's mansion, they were already busting in, guns drawn.

Nicky cursed under his breath as he threw the Escalade into park. "Fucking figures."

I followed his line of sight and saw Freddy the Ferret standing in the doorway, cell phone at his ear, a shit-eating grin draped across his thin lips. But before I could respond, the sound of gunfire erupted from within the mansion.

"Sophia," I breathed, throwing open the door and leaping out. But before I could get very far, Nicky grabbed me around the waist and lifted me from my feet. I kicked and squirmed, struggling to get out of his hold. "Let me go! We have to help her!"

Nicky's arms tightened around me. "What are you going to do?" he hissed in my ear as two more loud pops fired off in the house. "You're not even carrying."

I instantly went still and waited for him to set me back on my feet. "She's a tigress," I reminded him, my voice tight with tears. "She'll attack them if they barge in."

"I know, baby," he whispered.

I sagged against him, glad his arms were still wrapped around me when the agents emerged from the house a few minutes later, dragging Sophia's body by her white hair and leaving a long red streak on the stone steps.

"What the hell are you doing here?" I shrieked, furious tears hot on my cheeks. I broke out of Nicky's hold and stormed toward them, shoving the agent who held Sophia's hair in his grasp. "You didn't have to kill her, you fucking asshole!" I shoved him again, then grabbed his hand, trying to pry his fingers loose. "Let her go, god-damn it!"

"Turn her loose, Pryor."

My head snapped up and rage filled my veins with furious fire when I saw Ian Spalding's smug, indifferent expression. Something between a growl and a scream erupted from my gut, burning my throat as I launched myself at Ian's throat, fully intending to rip it out. As it was, I was only able to get in a right hook to his jaw before someone grabbed me from behind and pinned my arms.

"Get your hands off her!" I heard Nicky growl. And then the guy holding me dropped to the snow, taking me with him. My head smacked into the ice, making the world go dark for a split second before I saw Nicky's face before me, his brows drawn together in concern. A shadow loomed up behind him.

"Watch out," I managed, my words slurred.

Nicky twisted up in time to catch the arm swinging toward him, then turned it with a jerk. The gun dropped and Freddy the Ferret face-planted in the snow next to me, his expression contorted with pain.

"Nicky, you fucking prick," he ground out. "I'll kill you for this."

"Well, I think we've had enough fun for one night, don't you?" Ian drawled, taking my elbow and helping me to my feet.

Nicky stood across from me, his hands raised in response to the three agents whose guns were now trained on his head. But the look in his eye told me he was about two seconds away from taking them down.

"Tell your goons to lower their guns," I said, my vision blurring annoyingly. "I just want to know what's going on."

Ian jerked his head toward his guys, who holstered their weapons and took a couple of steps out of Nicky's reach. Nicky hurried toward me and took my face in his hands, his worried gaze searching mine. "You okay, doll?"

I smiled in spite of the pounding in my head. Was I *okay*? How could I *not* be when he was looking at me that way?

"I need you to read her," Ian ordered, his words cutting across my moment of hopeful happiness. "Tell me what she was thinking when she died."

"Fuck you," Nicky snapped, his expression going deadly. "She's not doing shit for you. If you wanted to know what Sophia had in her head, you shouldn't have killed her."

"She attacked us," Ian said, his tone infuriatingly reasonable. "I couldn't allow her to kill my men."

"What the hell are you doing here, Ian?" I spat.

"Same thing you were, I imagine," he smirked. "Oh, yes. I saw you sitting there in the woods. Nice try, though." He blinked at me expectantly. "Now, the tigress?"

"Not until you show her the respect she deserves," I insisted, squaring my shoulders. "I'll call in the FMA to take care of her and the guards I'm assuming you knocked off to get to her, and then I'll read her."

Ian's lips flattened in an angry line, but he forced a smile and inclined his head. "Very well then."

I tried calling Red first, but the call went to her voice mail and I hung up before leaving her a message. I tried Al next, and he picked up on the first ring. "Hi, Al," I said, sniffing when the sound of his steady voice brought tears to my own. "I need a team out at Tim Halloran's place." I pegged Ian with a furious glare. "His girlfriend Sophia was murdered by the Agency."

"Murdered?" Ian hissed, as I pocketed my phone, not having waited to hear Al's response. "I told you—I had no choice!"

I ignored him and squatted down by Sophia. I hadn't known the tigress. Hadn't really even liked her when we'd chatted with her in Halloran's study. But as I looked down at her now, I felt such a weight of sadness, it nearly knocked me on my ass. She didn't deserve to be gunned down by these Agency assholes. No one did. And as I gently tilted her head toward me and looked into her eyes, a horrible foreboding began to creep just beneath my skin, making my muscles twitch with apprehension. I tried to shove the feeling aside and waited for the connection to begin with Sophia's mind, but it didn't come.

"That's weird," I muttered. I shifted positions and tilted her head at a slightly different angle. But had the same result. She was completely and totally blocked from my sight. I shook my head a little, trying to clear my own muddled thoughts, but the movement cost me my balance, and the next thing I knew, I was face-down in the snow again.

Nicky was there in an instant, helping me back to my feet. "You all right, doll?"

I tried to nod, but I swayed again. "Shit. I guess not."

"That's it, I'm getting you to the hospital," he informed me, bending to scoop me up into his arms. As much as I would've loved the whole romantic carry and snuggle back to the Escalade, I wasn't about to leave Sophia in the Agency's clutches. I wiggled out of his hold, dropping back to my feet.

"I can't leave yet," I told him.

"Trish—"

"I'm *not* leaving her, Nicky," I insisted, blinking rapidly to try to bring him back into focus.

"Nicky?" Ian repeated, a smug grin slowly curving his mouth. "Nicky *Blue*?"

Nicky eyed him warily, his muscles visibly tensing, preparing for a brawl. "In the flesh."

Ian pegged me with that cocky grin that I'd once, in a brief moment of weakness and profound naïveté, found so charming but which now turned my stomach. He jerked his thumb at Nicky. "So, this is the guy you were talking about in your sleep?"

My eyes went wide, but before I could really sink into my humiliation and get all comfy, Nicky snapped, "How the hell do *you* know she talks in her sleep?"

Ian's grin widened, and he shoved his hands in his pockets, puffing his chest out a little. "You didn't know I fucked her?"

"Shut up, you bastard!" I hissed, my heart shattering at the look of shock on Nicky's face.

"Oh, yeah," Ian drawled, apparently reveling in my complete and utter mortification. "I *totally* hit that."

I grabbed Nicky's arm and tried to pull him away, but he was anchored where he stood, his expression taking on a deadly look that frightened me a little, but apparently had no effect on Ian, who leaned in conspiratorially and whispered, "She might look innocent, my man, but she's a *freak* for it. You get a piece of that sweet ass yet?"

Nicky struck lightning-fast. His arm shot out, his hand grasping Ian by the throat and lifting him from his feet before he slammed him down on the hood of his car. Ian kicked wildly, clawing at Nicky's hand around his throat, ripping into Nicky's skin, but Nicky didn't even flinch. He narrowed his eyes at Ian, the rage in his expression twisting his features into a frightening mask. And for one brief moment, he was unrecognizable to me.

"Nicky, let him go," I said, trying to pull his hand away from Ian's throat. But his fingers only tightened. Ian's lips were beginning to turn an alarming shade of blue. "Nicky!"

He suddenly released the Ordinary and took a step back, pegging Ian with a murderous glare, letting him know that he'd take him down in a second if the asshole pissed him off again. "Apologize to her," Nicky hissed. "Right. Fucking. Now."

Ian coughed and sputtered and sent an unrepentant glare Nicky's way. "Go to hell."

Nicky took a menacing step forward, sending Ian stumbling backward into the car's grill. "Wanna try again, dickhead?"

Ian's mouth twisted into a furious frown, but then he straightened to his full height and smoothed his sleeves to regain his composure before forcing a mirthless grin. He inclined his head toward me briefly before grinding out, "Forgive me, Trish. What I said was in poor taste." Then he gestured to his men. "Let's get the hell out of here. We're not going to get anything from these stiffs."

I managed to stay on my feet long enough to watch the Agency bastards pile into their vehicles and take off. But the second they were out of sight, the world seemed to shift, and I listed, throwing out my arms to catch myself this time. Luckily, another set of arms was there to keep me from hitting the ground. And this time when Nicky scooped me up, I didn't protest. I rested my head against his chest, suddenly so tired I couldn't keep my eyes open any longer.

Nicky gave me a little shake. "Stay awake, doll. You need to keep those pretty eyes open. Can you do that for me?"

I nodded even as my lids began to drift closed again.

"Trish," he said, jostling me again. "Wake up. Come on."

"Can't," I muttered, alarmed to hear my words slurring. "So tired . . ." He somehow managed to get the car door open and set me inside, buckling me in. I squinted at him, trying hard to stay coherent. "So sick . . . of getting my head knocked around." I lifted some of my curls out of the way to show him the scar on my forehead from where one of Sebille's followers had slammed my head into the dashboard of his car last fall and split my skull open. It would've been a deadly blow if Sebille hadn't healed me just so she could try to kill me later.

Nicky smoothed his thumb over the scar, a soft look coming into eyes that had been murderous just minutes before. Then his hand cupped my face and his thumb smoothed across my cheek.

"You're bleeding," I murmured, catching a glimpse of a thin trickle of crimson where Ian had clawed at the back of his hand.

Nicky shook his head. "It's nothin', doll. Don't worry about it."

"Put pressure on it," I murmured, reaching into my coat pocket and pulling out the handkerchief I kept there, too foggy to realize what I'd grabbed until Nicky had already taken it from me.

He grinned a little as he smoothed his thumb over the *NB* monogram. "Where'd you get this?"

I narrowed my eyes as he went all fuzzy on me. "From you," I told him, suddenly feeling a little nauseated. I closed my eyes. "You gave it to me that day in my lab."

"And you kept it?"

I nodded ever so slightly. "Of course I did. It was from you. . . ."

I felt the back of his fingers drift down the curve of my jaw and opened my eyes. He was gazing down at me so intently, my breath caught in my chest.

"Trish—"

"What the hell happened here?"

Nicky closed his eyes for a beat, then pulled back from me. "The

Agency," he explained to Nate, who'd suddenly appeared beside him. "They came in guns blazing. Killed Sophia and the guards. Trish called it in to Al Addin a few minutes ago."

Nate nodded, then cast a concerned look toward me. "Did they hurt Trish?"

Nicky's face suddenly went dark again. "No. I got into it with one of the agents and she was in the middle of it and got a concussion. It's my fault she's hurt."

Nate leaned into the car and gave me a comforting smile, patting me on the thigh. "I've got this," he assured me. "Let Nicky get you outta here, okay?"

I nodded, then rested my head back against the seat, relieved to be able to turn the crime scene over to someone else and wishing like hell that I knew what Nicky had been about to say. Unfortunately, any hope I'd had of him renewing the conversation was extinguished the moment unconsciousness wrapped me in its arms and dragged me down into its dark embrace.

Chapter Nine

"I'm fine," I insisted as we drove away from the hospital a couple hours later. "Really."

Nicky's grip on the steering wheel tightened. "You shouldn't be," he replied. "You had one hell of a concussion. Tales heal fast, but they should've kept you longer. What if they sent you home too soon and something happens? I don't trust that hack doctor."

"Dr. Knowall might've been a total sham in Make Believe," I conceded, "but he's earned a legitimate medical degree from both the Ordinaries and Tales since coming here."

I honestly was just as surprised as Nicky that I'd only had to spend two hours in the Tale hospital before they assured me everything looked fine and I was free to go. But I'd taken a look at the X rays myself, had gone over all the other tests, and I would've made the same diagnosis.

He shook his head. "I still don't like it. And that Agency cocksucker better hope he never crosses my path again. Did you really sleep with that asshole?"

I sighed, hating to admit to my serious lapse in judgment. "Unfortunately."

"What the hell did you see in him?"

I shrugged. "I don't know. He was hot and I was lonely, I guess."

We didn't speak for most of the drive back to Nicky's. Now that my brain was fully functioning again, I was so humiliated by what

Ian had divulged, I couldn't even look at Nicky. I watched the land-
scape zip by, wishing the drive was just a little longer and not looking
forward to the uncomfortable conversation that was going to have to
take place at some point. I had no idea how I'd even begin to explain
to Nicky why I'd been talking about him in my sleep. *Gee, Nicky, I've
been secretly in love with you for decades,* was just this side of pathetic.

"So, is it true?" Nicky asked suddenly, making me start and bump
my head against the passenger window.

"Freaking hell!" I muttered, rubbing my head where I'd smacked
into the glass. "Is what true?"

"That you said my name in your sleep when you were with Ian?"

Oh. Wow. Okay. So we were going to do this now. Awesome.

I swallowed hard, but my mouth was dry and my answer came out
as a quiet rasp. "Apparently."

"So . . ." he drawled, a slow grin curving his lips, "does this mean
you've had a little *crush* on me for a while, Trish?"

"Oh, God," I muttered, my face instantly on fire. I glanced out
the window, briefly wondering how much it could really hurt if I
bailed out.

"It's okay, you can say it," he teased, then added in a ridiculously
high-pitched voice that was supposed to be all girlie, " 'Yes, Nicky,
I've had a crush on you for *ages.* You're so *handsome.*' Go ahead. It's
easy."

I cast a tortured look his way, wondering if he knew just how
close to the truth he was. "Could we just drop this, please?"

He shook his head, his grin growing, as impossible as that
seemed. "Nope, not until you admit you like me."

"*Like* you?" I repeated. "Are you kidding me? What are you,
like *ten*?"

He chuckled. "Dear Trish—do you like me? Check *yes* or *no.*"

"Oh, my God," I groaned, rolling my eyes. "This is ludicrous."

"Then stop avoiding the question," he prompted with a laugh.

I punched him in the shoulder, which served only to make him
laugh harder. "Would you shut up?"

"Just say it."

I crossed my arms over my chest and lifted my chin a notch. "I'm
not saying it. You can just sit there and stew in curiosity."

"Why won't you say it?"

"Why should I?" I countered.

"Why *shouldn't* you?" he shot back. "You really can't deny I'm irresistible, doll. Charming, funny . . . devilishly handsome, too. Oh, and humble."

"Oh, yes, *humble*," I mocked. "We can't forget *that* one."

Nicky sent an expectant glance my way. "So . . . ?"

"Good Lord," I huffed. "Fine! *Yes,* Nicky, I've had a *crush* on you for *ages*."

He grunted, but was still grinning. "Good." And that was it. No more questions. No more discussion. He dropped it just like that.

Which was totally infuriating.

Good? *Good?* What the hell did he mean by *that*? Was it just his male ego strutting around, metaphorical chest puffed out, because he could hold it over the other guy's head? Or was he actually glad that I'd been dreaming about him? If so, why didn't he ask me more? Why didn't he ask me what I'd been dreaming about? If I'd dreamed about him often? He didn't even ask me how long I'd had a crush on him, for crying out loud. Criminy!

I sat in the passenger's seat torturing myself the rest of the way to Nicky's, trying to analyze the inflection in his voice in that one simple word, the expression on his face. But when he pulled through the gates, I still hadn't reached a satisfactory conclusion. I was scowling so intently that when I didn't immediately get out of the Escalade, Nicky came around and opened my door.

"Trish?" he said softly, the levity we'd shared gone now. "We're here, doll."

I turned my scowl on him, but the tender look in his eyes dissipated my irritation in an instant. "Sorry," I muttered. "Lost in thought."

He took my hand and helped me out, then led me up the steps, my hand still clutched tightly in his. I expected him to turn me loose once we were inside, especially in light of what his teasing had goaded me into admitting, but instead of releasing my hand, his fingers shifted, twining with mine more securely than ever. Without a word, he led me into the kitchen and only then did he release my hand so that he could help me out of my coat. Then he pulled out one of the chairs at the island bar and handed me up before turning away and busying himself at the stove.

I propped my chin on my hand, watching him open and close cabinet doors and rummage through the pantry until he found everything he was looking for. Twenty minutes later, he set a steaming mug of hot chocolate in front of me along with a plate of herbed cheeses, crackers, and an assortment of fresh fruits and vegetables.

"Sorry it's not more," he said with a shrug of apology. "I'm not exactly a gourmet."

I offered him a grateful smile. "This is perfect. Thank you."

I took a sip of the hot chocolate, loving the path of warmth it left as it traveled down my throat and into my stomach. But that heat was nothing to what lanced through me when Nicky scooted the other bar stool close to mine and took a seat next me, silently sipping at his own mug, his elbow touching mine, his fingertips occasionally brushing against my own when we happened to reach for the same strawberry or slice of cheese. And when the food was gone and our mugs were empty, we remained there in companionable silence, elbow to elbow, shoulder to shoulder, knee to knee. At some point, I leaned my head against his shoulder, and I heard him sigh before he dipped his head to press a lingering kiss to my curls.

It was a perfect moment. One of the few in my life up to that point. I wish I could've frozen that moment in time, kept it from ever moving on, but eventually I heaved a sigh of my own and lifted my head.

"Nicky," I whispered, not sure what I planned to say next. I think I honestly just wanted to hear his name on my lips. But when I caught a glimpse of his dark frown, I knew our moment was over.

"I need to go out for a while," he announced suddenly, gathering up the dishes and carrying them to the sink. "Will you be okay here by yourself?"

"Where are you going?" I replied, ignoring his question.

He shrugged evasively. "Just out. I have some things to take care of."

The edge of his voice told me what he had in mind. "You're going hunting," I guessed. "You're going out looking for Dracula."

He glanced my way and I could tell he was about to lie to me, deny what he was planning, but he must've thought better of it. "Yeah. But the first thing I want to do is pay a visit to Happy Endings and find out how the hell Aloysius knew to take off from Halloran's before the Agency showed up."

"Maybe it was just a coincidence," I suggested.

"Maybe," Nicky agreed. "But I plan to ask him anyway. And I don't plan on asking nicely."

I hopped down from the bar. "Then I'm going with you."

"No way," he shot back. "You're staying here where it's safe."

"You have no idea if it's safer here than anywhere else," I countered. "I was attacked in my apartment—up until then, I'd thought it was pretty safe, too."

"This is different," he mumbled, rinsing out our mugs. "You have no idea what I've seen when hunting."

"Don't I?" I said, coming over to stand at his elbow. "You don't think I've seen some pretty freaky shit over the years?"

"It's not open for discussion," he insisted, his tone leaving no room for argument. Too bad I wasn't listening.

"This is my *job,* Nicky," I reminded him. "I'm *supposed* to help bring down the bad guys. You don't think the crime scenes I visit have the potential for danger? It's what I'm trained to deal with. If anyone should be staying at home, it's you! You need to stay out of it and leave things to the professionals."

At this his eyes went wide. "The professionals? Because you guys are doing such a bang-up job bringing Drac down?"

I pressed my lips together, trying to bite back my angry retort. I counted to five as he went around me to grab his jacket, then said between clenched teeth, "You are going to get yourself killed."

"*I'm* not the one I'm worried about getting killed!" he retorted, his voice so loud it echoed in the enormous kitchen. "I'm not letting you come with me. It's too dangerous!"

I slapped my hands on my hips. "You can't be serious!"

"Serious as a heart attack." He shrugged into his jacket. "You're staying here and that's final."

"Goddamn it!" I yelled, slamming my palm down on the counter. "Stop treating me like a child!"

He jerked back a little at my accusation. "What the hell are you talking about? I'm not treating you like a child."

"The hell you aren't!" I stomped toward him, hands back on my hips. "What with the whole *crush* thing in the car. *Crush,* Nicky? I'm not a little schoolgirl who has *crushes,* okay? And you're always 'doll' this and 'honey' that! Then there's the tugging on my ringlets. I *know* they look ridiculous, okay?" My hands were flailing around now in frustration. "I *know* I look like a naive little girl because of the freaking ringlets, but I'm a grown *woman,* Nicky. In case you hadn't noticed, I have boobs and everything. Oh, and by the way—they're really *nice* ones!"

My chest was heaving from my angry—and somewhat incoherent—outburst as I stared at him, waiting for him to respond. But he just returned my gaze, his expression blank. Then his lips twitched at the corners and his eyes twinkled. "I've noticed," he said finally.

I frowned. "What have you noticed?"

He sauntered toward me, his lips curving into a full-blown grin now. When his body was just inches from mine, he slipped his arm around me and pulled me closer. "I've noticed you're a grown woman," he said, his voice low. His gaze flicked down to my chest, which was heaving now for another reason. "That you're *all* woman."

"Yeah?" I managed to choke out. "In spite of my ringlets?"

"I like your ringlets."

"You do?"

He nodded and dipped his head until his lips were near my ear. "But you're still not going with me." He chuckled and abruptly released me, no doubt planning to leave me all gaspy and breathless, but two could play this game.

Before he could walk away, my hand shot out and I grabbed the front of his shirt, jerking him back to me. His eyes went wide as I leaned into him, pressing my body into his. "Nicky," I whispered, my mouth close to his. God, it was torture not to lean all the way in and steal the searing kiss that was smoldering in the air between us. But that wasn't part of the game. "You need me."

His powerful body shuddered a little as he swallowed hard and ground out, "Yeah?"

"Mmm-hmm," I replied as I slid my hand into the pocket of his jeans, eliciting a hissed curse from him. "You just don't realize how badly."

His voice was shot to hell when he said, "Oh, I think I know, doll."

"Good." My fingers closed around his car keys and jerked them out of his pocket at the same moment I pushed him away and snatched my coat off the back of the bar stool. "It's settled then. I'm going with you."

I slung my coat over my shoulder and sashayed from the kitchen, swinging my hips in triumph. And when I cast a glance over my shoulder, I watched Nicky's dumbfounded look change into one of bemusement and then amusement as that smile I adored broke over his face.

"Holy hell," he chuckled, shaking his head. "I guess you are."

Chapter Ten

As we stood in the shadowy parking lot of the deserted office building across from Happy Endings, I turned up the collar of my jacket, unable to shake the feeling we were being watched. Nicky must've felt it, too, because I saw him scan the darkness with his sharp gaze, searching for any indication of who might be lurking in the shadows. But apparently satisfied that we weren't in any immediate danger, he opened the back of the Escalade and lifted away the spare tire cover in the floor to reveal a veritable arsenal.

"What do you want?" he asked, stowing a pair of wicked-looking knives in a holster he'd slipped on over his T-shirt. He loaded a fresh magazine into his Glock, then tucked it in the back of his pants. He pegged me with an expectant look as he slipped back into his leather jacket. "See anything you like?"

Aside from those sexy biceps and rockin' pecs?

I forced myself to focus. "You want me to carry a gun?"

He shrugged. "Gun, knife . . . makes no difference to me. But if you're going, you're going armed."

I cocked my head to one side. "We're going into a brothel, Nicky. What could possibly happen?"

"Let's just say not everyone there will be happy to see me." He turned back to his arsenal and selected a pistol from one of the foam inserts and quickly jammed a magazine into it, then slipped his arms inside my unbuttoned coat and around my waist to tuck the gun into the back of my jeans. His hands lingered for just a moment against the small of my back. "Stay close to me, doll."

I nodded, my hands drifting up to rest against his chest. "I think I can manage that."

The slow smile that curved his lips ended on a wink, but then he abruptly released me and slammed the door. "All right then, let's do this." He grabbed my hand as we climbed the steps to Happy Endings' red door, giving the valet a sharp nod. The kid ducked his head and turned away, obviously knowing better than to question Nicky. We stood on the top step for a moment while Nicky blew out a breath and rolled his neck. Then he pressed the doorbell and loosened his shoulders while we waited.

I frowned a little watching him. Good Lord. Was he seriously *limbering up*? What exactly *did* he expect to happen? Luckily, I didn't have much of a chance to think about it before the door swung open to reveal one of the seven dwarves who helped run the place.

"Hey there, Pete," Nicky said with forced politeness. "Ted have the night off?"

The little man with a long blond braided beard and bushy unibrow gave Nicky and me the once-over before grumping, "What the hell are you doing here, Nicky? You've got one helluva lot of nerve showing your face around this place."

"I wanna see Snow," Nicky told him.

Pete grunted. "She's not here." He tried to slam the door shut in our faces, but Nicky caught the edge of it and shoved, sending the man stumbling back several feet.

"Bullshit. I know she's here." Nicky pulled me inside with him and strode down a short hall to the waiting room. He glanced around quickly, then headed for a door of reinforced steel across the room. "Buzz us in."

Pete rushed forward and blocked the door. "Why the hell should I let in you and your little lemon tart here to see Snow after what you did?"

Nicky cast an uncomfortable glance my way. "That's ancient history," he mumbled. "Now, you gonna take me to her, or am I gonna have to go exploring on my own?"

Pete grunted again, apparently starting every answer this way. "Fine," he spat. "But don't say I didn't warn you if she cuts your nuts off and rams 'em down your throat."

I sent a wide-eyed glance Nicky's way, wondering what the hell he'd done to piss off Snow White so much that she'd want to relieve him of his dangly bits. A buzzer sounded as Pete pressed a button under the counter that released the inner security door, rescuing me from further speculation. Nicky pulled open the steel door and motioned for me to go first.

"Just him," Pete barked, throwing out an arm to block my entrance. He gave me the once-over again, more thoroughly this time, lingering on my chest longer than I liked. "You can stay here and keep me company."

"Uh, thanks," I demurred, "but—"

He sidled a little closer, wedging himself in between Nicky and me. "Ah, come on, baby. You don't know what you're missin'." He wagged that massive caterpillar on his forehead at me. "You ever had a dwarf go down on you? I promise it'll be like nothin' you've ever experienced before."

"Back off, Pete," Nicky growled. "She's with me."

Pete shrugged. "Not usually what I'm into, but I'm game. Hell, you're a good enough lookin' guy even if you are a dickhead."

Nicky pegged Pete with a murderous glare and ushered me inside. "Don't make me kill you, Pete." He slammed the door behind us but not before I caught a glimpse of Pete wagging his tongue at me in what had to be the most disgustingly obscene gesture I'd ever witnessed.

Trying not to dwell on the skeezy dwarf, I turned my attention to the dim halls of Happy Endings. If the road to hell was paved with good intentions, the road to depravity was apparently paved with red shag carpet and black wall sconces blazing the way like runway lights. And if there'd been any doubt about what kind of establishment we'd entered, the moans and cries of passion seeping out from under closed doors would've clued me in.

"Wow," I muttered, trying to swallow the little bit of vomit that had risen in my throat. "Why do I feel like I just stepped into an upscale porno?"

Nicky snorted with quiet laughter. "Seen a few of those, have you?"

I felt the heat rising to my cheeks and was glad for the dim light in the hallways. Okay, so maybe I'd switched the TV to Cinemax a few times in recent years when the loneliness had gotten to me and the ache in the center of my chest—and other areas—had been too much to bear. Honestly, though, I hadn't really needed the stuff on cable to provide inspiration. All I had to do was close my eyes and remember my latest dream about Nicky.

Luckily, Nicky was more intent on finding Snow White and her lover than finding out about my history of sexual solitaire. I had to jog a little beside him to keep up with his long strides as he navigated the halls. Obviously, he knew his way around the place.

"So," I said, drawing out the word, "I guess you've been back here before?"

Nicky glanced down at me, his cheeks going a little crimson. "I hung out with Snow for a while, but it was a long time ago."

I felt my chest constrict. I'd known about him and Red and had made my peace with that, but the unexpected news that Snow White had found pleasure in Nicky's arms while I was lying cold and alone in my bed most nights, with nothing more than my fantasies to keep me company, was like Truth had shoved her hand into my chest and given my heart a good squeeze just to remind me that I was her bitch.

When my steps faltered, Nicky moved closer to my side and dipped his head. "Ah, shit," he muttered. "Trish, it's not what you think—"

"It's fine," I said in a rush, cutting him off and picking up my pace. "You don't need to explain."

I heard his quick steps as he followed. He grabbed my arm and gently pulled me to a halt. "You don't understand—"

"Really, Nicky!" I interrupted, glancing up and down the hall, wishing someone would come out of one of those doors and keep him from saying anything more. "I don't want to hear this."

He lifted my chin with the edge of his hand and I was surprised to see the pain in his eyes. He looked tortured, torn. "What I was going to say is that nothing ever happened between Snow and me—and she's pissed as hell about it. I hung out here now and then back in the day 'cause Snow was a friend. But that's all she's ever been."

I tried to look away, but he gently guided my face back to him. The way he was looking at me now made my heart trip over itself. Something shifted in the air between us, and the tug in the center of my chest pulled me closer to him, but this time I didn't resist. I began to tremble a little as his head dipped toward mine.

"Well, if it isn't Nicky Blue . . ."

Nicky cursed under his breath and let his hand drop away from me before forcing a rakish grin. He turned and spread his arms wide. "Hello, Snow," he drawled, going to her and enveloping her in a brief hug as he pressed a kiss to her cheek. "You're looking as beautiful as ever."

Olivia "Snow" White gave him a sultry smile and a wink that would've melted a lesser man. "Flatterer."

God, no wonder her business was thriving. . . .

She leaned out around Nicky's shoulder and gave me a sweet little smile that didn't fool me for a minute. "And who's this?" She gasped theatrically and rushed to me, taking hold of my upper arms. "Is this Trish Muffet? I recognized you from your sweet little ringlets! Oh, my darling—if things don't work out at the FMA, you really *must* come work for me! I have men who love the whole little schoolgirl look!"

I managed a smile in return, but was *so* not in the mood to be patronized. "Oh? Do they get tired of a used up, has-been princess who'd spread her legs for anyone?"

She laughed, but there was no amusement in it. "Not as tired as they get of a cock-tease whose legs have to be pried open with a crowbar."

I batted my lashes and smiled sweetly. "I'd rather hand out crowbars to pry open my legs than 'now serving' tickets to the turnstile in my vagina."

I caught a brief glimpse of Snow's enraged expression just before Nicky stepped in front of me, his chastising look negated by his unsuccessful attempt to smother a grin. "Try to play nicely," he whispered. "We need information, remember?"

I rolled my eyes and heaved a sigh. It might've been a lot easier to let Snow's insults roll off my back if I hadn't known that she'd wanted to be flat on hers with the man I was not-so-secretly in love with. And to see her standing there in her black negligee, looking absolutely stunning and sexy, while I stood there pouting in my boring-as-hell jeans, sweater, and standard issue pea coat didn't help boost my confidence in spite of all Nicky's assurances he wasn't—and never had been—interested in the sultry madam. At least I'd traded my snow boots for the lug-soled biker boots Lavender and Seth had sent me for Christmas. That was something, I guess.

Beatrice...

My head snapped around toward the sound of the voice that seemed to be just over my right shoulder.

"Trish?"

She's not the one he wants, the voice reminded me. *She's not the one I want....*

"Trish," Nicky said again, taking hold of my arms and bending to peer into my face intently. "You okay, doll?"

I glanced over my shoulder again, half expecting to see the mystery man slipping out of the shadows to stand beside me and laugh at the confused expression on my face. But of course there was no one there. I gave my head a quick shake, then offered Nicky a weak smile. "I'm fine." He looked unconvinced, so I patted his chest lightly and forced my smile to be a little stronger. "Really, Nicky, I'm fine."

Snow coughed pointedly behind us. "Did you actually want to see *me,* Nicky, or were you and your girlfriend planning to pay for a little fun? I have a business to run. And, frankly, darling, as reluctant as I am to turn away a paying customer, I'd much rather tell you to go fuck *yourself.*"

"Playing nicely, was it?" I snarked at Nicky.

He groaned and took my hand in his, keeping me close to his side when he turned around to face Snow. "Maybe we could chat in your office?"

Snow inclined her head and pivoted with a flounce of black chiffon, motioning us to follow. "I'll give you ten minutes."

"Works for me," Nicky said with a shrug. "Might want to ask Aloysius to join us."

Snow visibly stiffened, but she didn't even spare a glance over her shoulder as she glided down the hall. "Why ever would you need to speak with Ally?"

"Tim Halloran's dead," Nicky told her.

This brought Snow's feet to a halt. She waited just a beat before turning around, no doubt to dampen the joy she felt at hearing the crime lord had bought it. "How very unfortunate."

"What's unfortunate is that Sophia is dead as well," I said, watching her expression. "She was killed in an Agency raid on the compound. A raid from which your lover was curiously absent."

She cast a quick glance up and down the hallway, then grabbed

Nicky's arm and pulled him after her as she hurried down the hall. I found myself jogging again to keep up and was glad when Snow threw open a set of intricately carved double doors and ushered us inside. I was a little shocked at the opulence of the room, from crystal chandelier to plush furniture, but my shock paled in comparison to what Snow apparently was experiencing.

"There must be some mistake," she said, not nearly as confident now as she'd been in the hallway. "Sophia wasn't supposed to be harmed. That was the deal."

Nicky gave her a stern look that would've shaken even the most hardened criminal. "I think you'd better start talking."

"Ally has been trying to get out from under Halloran for years now," Snow explained. She sat on her white settee, her head hanging. "He'd been skimming from Halloran's coffers, saving the money so that we could start a new life together. But after all the shit with Sebille Fenwick two years ago, Halloran started watching things much more closely. Ally and I had to put our plans on hold."

"So you thought you'd have the Sandman knocked off?" Nicky demanded.

She lifted her head, her eyes pained. "It wasn't like that," she retorted. "Someone approached Ally and asked him to set up a meeting with Halloran. They had a business proposition for him."

"And was this someone from the Agency?" I asked.

Snow nodded. "It was some guy named Norman Fredericks. Ally said he used to work for Halloran but had gone to work for the Agency."

Nicky shook his head. "That fucking ferret."

"Ally said Halloran came back from the initial meeting talking about how a new day would soon be dawning," Snow continued. "He told me the Sandman said the deal he'd been offered was huge, that it would change everything. Ally was worried that if Halloran became even more powerful, we'd never get out from under him."

"What was the deal?" I questioned. "Did Aloysius tell you?"

She shook her head. "He didn't know the specifics, but he thought it might have something to do with supplying fairy dust to the Agency."

I heard Nicky curse from his seat next to me, putting into words exactly what I was thinking. If the Agency was trying to get their hands on fairy dust, which had been expressly forbidden by their treaty with the FMA, there was no telling what they were planning.

"So how did the deal go south?" I prompted.

Snow heaved a long sigh. "Ally—"

"Olivia."

Snow bolted to her feet at the sound of her lover's voice. And so did Nicky, his gun already in his hand and aimed at Aloysius as the gangster emerged from his hiding place in Snow's closet holding a gun of his own.

Late to the party, I shot to my feet as well, glad Nicky had insisted I bring along the pistol tucked in my waistband. For the moment, I left it where it was, though, as a tactical edge.

"Don't say another word, baby," Aloysius ordered, slowly circling around to where Snow waited, her expression growing increasingly panicked.

"Ally, please," she begged, clasping her hands together at her chest. "Just tell them what happened. You did nothing wrong."

Aloysius grunted. "Tell that to the FMA. I'm not letting them pin Sophia's murder on me."

"It's only a matter of time before Red Little comes calling," Nicky told him. "Do you want to deal with her instead?"

Aloysius snorted with laughter. "She's pregnant!" he retorted. "What's she gonna do?"

"She could still kick your ass, and you know it," Nicky insisted. "Now put down the gun and tell me what the hell happened with Halloran's deal. I'd hate to have to shoot you and ruin Snow's white carpet."

"Ally, listen to him!" Snow entreated. "Please, baby—for *me.*"

Aloysius's grip tightened on his gun for a split second, but then he held up his hands and let it slip down onto his finger. I rushed forward and took the gun, ejecting the magazine and the bullet in the chamber before tucking it into my coat pocket for safekeeping.

"Looks like you gotta brain after all," Nicky said. "Now sit your ass down and start talking."

"It's like Snow said," Aloysius began. "We've been trying to start a new life. We thought maybe we'd open up our own escort service, fall back on what I know. It's not like I can just go around shooting people in the ass with magical arrows like I did in Make Believe—"

Holy shit! Aloysius was a freaking cupid?

"—so with Snow's business experience, we figured we could make a go of it. But we needed resources to start a business and I wasn't going to let Snow carry me financially. I had to contribute something."

"So you thought you'd double-cross your boss and put him out of the picture?" I asked. "Having him killed seems a bit extreme."

"That wasn't the plan," Aloysius ground out. "He was supposed to be ruined financially. They were supposed to sabotage his business. I don't know what the hell happened with those vampire chicks. Freddy the Ferret called me after Halloran bit it and told me they were going to be bringing in Sophia."

"Why?" I demanded. "What would they want with her?"

Aloysius shook his head. "No fucking clue."

Nicky tapped his gun with his fingertips. "Sure about that?"

Aloysius thought for a moment, then ran a hand down his face. "Okay, so Sophia was pissed when she found out the Sandman was fucking around on her. I told her who he'd been with. I happened to overhear a conversation between her and that one agent. What's his name . . . ? Spalding. He paid her a visit one day when Halloran was out, and . . . well, they spent a few hours up in her room. When he was leaving she warned him if he didn't hold up his end of the deal, she'd tear him limb from limb and eat his cock for breakfast."

"Good God," I breathed. "Ian took her out to keep her quiet."

"When you guys showed up, I figured it was only a matter of time before the Agency showed up, too," Aloysius explained. "That's why I took off. I put a few things in order, then I came to get Snow so we could get the hell outta here."

"Please, Nicky," Snow pleaded, gripping Aloysius's hand. "He didn't intend for anyone to get hurt. We just wanted out. We were planning to leave tonight, but you showed up and I had to pretend that everything was business as usual."

"Where are you gonna go?" Nicky asked. "The Agency has people everywhere. They'll track you down eventually if they want you bad enough."

Snow nodded. "We know. We just need a head start."

Nicky sent a glance my way and I saw conflicting emotions pass over his face before he turned back to Snow. "We can give you a couple of hours. After that, you're on your own."

"Thank you," Snow gushed, her voice thick with tears of gratitude—whether real or counterfeit, I couldn't tell. "I'll make it up to you, Nicky. If you ever need anything . . ."

Nicky stood, peering down at Snow and her lover, his shoulders square and strong, a force to be reckoned with. "Don't worry," he said. "If I want a favor in return, I'll find you."

Chapter Eleven

Nicky checked his watch for what had to be the thousandth time since we'd been sitting in the Escalade, keeping an eye on the front door of Happy Endings, waiting to intercept the Agency goons if they showed up before Snow and Aloysius managed to get out of town.

"It's been two hours," I assured him. "I don't think the Agency is going to show."

He checked his watch again as if by some miracle it had advanced more than fifteen seconds. "If nothing happens here in the next ten minutes, we'll head out. I can drop you at the house and still get some time in searching for Dracula."

"Bullshit," I said. "The deal was that I could come with you tonight."

"There was no deal," he shot back. "You . . . *distracted* me into agreeing with you."

I rolled my eyes. "I can't help it if feminine wiles are too much for you to handle."

"Oh, trust me, doll," Nicky drawled, his voice going low, "I can handle 'em."

I swallowed hard, the heated look he gave me setting my blood ablaze. To hide the flush in my cheeks, I turned my gaze back to the building across from us.

"So, you weren't kidding that Snow was pissed as hell at you."

Nicky sighed. "I knew Snow from before she went into the business. She was a sweet girl before that asshole husband of hers left her for the Ordinary dame. She needed a friend when things went south with her husband, needed some money to get back on her feet, so I helped her out. I had no idea she'd use the money to set up Happy Endings." He shook his head. "I tried to talk her out of it, offered to help her find something else, but she wouldn't accept any more help from me. I checked in on her now and then, though, made sure her business didn't get the wrong kind of attention. I didn't think it was anything, you know? Just being a good friend, looking after a Tale who needed it. But it was more serious for her. I sure as hell never intended to hurt her."

I turned my gaze back to him. "You don't need to justify anything to me, Nicky. I know you're not a love 'em and leave 'em kind of guy."

"That's what I'm trying to say, Trish," he said. "I'm *not*."

At this, my brows came together. "What are you getting at?"

"Once I get everything wrapped up here, I'm leaving."

"But you just got back!" I cried, my heart fluttering with panic. "You can't leave again. Not now."

"Why should I stay?" he asked, pegging me with a gaze so intense, I had to look away. "Give me one good reason."

I couldn't tell him the reason that was making my heart pound against the wall of my chest. So, instead, I opted for the obvious. "You have businesses to run. You can't just put all those people out of work because you have issues you're dealing with."

"Since Juliet died, I've been slowly selling off my business interests," he said. "What I couldn't sell quietly to my competition, I've been handing off to Eddie Fox to set him and Red's Gran up for life. I owe that guy a shitload—I make good on my debts. The house'll be last to go."

"But you love that house," I insisted.

He shook his head. "I did once, but not anymore. Too many memories I could do without."

"You're serious about this, aren't you?"

He nodded, his expression impossible to read. "How about you?" he asked, turning the tables. "Do you think you'd ever leave Chicago? Quit your job with the FMA?"

"I'm needed here," I told him. "I don't know anyone else who can do what I do when I read the dead."

"Is it just the dead?" he asked. "Or can you read the living, too?"

"Only if they let me," I said. "Well, most of the time anyway. Sometimes people let me in accidentally."

"What about me?"

I turned away to stare out the windshield. "What about you?"

"Have you ever read me?"

I shrugged, swallowing hard to remove the lump rising in my throat. "Yes."

"What did you see?"

But before I could respond, a shadowy movement a few doors down from Happy Endings set my hair on end and brought me to full attention. "There," I said, pointing. "In the shadows near the drain spout."

Nicky's face went deadly in an instant as he caught sight of the three figures slinking along the walls, the undulating shadows disguising them as they crept toward the alley. He threw open the car door and hopped out, hurrying around to the back of the Escalade. By the time I managed to climb out and join him, he'd already strapped on his belt loaded with both iron and wooden stakes and had added a quiver of arrows and his crossbow to his cache.

Without looking up from his weapons store, he snatched one of the iron stakes from his belt and passed it to me. "Keep this with you."

"I'm going to need more than a gun and an iron stake," I muttered, shoving the stake into my pocket. A deadly looking curved blade caught my eye, and I grabbed it before Nicky could voice the protest I saw forming on his lips. "Don't tell me I'm not going. We've already had that discussion."

He turned his eyes to the building, searching the shadows as he closed the hatch with a quiet *click*. "Shit," he muttered. "They're going up to the roof. I gotta get up there."

We padded across the street on silent feet until we reached the alley between Happy Endings and the massage parlor next door. He motioned for me to stay put and be his eyes and ears. Then, before I realized what he was doing, he fired a grappling hook gun, sending the hook flying up three stories.

"Where the hell did you get that?" I whispered.

He shrugged. "I know a guy." Then he was scaling the bricks like something out of a freaking comic book.

"Okay," I muttered. "The whole Spider thing makes sense now. . . ."

Beatrice . . .

I whirled around with a startled gasp at the sound of the voice behind me, my fear instantly replaced by irritation. "Where are you, damn it?" I mumbled under my breath, searching the shadows with narrowed eyes. Suddenly, the shadows shifted and a figure emerged—just an amorphous dark mist at first, but as it drifted closer, the mist began to solidify and take form before my eyes.

As it moved closer, I slowly edged back, the desire to finally get a glimpse of my mystery stalker keeping me from calling out for Nicky. But when my back hit the brick wall, I began to seriously rethink the wisdom of keeping quiet. I snatched the iron stake from my pocket and opened my mouth to yell for Nicky, but the shadow was on me in an instant, its hand muffling the sound of my scream.

Be still, he said, his voice in my head even though a full mouth began to take form in the mist. Then his dark gaze locked with mine. In the next moment, the man stood before me, fully formed, his black shirt gaping to reveal a sculpted chest.

"Come to me, Beatrice," he said, his velvety soft voice working its way under my skin and into every fiber of my being. A fog began to descend upon me, making the world around us go hazy, the edges blurry and indistinct. *"I need you. . . ."*

I tried to respond, to tell him to piss off, but I couldn't move, couldn't speak. And that gaze . . . it was infinitely dark and deep, and I felt myself drifting into it, a connection between us pulling me in.

No, no, no . . .

I tried to break away as ghostly images, mercifully indistinct, drifted to me. Scenes of violence and gore were lurking just on the periphery, but I couldn't quite make them out.

His icy cold fingertips lightly skimmed down the curve of my cheek to beneath my chin. His touch was tender, airy—and not quite solid. With a shock, I realized that the man standing with me was a creature of fog and mist. He wasn't really *there.*

The realization seemed to break whatever spell he had over me, and I blinked, severing the connection from my thoughts to his. And with an energy that erupted from deep within the center of me, I screamed, lashing out with the iron stake. He burst apart in a million atoms of shadow, and re-formed a few feet away, a smug smirk curling his lips.

"That's my girl. . . ." he taunted, slowly backing away. Then, with a quiet chuckle, he spun around and hurried down the alley.

Oh, hell *no!*

I'd be damned if he was going to get away that easily. I ran after him, my legs pumping as I raced to catch up with him. As the shadows in the alley began to grow deeper I slid to a stop, giving myself a mental smack upside the head. What the hell was I *doing*? Hadn't I just walked into a trap two nights before doing the same damned thing? I wasn't about to brand myself too stupid to live by falling for that trick again.

I glanced around, searching for any sign of movement. As I slowly began to back toward the street, I shifted the stake to my left hand and palmed the gun Nicky had tucked at the small of my back. "This isn't over!" I called into the darkness. "I'll find you, you son of a bitch!"

"Trish!"

I spun around with a start, gun out in front of me, ready to open fire. Nicky's hand shot out, grabbing the gun from my hand before it'd even registered that he was standing there.

"What the hell's going on?" he demanded, dragging me into his embrace. "Are you all right? I heard you screaming."

I nodded against his chest, which was damp with what I realized must've been vampire blood from his altercations on the roof. "He was here, Nicky," I told him. "Dracula was here."

Chapter Twelve

Nicky was pacing furiously, a dark scowl on his face. "You should've told me."

"Why?" I asked from my seat on the sofa. When he came to an abrupt halt and pegged me with a withering glare, I didn't even flinch. Meeting his gaze, I clasped my hands between my knees to hide the fact that they were still trembling.

"Why?" he repeated. "Because Dracula's been in your head, Trish! You know I've been tracking him for two years—you didn't think to mention he's been chatting with you?"

"We haven't been *chatting*," I corrected, trying to keep my voice level but rapidly losing my patience. "He's been *intruding*. It's not like I invited him in. Besides, I wasn't even sure who it was. I've never met Dracula—I have no idea what his voice sounds like!"

"You still should've mentioned it!" he raged, jabbing a finger at me. "Did you ever think that maybe we could've used this connection to draw him out? That we could've lured him into a trap?"

"No, Nicky," I spat. "I was a little more concerned about my *sanity*. So forgive the hell out of me for not thinking about how this development could've benefited *you*."

He ran a hand through his hair, his anger almost a palpable force in the room. "This is seriously fucked up."

"Tell me about it," I snapped.

He shook his head. "I have to catch him, Trish."

"I know."

Nicky cursed roundly, then strode over to the fireplace and slammed his hand against one of the bricks. A large section of wall slid away in response, revealing a room that looked like the freaking Bat Cave. I hurried in after him before the wall slid closed behind him. As I stood there in the center of the room, slowly surveying the massive cache of weapons that took up pretty much every square inch of the wall, he began to strip off all his weapons in short, angry motions.

"Are we not going back out?" I asked as Nicky packed away the last of his weapons. "I'm fine. We can try to track down the vampires you had to give up on the roof when you heard me scream."

He shook his head. "No, I won't find them again tonight. I have a feeling they were only that obvious to draw me away from you."

"I'm sorry, Nicky," I said, shoving my hands into my pockets. "I don't know how many times I have to say it."

He shrugged and slammed one of the display case doors. "Forget about it."

I wanted to forget about it, to feel like I hadn't just been a liability to his efforts that night, but his perma-scowl made it tough. The minute we left his weapons room, I made for the stairs, figuring it was probably best if I made myself scarce and let him brood in private. I had just changed into a T-shirt and pajama pants and was pulling back the covers to slip into bed when there was a tentative knock on the door.

I opened it, expecting to see Nicky in all his gear, prepared to tell me he'd changed his mind and was going out on the hunt again. But, to my surprise, he was leaning against the door frame wearing nothing but his jeans, as if he'd been in the process of undressing when he'd suddenly decided to drop by.

"Hey," I said as nonchalantly as I could manage while trying to keep from staring at his bare chest. I crossed my arms to keep my fingertips from going exploring.

He looked up at me from under lowered lashes. "Hey."

I waited to see if he'd say more, but he started to fidget with a little bubble of paint on the door frame, his brows coming together in a frown as if he was concentrating intently.

"So . . ." I prompted. "What do you want?"

He shrugged. "You know. I just wanted to see if you were doing okay. If you needed anything."

I waited a beat. "And?"

He huffed and gave me an irritated look. "And I wanted to say . . . You know . . ."

"Nope, sorry," I said, shaking my head. "I don't know. So if you have something you want to say, go ahead. Otherwise, I'm going to bed."

"I wanted to apologize," he said in a rush. When I didn't immediately respond, he finally met my gaze. "Did you hear what I said? I'm sorry."

"Yeah, I heard you."

"Do you have anything to say?"

"Not really."

He ran his hand through his hair, giving me a great look at those biceps in action. "I'm trying to apologize here, Trish," he snapped. "You're not making it easy."

"Nope," I agreed. "I'm not."

At this, his dark expression suddenly cleared and the corners of his mouth turned up in a smile. He cursed under his breath, shaking his head. "Fine. All right. I get it. I was an ass. I shouldn't have made it seem like I didn't care about what you've been going through."

"Thanks."

He nodded toward my room. "So, you gonna be okay in here tonight?"

I started to assure him that I was fine, but hesitated. A fact he picked up on immediately. He was already wearing a doubtful expression when I gave him a shaky, "Oh, yeah. Of course!"

Without a word, he grabbed my hand and led me to the bed. "Climb in."

"You really don't have to tuck me in," I demurred, even though having him there had instantly calmed my nerves.

He pulled the covers up over me, then flipped off the overhead light. For a moment, I wondered if he was planning to leave without so much as a "good night," but then he came back to the bed and stretched out beside me, propping himself up on his elbow so he could peer down at me. "Go ahead and go to sleep, doll," he said. "I'll stay right here with you."

My heart began to pound. "Nicky," I said, a little breathless, "really—you don't have to—"

He put a finger to my lips, silencing my protestations. "I know I don't have to," he replied. "Maybe I need this, too."

I held his gaze for a long, supercharged moment. But when the air began to crackle with tension, I swallowed hard, and turned onto my side, putting my back to him. I could still feel his gaze on me for a few minutes longer, but then he put his head down on the pillow next to mine and wrapped an arm around my waist, pulling me into the curve of his body. I tried in vain to ignore the nearness of him, to not think about the thin barrier of cotton material that separated my back from his chest. And I wondered what would happen if I rolled over to face him.

But before I could give it a try, his hand found mine in the darkness, his fingers twining with mine, and he pressed a kiss to the crown of my head. "Good night, doll."

If there'd been a window of opportunity to see where things would go, he'd just closed it. I took a deep breath and let it out slowly. "Good night, Nicky."

I woke slowly, gradually becoming aware but not sure what had awakened me. I opened my eyes and scanned the room, searching the heavy shadows. Birds chirped outside the window, alerting me it was morning, but thanks to the blackout shades, the room was still plunged in darkness. I also heard soft snoring. Frowning, I turned my head and saw Nicky lying on the pillow beside me. He was still dressed and on top of the covers, but his arm was lightly draped across me.

My stomach did its little fluttery thing at the realization that instead of leaving once I'd fallen asleep, Nicky had stayed at my side while I slept, watching over me and keeping me safe. If someone had told me a week ago that I'd be in Nicky Blue's house, sleeping in bed with him, I would've called her a liar—plus another couple of names that were even less complimentary. Then again, if someone had told me a week ago that I would be jumped by vampires, attacked in my apartment by a seriously pissed off ghost, and psychically invaded by Dracula himself, all in the same week, I wouldn't have believed that either. Guess life was just full of surprises. . . .

Feeling a sudden shift in the air, I shook off the last remnants of sleep and squinted into the darkness. There was a heaviness in the room that I couldn't quite place. All the hairs on the back of my neck jumped to attention, and my blood went cold. No, wait—it wasn't my blood. It was the temperature in the room itself that had plummeted several degrees. Next to me, Nicky shivered in his sleep.

I swallowed hard, then whispered, *"Nicky!"* My breath came out as a frosty mist that curled before my eyes.

Shit. Not good.

In a panic, I tried to get up, but I was completely paralyzed. I tried to call out to Nicky again, but all that came out was a strangled rasp. As I lay there, completely helpless, the shadows swirled and shifted, slowly taking form as they moved toward the bed. A moment later, the silhouette of a woman took shape at the end of the bed. I felt the mattress dip down by my feet as the shadow-woman put one knee on the mattress and then another and began to creep toward me.

In the next moment she was straddling me, her face just inches from mine. I was trembling so violently, I couldn't believe the shaking hadn't woken Nicky. As if the phantom had heard my thoughts, she glanced over at where he lay, then ran a ghostly finger from my forehead down along the bridge of my nose until she reached my lips. "Don't bother trying to call for him," she said, her voice edged with amusement. "He can't hear you. It's just you"—her finger continued down my chin and along the edge of my throat—"and me."

I wanted to look away, close my eyes, pretend this was just a dream, but I couldn't. It was as if she was controlling me.

She chuckled, a low, throaty sound. "No, silly girl, it's not *me* controlling you." She bent forward until her lips were near my ear. "It's the master," she whispered, her breath an arctic blast on my skin. "You tasted the blood of one of his children. And now you are his."

My eyes went wide, remembering how, in desperation, I'd bitten the vampiress the other night, how her blood had flooded my mouth when my teeth had broken her skin.

"You weren't the one he was hoping for," she giggled, "but after meeting you face to face last night, he thinks you'll be a lovely addition to the family." She shifted and pressed her lips to mine in a slow kiss, then grinned down at me. "Oh, we're going to have *so* much fun. . . ."

She turned her head to regard Nicky for a moment, her blond hair sweeping across my face. "What do you think," she taunted, "should we bring Mr. Blue into the family, too? He'd be such a delightful plaything for the other girls. So handsome and strong." She giggled again and gave me a lascivious wink. "They'd enjoy sucking him dry in more ways than one."

Fury so powerful engulfed me, it shattered the hold over me. My arm shot up and grasped her throat, and I flipped her onto her back, now sticking my face into hers. "You and whatever vampire whores Dracula has recruited will stay the hell away from Nicky Blue, or you'll have to deal with me."

The ghost merely laughed, her eyes twinkling with amusement before she dematerialized and re-formed beside the bed, safely out of my reach, proving just how empty my threat was. She adjusted her fluffy pink sweater and pulled her miniskirt down a notch before giving me a patronizing grin. "I'll be seeing you soon, sweetie!"

"Don't count on it," I hissed. "I'll take on that son of a bitch Dracula any day, any time. You tell him to bring it on."

She suddenly swooped forward, her face morphing into a horrifying replica of Sebille Fenwick's rotting corpse, somehow knowing about the nightmares that had plagued me for the last few months. Then she grabbed *my* throat and squeezed. I clawed desperately at her ghostly hands, doing nothing more than scoring my own skin with my fingernails.

"Do not underestimate the master," the phantom warned, her breath rank, making me gag. "You *are* his, Trish. And you'll be joining him *very soon.*"

With a parting cackle, she flung me backward, but instead of hitting the mattress, I kept falling, the darkness growing deeper. Screaming, I threw my arms out to my sides, desperately grasping for anything to stop my descent. My nails dug into something soft and foul. *Was it dirt?* Just when it felt like I would fall forever, I suddenly hit bottom, and the air was forced from my lungs.

"This isn't real," I panted, squeezing my eyes closed with relief. "It's just a dream. It's all just a dream. Wake up, Trish."

But when I opened my eyes again, I was still lying at the bottom of a freshly dug grave hundreds of feet deep. "It's just a dream," I ground out, balling my hands into fists. "Wake up!"

I suddenly felt an arm snake under my back and around my shoulders. With a gasp, I rolled toward my unexpected companion in the grave and found myself lying on top of him, his blazing red eyes burning into my soul. "What the—"

"Hello, little one," came the low, hypnotic voice, the tendrils of sound wrapping around me, drawing me closer.

I was still screaming when his fangs plunged into my throat.

"Trish!"

I jolted awake, my arms flailing wildly, the scream still burning my throat.

"Trish, it's me! It's Nicky!"

The sound of Nicky's voice brought me out of the fog of fear and desperation. I snapped my jaws shut, my scream abruptly cutting off, and blinked at him in confusion. He was sitting on the edge of the bed, wearing nothing but a towel wrapped around his waist. His dark hair was wet and droplets of water glistened on his skin.

I shook my head as I sat up, not understanding. "What's going on? You were just here. On the bed beside me."

His brows came together in a frown. "I got up a couple of hours ago, doll. You were sleeping so soundly, I didn't want to wake you up."

I shook my head again, more vehemently this time. "No, that's not—" I bit off my words. Realizing it really *had* all been a dream, I let out a sigh of relief so deep my shoulders sagged, suddenly feeling boneless. "Nightmare," I muttered around chattering teeth. "I must've had a nightmare."

"Want to talk about it?" he asked, tucking a ringlet behind my ear.

I shook my head. "No. Not yet. I just—" *I just need you to hold me,* was what I wanted to say, but I bit off my words, not wanting to admit how rattled I was.

But to my surprise, Nicky pulled me into his arms anyway, pressing me close to his bare chest. "You're safe now," he murmured against my hair. "I gotcha."

I closed my eyes and leaned against him, letting him hold me and trying not to think about the fact that my cheek was resting against his fabulously sculpted chest, or about how right it felt with his strong arms wrapped around me. After a moment, I tentatively slipped my arms around his waist and curled into him a little more.

His heart began to pound faster in my ear and his arms tightened around me. Then his hand started moving in a slow circle on my back, just a small gesture of comfort, but it sent a lance of white-hot heat through my body, slamming me with the ache I experienced every time I fantasized about just such a scenario. I let my eyelids flutter shut, focusing on the gentle pressure of his hand on my back instead of the increasingly persistent heat between my legs.

Oh, God . . . please don't let this be another dream. . . .

I felt him swallow hard; then his hand roamed a little lower, tentatively at first, but soon he was skimming across the curve of my ass and down my thigh. My pulse was racing so rapidly as he eased me back onto the mattress that I could hardly breathe. I looked up at him, meeting his gaze. His eyes seemed brighter, filled with a fiery desire that startled me. I caught a glimpse of what was going through his mind—just a flicker. But I didn't need to see beyond his mental defenses to know what he wanted at that moment—the rock-hard length pressing into my thigh was a damned good indicator. And I was *so* onboard with where his thoughts were going.

His hand slid back up my thigh over my hip and to my ribs as he shifted, scooting up a little to stretch out on the bed beside me. I kept one arm around his waist, my fingers splayed across his back, and let my other hand drift up along his muscled forearm to his bicep where a beautiful Celtic design marked him up to his shoulder and around to his back. I traced the tattoo with my fingertips, gliding lightly over his skin. When I reached the nape of his neck, his lids snapped shut briefly, his lips parting in a sharp exhale. And when he opened his eyes again, I shuddered at the intensity of his gaze.

My God—was this really happening? Was I actually lying on a bed in Nicky Blue's arms, his body pressing against mine, *straining* toward mine? After so long dreaming of such a moment, was it actually happening?

But just as I began to doubt that I was awake, the increasingly agonizing ache at the center of me assured me that this was no dream. He was right there, staring down at me, wanting me, just as much as I wanted him. I grasped the nape of his neck and urged him toward me, desperate to feel his lips upon mine, to slake some of this heat building inside me before I went up in flames and was reduced to a smoldering pile of ash.

His gaze flicked down to my mouth.

God, yes! Yes! Finally . . .

I let my lids flutter shut as he pressed a whisper of a kiss to my lips. Just a tender brush of his mouth against mine. And not nearly enough. On the next pass, his lips lingered a little longer, testing, teasing. And again, even longer this time. He lifted his head for a moment, meeting and holding my gaze. There was something there, something I couldn't quite see. Was it caution? Fear? But before I could look closer, there was a sudden shift in his gaze as if a switch had tripped, and then his mouth was on mine again. And he was done messing around.

This kiss was possessive, demanding. His mouth claimed mine as no man's ever had, drawing out of me a fiery passion I'd never experienced before. I clung to his lips with each pass, gasping, breathless, hardly daring to believe that it was really Nicky's mouth devouring mine. I nipped at his bottom lip, then sucked it into my mouth, making him moan.

He shifted position again, rolling on top of me so he was between my legs, his hips pressing into me in urgent need. "Jesus, Trish," he groaned before his mouth captured mine again, his tongue slipping between my teeth in an insistent caress.

My God, as kisses went, it was off the charts. I could've gone on kissing him for hours, days! Even without his hips grinding so maddeningly against mine, I was on the verge of coming just from the way he was making love to my mouth. And when he began pressing those fevered lips to my cheeks, my jaw, it was just as intoxicating.

When his hand finally slipped up under my T-shirt and caressed my skin, I thought I was going to come undone. I shuddered, a precursor to what was building deep inside, when his thumb passed over my nipple. I choked back a moan and arched my neck, granting him access to the curve of my throat, dying for him to explore every inch of me, place those hot kisses on my skin over and over again.

But Nicky's hand instantly stilled. His lips hovered near my skin as he whispered, "What the hell?"

I swear my heart stopped for a full three seconds. "Nicky?"

He slowly drew back, his brows pinched together as he reached up and pulled the collar of my T-shirt away from my neck. "Did one of those vampires get a taste of you the other night?"

I began to tremble. "No." I swallowed, but my mouth was so dry it didn't do any good. "Why?"

He ran his thumb across my skin and gave me a look so full of pity and disappointment, it made my heart shrivel. "I think maybe you'd better tell me about that nightmare."

My heart dropped, and when he started to draw away I shook my head. "No," I said. "Not now."

He frowned. "What—"

I grasped the back of his neck and pulled his mouth down to mine. I'd waited for far too long to be in his arms to let this opportunity pass by. I was taking him. I didn't give a shit what happened afterward, but for now he was mine. And I'd be damned if some fucking vampire was going to ruin it for me.

To my relief, Nicky responded to my harsh kiss with his own hot enthusiasm, and the marks on my neck were forgotten as his hands began to roam again. And when his hand slid down my belly and slipped under my waistband, I was shattering apart even before he reached the tight little bud of nerves that was screaming for his touch. Then his fingertip began to move in a slow, deliberate circle, and I was shattering apart all over again, my body curling up into his before arching back again.

"Oh, yeah," he hissed in my ear, his fingertip unrelenting, winding me up again. "That's it. Come again for me, Trish."

I honestly didn't think it was possible, but when his hand slid down farther, delving deeper into my wet heat, I was ready to go yet again. First one finger and then another slid inside me, slowly advancing and retreating.

Writhing against his hand, panting with need, I slid my palm down to where his erection had escaped the folds of his towel and took him in my hand, making him jerk and squeeze his eyes shut on a juicy curse. Impatient for more, I grabbed his towel with my other hand and tore it off, then gripped his bare ass. And, holy hell, what a fine ass it was.

"I need you inside me, Nicky," I gasped. "Right. Now."

His fingers plunged deeper as his mouth curled into a smug grin. "I thought I was already inside you," he said, punctuating his words with another thrust.

I moaned, closing my eyes and rolling my hips against his hand.

But then he suddenly withdrew. My eyes snapped open to see what was wrong, but before I could ask the question, he was yanking my pajama pants down and tossing them aside.

"Oh, God," I gasped as he sat back on his heels and grasped my hips, jerking me toward him. In the next instant he was plunging deep, filling me, his powerful thrusts creating a blissful friction that sent me careening over the edge again within seconds. My release was so powerful, it made him groan and pitch forward to brace himself on his elbows.

"My God, it feels good inside you," he murmured.

I tried to respond, but all that came out was a gasp as he shifted ever so slightly, hitting a spot that set off an explosion of light in my head. He chuckled at the choked scream that came next, obviously enjoying the way his body was affecting mine. His smug pleasure set off something inside me, something savage and animalistic. Without thinking, I bit his shoulder. Hard. Hard enough to break the skin.

"Ow! Shit!" he shouted, flinching away. He went completely still and pulled back to gaze down at me, a startled expression on his face.

I stared at the tiny drop of blood on his skin, horrified at what I'd done. "Oh, God," I breathed. "I'm so sorry. I don't know what—"

I didn't get a chance to complete the sentence before Nicky's mouth was on mine again, his kisses rough and harsh this time. And when he grabbed my hands and pinned them over my head and began to move his hips once more, the source of his startled expression was now clear. He wasn't surprised that I'd bitten him; he was surprised that I liked it as rough as he did. And, honestly, that was as much of a surprise to me as it was to him. But I loved it. I loved his hard thrusts. I loved how his muscled body overpowered mine. And I loved it when his teeth nipped and teased my skin, drawing out the kind of pleasure I'd only dreamed of.

And when Nicky finally let go, his release was so powerful, his strangled scream echoed off the bedroom walls. And it was the most beautiful sound I'd ever heard. Even reliving the sound in my head as he lay there, collapsed in exhaustion in my arms, my body cradling his, made me want to go at it all over again.

To my mortification, my muscles began to twitch, grasping onto his shaft, begging for more. His soft chuckle rumbled in his chest, and when he lifted his head to peer down at me, he was grinning from ear to ear.

"You're going to be the death of me, doll," he drawled.

Now it was my turn to chuckle. "Yeah?"

He nodded and slowly withdrew. But before he could completely pull out, he thrust hard, making me gasp. And as he began to move again, he put his lips near my ear and whispered, "But what a way to go. . . ."

Chapter Thirteen

"It had to be Amanda."

"Amanda?" he repeated from where he sat at the kitchen bar, sipping the coffee I'd made us. "That Ordinary dame Dracula killed so he could use her ghost to try to bump off Caliban?"

I scraped scrambled eggs onto two plates already loaded down with toast and fresh fruit, then nodded. "One and the same. Looks like he's still using her to do his dirty work."

"So, do you think she was an early attempt to turn an Ordinary that went wrong?" Nicky asked. "Or do you think he intended to kill her all along?"

"I'm guessing the latter." I set the plates in front of him and climbed up onto the bar stool beside him, trying to ignore the fact that I knew he was going commando under his jeans. "When Tale vamps come over, we spend a lot of time rehabilitating them, teaching them to control their hunger, feed responsibly, so they can lead a normal life among the Ordinaries and not get into trouble. Part of that program emphasizes the fact that Tale vamps aren't able to turn anyone else so there's no reason to kill anyone."

"Is it true?" Nicky asked.

"As far as we know."

He blinked at me and said around a mouthful of strawberries, "No one ever bothered to test the theory?"

I shrugged. "Who would you have us use as test subjects? Had the experiment gone wrong, it would've resulted in the death of a Tale. And if it had worked, we would've had more vamps to deal with and no deterrent to keep them from turning whoever they wanted, whenever they wanted."

"And no one ever questioned this?"

I pressed my lips together for a moment. "As Al says, 'You tell someone something often enough, they'll start to believe it.' But I think we honestly all believed it, too. I mean, it's never happened."

"Until now."

"What do you mean?"

He polished off the fruit and started in on the eggs. A moment later he finally answered, "These vamps I've been chasing—there's something strange about them. You know that. They don't have a normal Tale signature. I think he's turning Ordinaries."

"We have no proof of that," I reminded him. "And if it *has* happened, the FMA will handle it. That's why we have rehabilitation programs in the first place."

"You know, the FMA has a bad habit of trying to regulate every aspect of our lives," Nicky mused. "Now that we're here, we're supposed to be able to write our own stories, find our own voices. Maybe they should be a little more hands-off and let us all deal with things ourselves."

"Careful," I retorted, jabbing my food with my fork, "you're starting to sound a lot like Sebille Fenwick and her fanatical pals." My hands stilled the moment I said it, not needing to turn around to know how much my words had cut him—I felt it in the air. But he didn't say anything. It wasn't until the dishes were cleared away and all evidence of breakfast disposed of that Nicky spoke again.

"Listen, I'm sorry about earlier," he said, running his hand through his hair. He leaned a hip against the counter and regarded me with a frown. "You know, in the bedroom."

I froze, my stomach plummeting. "What?"

He crossed his arms over his chest. "I shouldn't have let things go that far."

I let out a shaky, nervous little laugh and waved away his comment, trying to act nonchalant, especially in light of my misstep a moment before. "Don't worry about it."

Seriously. Please *don't worry about it. . . .*

"No, I owe you an apology," he went on, shaking his head a little. "You were vulnerable and I took advantage of that."

"No, no, Nicky," I said quickly. "Really, I—"

"Hell, I'm just sorry, Trish," he said on a sigh. "It was an asshole thing to do. Won't happen again."

My shoulders sagged, wondering if we'd be having a different conversation about what had taken place if I hadn't just compared him to his wife's murderer. "Right."

He shook his head again as if he was completely disgusted with his behavior. "I just . . . I think I've been getting in your head for so long, I feel like I *know* you."

"I know the feeling," I muttered.

"The thing is," he continued, "I've been coming on to you since that night in your apartment, and I had no right. Not when I'm getting the hell outta town as soon as this shit is over. It's not fair to you. I wasn't good enough for you the day I met you, Trish—and I'm sure as hell not good enough for you now."

I shook my head, confused. "On the day you met me?"

He nodded. "That day we came over. I saw you lying there in that field and there was something . . . I don't know. I felt a connection when you looked at me, doll. It was like nothin' I'd ever felt before or since. Hell, you probably don't even remember."

Was he kidding?

"I remember," I breathed.

His brows lifted and a smile teased at the corners of his mouth, but he quickly shoved it away, resuming his scowl. "Yeah, well, I wanted you so bad at that moment, wanted to keep feelin' that way, I didn't even think before I asked you to come with me. I just . . . I just wanted to hang on to that. But when you refused so damned politely, I realized you deserved a helluva lot more than some two-bit thief could offer. You still do. 'Cause when you get down to it, Trish, I'm still the same guy I was that day."

"Good," I said, my heart hammering at his confession.

His brows flinched together. "What?"

I closed the distance between us in a few quick steps and grabbed the front of his shirt, pulling him to me and pressing a hard, hungry kiss to his mouth. When he abruptly broke the kiss and looked down at me, he was panting, his pupils dilated with desire and wide with disbelief at the same time.

"Trish," he stammered, "I—"

"Shut up, Nicky," I interrupted. "And kiss me again."

He didn't need any urging. And soon we were easing down onto the kitchen floor. I remember that the terra-cotta tile was cold against my back, but then all other thoughts ceased except for the feel of Nicky's hands skimming across my skin, the warmth of his body as it pressed against mine, the pleasure he brought me as we made love there on the kitchen floor. As rough as the sex had been earlier, I was surprised at how gentle he now was, how tender and loving was each caress.

At some point we ended up back in the bedroom and when we finally collapsed into each other's arms, I still found myself wondering if I was trapped in some wonderful, blissful dream and if any moment I would wake up and realize that I was still alone, cold and lonely, in my own little bed in my apartment.

Nicky pressed a kiss to my shoulder and then peered down at me, his brow furrowed. I reached up and cupped his cheek, smoothing my thumb across his skin.

"Hey there," he said. "Welcome back."

"Sorry?"

"You drifted away from me there for a minute," he explained. "Where'd you go?"

I sighed. "Got lost in my thoughts, I guess." I ran my fingertips along the tattoo at his shoulder, then, suddenly seeing the picture in the design, I blinked at him in dismay. "This is a spider."

He nodded. "Took a helluva long time to get the damn thing to stay. My Tale body kept trying to heal it before the guy could finish."

"So, why a spider?" I asked. "You're not taking the nickname the Agency has given you that seriously, are you?"

Nicky grinned. "They didn't give me that nickname. That's what I told them to call me."

I shook my head, confused. "Sorry—what?"

"When I figured out that they were on to me, I decided to leave them a little calling card and signed it *The Spider*."

"But why?"

"I guess I've thought of myself that way for a while now," he sighed, lying back against his pillow with his arm behind his head. "I mean, I frightened Miss Muffet away on my first day in the Here and Now, didn't I?"

My heart hopped up into my throat, making it hard for me to get my voice past it to ask, "So the tattoo, it was . . ."

"It was a reminder," Nicky finished. "A reminder of everything I wanted and didn't deserve."

"Oh, Nicky," I breathed. "You don't understand. I didn't say no to you that day because I thought I was too good for you or because I was afraid of you. I—"

The doorbell suddenly sounded, cutting me off.

"Who the hell got past my gates?" Nicky mumbled. He pressed a kiss to my lips, then threw back the covers. "Stay here, doll. I'm going to go see who it is."

I grinned as he strolled, naked, toward the bedroom door. "You might want some pants, lover."

He gave me a wink. "Don't think the Bible thumpers want to get a good look at this?" he asked, sweeping his arm down his torso.

I giggled and lobbed one of the pillows at him. "Put some clothes on and see who's at the door. Then you'd better get that fine ass back in here. I'm not done with you yet."

His brows shot up as the doorbell rang again. "Well, that's an offer I can't refuse."

I was still grinning when I heard the thunderous pounding on the front door. "Damn," I muttered. "Insistent little bastards."

I heard Nicky open the front door and then male voices. I sat up, listening intently, but I couldn't make out what was being said. Then there was a loud crash and a chorus of shouts.

"What the hell?" I muttered, throwing off the covers and grabbing a shirt and pair of pajama pants from my suitcase. I raced down the stairs, not giving a shit what might be waiting for me. My only concern was for Nicky's safety.

When I reached the bottom of the steps, I slid to a halt, quickly assessing the situation. Four FMA agents were laid out on the ground, two of them apparently unconscious. Another three were pinning Nicky against the wall, while another tried to put handcuffs on him.

My God—they'd sent eight agents? What the fuck?

I raced forward, grabbing one of them by the scruff of the collar and jerking him away. "What the hell are you doing?" I demanded.

The guy I'd grabbed pivoted and took a swing at me, but I ducked his arm and came up swiftly, pinching each side of his trachea with my fingers, cutting off his air just enough to quiet him down. "Somebody explain this shit right fucking now!"

The guy who'd been putting handcuffs on Nicky took him roughly by the upper arm and turned to face me.

"McCain?" I gasped. "What are you doing here?"

"I could ask you the same thing," he shot back, his tone condemning. "Married to the job, huh?"

"Don't worry about it, Trish," Nicky said around a split lip that was already swelling. "I've gotten out of worse."

"Worse?" I repeated. "What the hell is happening here? Why are you guys taking him in?"

"Apparently, he roughed up one of the guys from the Agency," McCain explained as the other agents helped their comrades who were coming around and trying to get to their feet.

"What?" I shrieked. "That's bullshit! Nicky was protecting *me*. That asshole Spalding and his boys took out Halloran's girlfriend and her bodyguards and then got rough with me when I showed up."

McCain shrugged. "Sorry, Trish, that's not the story they told Al. He ordered us to bring Nicky in."

I blinked at him in disbelief, my chest constricting with that particular brand of pain that went along with betrayal. "Al did this?"

McCain nodded. "You'll have to take it up with him. In the meantime, I gotta take in your—what?—*boyfriend*?"

When I pressed my lips together in an angry line, McCain shoved Nicky toward the open door.

"Wait!" I snapped. "You could at least let him put on some shoes and a shirt, you jackass! It's February, for God's sake."

McCain pegged me with an irritated glare, but said, "Fine. You have two minutes to get him something to put on."

I raced back up the stairs and grabbed one of Nicky's black turtleneck sweaters from the shelf in his closet and a pair of socks and combat boots.

"You wanna take these handcuffs off, pal?" Nicky asked when I returned. "I don't mind Trish *undressing* me, but dressing me's a different story." When McCain looked like he was going to tell him to fuck off, Nicky added, "I promise to be a good boy. There's a lady present and all that."

McCain huffed, but took out his key and unlocked the handcuffs. The instant he did, the other agents pulled their guns and trained them on Nicky as a further reminder that he needed to behave. Nicky quickly pulled his sweater over his head and ran his hands through his dark hair. Then he sat down on the stairs to put his shoes on. I sat down next to him, watching his face intently, but never once did he look concerned until he glanced my way. Then his brow furrowed and he paused to put an arm around me and draw me close.

"Everything will be okay," he murmured against my hair. "I promise. This is nothing, Trish. I've been through it before."

"I'll be right behind you," I assured him. "I'll talk to Al and get this straightened out."

"Come on, Blue," McCain snapped. "Time's up."

Nicky stood and pulled me up with him, then took my face in his hands and pressed a tender kiss to my lips. "I'll see ya soon, doll."

I nodded. "You'd better."

Nicky turned and put his hands behind his back for McCain to put the cuffs back on, and kissed me again as they clicked into place. Then he gave me a grin and a playful wink before McCain led him out the door. They all loaded into the SUVs and slammed the door on Nicky, blocking him from my view. McCain was opening the door to get in when he saw me standing in the doorway and paused. I heard him curse under his breath and then he was striding toward me.

I spread my legs in an attack stance in case he'd decided to try to take me in, too, but he shoved his hands deep in his coat pockets and ducked his head a little. "Be careful, Trish," he said quietly. "Spalding's gunning for Nicky big-time after what happened. I don't want you getting caught in the middle."

"Gee, McCain," I spat, "I didn't know you cared."

He gave me an apologetic look. "I *do* care," he muttered. "A lot. I'm sorry things had to go down this way."

I crossed my arms over my chest. "Me, too."

He heaved a sigh. "Just be careful. That's all I'm saying."

The guy looked genuinely sorry for what he'd been sent to do, but that did little to help dampen the anger that was boiling up inside me.

Without a word, I slammed the door in his face and made my way up-stairs to get dressed, my mind churning with the facts that I knew.

Spalding had it out for Nicky because of me, and Al had rolled over to take it up the ass from the Agency. I couldn't believe that he'd give up one of his own with so little resistance, but if he thought I wasn't going to have a thing to say about it, he could think again. I had so much to say, in fact, I hoped I still had a job when I was done.

Chapter Fourteen

"This is bullshit!"

Al Addin looked up from the paperwork on his desk and regarded me calmly. "I remember the days when you used to knock."

"I remember the days when you used to have a pair," I shot back.

His eyes flashed with mild anger, but he gestured toward the chair across from him. "Have a seat, Trish."

I slammed the door and stormed over to the chair but didn't sit. Instead, I crossed my arms over my chest and glared down at him. "Nicky didn't do anything wrong. Spalding's just pissed because Nicky cleaned his clock in front of his men."

"Yes, he is," Al agreed. "And if it'd been you who'd done it, we'd be having a very different conversation. But Nicky Blue is a known crime lord. I can't protect him the same way I can protect you."

"*Protect* him?" I echoed, incredulous. "You call sending eight men barging into Nicky's house to rough him up and bring him in *protecting* him?"

"Roughing him up wasn't part of the plan," Al assured me, leaning back in his chair and giving me that look of his that made me a little jumpy. He only used it when he was righteously pissed off—and it was generally the only indication that he was. "I'm afraid things weren't fully explained before one of the Enforcers decided to act. I believe he's still recovering from the broken jaw Nicky Blue gave him, but the doctors tell me he'll be fine."

"So, what was *supposed* to happen?" I demanded.

Al steepled his fingers. "We were supposed to be taking Mr. Blue into protective custody under the ruse of charging him for the assault on Agent Spalding."

I frowned in confusion and dropped into the chair Al had offered earlier. "Protective custody? Why?"

"The Agency wants Nicky's head on a platter," Al said on a sigh. He picked up a manila folder and tossed it to the edge of his desk. "Apparently, they don't take kindly to Tales interfering with their investigations."

I tentatively opened the folder. My eyes widened when I saw the photographs inside. There was one of Nicky fighting in the alley the night he'd rescued me. One of him carrying me to the Escalade after I'd been attacked at Halloran's. Another of us walking into Happy Endings. Another one of him crouching along the roof of the building as he pursued the vampires that night. And another of us as we stood together, his arm inside my coat. It captured the moment when he was slipping a gun into my waistband, but it looked far more intimate—and the look being exchanged between us, although it brought a smile to my lips, was so intense it didn't do much to illustrate the truth of what had been happening. But the last photograph was the most infuriating. It was of me, pressed against the alley wall, a dark, formless mist pressing into me, my eyes wide with terror.

One of the Agency goons had been there, watching the whole time, and hadn't come to my aid. I had to wonder, if Drac had decided to rip my throat out, would the goon have just watched me bleed out through his camera lens?

"How long have they been following us?" I asked, my mouth dry, wondering what else they might have pictures of but just hadn't shared.

Al shook his head. "No clue. And I'm not entirely sure which of you was the initial target of their surveillance. But until we sort this out and smooth things over, I need to ask you to stay away from Nicky Blue."

My head snapped up. "Pardon me?"

"I can't have one of my employees consorting with someone like Nicky," he explained.

"That's a load of horseshit," I snapped. "Red was with Nicky on and off for years back in the day."

"That was different."

"Why?" I countered. "Because it was Tess?"

"I'm not playing favorites," Al insisted, his voice getting louder. "I've never been able to control Red."

"Oh, but you can control *me*?" I yelled, launching to my feet. "Fuck this."

"Trish!" Al shouted, bringing me to an abrupt halt. "I am saying this for your own good. Nicky Blue is trouble. I don't want you getting caught up in it."

I turned back to face him, my heart aching. "Al, you have been my friend and mentor since I came over. When I was lost and afraid, you took me under your wing and showed me that I could have a purpose here, that I didn't have to be a victim of my past and the darkness that haunted me, that I could *use* my experience to help others. I've looked up to you and loved you and have done everything I can for you. But I can't give you this."

Al came around his desk and took my face in his hands. "I'm not asking, Trish. I'm ordering."

I met his gaze and held it, something I'd never done before. And, to my surprise, I saw something there I'd never seen. Had never even guessed. "Are you sure this is just about the Agency's complaint?" I whispered. "Or is there something else behind your order?"

His thumb smoothed my cheek and his gaze dropped briefly to my mouth before he squeezed his eyes shut, forcing away the impulse that had apparently weighed heavily on his heart for a long time. "You work for me, Trish."

I sighed as his hands fell away, hating that I had seen the secrets of his heart when he had worked so diligently to deny them, to remain professional and never hint at how he felt about me. Then I stood on my toes and pressed a lingering kiss to his cheek, a parting gift before I said, "Not anymore, Al."

His eyes snapped open. "What?"

"I quit."

I trudged down the corridor to Mary "Contrary" Smith's office, hoping to catch our prosecutor at her desk to plead with her to release Nicky to my custody before word spread that I'd quit. If I was lucky,

Al had been too rattled to call her right away and I still had a little time before all my credentials were revoked.

I hated to have to do that to the guy, but it was clear that his lack of support for my burgeoning relationship with Nicky was partially motivated by his secret feelings for me. Granted, he was pissed about having to get into a power struggle with the Agency over what was going on with the vampires and Nicky's vigilantism and was genuinely worried about me getting in the middle of all that, but he also was furious that I'd take up with someone the FMA had been watching very closely since the nineteen-twenties without being able to make any charges stick.

When I told him I quit, the look of pain and sorrow on his face was almost more than I could take, and I nearly retracted my resignation. But I held my ground in spite of Al's attempts to persuade me to stay. Now I just had to get Nicky the hell out of there before he was beyond my reach.

To my relief, Mary was sitting at her desk, her manicured nails clacking away rapidly on her laptop, her lovely brow furrowed in a deep frown. "Well, you've certainly made a mess of things," she snapped the moment I darkened her door.

I blinked at her, surprised she'd even noticed me. "Sorry?"

She glanced away from her screen and gave me a mildly reproachful look over the top of her naughty librarian glasses. "Al called me."

Oh, shit.

I swallowed, trying to act nonchalant. "Oh? What did he say?"

"He said that under no circumstances was I to release Nicky Blue to you." She pushed back from her keyboard and swiveled her chair so she could face me. "He said it was for your own protection."

I rolled my eyes. "Come on, Mary—"

"I told him it was too late," she interrupted. "I'd already released him."

I gaped at her in dismay for a full five seconds before I was able to say, "What? When?"

"We hadn't even processed him when I received a call from the head of the Tribunal, demanding I release Mr. Blue at once," she explained. "He must have some friends in pretty high places to move that fast. I didn't even file the paperwork until about an hour before Al sent the boys to pick Nicky up. Someone was already talking to the right people before we'd even brought him in."

No wonder Nicky hadn't been concerned.

"So . . . what did Al say to that news?" I asked.

Mary shrugged. "What could he say? We'll still go through the motions of a hearing and all of that to appease the Agency, but it's pretty clear how it'll come out."

I tried not to let my relief seep into my voice when I asked, "Where's Nicky now?"

A rare smile tugged at the corner of Mary's mouth. "Down in processing, I imagine."

I nodded. "Thanks, Mary. I owe you one."

Mary shook her head. "No, you don't. Now, get the hell out of here before any other shit hits the proverbial fan. I'll see what I can do where Al's concerned."

"Why?" I asked, not meaning it to come out so incredulously. I grimaced and quickly amended, "Sorry, no offense—but it's just that you're not exactly known for your altruism, Mary. Why help me—or Nicky for that matter?"

"You deserve to be happy, Trish," she said, her words clipped. "Everyone does. Al's been hung up on you for a hell of a long time—"

"How did *you* know that?"

"—and it's time he moved on, don't you think?"

I studied her for a moment, understanding dawning. "He'll probably need someone to talk to, you know. Someone to assure him this is all for the best."

She nodded. "Yes, I think you're right."

"Well, I hope he listens to what you have to say," I told her, meaning it. "I do care about him, you know."

"So do I." She jerked her chin toward the door. "Now, get the hell out of here and go find Nicky. I have somewhere I need to be."

I offered her a smile and hurried away from her office to the processing area, but the person at the desk told me that Nicky was already released to a tall gentleman with gray hair.

Eddie Fox.

I should've known that Nicky's loyal second-in-command would've been the one handling things. No one knew exactly where

Eddie had come from, but everyone knew him to be a friend to Nicky and a savvy businessman who had helped Nicky run his empire for decades. Even since taking up with Red's Gran, he'd continued to be the face of Nicky's business enterprises. And I had no doubt that if there were any strings being pulled, it was Eddie doing it.

Now I just had to figure out where the hell they'd gone. Would Nicky have headed back home or gone elsewhere? He knew I'd be following him to headquarters, so I found it hard to believe he'd leave without trying to track me down or give me a message. I grabbed my cell phone from my pocket and started to dial him but then realized I had no idea what his cell phone number was.

It was also at that point that I realized I had five missed calls—all from the same person. "Oh, shit," I muttered, noticing the date. I quickly hit the Call Back button on the touchscreen and waited.

"It's about damned time!" Lavender Seelie snapped when she answered. "I was about ready to send out a spell to search for you! Is everything okay? Seth and I stopped by your apartment and it looked like a tornado had hit. I've been trying to get in touch with you all morning! I even thought about calling Tess precoffee to see if she knew where you were."

I laughed a little in spite of her obvious concern. "You *were* desperate if you thought about calling Red in the morning. She only gets one cup of coffee per day with the pregnancy, you know. She's already a little testy."

"This isn't funny, Trish," Lavender retorted. "We were worried. My magic has been popping sparks all morning."

I ran a hand through my curls, feeling like the worst friend alive. "I'm so sorry, Lav—there's some really crazy shit going on right now. I totally forgot that you guys were going to be in town today. Where are you right now?"

"At FMA headquarters," she said. "I had to give my statement for James Charming's hearing on the fraud and racketeering charges."

I had to grin a little at this news. Cinderella's ex-husband and Lavender's former employer deserved everything he got, including the years he was looking at in FMA prison for all the shady deals he'd cut in the past and the people he'd screwed over. He'd already been serving time for his assault on Lavender the previous fall, so it looked like he might be hanging out in a cell for a good long while.

"I'm at headquarters, too, but I'm getting ready to leave," I told her. "I can meet you in the lobby if you're finished with everything."

"See you there in five," she said before hanging up.

I was so relieved to see Lavender and Seth standing in the FMA lobby that I had to choke back tears as I hugged them both. "God, it's so good to see you guys," I said, blinking the blur from my eyes.

"What's going on, honey?" Lavender asked, putting her arm around my shoulders and leading me toward the doors that opened up to the street.

I covered my face with my hands for a minute, wondering where the hell to start and desperately wishing I had Nicky with me at that moment to at least remove one concern. "I can't talk here," I said, glancing around. "Can we go somewhere else?"

She nodded. "Of course! Have you had lunch yet?"

I shook my head. "No, I—"

"Not leaving without me, are you, doll?"

I whirled around at the sound of Nicky's voice and relief washed over me like a tidal wave when I saw him strolling toward me, wearing that lopsided grin of his. I rushed to him, throwing my arms around his neck and squeezing tightly as his arms came around me and he buried his face in my hair.

He chuckled a little as he pulled back to peer down at me. "Don't think I could ever get tired of you throwing yourself in my arms."

"Where the hell have you been?" I demanded. "Mary told me they released you almost right away."

He shrugged. "Had to stop by and say hi to an old friend, thank him for doing me a favor."

I frowned at him, curious whom he meant and assuming he was talking about one of his friends in high places, but before I could ask about it, I heard a polite cough behind me and turned to see Lavender standing there, trying unsuccessfully to hide a smile. "I see you *do* have a few things to tell me about," she drawled. Then she grinned at Nicky. "Hey there, stranger. We were just going to take Trish to lunch. Care to join us?"

"I don't like this," Lavender was saying, shaking her head stubbornly. "You can't do this on your own. It's not safe—especially now that you've quit the FMA."

"We're just looking for answers right now," I assured her. "There's more going on than Al understands. The Agency isn't being straight with him, and for all their claims of trying to stop the vampires that have been popping up all over the place, they haven't actually done much. They didn't do a goddamn thing when I was being attacked."

"Maybe they didn't want to get involved because Dracula is a Tale," Seth offered. "You said the FMA and the Agency have an agreement to stay out of each other's sandbox, right?"

Nicky was frowning, his expression darker than I'd ever seen it. I wasn't sure if he was more upset about the pictures Al had showed me or the fact that I'd quit my job over him. Both had brought out a flash of rage in his eyes that made me a little nervous. I was still getting to know him, still trying to understand him completely in spite of everything I'd already seen of his soul. There were still places that had been out of my reach, dark corners that my sight hadn't penetrated. And he was careful to keep those hidden.

"I don't think that agreement means shit to the Agency," I said. "They obviously didn't care what lines they were crossing when they showed up at Halloran's and took out Sophia."

Lavender glanced between Nicky and me, her concern written all over her face. "Okay, so how can we help?"

"You can't," Nicky snapped before I had a chance to respond. "I don't want to involve anyone else in this."

"Well, I think it's a little late for that," Lavender shot back. "We care about Trish."

"You think I don't?" he spat.

Lavender met his gaze evenly. "I've known you for a long time, Nicky Blue. And I know a lot *about* you, more than you probably realize. If I thought for a second that you were just dicking around with Trish and felt nothing for her, I'd have already turned you into a toad and sent you hopping. So stow all this brooding bullshit and tell me what we can do to help you out. Otherwise, you can get used to dealing with warts."

Nicky's eyes narrowed at her as if he was trying to figure out whether she would carry out her threat, but then his face suddenly broke into a smile. "Glad to see you're back to your old self, Lav."

She winked at him. "Back atcha. So, what do you need?"

"Gideon still hasn't gotten back to us about the audience with your father," I reminded her. "Could you get us in to see him?"

Lavender's smile faded to a grimace. "I can, but you'll have to see my mother, too, I imagine."

I heard Seth groan, but gave Lavender a terse nod. "We'll just have to grin and bear it."

Nicky glanced at all of us with a confused frown. "Come on—it's *Lav's* mom," he said. "How bad can she be?"

Chapter Fifteen

"Are you sure about this?" Lavender asked sotto voce, taking my arm as we walked up the marble steps to her parents' manor.

I nodded. "If dealing with your mom again means we'll get a few answers, then I'll suck it up."

"That's not what I mean," she said, glancing over her shoulder where Seth and Nicky were hanging back while Seth filled Nicky in on what to expect from the Seelies. "I'm talking about Nicky."

I frowned at her. "He's not what a lot of people think."

"I know that," she replied. "He's a great guy at heart. But he's been through some serious shit, Trish. I don't want you to be his rebound. I know how much you—" She paused for a moment, considering her words. "I saw his handkerchief last fall when you were asking me about how it felt being with one of Red's exes, remember? I knew then that you were in love with him."

I felt my cheeks going warm. I knew exactly which conversation she was talking about. "It's not what you think," I mumbled.

"For your sake, I hope not," she said on a sigh. "Just be careful, sweetie. I don't want you to get your heart broken."

Before I could respond, the twelve-foot-high doors to the house swung open and a brightly dressed man bowed deeply to Lavender. "Greetings and welcome, Your Highness. Your father awaits you and your guests."

"Thank you, Felix," she said with a smile. Then she turned and motioned to Seth to get his ass up the stairs. Her fiancé sighed and exchanged a glance with Nicky. They both looked like they were heading to the gallows as they trudged up the stairs.

The opulence of Seelie Manor was truly breathtaking. The marble floors were so polished we could see our reflection in the stone. The crystal chandeliers were delicate and looked more like dew-laden spiderwebs than light fixtures. And the magnificent sculptures that lined the domed foyer were so lifelike, I half expected them to rush forward to greet their beloved princess.

We waited for just a few moments before a towering man with dark hair and a sparkling blue gaze swept into the room and spread his arms wide. "Hello, petal!" he said, his booming voice echoing off the marble. "I am delighted that you could visit us after all!"

"Hi, Dad," Lavender said, hugging him tightly.

The man then turned his smile to his future son-in-law. "Seth, m'boy—good to see you. Treating my daughter well, I see. She's absolutely glowing!"

I hadn't noticed it before, but Lavender *had* taken on a slight purple glow just under her skin and her eyes were brighter than I'd ever seen them.

"Absolutely, sir," Seth replied, shaking the king's hand. "You've no worries there."

"Of course, of course!" He clapped Seth on the back, then turned to Nicky and me. "And who have we here?"

"Dad, you remember Trish Muffet," Lavender said. "She is to be one of my bridesmaids this spring."

"Oh yes, yes. Of course. My apologies." He leaned in and whispered, "I've been trying to stay out of all that business. Mab can be very particular, you know."

"So I've heard," I said with a tight smile.

He chuckled. "Oh, I'm sure you have. I'm sure you have."

"And, Daddy, this is Nicky Blue," Lavender told him.

The king's response to Nicky wasn't nearly as warm. He looked down his nose at him, sizing him up. "Mr. Blue," he said, shaking his hand. "I understand you wished to have an audience with me."

Nicky gave him a terse nod. "Yes, sir, I did. I still do."

The king regarded him for a moment. "Gideon tells me he owes you a debt of gratitude for assisting him the other night."

"He hardly needed my help, sir," Nicky demurred.

The king laughed in a short burst. "I daresay he didn't. Gideon is a force of nature. But you offered your assistance nonetheless. And for that I am grateful. You have done me a favor, have shown your friendship, and now I will show you mine. I will see you."

"Thank you," Nicky said, inclining his head. "I appreciate your generosity."

The king swept his arm toward the arch that led from the foyer. "Well then, shall we?"

We followed the king into a dining room that held a twenty-foot-long table already laid out for a feast.

"You didn't have to do all this for us, Dad," Lavender said, her eyes wide.

The king gave her a somewhat put-upon look. "The girls are visiting."

I glanced at Lavender. "The girls?"

She rolled her eyes, but before she'd even had a chance to explain, we heard a chorus of giggles and a dozen or so young women came hurrying into the dining room, twittering and chattering like a flock of birds.

"These are my sisters," Lavender announced on a sigh, as they bounded into their seats at the table and offered up sunshiny waves before pointing at Seth and Nicky and giggling behind their hands.

"I thought Poppy was your only sister," I said as the king swept an arm and motioned for us to join them at the table.

Nicky and Seth pulled out chairs for us and waited for Lav and me to sit before taking the seat on either side of us. Two of the girls from the other side of the table immediately hopped up and came around to nestle in close to the guys, their cheeks flushed and eyes glowing with amorous intent.

Lavender sent a glare of warning at the one next to Seth, which made her instantly wither and resign herself to batting pretty orange eyelashes at him. "They're my half sisters," she ground out as she turned back to me. "Let's just say Puck comes by his wandering eye honestly."

"Oh." I glanced down at the king, who was looking more than a little irritated with the silly brood he had sired. Guess what goes around comes around. . . .

"Lavender," Seth said, leaning a little away from the doe-eyed gaze of his companion, "would you care to introduce your siblings?"

She huffed. "I guess." Then she went around the table in rapid fire. "Ivy, Lilly, Daisy, Rose, Pansy, Flora, Blossom, Petunia, Hyacinth, Iris, Dahlia." Here she paused and sent another look of warning to the woman beside her fiancé. "And your little *friend,* Seth, is Calla."

Calla twisted her face into a grimace and stuck out her tongue at her elder sister. She looked like she was about to say something petulant and snotty when she suddenly straightened and snapped to attention, as did all of her sisters. I glanced around to see what had happened to settle them down in an instant, but the reason was immediately evident.

Standing in the doorway in all her imperious glory was Lavender's mother, Queen Mab, her beauty as stunning and unchanging as the first time I'd seen her. The king rose to his feet and took Mab's hand to escort her to her seat at the other end of the table, then kissed her fingertips with an adoring gaze before leaving her side. Mab slowly surveyed the king's brood with barely disguised disgust and then turned her golden eyes upon her own daughter.

"Hello, Lavender, darling," she said with a hint of a smile. That trace of warmth vanished in an instant when she glanced at Seth and gave him a nod. "Werewolf."

He forced a strained smile. "Your Majesty," he replied with a polite nod, although his tone clearly conveyed *Bitch.*

The queen bristled, but before she could send an angry retort his way, Lavender piped up, "Mother, you remember my friend Trish Muffet, of course."

Mab narrowed her eyes at me as if she was deciding whether or not she cared to admit it. "Of course."

"And this is our friend, Nicky Blue," Lavender introduced.

Mab clucked her tongue. "Perfect. Another nursery rhyme at my table."

"Mother!" Lavender hissed, her magic sending up a crackle of electrical charge at the insult, a tiny pop of purple spark shooting off and landing on my hand. I winced and sucked in air through my teeth, rubbing at the skin where it had burned me. "Mr. Blue has business with my father."

Mab lifted her brows at her husband. "Indeed?"

The king lifted his goblet of wine. "Mr. Blue recently did me a courtesy, Mab. He is now a friend of ours."

She made a little noise but said nothing.

"I welcome *all* of you to my table," the king said, looking pointedly at his wife. "Let us feast and then we shall discuss whatever business brings you here. I—"

"Sorry, sorry!" came a cheerful voice from behind me.

I turned to see Lavender's sister Poppy rushing into the dining room, her bubblegum pink hair a bit disheveled, her clothes not quite in perfect order. And to my amazement, she wasn't alone. Beside her, looking a great deal better than when last I'd seen him, was J.G. Squiggington, the former publisher of *The Daily Tattletale*, whose brain had been pretty much turned to mush by a fairy dust overdose courtesy of Sebille Fenwick.

"J.G.?" Lavender gasped.

He gave us a boyish smile in response. "The one and only—thank Christ, most people would say. Am I lyin'?"

"Not in the least," I heard Mab mumble.

"You look fantastic!" Lavender gushed, hurrying over to give him a quick hug. "The treatments with Poppy are going well?"

Poppy flushed very prettily and cast an adoring look at J.G. that was hard to miss. "Totally."

Lavender drew back and glanced at her sister and J.G. "Oh?"

Poppy suddenly jumped up and down with a quick clap of her hands and threw her arms around her sister. "I have some, like, *totally* awesome news!"

I exchanged a glance with Nicky, suddenly feeling a little uncomfortable at the tension I could feel in the air. "You know," I said, scooting my chair back, "maybe Nicky and I should—"

"We're getting married!" Poppy announced.

Lavender's face went slack. "Wow. That's . . . well . . . I'm happy for you guys, I guess, but are you sure that's a good idea? I mean, J.G. was in pretty bad shape. . . ."

J.G. put his arm around Poppy's waist and drew her close, planting a big wet one on her cheek. "And I still would be if it wasn't for this gal right here! She's the shit—and seriously fuckin' hot, too, you know what I'm sayin'?"

"Oh, God," I mumbled when I saw the king's jaw tighten ominously. "Nicky."

He nodded and pushed his chair back from the table.

"And here's the best part," Poppy was saying as Nicky and I stood to go, "we thought we'd do a double wedding with you and Seth!"

"Ah, shit," I breathed.

"I beg your pardon?" Lavender gaped, purple sparks dancing all around her now.

"Over my dead fucking body!" Seth snapped, standing abruptly, his eyes glowing with anger.

"Seth, honey," Lavender said with a glance at her parents. "Please."

"No, Lav," he replied, his voice growing louder. "Now, if you two want to get married, have at it. Good luck and congratulations! But you are not hijacking our day."

Poppy's eyes welled up with tears. "But I thought you'd be happy."

"Happy?" Lavender screeched. "Are you *serious*? Why would I be happy about having to share my wedding day?"

Nicky and I started edging to the door, hoping to duck out before magic really started flying.

"Ms. Muffet and Mr. Blue," the king's voice boomed. "Please do not leave on account of my children's little squabble."

"Oh, yes," Mab interjected. "By all means—please stay and witness the tragedy that is my family. I sit here surrounded by my husband's bastard daughters and my future sons-in-law who are a werewolf and a gossip peddler. Yes, *do* stay and add your own low-born blood to my lovely assembly."

Now it was the king's turn to launch himself to his feet. "Mab! I would speak with you. Privately."

Everyone in the room went instantly still, their eyes focused on the king and his queen. Mab rose to her feet in a shimmer of golden fairy dust that just about made J.G.'s eyes roll back into his head. Then she peered down her nose at each and every one of us before sweeping from the room.

The king made a courteous bow and offered us a smile. "Please," he said, gesturing to the table, "enjoy the feast. I shall return momentarily."

"It was Mother's idea," Poppy said quietly as soon as their parents had left the room.

Lavender shook her head. "I'm sure it was, dearest. You and J.G.—well, I wish you every happiness. If you love each other, then I'm excited for you. But you deserve your own day."

As they all resumed their seats and began to eat in silence, Nicky and I looked at each other again, weighing our options. Part of me wondered if we should still slink out and leave the family to settle their issues in private. But then another part of me didn't want to squander the chance we had to speak with the formidable king and possibly get some answers to our questions about what was going on with the Agency.

"Please stay," Lavender said, grasping my hand in hers. "I haven't seen you since you left The Refuge."

My gaze snapped toward where Poppy was cooing over J.G., trying to sooth the sting of her mother's tirade. *The Refuge.* "J.G.," I said, "when you were investigating Sebille Fenwick and the cult at The Refuge, did you come across any information on Dracula?"

J.G. shrugged. "Yeah, sure. They were in league for a while."

I nodded. "We need to chat."

"That bloodsucker was a helluva lot better at covering his tracks than Sebille," J.G. said, snipping off the end of a Cuban cigar that had been part of the king's personal stash in the study. "I couldn't ever find out anything concrete on the guy—just rumors and innuendo. That kinda shit. Nobody was willing to flap their gums and risk ending up dead, you know what I'm sayin'?"

"That must be what I was picking up on when I was asking around during the werewolf murders," Nicky mused. "Nobody was talking. Nothing tips me off faster that something big is going on than when Tales won't talk about it."

J.G. grinned around the cigar as he lit it up. "I like you, Blue. I don't care what anybody says."

Nicky jerked back a little. "What are people saying?"

"So how do we get them to talk?" I said in a rush before J.G. could spew out whatever gossip he'd heard about Nicky.

"Just gotta ask the right questions of the right people," J.G. said. "I was focusing on Sebille before, not that bloodsucker Dracula."

"And who would those right people be?" Lavender asked. "Trish and Nicky need something to go on."

J.G. blew out a long curl of smoke and nodded. "If it was me, I'd start with Renfield."

"Renfield?" Seth scoffed. "That guy's freaking crazy. He lived in The Refuge for a while after Dracula went off the grid. But he started wigging out again and had to be sent back to the Asylum. No offense, J.G."

J.G. shrugged. "Don't worry about it. I was in the room next door to the guy and had to listen to him rant and rave all fuckin' night. Thank Christ Poppy came along and got me the hell outta there." He sent a wink her way that made her blush fiercely. I had to wonder if I ever turned that particular shade of red when Nicky looked at me.

"So, we'll make a trip to the Asylum," I said with a determined nod. "Renfield might be a total lunatic, but if he can help us track down Dracula's lair, then it'll be worth the visit."

J.G. shook his head. "Nah, he's not going to know how to find Dracula. The count wouldn't trust that crackpot with anything like that. If you want to find the lair, you're going to have to track down whoever built it. It's a shitload of dirt to move around, so it'd be a big job."

"Everyone knows Dracula is wanted by the FMA," I said. "Who would take on a job like that?"

Seth and Nicky exchanged glances, and I heard Seth curse under his breath before they said in unison, "The Piggs."

I frowned. "I thought the Pigg brothers were indicted for fraud for their shady home building practices before the housing bubble burst and were serving time in the Ordinary prison system."

"They got out a little over a year ago," Nicky said. "Perfect timing."

"Just don't tell 'em you know me," Seth warned. "If they find out they'll send you packing."

"What the hell happened between you guys anyway?" Lavender asked. "You never have told me."

"Let's just say when I was first a wolf, I sometimes had a tough time determining what was off-limits for dinner," Seth replied. "It was all a big misunderstanding."

"You almost *ate* them," I pointed out with a grin. "I think that goes beyond a misunderstanding."

Seth gave me a sardonic look. "Have you ever *met* the Piggs?"

I was about to ask what he meant when the study door opened and the king entered, his manner more aloof than it had been before. "I apologize for the disruption during your dinner," he said to all of us, pointedly waiting for J.G. to vacate his chair behind the desk. His future son-in-law stared at him for a moment, but then finally caught on and hopped up and turned the chair toward the king.

"Sorry there, Pops," he muttered. "Plant it right there."

The king heaved a sigh, then shook his head a little before assuming his seat and peering out at all of us, waiting for us to begin. When none of us immediately spoke up, he inclined his head toward Nicky. "My apologies to you in particular, Mr. Blue. You are a guest in my home, a friend now by virtue of your assistance. Please, tell me what it is you wish to know."

Nicky scooted to the edge of his chair, his demeanor suddenly changing. He was in business mode now, ready to parley with an associate. He offered the king a smile that was charming, but there was something dark about the edges—something deadly and determined. This must be the Nicky that people who knew and feared him had always seen. It certainly wasn't the tender, caring, loving man I knew so intimately now.

"Gideon told us that you have a little problem with someone selling D on the black market and trying to implicate your operation," Nicky said.

The king inclined his head. "This is true. Gideon was sent to gather intelligence to help identify those involved. When I am satisfied that I have the facts, I shall handle it. And swiftly." The king smiled, but there was no mirth in his eyes. I had a pretty good idea of just how he planned to go about taking care of the dealers who were interfering with his business.

"I have no doubt of that," Nicky told him. "I respect you and honor your decision. But may I ask, as a friend, why you refuse to let the FMA get involved?"

The king shifted, casting a meaningful glance my way.

"I quit this morning," I told him. "You can speak freely, sir."

He clasped his hands over his stomach, then looked at his younger daughter and her fiancé. "Poppy, why don't you take Mr. Squiggington to the gardens? I imagine he could use some fresh air. Good for the constitution."

Poppy obediently hopped to her feet and dragged J.G. from the room, shutting the door behind her. As soon as she was gone the king sighed. "Poppy's a good girl," he mused. "I hope that little shit will make her happy. He seems to love her, so I grant him leeway. But he is still a bit *off* from his experiences. I would rather not have him present when we discuss these things. I hope I do not offend."

Nicky shook his head. "That's your prerogative, sir. I defer to you in that matter."

The king chuckled. "I like you, Mr. Blue. You understand respect and honor. This is why I will tell you what I know."

Nicky spread his hands in gratitude. "Thank you, sir. I hope I prove to be worthy of your praise."

The king rose from his chair and strolled to a liquor cabinet. "Do any of you care for a drink?" Not waiting for an answer, he poured out four snifters of brandy and handed one to Seth, Nicky, and me, then filled a tumbler with sparkling water and gave it to Lavender, pausing to press an adoring kiss to the top of her head before lifting his own glass. "*Sláinte chuig na fir, agus go mairfidh na mná go deo.*"

I glanced to Lavender for the translation and saw her grinning fondly at her father. "Health to the men, and may the women live forever."

He patted her cheek. "Lovely girl." His expression then grew solemn again as he perched casually on the corner of his desk. "I have no doubt that the Agency is behind the black market distribution of fairy dust. I know that Tim Halloran was in discussions with them but, although he was an annoyance, he was hardly a threat to my operations. The Agency, on the other hand, is a formidable force. That being said, I refuse to go to the FMA about it because I believe the organization has been compromised."

I blinked at him in amazement. "Compromised? What do you mean? Someone in the FMA is dirty?"

"Exactly so."

"Do you know who it is?" Seth asked.

"Not yet," the king admitted. "That is what Gideon was trying to uncover. We know that those Tales who were installed with the Agency to be liaisons are working against their own brethren—"

I immediately thought of Freddy the Ferret and his pals and had no doubt of the king's assessment.

"—but I believe there are those within the FMA who are also working against us."

"Why do you think so, sir?" I asked.

He took a sip of his brandy and hissed a little as it went down. "Al Addin has been very cozy with the Agency in recent years. There once was a time when he would stand up for us, fight for our right to exist without the Ordinaries' interference, but he is being worn down, persuaded that it is not to our detriment to go along with the Agency, grant them access to us, to our secrets."

"You can't possibly believe that Al has betrayed us, can you?" I demanded, my voice edged with anger. For all Al's faults, I couldn't believe that he would sell out like that.

"Perhaps the Agency is simply putting a great deal of pressure on him, Dad," Lavender piped up. "I mean, the times have changed considerably since we came over. It's growing increasingly difficult for us to stay hidden. The revolution that was brewing in The Refuge was hardly an isolated incident. As you know, there are other groups pushing for the same thing. Perhaps Al is just doing what he has to do to keep us all as safe as possible."

"I am willing to give him the benefit of the doubt because of the kindness he has shown you over the years, petal," the king admitted. "But the FMA has a list of all of my distribution centers, my distribution schedule, the transportation routes. They are operated secretly for good reason, but I am required to report all of my activities to the FMA in order to be in compliance with our laws. My transports have been robbed on several occasions in the last two years and I am certain it is this product that is being distributed to the Ordinaries."

"But why would the Agency want to do that?" I asked. "What do they have to gain?"

"Fairy dust is used as therapy for the most volatile Tales," the king reminded me. "If my business had to be shut down because I was no longer in compliance, we would have significant problems."

I thought about the repercussions of a sudden shortage of fairy dust. Those who took it for "medicinal" reasons would be in a panic from the withdrawal symptoms and would search out any black market source they could find—and who knows what kind of deals they'd make, what they would give up, what secrets they would divulge to the Agency to get it. And I didn't even want to think about what would happen if fairy dust was no longer available to the population in the Asylum.

"Shit," I muttered. "What the hell are they trying to do?"

"Break us down," Seth said, "destroy our unity. The only reason we've made it this long without discovery is because we've stuck together—even when we were fighting among ourselves."

Nicky nodded. "Get us fighting over the right thing, and they can swoop in and start recruiting."

"And gathering specimens," I breathed.

The king's brows lifted at this. "Specimens?"

I glanced around at everyone before my gaze settled on Nicky. "They've been trying to get Al to hand over one of us for a long time. They want to study us, dissect us, figure out what we're made of, how we're different. Al has always refused. One of them—Agent Spalding—got to me a little over a year ago and . . ." I paused, wondering what I should divulge. "Well, he tricked me into trusting him so he could try to get information about my ability to read the dead. He didn't find out what he wanted, though, and I caught a glimpse of what he was up to, so he finally gave up trying. But they almost nabbed Nicky this morning. Al took him into protective custody to keep him safe."

"Protective custody?" Nicky repeated. "Is *that* what Al called it?"

I averted my gaze and looked at the king instead. "With so much at stake, with so many of us at risk of being taken and abused by the Agency, I'm sure you can understand why it's so important to work together and not allow them to plant the seeds of distrust."

The king narrowed his eyes at me, regarding me for a long moment. "I will reserve judgment at present," he finally announced. "But I will be watching, madam. And if I sense any threat to my family or my business interests, I guarantee that I will deal with it swiftly."

And without mercy, I imagined.

I gave him a terse nod. "Of course. That's all anyone can ask."

When we all said our good-byes to Lavender's father, I was surprised to see that the king seemed genuinely disappointed that we were leaving. He hugged Lavender and brushed a kiss to my fingertips with a very gentlemanly bow before shaking hands with Seth and Nicky. But his final words were for Nicky.

"Be careful, Mr. Blue," he said, his blue eyes pegging Nicky with a look of warning. "I do not generally enter into a deadly game until I am sure I know the situation well and am assured of victory. And there are many unknowns in this instance."

Chapter Sixteen

Lavender finished tying the small braid of hair around my wrist and sighed. "There you go, sweetie. That should help protect you when you're out and about, make you a little less vulnerable."

I nodded and looked down at the talisman she had imbued with her magic and friendship to try to keep me safe. "Thanks, Lav." I looked up and frowned at the gap in her purple locks. "Sorry about your hair."

She shrugged with a grin. "It'll grow back." She snapped her fingers and hair quickly sprouted, growing longer until the new lock was even with the rest. "See?"

"So, will this keep away the dreams, too?" I asked Lavender.

She worked her mouth a little in thought. "No, probably not. Not much I can do about invasions of that variety. Your defenses are down when you sleep, so it's easy for Dracula to come in, magic talisman or not. Just keep Nicky close. That'll help."

"What about ghosts?" I asked. "What do I do if Amanda comes back?"

Lavender's eyes narrowed. "Ah, yes, Amanda. Freaking ghosts—they're a pain in the ass. Do you have any sage handy?"

I glanced at Nicky, who shrugged and shook his head. "Hell if I know."

"Okay, well, I know one spell that might keep anything from

physically crossing your threshold," Lavender said, nodding. She grabbed the edges of her shirt and pulled it over her head, then started shimmying out of her skirt before Seth rushed forward to block her from Nicky's wide eyes.

"Whoa, whoa, whoa!" Seth cried. "What the hell are you doing?"

She looked at him like it was the most obvious thing in the world. "I'm going to put a protection spell around the house like I did at your cabin last fall."

"And you have to be naked?" he whispered, jerking his head toward Nicky.

"Oh, Seth, for crying out loud," she laughed. "Nicky doesn't care what I look like naked."

Seth turned around with a protective snarl, his face beginning to shift a little ominously, and Nicky threw up his hands.

"I'm turning around," Nicky said, making good on his words. "Promise not to peek."

"Sorry, Nicky," Lavender said as she finished stripping off her clothes. "The full moon is coming in a couple of days and Seth gets a little more territorial than usual."

A low, hungry growl began to vibrate deep in Seth's chest as he took in Lavender's gorgeous body. I didn't know for sure, but I was guessing that ramping up his territoriality wasn't the only effect the full moon had on him. In the next instant, Seth pretty much confirmed my theory when he gathered Lavender in his arms and kissed her savagely as he pressed her against the wall. He hefted her up and wrapped her legs around his waist, pressing even closer.

Holy shit.

"Um, Lav," I stammered, "do you two, um, need to . . . you know . . ." Nicky started to turn around to see what was happening, but I pushed his head back so he was facing away. "Don't even think about it."

"Sorry, Trish," Lavender gasped as Seth left her mouth to nip at her neck. "We might need a few minutes."

I tore my gaze away, feeling like a total voyeur, and grabbed Nicky's hand. "Come on," I whispered. "Let's go."

"Where?" he asked, starting to turn his head again.

"Do you want Seth to rip your throat out?" I hissed. "Come on!" I pulled him out of the living room and shut the double doors behind us.

"What the hell was *that* all about?" Nicky asked, staring at the closed doors.

"I guess it's a werewolf thing," I said, trying not to hear the noises of passion coming from the other room. It made me want nothing more than to drag Nicky upstairs and see if he had a little inner wolf in him, too—especially considering the sexy beast I already knew him to be—but we had work to do and I had a feeling time was running out. "Maybe now would be a good time to visit the Asylum."

He shook his head. "Damn. Guess so."

I smothered a smile at his dazed look. "Come on, lover," I cooed. "The sooner we get back, the sooner we can have a little fun of our own."

Nicky's head bobbed in a nod. "Works for me." He suddenly pivoted and picked me up, throwing me over his shoulder.

I laughed. "Nicky, what the hell are you doing?"

He strode toward the front door, his long strides thundering on the hardwood floor. "Just speeding things up," he replied, yanking open the door. I laughed again as he hurried down the steps, making my upper body bob with the motion. Then he plopped me down next to the Escalade and pressed a hard kiss to my lips. "Those folks at the Asylum can have one hour with you. Then you're mine."

I grinned and returned his kiss with a slow, sultry one of my own. "I'm yours anytime you want me, lover."

Nicky groaned, then broke away, slipping a little on the ice and snow in his haste to get around to the other side of the SUV. He hopped in and shoved open my door from the inside, then offered me that mischievous grin that assured me he was up to no good. "What are you waiting for, doll? Tick tock."

For all the levity we'd shared before we reached the Asylum, the moment we arrived at the entrance of the secluded estate nestled deep in a hundred acres of forest in northern Illinois, it was impossible to be lighthearted. There was a heaviness in the air that weighed down on us, growing more profound with each step.

"How the hell do people work here every day?" Nicky muttered as we climbed the stone steps. "This would depress the shit out of me."

I shook my head, wishing we'd waited until it was daylight to visit, but there was no way I was going to bail after we'd come all that way. Besides, I had a feeling that when Dracula realized he couldn't get into my thoughts, he wasn't going to be very happy. And an unhappy Dracula was something I wanted to avoid.

The Asylum had existed in its current form for over a hundred years, and some of its residents had been there for that long. The FMA tried to rehabilitate those who were brought to the Asylum for treatment, but, sadly, few were as successful as J.G. seemed to be. This was hardly my first trip to the last resort for many Tales who were deemed either too dangerous or too unstable to be left in the general population of the FMA prison, but no matter how many times I had to visit, I never got used to the ominous feeling that pervaded the building.

I shuddered when Nicky pounded a fist on the front door and I heard the knock echoing through the hallways. Sensing my uneasiness, Nicky took my hand in his, giving it a squeeze.

"You okay?" he whispered.

I nodded and swallowed hard. "Yeah, I'm good. I just hate this place. Too many opportunities to catch a glimpse into one of the patients' thoughts when I'm not expecting it."

"Are you sure you want to go inside?" he asked. "I can talk to Renfield myself."

But before I could respond, the door swung open to reveal a very austere woman in a plain black dress, her gray hair pulled back flat against her head in a tight bun. Her face was pinched and unfriendly as she looked us over.

"It's after hours," she snapped. "No visitors."

I offered the matron a smile. "I'm Trish Muffet," I said. "I've visited here before on FMA business."

"Don't care who you are," she said. "After hours."

Nicky leaned against the door frame, giving her his patented smile. "You won't let us in for just a few minutes?" he drawled. "We promise not to cause any trouble. I'd consider it a personal favor."

The matron seemed to cave a little. "I really shouldn't. . . ."

He bent forward a little toward her. "Hang on—it's Mrs. Reed, isn't it? From *Jane Eyre*?"

She lifted a single brow. "What of it?"

He nodded. "I thought I recognized you. A woman of your impeccable breeding and stature—how did you end up being the matron of the Asylum?"

She straightened, obviously flattered by his notice. "It seems my lot in life to be forced to look after monsters," she told him, smoothing the front of her dress, which was a far cry from the type of attire she'd been used to in her story.

"A great injustice," Nicky said, shaking his head. "You were intended for a life of ease, not working in a place like this."

"Exactly so." She glared at us for a moment, then stepped back, opening the door wide. "I suppose I can let you in for a little while. Just don't upset any of the inmates."

"We only need to see one of them," Nicky assured her. "Renfield."

Her brows shot up. "That man is completely deranged. Why would you want to see him?"

"I'm sorry, but that's classified," I told her. "Just tell us where he is and we'll find our way."

"Third floor," she spat, obviously not as impressed with me as she was with Nicky. "Cell forty-two."

"Insufferable woman," I muttered as we trudged up the stairs to the upper levels. "How *dare* she call the patients here monsters? Only some of them are completely beyond help. If anyone's a monster it's *that* detestable woman. The way she treated Jane Eyre . . . How could you possibly be polite to that harpy?"

"I've had to be polite to a lot of assholes over the years, doll," Nicky said. "It makes my ass twitch every single time. But if you want to get anywhere, you sometimes have to dance with the devil."

We were silent as we navigated the dim, clinically sparse halls of the Asylum. The dirty light cast by the bare bulbs spaced in even intervals along the ceiling cast dark shadows, creating corners that weren't there and bathing the passageway in an eerie, murky glow. I edged a little closer to Nicky and he reached for my hand, clasping it tightly in his.

There were unintelligible mumblings floating toward us and beneath the static of voices I heard a woman keening in sorrow, another weeping, punctuating her grief with sharp yowls that made me start each time her mournful screech split the air.

Nicky's fingers tightened around mine. "Here's forty-two," he said, jerking his chin toward the number hanging over a heavy steel door with a barred window.

I nodded. "Okay, let's get this over with."

Nicky blew out a sharp breath, then slid the blind to the left and peered through the bars. "Renfield." There was a scrabble of movement inside but no response. "Renfield, we want to talk to you."

We waited in tense silence, listening for any response. Suddenly a face appeared at the bars, making Nicky jump, which startled a little yelp out of me. I clutched at his arm, my heart racing.

The grimy face before us twisted into a grotesque smile, revealing filthy, rotting teeth. He chuckled, the sound as harsh as sandpaper. "Have come to visit me, have you?" he rasped. "Come to talk to the freak?"

"We need to know about Dracula," Nicky said, cutting to the chase. "We need to know where he is, what he's planning."

Renfield chuckled again. "You won't find the master," he assured us. "Not until he wants to be found. And then he'll find *you*." He looked pointedly at me. "But you already know that, don't you?"

Renfield suddenly darted to one side and there was a soft shuffling inside the cell. A moment later he reappeared, chewing on something crunchy. His eyes rolled back into his head as his lids fluttered shut, and he moaned with ecstasy. "The blood is the life," he murmured. "The blood is the life. . . ."

I gagged a little, trying in vain not to imagine what manner of creature Renfield had just ingested. I'd read his story and knew his obsession with consuming insects and whatever else he could get his hands on in the assumption that it would make him stronger, grant him a measure of immortality.

"Renfield," Nicky said, "could you tell us what you know about Dracula? Has he communicated with you lately?"

"He has promised me life!" Renfield rasped, grasping the bars of his cell. "He will come for me when he is ready for me to do his bidding and free me from this damnable place! And he will make me an immortal with his blood. He has told me so!"

"He can't make you any more immortal than you already are," I told him. "We're Tales, Renfield—we don't age here. We don't die except under very extreme circumstances."

Renfield blinked at me, his unfocused gaze suddenly becoming laser sharp. "You are wrong, pretty girl. The master can make me stronger, can teach me the ways to find the blood that gives life. He has promised it."

"When did he tell you that?" I asked, beginning to wonder if Renfield even realized he was no longer trapped within the pages of his story. It was possible he could no longer differentiate between what had occurred in his novel and what had taken place since coming over.

Renfield ignored the question and instead looked me over, his head cocked to one side as he studied me. "You remind me of her," he said. "That Mrs. Harker who came to see me once. You do not resemble her—no, no. Not in that way. But you have a sweet face, a beautiful face. And you, too, have heard his voice, haven't you?"

My blood ran cold at his words. "Yes. I've heard it."

Renfield shook his head. "A pity, madam. He will never let you go once you've heard his voice in your head. I have heard it, you know. Have heard it howling on the winds that seep through the cracks of this very building. Have heard it in the stillness of the shadows. He draws ever closer. And soon he will come for me. As he will come for you, too."

Nicky bristled at my side and pulled me a little behind him, shielding me from Renfield's view. "Talk to *me,* you lunatic."

Renfield's eyes trained on Nicky now. "You come to me, demanding answers, but you ask the wrong questions, sir. You have not asked me what it is you truly need to know."

"And what's that?" Nicky demanded.

Renfield's parched lips spread into another grotesque smile, his skin cracking and beginning to bleed. "Ah, but you bring me no gifts to tempt me to answer. I have asked over and over for a little kitten to love and care for, but I have received none. Am I to be denied even an ounce of affection?"

"You'd just eat it, you sick son of a bitch," Nicky replied.

Renfield sighed dramatically. "Such is my existence. I am misunderstood, madam. Do you not see that?"

I edged out from behind Nicky and approached the door. "I can't offer you anything, Renfield," I admitted. "But will you tell me what it is you know about your master and his plans? I'm afraid lives depend upon it. Perhaps even mine."

He beckoned me closer, glancing from side to side as if he expected someone to suddenly appear inside his cell. I took a cautious step forward, shaking off Nicky's restraining hand. Renfield beckoned again, more urgently this time.

"Give me your hand, pretty lady," he demanded.

I lifted my hand, but Nicky grabbed my arm. "Trish—"

I shook my head at him. "It's fine." I slipped my fingers through the space between the bars.

Renfield grasped them with a lascivious little gasp and began stroking them with his own filthy fingers. I resisted the urge to recoil from his touch, determined to see where this would go.

"Such lovely fingers," he murmured. "I can hear the blood coursing through your veins. Little rivers of power and vitality. So much life . . ." To my horror, he closed those disgusting lips around my index finger and sucked in one long motion, his tongue savoring the taste.

"Jesus Christ," Nicky spat, balling his hands into fists, straining to keep from bolting forward and tearing my hand from Renfield's grasp.

But I shushed him. "What do you have to tell me, Renfield?" I ground out, swallowing the bile in my throat. "Please, I must know what your master has told you."

He pulled my finger from his mouth with a little *pop*. "You already know what I know," he said, leering at me. "You've tasted the master's blood. And he has tasted yours."

I shook my head. "No. That's not true."

He chuckled. "Oh, but it is. You've felt his bite. You have his mark upon you."

"That was a dream," I insisted. "The mark I had has faded. It was probably just psychosomatic."

Renfield went back to stroking my fingers, his eyes taking on a disturbingly hungry look. "So you say . . . but you've tasted of him, madam," he assured me. "You took his blood into you, have brought part of him into your body." His grasp on my hand suddenly tightened to the point of pain and he jerked me forward, knocking me off balance. When I fell against the door, he grasped a handful of my hair. Nicky bolted forward in an instant, working to pry the man's fingers loose.

"Do not deny him!" Renfield shouted. "Do not deny him, madam! He is the giver of life. The blood is the life! The blood is the *life!*"

Nicky finally managed to free me and jerked me out of Renfield's reach. "Are you all right?" he asked, his brow furrowed with concern.

I nodded, my eyes still on Renfield, who was sobbing hysterically now. "She doesn't listen!" he whimpered. "She denies you, master! Leave her in peace, I beg you! Leave her be!"

I began to tremble as his deranged wailings continued. "Renfield—"

He lunged at the bars again, clinging to them and pressing his face against the iron until for one crazy moment I thought his head might actually squeeze between them. "What the master wants the master gets. He will not be denied, madam. The red one he loved denied him and he went mad with grief. And now he will seek revenge upon you all! You will be sorry you denied the life giver! Flee now while you can! Flee! Fly like the sparrows I would consume for the life they give. I pray I never see your sweet face again, madam!"

"What revenge?" I demanded. "What is he planning to do, Renfield? You *must* tell me if you want me to be safe."

He shook his head, his tears leaving streaks on his grimy cheeks. "You are lost, madam," he sobbed. "Lost!" Then he stabbed Nicky with an accusing glare. "This is *your* fault, sir! You brought this sentence upon her head."

When Nicky didn't immediately respond to refute the nonsense Renfield was spewing, I glanced over at him, startled to see that he had gone pale, a tense expression of concern furrowing his brow. "Nicky?" I whispered, placing a hand on his arm. "Are you okay?"

"You, who call yourself the Spider," Renfield raged on, his face twisting in disgust. "You slink along in the shadows, chasing the master and trying to destroy what he has built. But the master has told me all about you—you are no *spider*! You do not consume the blood that is life! You only take, take, take until the blood flows— wasted—on the ground! He would've left her alone if you had not interfered, but he saw what was in your heart! And he will rip it from your chest, sir. He will devour it before your eyes and revel in your horror and sorrow as he has before!"

"You, there!"

Nicky and I glanced up at the man in scrubs who was jogging down the hall toward us. "What the hell are you doing here after hours? You're riling up the patients."

Nicky took my hand and made for the stairs, shouldering past the orderly. "We were just leaving."

We bolted down the stairs, Nicky fairly dragging me after him. "Nicky!" I gasped, out of breath from our mad dash. "Stop!"

"I'm getting you the hell out of here," he mumbled, pulling me out the front door and shoving me into the waiting Escalade. When he got behind the wheel, he sat there for a full five minutes, hands grasping the steering wheel so hard his knuckles were white.

I sat in silence, waiting for him to explain what had just happened, but his frown only seemed to deepen. Finally, I couldn't stand the silence any longer. "Nicky, honey, are you okay?"

He started at the sound of my voice, then threw the SUV in gear and stomped on the accelerator, not so much as glancing my way as he sped back toward Chicago. I waited until we were on the interstate and his shoulders started to relax a little before I said, "So, what was that all about?"

He shrugged. "Renfield's a fucking lunatic. Who knows what the hell he was talking about?"

"Well," I said, "considering you bolted out of there like your hair was on fire and your ass was catching, I'm guessing *you* do."

Nicky's jaw twitched as he ground his teeth. "Trish—"

"Don't even finish that sentence," I interrupted. "I can tell by the tone of your voice that you're about to give me a load of bullshit. I'm not about to just turn a blind eye to what's going on, Nicky. There's more to the story than you've told me. So you either spill it right now, or you can drop me off at my apartment and bring me my cat. We're done."

It pained me to have to draw such a hard line, but I'd seen just how smooth and charming Nicky could be. And he sure as hell had proven he could charm the pants off me. I wasn't about to fall for his bullshit and pretend everything was hunky-dory. He'd pulled that with his wife and I'd seen where it had gotten them—even if he didn't.

He heaved a resigned sigh and cast a glance my way, looking at me for the first time since we'd left the Asylum. Then something in his expression changed dramatically. It fell. The strength and devil-may-care defiance I'd seen there from the moment I'd met him vanished, and he suddenly looked . . . scared.

"Nicky, what is it?" I asked, my tone gentle now.

He reached for my hand and brought it to his lips, pressing a lingering kiss to my fingertips. "I never meant to involve you in this. I just wanted . . ." He shook his head.

"Nicky, whatever it is, you can tell me," I assured him.

He remained silent for so long, letting my words hang in the air, that I'd begun to believe our conversation was over. But when he took the exit for his house, he finally said, "Dracula came to visit me when I was in the hospital."

Chapter Seventeen

I blinked at him in disbelief. "What? With everyone looking for him, he had the balls to come see you?"

"At first I thought I'd imagined it," Nicky admitted. "I mean, I was half dead, lying there in the hospital bed pumped full of fairy dust to keep me calm so I could heal, and he just showed up at the side of my bed. And he was grinning. That motherfucking bastard was *grinning.*"

"Oh, Nicky . . ." I put my hand on his thigh, and his fingers found mine, giving my hand a squeeze. "What did he want?"

"He wanted to gloat," Nicky ground out. "He and I had been vying for some of the same business interests. When I helped Red track down the information she needed, it gave Dracula the excuse he needed to order Sebille to take me down. Well, we know how that turned out."

I wanted to tell him that he didn't quite know as much as he thought he did, but I bit back my words. "Did he try to hurt you?" I asked, my protective instincts for the man I loved making my words come out more harshly than I'd intended.

Nicky grinned and reached over to cup my cheek for a moment. "No, doll—not physically. He wanted to drive the point home that he could take away anything or anyone I cared about. The bastard got down in my face and told me all about what he planned to do to Red once he had her in his clutches, once he'd finished playing their little game. And he told me there was nothing I could do to stop him."

"Was that why you left town so abruptly?" I asked.

He nodded. "I wasn't about to let him hurt anyone else I cared about. I was determined to take him out or die trying. I left a note for Red and stayed away. A few days after I left, though, I contacted Nate to let him know what was doin' so he could protect Red. That was the last time I made contact."

"I'm guessing that's when Nate came to me and asked me to hide any leads from Tess," I mused, going over the time line of events in my head.

Nicky nodded. "Probably so."

I frowned at him. "And then what?" When he didn't respond, I added, "Because, as infuriating and frightening as Dracula's hospital visit must've been, I'm guessing that's not everything that transpired."

"No. Not everything." He lapsed into silence again, his lips pressed together in a grim line. I waited patiently to hear more, not wanting to rush him but not about to let him off the hook that easily. My gaze on him was so intent that I didn't notice he'd pulled off the main road and onto a gravel access road until the Escalade slid a little on the ice, slamming me into the door when the back end fishtailed.

"Where are we going?" I asked, glancing around us.

"I'm taking you in the delivery entrance," he answered. "I don't want to go in the front door in case Lavender's spell isn't up and running yet."

I glanced around us, my eyes searching the dark woods that lined the road, half expecting something to come charging out at us. Being on the access road made me one hell of a lot more nervous than walking through the front door. Unless . . . "Do you know something I don't?"

Nicky glanced in the rearview mirror. "Someone was following us after we left the Asylum," he divulged. "I think I lost him a few miles back. But it's not like where I live is a secret, and seeing as how your FMA pals fucked up my gates getting to me earlier today, I'm not taking any chances on someone camping out in the front yard, waiting to have another go."

As he pulled into a circular drive behind his mansion, I turned in my seat to pin him with an expectant look. "Okay, so, do I get to hear the rest of the story now that we're safely at home?" My eyes widened when I realized what I'd said and quickly amended, "I mean, now that we're at *your house.* Sorry."

Nicky's lips twitched at the corners and he leaned over to give me a quick kiss that rapidly turned into a slow one. When he finally pulled back, he was grinning. "I like the thought of you calling this place home."

My stomach fluttered with joy and I wanted nothing more than to drag him back to me for another kiss, but I leveled my gaze at him instead. "You're changing the subject, Nicky Blue."

Miffed at being called out, he shoved open the car door and reached under his seat, pulling out a Glock and keeping it down by his side as he came around to the other side of the SUV to help me out. As he led me to the door, his eyes scanned the darkness, searching for any movement.

Once we were safely inside, I grabbed his free hand and pulled him to a stop. "I'll let it go for now because Lavender and Seth are here. But, make no mistake—this conversation isn't over."

He heaved a sigh and led me through the house until we were in the main wing. When we reached the living room, Seth and Lavender were snuggled up on the sofa—fully clothed, thank God!—and murmuring softly to each other. Nicky coughed, looking uncomfortable with intruding on their quiet moment.

But when Lavender's head popped up, she was grinning and glowing more than a little. "Hey there! Where have you two been?"

"The Asylum," I told her. "We went to visit Renfield."

"Did you find out anything?" Seth asked, looking less murderous than the last time we'd seen him.

I exchanged a glance with Nicky. "Nothing concrete. Just the ravings of a madman."

Lavender extricated herself from her fiancé's grasp and came to envelop me in a hug. "Oh, honey—I'm so sorry. Do you want me to try a spell on him? I might be able to come up with something that would make him coherent for at least a few minutes."

I shook my head, not sure that even a spell could make sense of what was in Renfield's head. The man was too far gone to be able to separate fiction from reality. Anything he told us under Lavender's influence might come out sounding rational, but I couldn't depend on the information being reliable. "Thanks anyway, Lav. We still have the Pigg brothers to talk to tomorrow. Maybe we can get something more from them."

She nodded. "Well, I put the spell around Nicky's house, so that should keep anyone—human, Tale, or otherwise—from physically crossing the barrier if they have malice in their hearts toward either of you."

"Thanks, Lav," Nicky said, putting his arm around my shoulders and drawing me close, his expression still solemn.

"Anytime," she said slowly, narrowing her eyes. She obviously was picking up on his dour mood, too.

Seth extended his hand to Nicky. "I wish we could stay longer and help you out, but we've got to stop by Red and Nate's before we head back to The Refuge."

"Forget about it," Nicky told him. "We'll be okay."

"And, uh, sorry about earlier," Seth said, his ears turning red. "The things that woman does to me . . ."

A smile tugged at the corner of Nicky's mouth as his arm tightened around me. "No need to explain."

Lavender suddenly threw her arms around my neck, hugging me tightly. "Damn it! I don't want to leave you like this! You need a fairy godmother now more than ever."

I hugged her back, basking in the warmth of her love and friendship, drawing it around me like armor. Then I pulled back and gave her a wink. "I know how to reach you if I need you."

She nodded, then hugged Nicky. "Take care of her," she ordered. "My threat to turn you into a toad still stands." When she stepped back she fixed him with a firm gaze. "You have a friend in my father and in Gideon. Keep that in mind."

Nicky and I waved good-bye to them from the doorway as they drove off, and I could feel Lavender's magic crackling around me, seeping deep into the ground and extending far up into the sky. I couldn't help but smile. Perhaps I'd sleep well tonight after all.

The second the door closed, Nicky's arms came around me, pulling me into his embrace so he could press a kiss to the curve of my neck. "Alone again," he murmured against my skin.

I closed my eyes, leaning against him for a moment, loving the tantalizing warmth spreading through my body at his touch, but then I remembered that we had some unfinished business. I ducked out of his hold and turned to face him. "Yes, we are," I said. "And I believe you have something to tell me."

Nicky cursed under his breath and strode down the hall toward the kitchen, shrugging out of his coat as he went. He threw it over the back of one of the dinette chairs and started rummaging through the cupboards.

"Nicky," I said, sitting at what was becoming my normal seat at the bar, "whatever it is you have to tell me can't be that bad!"

"No?" he called over his shoulder, slamming a pot on the stove and pouring a generous amount of milk into it.

"Jesus, Nicky!" I cried. "Just tell me what the hell Dracula said to you! You're being ridiculous."

Nicky's shoulders bunched as he added cocoa powder to the milk. I could feel the tension and anger rolling off him, but he didn't turn around until he'd poured the steaming hot chocolate into a mug. He set it in front of me and then finally lifted his eyes to me, capturing my gaze. The pain I saw there was heartbreaking.

"He looked into me, Trish," Nicky said. "It was kinda like you do, except not as . . . welcome. It tore at me, like he was ripping my soul apart. He was searching for something—hell—my weakness or somethin'. I don't know." He ran a hand down his face, looking more haggard and weary than I'd seen him before. "And he found it."

"Your love for your friends," I guessed.

Nicky shook his head. "More than that. He saw how much I hate being powerless. I grew up powerless—just a nobody Rhyme with no future. When I came here, I knew I was gonna change that, and I did. There's nothin' I can't handle, nothin' I can't make happen. But I couldn't save Jules. I couldn't protect Red. And he saw that fear in my heart."

I didn't know what to do to comfort him, so I reached out and twined my fingers with his. He offered me a weak smile and pressed a kiss to the back of my hand.

"So all this time, you've been tracking Dracula down, trying to prove that you're not powerless," I said. "You've done everything you can, Nicky. Hell—you've done more than anyone else has been able to."

He shook his head. "But it's not enough. That asshole is still out there, doing God knows what, and I can't do a goddamned thing! I'm supposed to be avenging Juliet's death, and I can't even get close to the son of a bitch! What the hell kind of husband can't avenge his wife's murder?"

I pressed my lips together, choosing my words carefully. "Nicky, maybe you're doing this for the wrong reason."

"Wrong reason?" he cried, pulling his hand from my grasp. "What better reason is there? That woman stood by me no matter what, no matter who I was. And how did I repay her? I got her killed."

"*You* didn't get her killed—"

"No?" he raged. "Whose fault was it then? Red's? That's bull-shit!" He slammed his fist on the counter, jarring my hot chocolate and making it lap over the edge. "I didn't have to bring her here that night. I didn't have to choose her needs over those of my wife's. I could've put her up in a hotel, for chrissake!"

"It wouldn't have made any difference!" I yelled, fed up with his misguided self-flagellation. "Jesus, Nicky! Red was never the target. It was you all along—and not because you helped Red with the case!"

Nicky's face went slack. "What the hell are you talking about?"

My stomach dropped at warp speed. "I'm sorry," I said, scooting off the bar stool. "Just forget I said anything."

"Like hell," he called after me as I rushed from the room, morti-fied that I had let the truth slip out. "What did you mean by that?"

"Nothing," I snapped. "Just leave it alone, Nicky."

"The hell I will." He grabbed my arm and spun me around to face him, his body curving menacingly around mine as he backed me against the wall. "Now, what did you mean?"

I closed my eyes for a moment, preparing myself for what I was about to do to him. I couldn't even look at him when I said, "Nicky, Juliet put a hit out on you."

I felt his breath burst from him like he'd been punched in the gut. It was only then that I opened my eyes and met his gaze. It was as pained and as confused as I'd expected. My heart shattered, the jagged pieces tearing the hell out of my soul on the way down.

"Why would you say that?" he breathed. "Why would you do that to me, Trish?"

I shook my head. "Nicky, I didn't want to tell you, but I couldn't let you continue to beat yourself up over her death. It was *her* deci-sions, *her* malice, that brought Sebille here that night."

"It's not true," he said, backing away from me. "It can't be. Juliet wouldn't do that!"

I followed him as he retreated down the hall. "She was jealous of how you felt about Red. She was convinced you were still sleeping with her."

"I never cheated on Jules," he spat.

"I know that," I assured him, "but Juliet was insecure. She never believed that you loved her. She thought you were always wishing you were with someone else."

This brought Nicky up short and the blood drained from his face at an alarming rate, just as it had at the Asylum. *Had* he always been wishing he was with someone else? The look on his face said that little nugget had hit a bit too close to home. Maybe he was still in love with Red. That cheery thought brought my misery to a whole new level.

"Nicky, I'm so sorry to tell you all of this," I said, knowing the words sounded like hollow platitudes. "I feel like I'm ripping your heart out. But I wouldn't lie about this. I saw it all in Juliet's eyes before Nate came to collect her. She was the one who tipped off Sebille and Dracula that you were helping Red in the investigation. The whole flirtation with you in the car on the ride home was just to throw you off balance, get you off your guard so that when you opened the door you wouldn't be expecting an attack."

Nicky's shoulders sagged and he ran a hand through his hair. "You know about what happened on the ride home that night?"

I nodded. "Yeah."

"What else did you see?" he asked, no inflection in his voice.

"Nicky—"

"Don't lie to me, Trish." His expression had gone cold, his voice devoid of warmth. "What the hell else did you see?"

I sighed and then admitted in a whisper, "She'd been sleeping with Dracula for several months."

Nicky laughed, his normal deep rumble now edged with sorrow. "No wonder the son of a bitch stopped by the hospital to gloat. He'd been fucking my wife all that time."

I went toward him slowly, not sure how my offer of comfort would be received. But he didn't retreat from me this time. And when I placed my hand over his pounding heart, he looked down at me for a long moment.

"Why didn't you tell me all this sooner?" he asked.

"I didn't want to hurt you. I'm so sorry."

"Sorry you told me?" he asked. "Or sorry that I'm a pathetic fucking asshole?"

"Sorry that your heart is breaking."

He shook his head. "No, it's not breaking," he said, gently putting me away from him. "If anything, it just got even harder." He took his keys from his pocket and headed for the front door.

I followed, having to jog a little to keep up with him. "Where are you going?"

"I need to be away from here," he ground out as he wrenched open the door.

My heart began to hammer in panic at the murderous look in his eyes. "Nicky, wait! Please don't go out when you're like this."

He shot me a dark look. "Don't wait up."

The sound of the door slamming echoed throughout the foyer like a gunshot.

Chapter Eighteen

Not knowing what else to do and too worried about Nicky to really do much of anything, I wandered around the mansion, peeking into various rooms and exploring as I hadn't had a chance to do before now. The house was as lovely as I'd expected, each room impeccably decorated, but few looked lived in—and none but Nicky's living room and his bedroom even hinted at his presence. It was very clear that this had been Juliet's house, even if she'd hated it.

After exploring for more than an hour, I went back to the kitchen and filled Sasha's food bowl. She appeared out of nowhere at the sound of the crunchy little bits hitting her dish and twined about my ankles a few times, purring loudly as if in apology for having been so absent. But then I was promptly forgotten in favor of her dinner. I shook my head with a little laugh and scratched behind her ears while she ate.

"Have you been busy exploring, too?" I murmured. "Quite a bit more room than my rinky-dink apartment, eh, baby?"

Her purring increased in volume in response, but that was about the best I could hope for from her at the moment. She was clearly more interested in her Friskies than anything I had to say.

My cell phone rang, startling me. I snatched it out of my pocket, hoping maybe it was Nicky calling to apologize for being such a jackass, so I was surprised to hear Lavender's voice instead.

"Hey, Lav," I said, frowning. "Everything okay?"

"Not exactly."

I instantly tensed. "What's wrong?"

"It's Tess," she said, her voice strained. My stomach plummeted as she went on. "She started having contractions again, so Nate rushed her to the hospital." Lavender sniffed. She'd been crying. "Something's wrong, Trish. And no one knows what. Red hasn't told the doctors"—her words trailed off and her voice was quieter when she continued—"about Nate's *condition*. I've cast a spell to try to prevent her from going into labor, but I don't know how long it will keep things at bay."

I set my jaw, my teeth grinding, damning Nicky for storming off and leaving me stranded. I needed to be there with Red. With my friend. With *our* friend. And he was out hunting, tracking down vampires who might or might not be linked to Dracula in an effort to avenge the woman who'd wanted him dead.

"Send someone to get me, Lav," I ground out, concern for Red and anger with Nicky constricting my chest until my lungs felt like they were going to pop. "Right. Now."

Gideon released me from his hold the moment we slipped through the veil of time and space and into the hospital's corridor. A second later, my lungs caught up with me. I bent forward to brace my hands on my knees, gulping greedily at the air.

"Sorry," Gideon grinned. "I forgot I was popping your cherry."

I gave him a sour look but chuckled in spite of myself. I couldn't help but like the normally stoic bodyguard. I took another deep breath, then stood and patted his massive chest. "Thanks for the ride, big guy."

He gave me a terse nod. "Anytime. All you have to do is call."

Then he vanished between the dimensions, leaving a momentary void in the air that snapped closed with a quiet *pop*.

I hurried to the nearby nurses' station and thought I was going to have to throw down when the nurse tried to tell me some shit about visiting hours being over. But apparently my profanity-laced threat to rip off her arms and shove them up her ass persuaded her to make an exception in my case.

I barreled into Red's hospital room, jolting to a halt when I saw it crammed full of people—which based on the look on Red's face was driving her more than a little crazy. My God—it looked like everyone in her life was packed tightly into the room; the only face noticeably absent was Nicky's. And Red noticed it, too, when she saw me enter the room alone.

I squeezed by Gran and Eliza Bennet-Darcy and briefly met Al's furious gaze—gee, glad there were no hard feelings there—before making my way to Red's side to take her hand.

"You know," I drawled, "if you'd wanted to get us all together, you could've just thrown a dinner party."

She attempted a saucy grin, but it lacked conviction. "Since when have you ever known me to do things the easy way?"

"Thanks for coming, Trish," Nate said from the other side of the bed, where he sat gripping Red's hand so hard his knuckles were white and hers had to be aching. His face was haggard with concern and his eyes looked like he was ready to rip someone's soul out just to relieve a little tension.

Time to get to work.

"So, you think we could chat for a few?" I asked, trying to keep my voice light.

Red nodded. "Yeah, sure. All this hovering and hand wringing is making me fucking crazy."

"But, Tess, darling," Gran began, "I cannot *possibly* leave you right now."

Lavender stood up from where she'd been sitting on Seth's lap and put an arm around Gran's shoulder. "Come on, Tilly," she said, grinning. "I'm sure Eliza and I can find you some coffee that doesn't taste like diesel fuel somewhere in this place."

Eliza gave Gran one of her warmest smiles, her fine dark eyes twinkling with affection. "Most assuredly so."

"Coming, gents?" Lavender said pointedly as she and Eliza led Gran from the room. Seth immediately hopped up and followed them out, the other men filing out behind him, leaving me with just Red and Nate.

The minute they were gone, Red's eyes welled up with tears. "What the hell is going on, Trish? The baby can't come this soon!"

I shook my head, then placed a hand on her belly. "I don't know, honey. But will you let me take a look?"

Red threw her arms out in frustration. "Why the hell not? Everyone else in this place has taken a look. For a while there I thought we ought to be charging for a peek at my uterus."

I chuckled. "That's not what I meant. I just want to look in your *eyes*. Maybe I can pick up on something that the doctors are missing."

Nate smoothed Red's hair lovingly when she looked a little nervous at the prospect of letting me into her head. "I'll be right here, sweetheart."

Tess nodded. "Fine," she said with a somewhat reluctant shrug. "But be gentle with me, Trish. It's my first time."

I groaned at her attempt at humor, then sat down on the edge of the bed, locking onto her gaze. I felt the connection starting, but she glanced away, averting her eyes.

"You're going to have to *let* me in, Tess," I told her. "I can't force it on the living . . . or the sane."

Her gaze darted almost imperceptibly toward Nate, then back to me. She was hiding something. *Shit. It had to be bad if she was keeping something from Nate. . . .*

"You know," I mused aloud, "maybe you should leave me alone with her, Nate."

The shadows haunting him gathered in a tumultuous cloud. "No way."

I motioned for him to join me a few feet away and turned my back to Red so I could whisper, "She's worried about you."

Nate frowned. "Worried about *me*?" he repeated. "*She's* the one in the hospital bed. Why the hell would she be worried about *me*?"

I put my hand on his arm. "She is concerned about the pain this is causing you. She loves you so much that your pain is her pain—and she has enough to deal with right now. I need you to be strong enough to trust me and let me see if I can help her."

Nate's black gaze bored into me for a long moment before he finally nodded. He went to Tess and whispered lovingly into her ear before pressing a tender kiss to her lips. "I'll be right outside."

As soon as he left, I pegged her with a sharp look of rebuke. "So, who's keeping secrets *now*?"

She glanced toward the door, her expression uncharacteristically pained. "I couldn't let him know, Trish. He'd go through the fucking roof. I haven't got anything concrete yet—just images and impressions that have been coming to me in dreams. But I think Vlad is coming for me. He's pissed that I haven't come after him in spite of all the stuff I know you and Nate have been hiding from me."

My eyes widened. "I have no idea what you're talking about."

"Are you serious?" she drawled. "You're the worst liar in the world, Trish. I've never seen anyone with a worse poker face. And Nate evades like nobody's business when he's hiding something. It didn't take a genius to figure out what you two were up to. So I played along to see what would happen—especially after I found out I was pregnant. I might be reckless with my own life, but there's no way I would put Nate's child in harm's way."

"I'm sorry, Tess," I said. "We should've given you more credit."

"Yeah, well, we'll chat more about you and Nate keeping all this from me later on," she assured me. "But right now, you need to help figure out what Vlad's up to. This shit's getting too personal and I can't take on that sadistic bastard on my own right now."

I nodded. "I swear to you, I will do everything in my power to keep you and your baby safe."

Red huffed, then pressed her lips into an angry line. "This is bull-shit," she muttered. "I'm not some goddamn damsel in distress. I should be the one doing the protecting."

I squeezed her hand. "Tess Little, you have spent almost two hun-dred years protecting us. It's time to let some of us return the favor."

The look of gratitude she gave me was so unexpected, my lips were trembling a little when I locked onto her gaze once more. This time when the connection started, she didn't fight it.

I plowed through her memories, blushing a little at the glimpses I caught of her most intimate moments with Nate. I was glad to see that her pregnancy hadn't put a damper on their sex life, though. At all. *Damn.* I was beginning to wonder if I'd get a glimpse of anything helpful regarding the problems with the pregnancy when I suddenly found myself drifting. No, not drifting . . . *floating.* My entire body grew warm as love and peacefulness enveloped me. So much love. I'd never felt such contentment. Then I hiccupped.

What the hell?

I peered in deeper. It was only then I realized it was no longer Red's thoughts I was reading but those of her unborn child. A smile tugged at my lips. He was anxious to come out and greet his parents, whose love he felt so intensely. I shuddered at the force of that love, tears coming to my eyes. He was going to be one very lucky boy.

But then there was a sudden disturbance in that perfect, all-encompassing cocoon of love. A ripple of hatred, fear, and jealousy hit me so hard, it physically knocked me back, but I didn't release the connection in spite of Red's hiss as a contraction hit her hard.

"It's all right, little one," I cooed in my thoughts. "Don't be afraid. You're safe."

"Talk to him, Tess," I said aloud.

"Him?" she echoed. "Him, who? Vlad?"

She started to look away, but I took her face in my hands, keeping her from breaking the eye contact. "Talk to your *son*, Tess—he needs to hear your voice."

"Son?" she said, her voice a little tight. "We're having a boy?"

"You didn't know?"

She shook her head, looking a little dazed. As she began to rub her tummy and talk to her son—albeit, a little awkwardly at first—I continued searching.

Suddenly a monstrous face, twisted and distorted with fury, loomed before me, making me cry out in surprise. I clamped a hand over my mouth when I felt Tess tense so I wouldn't alarm her further.

The face smirked and then it was no longer just a face but the whole man, his perfectly sculpted physique at odds with his hideous, batlike visage as he prowled toward me. His lips curled into a grotesque smile. It was only then that I recognized him from our encounter in the alley.

"Vlad," I breathed. "My God."

His smirk grew. "Beautiful, aren't I?" he snarled. "Have you ever seen a face like mine?"

Only in my nightmares.

"What the hell happened to you?" I asked, my heart pounding with fear as he edged closer and began to circle me like a predator coming in for the kill.

"I have become a product of my environment, Beatrice," he snapped, spreading his arms. "I am a creature of the darkness, a man denied what he needs to survive and left to become a monster!"

I shook my head, not understanding. "You brought this darkness upon yourself. You turned Red's love into hatred by your actions."

He snarled, snapping at me like a wild beast and beating at his chest. "*My actions*," he hissed. The circle he walked around me was growing smaller with each pass. I turned with him now, careful to keep him before me. "It is not *my* actions that have brought me to this. I tried to protect her, tried to warn her . . . but she wouldn't listen. They never listen. I call and no one hears!"

The guy was obviously descending into madness, his rant not making much sense. "Vlad," I said, trying to keep my voice even. "What is it you want from Red? What is it you want from *me*?"

He rushed me with a roar that sent me stumbling away, but not quickly enough. He grabbed me by the throat and walked me backward until we were standing in what looked like a basement or cellar. It was dark, but I didn't need light to know we were not alone; there were others lurking in the shadows, their eager, bloodthirsty hisses making my skin prickle with fear.

But I didn't have time to dwell on the quiet shuffling in the shadows. Vlad's breath reeked of death when he shoved his face close to mine. "Do you know what it's like to never have a voice, Beatrice?" He didn't wait for my response before he barreled on. "I was portrayed as a monster in my story. I never was given a voice to tell my side of the tale. I was portrayed as a *villain*, a *fiend*!" His expression twisted with bitterness and disgust. "But who does Stoker let speak? That simpering idiot Harker. *Harker!* That changed when I came over. The ones who loved me made it so. I was transformed into a man—not just a monster."

Whoa. Dude was way *gone. . . .*

"Have you ever loved completely?" he asked, his voice taking on a haunting sorrow at the sudden shift in topic. "To want so desperately to be seen for who and what you truly are, only to be misunderstood?"

"Yes," I said, thinking of Nicky and his anger over my revelation about Juliet. To him, I had become a monster who had sullied the saintly image of his wife. "Yes, I know what it's like."

Something changed in Vlad's expression then—it was twisted with sorrow and desperation. "Come to me, Beatrice," he pleaded, repeating the phrase he'd been calling out to me. "You are the one I need. Come to me."

It was disconcerting to see a man known for his power and prowess reduced to such a pathetic, despondent specimen, but I was feeling a little short on sympathy considering the hell he'd been putting everyone through. "I'm not doing shit for you until you leave Red and the baby alone."

He roared with rage and shoved me away. "You cannot deny me!" he fumed. "You have tasted the blood; it courses through your veins even now. Tell me, Beatrice, how did Nicky Blue's blood taste on your tongue when you bit him? How did it make you feel? Did you come for him, little one? How many times?"

I blinked at the surreal Hannibal Lecter moment we seemed to be having. If he so much as hinted at Chianti and fava beans, I was outta there. "How did you know about that?" I asked, my voice hoarse from the fear that was choking me.

He chuckled, a dark, grating sound that made me shudder, and was on me again in an instant. "You are *mine,* Beatrice. I have tasted you. And you have tasted me. We are one."

I shook my head. "Bullshit."

He ran a finger down the length of my jugular, his fetid lips close to my ear. "Come to me, Beatrice. Free me from this prison of darkness, and I will keep the spiders at bay. They will never plague you again."

Shit. He knew about the spiders, too?

"You know what it's like to be in a prison of darkness," he continued. "How long did they lock you away in that room after you saw the spider and lost your little innocent mind?"

I began to tremble as he spoke, the memories of that horrible time all too real. The closeness of the cellar, the terror that made my heart beat so frantically in my breast. My heart began to thunder again now as the fear flooded my veins.

"How long did your father listen to your screams, Beatrice?" Dracula whispered. I squeezed my eyes shut and turned my face away. "How long did you claw at the walls of your dark prison, desperate to escape the madness?"

Sweat trickled down my back, making me shudder. "Piss off," I spat, sick of playing games with this bloodsucking sociopath. I ducked out of his hold and backed away. "You think throwing my past in my face is going to make me come to you? You've been tormenting one of the only people who ever gave a damn about you—and putting her unborn child in jeopardy! And you dare to ask for my help? Fuck you! You want me, you're going to have to come and get me, you candy-ass leech."

He charged then, his long white fangs glistening with saliva and poised to strike. With a gasp of horror, I broke the connection, stumbling back and tripping over a chair, overturning it in my haste to get away.

Red's eyes were wide as she peered down at me on the floor. "What the hell just happened?"

Good question.

I was trembling so violently, I had a difficult time pushing myself to my feet. "I think I might've talked Vlad into leaving you alone."

She narrowed her eyes at me, no doubt wondering what I was leaving out. "Yeah?"

I forced a smile and nodded. "I think he's probably going to be moving on."

She gave me a knowing look. "Just like that."

I nodded again, my smile feeling a little grotesque. "Here," I said, slipping the bracelet of Lavender's hair from my wrist and sliding it onto Red's. "Take this, just in case I'm wrong. Lavender gave it to me for protection, but I think you need it more than I do." When Red looked like she was about to protest, I bent and pressed a kiss to the top of her head. "Just take it. Don't make me kick your ass."

She grunted. "As if."

Chapter Nineteen

Lavender wasn't thrilled about my handing over the enchanted bracelet to Red until I told her what had transpired while I was communing with Dracula somewhere in the miasma of Red and her baby's thoughts.

"Let Seth and me take you home," she said.

I shook my head. "No, that's okay. I'll just take a cab to Nicky's."

She and Seth exchanged a glance at the mention of Nicky's name. "Trish—"

"I'll be fine," I told her, exhaustion suddenly making my limbs as heavy as concrete. "I'm sure Nicky will be back soon."

"Well, at least let me make you another bracelet before you go," Lavender huffed, clearly not pleased with my stubbornness.

"Thanks, Lav," I said, surprised by how tired I sounded, "but I need to find out where Dracula is. And if getting into his head—and letting him into mine—is the way to go about it, I'm just going to have to take that risk."

Lavender cast a pleading look at Seth, but instead of trying to talk me out of going, he just took me by the shoulders and bent down a little so he could look directly into my face. "Call us if you need anything," he ordered. "No matter what, no matter when. We're going to hang out here a little longer so Lav can keep an eye on Red."

I nodded. "Keep an eye on Nate, too," I said. "He's in a pretty volatile state right now after what I've told him."

Yeah, it had been *loads* of fun for all of us to have to play one big round of truth or dare with Red. The rules of the little game were crystal clear: We could either tell her the truth, the whole truth, and nothing but the truth, or dare to lie to her again and risk a serious ass-kicking by one righteously pissed off, hormonal, pregnant Tale.

We went with truth.

None of us had much of a warm and fuzzy feeling after that, but at least I felt like I'd done what I could to deflect Vlad's wrath away from Red and focus it wholly on me.

Fuck. Me.

The cabbie who drove me back to Nicky's refused to drop me at the doorstep, apparently having heard that the house belonged to a man of Business. So the asshole dumped me at the gates and left me to trudge up the long driveway to the front door. Thank God I hadn't bothered locking the door when I'd left. I figured Lavender's spell would keep out anyone who had a dark purpose for being there.

Sasha greeted me at the door as if she owned the place, purring loudly as she wound around my ankles. But before I could scoop her up for a little comfort cuddle, she took off like a shot and disappeared down the hall.

With a sigh, I went upstairs, desperate for a little sleep, and found myself hoping that my dreams would be the same old nightmares—at least I knew when I woke up from those I wasn't going to be attacked by something waiting in the shadows.

To my surprise, I wound up in Nicky's bedroom instead of the guest room down the hall. I was so tired and so lost in my foggy thoughts, I wasn't even sure how I got there. But once I stepped across the threshold, my desire to have Nicky there with me hit me so hard, I could hardly breathe. I'd always prided myself on my strength and independence, but—damn it!—I wanted him with me, holding me and pressing his sultry kisses to my skin. I wanted to hear his voice telling me that everything would be all right. And I wanted to hear that he loved me, that we had a future together.

I swiped angrily at the tears stinging my eyes. *Shit!*

Exhaustion completely taking over now, I lay down on his bed and kicked off my shoes, then pulled the down comforter over me, inhaling deeply and letting Nicky's masculine scent envelope my senses.

A knot in the center of my chest tightened as I pictured the look on his face just before he'd stormed out. I wished I could take him in my arms, soothe away the pain he was experiencing at finding out the truth about his beloved wife, but I knew it was something he'd have to work out on his own. There was nothing I could do but wait and hope that he didn't let his fury and heartbreak over Juliet's actions affect how he felt about me.

Of course, who the hell knew *how* he felt about me? He hadn't put it into words. There was no question that he was attracted to me, that he cared about me, but did it go beyond that? He was leaving soon and had tried to deny the attraction between us because he didn't want me to be hurt when he left. But that only told me he wasn't a total asshole—not that he was in love with me.

I tossed and turned for a few minutes, trying to get comfortable on Nicky's bed and not having much luck. After an hour of sleeplessness, I finally realized that no matter how I shifted positions, I wasn't going to be able to sleep without Nicky there. With a huff, I threw off the comforter and sat on the edge of the bed, letting my legs dangle over the side. I put my hand to the back of my neck and rubbed at the knot of tension there, then rolled my head a few times.

"To hell with it," I muttered. "Might as well go watch some—"

A sudden pressure around my ankle cut off my words with a gasp. *Oh, Jesus.*

My gaze snapped down and I cried out in terror when I saw the hand encircling my leg. I tried to pull my leg loose, but the grasp was relentless, the bony fingers digging into my skin through my jeans. I drove my other foot down the inside of my calf over and over again, trying to pry the fingers off, but they dug in, holding fast.

"Oh, God!" I whimpered, frantically searching the darkness for something I could use as a weapon and continuing to pull against the hold on my leg. I glanced at the bedside table and leaned forward, jerking open the little drawer and rummaging through it in desperate haste. My hand had just closed around the familiar heft of the grip of a gun, when I pitched forward and face-planted on the carpet.

To my horror, I started sliding backward, the unseen assailant dragging me under the bed. I screamed and twisted onto my back, using my other leg to brace against the bed to keep me from sliding under even further. From the shadows came a low growl, and the pull on my leg increased, the joints in my leg straining to the point of pain. I gritted my teeth, straining with all my might, knowing if that thing pulled me under I was doomed. I had to stay out here where I at least had a fighting chance. With trembling hands I aimed the gun and squeezed the trigger. But I heard just a click in response.

Shit! Safety.

I flipped the safety off and fired into the darkness. The sharp crack of the gun split the air. I heard the bullet strike something, but I couldn't tell if the savage growl I heard in response was from the creature being hit or just becoming righteously pissed. Unfortunately, it jerked harder and I felt something pop in my hip as a fierce pain shot through me, bringing me toward the edge of blackness. Screaming now in rage, I unloaded the rounds, firing rapidly into the shadows under the bed, hoping like hell that one of the bullets hit home.

But as I fired, the creature merely grabbed my calf with its other hand and began to pull its way up my leg, hand over hand, that blood-chilling growl growing in volume. I was out of ammo, kicking and fighting, but I could tell I was losing ground. I tried to scoot back, using my elbows, but it was now at my knee, my thigh. . . .

Those horrible claws dug into my waist and jerked me sideways and into the claustrophobic darkness beneath the bed. And there in the blackness I saw a face, its features distorted and monstrous. Red eyes blazed like hellfire as it glared at me. And when its mouth curved into a hideous smile, its white fangs grew longer even as I watched.

"Jesus, no," I whimpered.

Dracula laughed as he edged up my body, his hands rough as they skimmed up my belly and found my breasts. "Come to me, Beatrice," he growled. "Come to me now. . . ."

I awoke with a start, bolting upright. Instinctively, my hand flew up to my neck to search for the evidence of Dracula's assault upon me, but I found nothing there. I sagged in relief and dropped back against Nicky's pillows.

It had been a dream. Just a dream. A horrible, terrifying dream, but nothing more.

Thank God.

I rubbed the inside of my wrist against my forehead, not surprised to find my hairline drenched in sweat. My clothes clung to me and I began to shiver in spite of the thick down comforter that still covered me. With a deep breath, I threw off the covers and then bolted from the bed, taking several quick steps away from it before pausing to look back and make sure nothing waited to grab me and drag me under again.

I leaned against the wall and heaved a sigh, then laughed a little at myself. "Don't be such a baby, Trish." I chuckled, trying to reassure myself that I was being ridiculous. I was a grown woman, for crying out loud! I was a little old to be afraid of monsters hiding under the bed. And then I turned on the lights.

It was at that point that I tasted a distinct coppery taste in my mouth. I touched my fingers to my tongue and was startled to see blood on my fingers when I pulled them away as I had the other night in my apartment. "What the hell?"

Wondering if I'd bitten my tongue during my nightmare, I headed to the bathroom and filled my palm with water, then filled my mouth. When I spit it out in the sink, streaks of red clung to the sides of the porcelain as they made their way to the drain. Frowning, I looked in the mirror, crying out when I saw my mouth filling with blood. Gagging, I spat into the sink again, then turned on the water and filled my cupped hand, rinsing out my mouth and spitting once more. But the more I tried to stop the blood, the more it came, spilling out over my lips and down my chin, dripping onto the porcelain in horrifying crimson streaks.

I choked and sputtered, the blood now coming so quickly I couldn't get it out of my mouth fast enough.

Oh, God. . . .

Tears of panic blurred my vision as I groped for the hand towel hanging on the rack, using it to try to absorb the blood and keep me from drowning. But it wasn't working. I choked again as blood flooded my throat. Desperate to clear my airway, I coughed in a violent burst, spraying blood onto the mirror, and caught a glimpse of my frantic, wide-eyed expression in spite of the blood obscuring my reflection.

I whimpered, feeling my lungs growing heavy as they filled with fluid. But then my father's words drifted to me as if whispered in my ear:

You must control your fear, Beatrice, or your fear will control you. Never let your mind slip into the abyss where chaos reigns. . . .

I closed my eyes, trying to regain control, bringing my racing heart back to heel. With one last sputtering cough, I opened my eyes again, determined to take on my tormenter with my last ounce of strength.

But the blood was gone. The bathroom was pristine once again. My face and hands were no longer covered in red. I swallowed, a faint metallic taste the only evidence that anything had even occurred. My knees went weak with relief and I sagged against the vanity, bracing myself for a moment, my head hanging down between my shoulders. After a deep, cleansing breath, I lifted my head again and met my own eyes in the mirror.

"What the hell was that all about?" I whispered, my throat still tight with lingering fear. As if in answer to my question, a streak of blood suddenly appeared on the mirror. Then another. And another. I began to tremble as I watched the blood trickle down, forming letters, until a single word materialized.

Mine.

I slid to the ground, my legs no longer able to hold me. Trembling, I tried to pull myself back to my feet so I could get the hell out of there, but nothing seemed to work. Then it hit me—I was in shock. I needed to get to my phone and call—

Who?

I wanted Nicky. I wanted to hear his deep voice calling me "doll." I wanted his strong arms cradling me against him. I wanted him to smooth my curls and kiss my lips and tell me I was safe. But he'd left me. Abandoned me. I was completely alone.

No. I wasn't *alone.*

There was someone I could call on. Anytime.

Mustering what strength I could, I pulled myself up to the sink and turned on the hot water full blast, letting the steam build and cloud over the mirror as Lavender had once taught me.

"Trish!"

I started at the sudden sound of my name. "In here!" I called from where I had collapsed roughly thirty seconds before.

Damn, he was fast!

Gideon burst into the bathroom, his sunglasses hiding his eyes, but his concern evident in the scowl he wore. Without a word, he bent and scooped me into his arms, carrying me out of the bathroom and into the hall as if I weighed nothing.

Too bad I wasn't in the mood for a rebound at the moment. I totally would've gone for the whole strong, silent, ass-kicking vibe

Gideon had going for him. As it was, I was just damned relieved to have him there. I rested my head against his chest as he swept me down the stairs.

"You're safe now," he said, his voice clipped as we reached the foyer. "I'll take you to my king."

"Like hell you will."

My eyes snapped open. Nicky stood in the doorway, his clothes torn and bloody, proof he'd had his own hellish night. His fists were clenched at his sides, near his weapons, ready to go medieval on Gideon's ass. My heart did a cartwheel of joy, but the rest of me was still too hurt and angry to let on how happy I was to see him.

"I suggest you step aside, Blue," Gideon said, his tone even and unconcerned, yet uncompromising. "She was in trouble and called me to her. I am bound by honor to offer my protection and will do so. I will take her to the safety of my king's estate, and then she may grant you an audience there. If she wishes."

"Grant me an *audience*?" Nicky echoed, his Chicago accent growing thicker in his anger. "Fuck you, Tiny. If she's in trouble, she can count on *me*."

Gideon regarded him mildly. "Obviously not."

Nicky looked like Gideon had just punched him in the nuts. But Gideon wasn't done yet.

He carried me forward until he was up in Nicky's grill, glaring down at him from his towering height. "If I were to have the love of such a woman," he growled, "I would do *anything* in my power to protect her, no matter the cost."

I thought of the story Lavender had once told me about her relationship with Gideon and how he had risked his life to stand beside her when she was on trial for transplanting us all. I had no doubt that Gideon meant what he said. Whoever eventually caught his heart was going to be one seriously lucky gal.

But there was really only one set of hearts I was worried about at the moment. And mine was still too hurt to play nice. "Let's go," I murmured when Nicky merely stood there, his jaw clenched in anger at being called out.

The next thing I knew, I was standing in a bedroom the size of my entire apartment. A fire burned in the fireplace, casting soft amber light throughout the room.

"Is this the king's estate?" I asked, the rather masculine decor a little on the tame side compared with what I'd seen when I last visited the mansion.

"Not exactly," Gideon mumbled, still holding me in his arms. "I did not want to disturb the family, so I have brought you to my home on the estate instead."

I glanced around. "Is this . . . um, *your* bedroom?" I asked, suddenly feeling a little awkward.

"What if it is?" he asked, pegging me with that gaze that was somehow still penetrating even behind his sunglasses. "Would you object?"

Suddenly his face felt a little too close to mine. "Listen, Gideon," I said as gently as I could manage, "you're a really nice guy, but—"

His chuckle rumbled deep in his chest. Then he lowered me to my feet. "This is one of my guest rooms."

I felt my face light up like an inferno. "Oh. Of course. I knew that."

He waved a hand toward a wardrobe that stood against one wall. "You will find anything you need in there," he assured me. "Feel free to take whatever you like."

"Thank you, Gideon," I said, still trying to recover from my embarrassment. "I really appreciate this. It seems like my relying on others is becoming a really bad habit." I sighed, thinking about how Nicky had taken me in just a couple of days earlier.

My sorrow and disappointment must've showed on my face because Gideon gently took me by the shoulders. "I have offered you my protection, Trish, and that offer does not expire. You are welcome to stay for as long as you wish." Then his lips curved into a grin and he gave me a little chuck under the chin. "But I have a feeling you may not need to stay long."

I frowned, intending to ask him what he meant, but he had vanished before I could utter a word. I went to the wardrobe he'd indicated and pulled open the doors, wondering what a guy like Gideon could possibly have lying around his bachelor pad when it came to the needs of an unexpected female guest, and so was startled to see quite a selection of jeans, T-shirts, sweaters, button-down oxfords, and shoes in my size and style.

"Damn," I muttered. "I want Gideon to be my personal shopper. This guy's good."

I pulled out the bottom drawer and found a stash of delicates and a few pairs of pajamas folded neatly in categorized stacks. There was also a little slip of dark green satin that caught my eye. I held it up and blinked in astonishment when I saw that it was actually a very simple but sexy nighty. Now, just who did Gideon expect me to wear this for? I glanced toward the door, wondering if maybe he hadn't been joking after all. But since it was warm in the room with the fire going, the flannel pj's were far from appealing, so I slipped out of my clothes and into the nighty, then crawled into bed.

As exhausted as I was, I was surprised not to fall asleep the moment my head hit the pillow instead of the twenty seconds it took. My sleep was deep and blissfully dreamless. So when I jolted awake sometime later, I wasn't entirely sure what had roused me.

I sat up in bed, drawing the covers close to my chest, searching in the dim light from the fire, which had burned down considerably. And when I saw the figure sitting in a chair in the corner, I had to cover my mouth to muffle the scream it startled out of me. But fear quickly faded as my heart began to pound, making my voice breathless when I gasped, "My God."

"Hi, doll."

Nicky stood up and came slowly toward me, his expression twisted with anguish. He'd changed, I noticed. He was in the usual jeans and turtleneck sweater that molded so well to his sculpted chest. I hated that he looked so damned hot—I wanted to be mad at him a little longer, but it was growing more difficult with each step he took.

"What are you doing here?" I managed to ask, my voice choked at the sight of him.

He spread his arms out a little. "I had to see you. I couldn't leave things the way they were."

"So, you came to apologize for being an ass?" I sniped.

His jaw tightened a little and he planted his feet where he stood. "I wanted to check on you, make sure you were okay."

Okay, so no apology forthcoming. . . . Got it.

I threw off the covers and got to my feet, crossing my arms over my chest in a huff. "Well, let's see," I drawled, "I was attacked by Dracula not once but *twice* after getting back from visiting our dear friend Red, who is in the hospital yet again because, as it turns out, Dracula has been attacking her and her unborn child, too!"

Nicky paled and blinked at me, clearly astonished. "Was he there? In the hospital?"

I gaped at him. Was he serious? I'd just told him that I'd been attacked twice and he wanted to know if Dracula had made a guest appearance at the *hospital*?

"No, Nicky," I spat. "He wasn't in the hospital. In fact, I think I've managed to draw him away from Red. Thanks for your concern about me, though. I appreciate it."

"Trish—" He took a step closer, but I held up my hand to stop him from reaching for me. I *so* wasn't in the mood for that apology now.

"Where were you, Nicky?" I demanded. "When Red was lying in the hospital and everyone else who cares about her was crowded around the bed, where were *you*? While I was struggling for my *life,* trying not to drown in the blood that was filling my lungs, where *were* you?"

He shoved his hands into his pockets and regarded me evenly, but said nothing.

"I needed you!" I hissed. "I couldn't even call you after the attack. The only person I could depend on was Gideon!"

His eyes flashed with anger, jolting him out of his silence. "What do you want from me, Trish?" he spat. "You tell me my wife took a hit out on me and you don't think that's going to fuck with my head?"

"Of course I knew it!" I yelled. "Why do you think I never said anything? I would do *anything* to save you pain! Don't you see that, Nicky?"

"Why?" he demanded, his voice tight. He closed the gap between us and took hold of my upper arms. "Why wouldn't you just tell me?"

I shoved him hard, pissed off that he could be so freaking dense. "Because I love you, you stupid son of a bitch! I always have!" Now that I was on a roll, I had to let it all out, all the pain, all the frustration from the decades of longing for someone I didn't think could ever be mine. "I fell in love with you the day we arrived when I saw the soul of you. It *killed* me to see you with Red all that time. And then when you married Juliet . . . I didn't think I could *ever* get over that pain, but I just wanted you to be happy. Then I saw you that day in the lab, and everything I'd been trying to forget came rushing back in an instant."

"Trish . . ." He reached for me, but I deflected his hand.

"When I saw what was in Juliet's thoughts that night, it broke my heart," I went on, not letting him derail me as the words came tumbling out. "Because when you're not being a total jackass, Nicky, you're the most noble, honorable man I've ever met. And you deserve to be loved by a woman who's worthy of you!"

He shook his head. "The things I've done—especially since Juliet died—I'm not the man I was the day we came over. You don't know me anymore. There's a lot I deserve, probably none of it good. But I know one thing for sure—I don't deserve *you*, Trish."

I grunted, disgusted with his self-pity. "Screw it," I muttered, going around him to get to the door. I didn't know where I was going; I just knew I didn't want to be there with him at the moment. "This is bullshit. I'm done."

"Trish!" Nicky called as I reached for the door.

"I don't think you could possibly have anything else to say to me," I shot back, hand on the doorknob. "I told you I love you, and you threw it back in my face. I think how *you* feel is pretty freaking clear. I see now that I'm just another notch in your belt."

"I wasn't finished," he said, suddenly standing behind me, his body wrapping around mine, his breath hot in my ear. I shuddered as his arm slid around my waist and pulled me into the curve of his body. "I don't *deserve* you, but that doesn't make me want you any less."

I peeled his arm away from me and stepped out of his grasp. "You *want* me?" I repeated, not about to let him off the hook that easily. "Is that the best you can do? Don't think you can just kiss me and make everything better, Nicky. I'm still pissed at you!"

He shoved his hands into his pockets, his expression more tortured than I'd ever seen it. "You have every right to be. I'm sorry. I'm *so* sorry. You never should've had to call Gideon. You needed me, and I wasn't there for you."

I crossed my arms over my chest. "And?"

He clenched his jaw, a fiery look coming to life in his eyes. "And, it would've killed me if you'd been hurt, if I'd—" His voice caught and he looked away for a moment and had to clear his throat a couple of times before he turned his gaze back to me and continued, "If I'd *lost* you."

I swallowed hard as he came slowly toward me. His steps were tentative, but as he took my face in his hands his gaze was so intense that I frowned at him. "Nicky? Are you okay?"

"Not without you," he ground out, cupping my face, his thumb caressing my cheek. He smoothed my hair, his amber gaze boring into mine. "Trish, when you saw my soul that day we came over, I saw *yours*, too. And I got another look that day you held my hand after the attack, kept me alive by what had to be willpower alone. But it wasn't until I started reading all those damned reports, getting into your head, that I really started to see what an amazing woman you are. And I don't know *when* it happened—hell, maybe it was when you threw yourself into my arms that first time—but somewhere along the way, I fell for you."

I blinked, tears blurring my vision. I couldn't believe what I was hearing, couldn't believe that the words I'd dreamed of for so long were hanging in the air between us.

"I love you, Trish," he said, his thumb skimming over my bottom lip. "And, I swear to God, I won't ever let you down again." Then he was kissing me, his lips so loving and tender, they stole my breath. If he'd never uttered another word of love to me, that kiss would have assured me what was truly in his heart. And when I snaked my arms around his neck, drawing him closer to me, his kiss became more insistent.

"Goddamn," he muttered against my mouth, his hands roaming over the satin of my negligee, "where the hell did you get this thing?"

I chuckled as I pressed a line of kisses along his jaw. "You don't want to know," I whispered, nipping at his ear. "Want me to take it off?"

"God no," he said, his voice gruff. "It's sexy as hell." His hands were rough as he shoved the nighty up, baring me to him. I gasped as he hefted me up and wrapped my legs around his waist, pressing my back against the wall. His mouth was on mine again as he tore at the fly of his pants. Then he was pressing into me, each rough stroke sending me careening toward ecstasy. I grasped fistfuls of his sweater, moaning against his kiss, urging him on. I came quickly, my scream strangled in my throat for fear of drawing Gideon's attention, but Nicky apparently had no such reservations.

"Damn," I panted, smoothing the damp hair from his brow. "Maybe I should take this nighty home with me."

He chuckled, already starting to grow hard again. "Doll, I'll buy you a whole frigging wardrobe of 'em." He kissed me then, slowly, languidly, his lips caressing mine. I groaned in protest as he pulled out, not wanting our lovemaking to end so soon, but then I realized he was shedding his clothes, leaving a trail as he walked me toward the bed. His sweater was the last to go.

I ran my hands over his chest and shoulders, loving the way his breath hitched a little at my touch. I pressed a kiss to his chest over his heart and let my hands smooth over his abs and down to his hips and then around to his back, pulling him to me.

"I want to hear it again," I said, peering up at him.

He pulled back a little. "Yeah? You don't mind me sayin' it over and over again? You don't think you'll get sick of me sayin' it?"

I shook my head. "Never."

He swept me up in his arms and tossed me onto the bed. I bounced once and was still giggling when he settled between my thighs. He was grinning when he pinned my arms over my head. "I love you, doll," he said, punctuating his words with a hard thrust. "My *God,* I love you."

I rolled my hips, arching into him, loving the way he filled me, body and soul. And when I rolled him onto his back, I met his gaze as I peered down at him. The connection I'd felt that first day we'd met jerked at the center of my chest and pulled him toward me until he was sitting up, our chests pressed close together, his arms wrapped tightly around me.

And when we finally collapsed together, panting, and he drew me into his strong arms, I didn't fear what the dreams would bring that night. Whether it was spiders or vampires or whatever else hell might decide to unleash, the man I loved loved me back, and nothing else mattered.

Chapter Twenty

I awoke to a quiet clinking in Gideon's guest room. When I bolted upright, I luckily remembered I was naked and held the covers over my breasts or the fairy bodyguard would've caught quite an eyeful.

Gideon held a finger to his lips and nodded to Nicky, who still snored softly on the bed beside me. Then he swept his arm toward the breakfast that was laid out on the table, which he'd somehow set up along with chairs while we'd slept. When I gave him a rather apologetic smile for the uninvited houseguest, he peered at me over his sunglasses, revealing his eyes for the first time. To my surprise, they were the color of molten silver and seemed to be morphing into a crisp arctic blue even as I watched. *What the hell?* He offered me a wink, letting me know he'd expected Nicky all along. Then he vanished.

Curious to see what Gideon had brought, I slipped from bed and tiptoed over to the table, the smell of bacon making my mouth water. My stomach grumbled when I lifted the silver lid that covered the nearest plate and saw a beautifully fluffy omelet, toast, and hash browns. And in the carafe in the center of the table was piping hot chocolate.

"How in the world . . ." I mumbled.

"I was just wondering the same thing." Nicky's voice so near my ear made me start with a laugh. "I was just thinking to myself, 'How in the world does Trish expect me to keep my hands off her when she's running around naked,' " he continued, pulling me into his arms and pressing a kiss to the curve of my neck.

"Well, I could put some clothes on," I told him, turning to face him and looping my arms around his neck. "But that would imply that I *want* you to keep your hands off me."

Nicky's kiss was hot on my lips, and the stubble on his jaw scraped against my skin as he pressed kisses along my neck and shoulder, down my stomach, the inside of my thigh. And when his tongue caressed the center of me, I gasped, my knees buckling. He chuckled as he sat me down in one of the chairs, then knelt before me, hooking my legs over his shoulders as his tongue resumed its caress. I writhed against his mouth, shattering apart with a loud cry, no longer caring if anyone heard.

As soon as Nicky stood, I pushed him down into the other chair and straddled him, groaning as he slid into me. "At this rate we won't eat breakfast before noon," I gasped, gripping the back of the chair.

Nicky took hold of my hips, making sure I didn't get any ideas about stopping now. "I wasn't hungry—not for breakfast anyway."

It probably *was* around noon by the time we'd managed to get enough of each other and take a shower—which probably should've been taken separately, considering lathering each other up was just too much of a temptation to resist. But, remarkably, the breakfast Gideon had set out for us was still hot when we finally sat down to eat. Gotta love fairy magic.

"So, what's the plan?" I asked Nicky after polishing off half of my omelet.

He took a long drink of orange juice to wash down the last of his breakfast, which he'd apparently consumed at warp speed, before answering. "We need to visit the Pigg brothers, find out what they know about Dracula's lair. Drac's obviously playing it safe by not coming out in person to attack you or Tess. If we want to take him out, we're going to have to track him down in the flesh."

I nodded. "Okay, so how do we find the Pigg brothers?"

Nicky shrugged. "Not too hard, really. I know a guy who's been my eyes and ears around this town for years. If anyone knows where to find the Piggs, Jack will."

"Jack?" I echoed. "Which one? There are like a hundred Jacks from fairytales and folklore. And every other rhyme is named Jack. You're going to have to narrow it down for me."

"Let's just leave it at *Jack*." Nicky leaned back in his chair, giving me a great look at his pecs. And suddenly I was hungry in an entirely different way.

Blushing at my insatiable desire for the man across from me, I quickly finished off my breakfast and went to the wardrobe to find something to wear. To my surprise, it now also held a collection of clothes for Nicky. I laughed, shaking my head. "I'll be damned."

Nicky joined me at the wardrobe, as astonished as I was. "What the hell? How did—"

I pressed a kiss to his cheek. "I'm learning that nothing about Gideon is quite what it seems."

Nicky grabbed a fresh set of clothes and gave me a warning look. "Yeah, well, he can be as mysterious as he wants as long as he keeps his damned hands off you."

I cast an arch smile his way as I pulled on my jeans. "Jealous?"

He ran his hands through his hair, causing a thick, dark lock to fall over his forehead, making him look way too rakish for his own good. "*Jealous* doesn't even begin to cover it. I could've murdered that bastard when I saw you in his arms."

I patted him on the chest. "No need for that, lover—your arms are the only ones I ever want around me."

When I opened the door a few minutes later, the object of our discussion was standing across the hall, leaning casually against the wall with his arms crossed.

"Gideon," I greeted, "we were just talking about you!"

The corners of his mouth twitched with the hint of a smile. Then he inclined his head toward Nicky. "I see you have . . . made amends."

Nicky shifted a little, still surly. "Something like that."

"Thank you, Gideon," I said, extending my hand. "I appreciate everything you've done for me."

Gideon took my hand and raised it to his lips, pressing a kiss to my fingertips. "It was my pleasure. If you have need of me again, you have only to call."

"Okay, okay," Nicky said, stepping in and taking my hand from Gideon's grasp. "That's enough of that. I'm grateful and all, but that gratitude only goes so far, Tiny."

Nicky was still frowning as we got into his Escalade, which Gideon, of course, had waiting and warmed up in front of his home when we opened the door. "How does he do that shit?"

"Anticipate what others need before they even know it?" I asked.

"Hell if I know. But now I see why the king likes having him around. Who better to protect him than a bodyguard who knows how to take care of the threat before it even happens?"

Nicky looked in his rearview mirror as we drove away, catching a glimpse of Gideon still standing in the doorway. "Yeah, well, everybody's got a blind spot."

I shuddered, wondering what manner of being it would take to get one up on Gideon. I hoped I wouldn't have to be around to see that happen. Or get called to the scene after the fact . . .

At some point during our drive I dozed off, my hand clasped in Nicky's. I wasn't sure how long we'd been driving when we hit a massive pothole that jolted me awake as my head bounced against the back of the seat.

Nicky cursed under his breath. "Sorry about that," he said, giving my hand a squeeze. "The roads in this part of town aren't for shit."

I sat up straighter, blinking away the last vestiges of sleep and looking around, trying to get a feel for our surroundings. The buildings were mostly boarded up, the result of the economic downturn that had put the businesses in the area under and left the buildings just empty shells, eerie reminders of what once had been. A few rusted-out cars lined the street, and trash blew across the dirty snow that spotted the sidewalk and gathered in the corners like arctic cobwebs. "Where the hell are we?"

"This is where Jack runs his operation," Nicky informed me. "Odds are good we'll find him lurking around here somewhere."

I caught a glimpse of a junkie sitting on the broken steps of one of the buildings, twitching and swatting at pests that only he could see. "Charming. Can't wait to meet this guy."

Nicky pulled up in front of a red brick building that looked like it might've been a store or a bank at some point in its history, but any indication of what sort of business establishment it once had housed had been peeled away by time and neglect.

Nicky reached under his seat and pulled out a Glock. He quickly ejected the magazine to make sure it had a full clip, then rammed it back in. He jerked his chin toward the glove box. "Grab the one in there and stick it in your pocket. They'll search us, but go ahead and let them take it."

I frowned at him. "Then why take a gun at all?"

"Lets 'em know we're not fucking around," he said, getting out of the car and keeping the gun down by his thigh.

Liking this plan less and less, I shoved the gun into my pocket and got out of the car, staying close to Nicky as we climbed the well-worn steps. He paused at the top of the steps and rolled his neck, then motioned for me to stay where I was beside the door and out of sight. Then he took a deep breath and kicked the door in, quickly firing off three shots.

"Hello, Jack," he said, his lips curling into a grin. "Good to see you again." He stepped over the threshold, his gun trained on a target I couldn't see. A few seconds later he called, "Come on in, doll!"

I swallowed hard, then peeked around the door, startled to see three burly guys nursing wounded shoulders, their guns lying on the ground at their feet. A series of tables along one wall were piled high with money—counterfeit, if I was to hazard a guess based on the equipment in the room. Sitting behind another table, his hands held up, was a man with a cocky, self-assured smile on his handsome face. His watery blue eyes sparkled with amusement, giving him a decidedly boyish look in conjunction with his carroty orange curls.

"Well, what have we here," he drawled. "You gonna introduce me to the dame, Nicky?"

"Trish, Jack. Jack, Trish," Nicky snapped. "Consider yourself introduced."

Jack's smile widened. "I'd stand and greet you properly, sweetheart, but your boyfriend has serious trust issues."

Nicky took a step closer, tightening his grip on his gun. "You double-crossed me on that deal with the Cyclops and nearly got me killed, you son of a bitch."

Jack spread his arms. "Ah, come on, Nicky," he drawled. "That was ages ago! Are you still holding a grudge over a little . . . misunderstanding?"

Nicky's jaw tightened. Apparently the answer to that question was a resounding *yes*. Feeling I needed to diffuse the situation if we were going to get the information we wanted, I stepped forward and gently put my fingertips on Nicky's gun, forcing him to lower it as I smiled at Jack. "Come now, gentlemen," I said. "We're all grown-ups here. I think we can have a civilized chat without dredging up the past, can't we?"

Nicky's eyes darted toward me briefly, and for a moment I thought he might debate that point, but he sighed and relaxed his shoulders. "Yeah, sure."

I turned my gaze to Jack, who just shrugged. "I can play nice. For now. I'll ask you to hand over that gun, though."

Nicky narrowed his eyes, but then grinned, and held up his hand, letting the gun dangle upside down from his index finger. One of the wounded guards snatched it from his hand, then placed it on the table in front of Jack. Jack rose from his seat and came around to where we stood, a shit-eating grin on his face as he got up in Nicky's grill. And for a second I thought they might take a swing at each other.

But then Jack laughed and grabbed Nicky, bringing him in for a brief man-hug, complete with smack on the back.

What the hell?

"Where the hell have ya been, you sneaky bastard?" he demanded, giving him a good-natured punch in the shoulder. "I thought you'd fallen off the face of the earth."

Nicky shrugged and shoved his hands into his pockets. "You know, doing the odd job here and there."

"Well, you coulda called me, let me know you were comin'," Jack admonished. "You didn't have to barge in and shoot my fuckin' guards and shit." Jack turned to me, shaking his head as he jerked a thumb at Nicky. "Always gotta make a statement, this one."

I frowned at them. "So . . . you guys don't hate each other? What about the double-cross thing?"

Jack waved it away. "That? That was just funnin'. I didn't mean nothin' by it. Nicky knows that. Hell—he's nearly got *me* killed dozens of times. Keeps me on my toes, you know what I'm sayin'?" He didn't wait for me to respond before turning back to Nicky. "So what's doin'? What brings you by now after being off the grid for almost two years?"

"I need some information," Nicky told him, his expression growing serious.

Jack nodded. "Why don't we go upstairs to my office?" We started after him, but he held up a hand and offered one of his boyish grins. "Sorry, but I gotta have my guys frisk your dame. Just business, you understand."

One of the guards reached out to pat me down, but Nicky intercepted his hand and twisted his arm so quickly the guy was face-down on the ground before he even knew what'd hit him. "Don't think so. Trish isn't business. Not to me. Your guys touch her, I break their arms."

Jack glanced back and forth between us. "All right. All right. No worries."

I let my breath out on a gasp, not realizing I'd been holding it. I sent a glance Nicky's way, wondering why he'd decided not to let them take my gun after all. From the look he sent back my way I could tell he might trust his friend Jack, but the guards were apparently a different story. Better safe than sorry, I guess. And seeing as how I was in Nicky's world at the moment, I sure as hell wasn't going to argue with his change of plans.

I could still feel the harsh gazes of Jack's guards on my back as we climbed the stairs to the second story, where Jack had set up an office. I don't know what I was expecting, but it certainly wasn't the rows of computers that were running scripts and calculations. One of them had the FMA's database displayed. And at another of the computers a young man with bright orange spiky hair was busy tapping away on the keyboard.

"I've almost decrypted these files, Dad," he said, without looking away from the monitor. He chuckled. "These idiots think they can keep me out? Don't call us 'nimble' for nothin'!"

Jack coughed and cast a glance at Nicky and me. "Why don't you take a break, Ethan? We've got visitors."

Ethan's fingers froze midstroke; then he typed a quick key combination, locking his screen before turning around to offer us the same boyish grin his father had. "Hey! Uncle Nicky! Haven't seen you in ages! Did that hack job I did for you a couple of years ago work out okay?"

I wondered if Ethan was the guy who'd hacked into some files for Nicky back on the Sebille Fenwick case when he was trying to help Red. Based on the way Nicky's face fell, I figured I was probably right on the mark.

"Yeah," he said. "Yeah, thanks, kid. Got just what we needed."

Ethan's smile broadened. "Sweet! You ever need anything else, you let me know. Always happy to help out my godfather."

My brows shot up. *Godfather?*

As Ethan headed for the door, Nicky grabbed the boy around the neck and ruffled his hair, then pressed a kiss to the top of his head.

"You stay out of trouble, you hear? Don't let your old man get you into any scrapes, or I'll kick your ass."

Ethan laughed, ducking out of Nicky's hold. "Yes, sir."

"So, how's Vera?" Nicky asked as we all took a seat.

Jack grunted. "As beautiful as the day I married her," he said. "Can't figure out why she'd stick it out with me, but I'd be lost without her. She's one helluva woman."

"Give her a kiss from me," Nicky said.

"She's pissed as hell you haven't been to Sunday dinner in so long," Jack told him. "You and Trish come over soon. Vera'll cook you up a feast."

Nicky inclined his head, that smile I was beginning to recognize as his business expression curving his lips. "It'd be our pleasure."

Jack put his elbows on his desk and clasped his hands, giving Nicky a rather pained look. "And, I'm sorry—but I gotta say it. We were real sad to hear about Jules."

Nicky shifted uncomfortably in his chair and cast a glance my way. "Forget about it."

Jack's brows twitched together in a brief frown, but it faded quickly on a nod. "So, what can I do ya for?"

Nicky leaned forward, definitely all business now. "I need to find the Pigg brothers."

Jack's face twisted. "Those fuckin' guys," he grunted. "Why the hell would you want to find them?"

"I think they're doing a job somewhere here in town, and I need to know where."

Jack shook his head and leaned back in his chair, lacing his fingers over his abdomen. "Let's say I know where they are. What then?"

Nicky shrugged. "Then I go have a chat with them. See what they have to say."

"Come on, Nicky," Jack drawled. "You and I both know how your 'chats' go. Hell, you shot up three of my guards, and I'm a friend."

"Just flesh wounds," Nicky argued. "They're all Tales. They've probably already healed."

"Not the point, Nicky, and you know it." Jack turned to me. "Talk some sense into him, Trish. The Piggs were indicted for fraud and sued for all kinds of shoddy building. But you think it made a dent in their wallets? They made their *real* money in the Here and Now working as cleanup men for criminals who could pay their fee. If there's a body someone doesn't want to be found, the Piggs know how to get rid of it. God knows how many people are buried in concrete around town."

"And you're worried about Nicky?" I asked, not bothering to disguise my doubt. I'd seen Nicky in action. I had no doubt that he could handle three brothers whose claim to fame in Make Believe had been building shitty houses and getting sideways with Seth Wolf. Sure, Seth was a werewolf, but Nicky was still a force to be reckoned with. No matter how I looked at it, I just couldn't share Jack's concern.

"Just tell me where I can find them," Nicky said. "And I'll take my chances."

Jack sighed. "It's your own necks, I guess. Last I heard, they were doing a job out in Oak Park. I'll have Ethan look up the address for you. Just promise me you won't get yourself killed, you stubborn asshole. It'd seriously piss me off."

Chapter Twenty-One

"I didn't know you had a godson," I said as we pulled into a half-built office complex in the suburbs where the Piggs had currently set up shop.

Nicky grunted but was smiling. "Jack and I used to hang out together in Make Believe. He was my partner in crime, literally and figuratively. Then he went and settled down with Vera." He chuckled. "I never figured Jack for a family man. When he came over about twenty years ago, he had a rough time finding good work. Then Ethan was born and Jack had even more of a reason to find something that would help him feed his family. He started doing all kinds of bullshit jobs for some pretty shady characters; damned near got himself killed pissing off the wrong people. I tried to get him to work for me and told him he could do whatever he wanted on the side for some extra money so long as it didn't get him in trouble with the Ordinaries or the FMA. But he thought there'd be more money in his own freelancing. Some friend I am, huh? I should've just *made* the stupid ass go straight and get a real job to keep him out of trouble."

"He could've taken you up on your offer," I pointed out. "You can't blame yourself for someone else's bad decisions."

He grunted again. "Nah, I could've pushed harder, insisted he get out of street scams and other shit. But I didn't want to lose his friendship. When it came down to it, I guess I was a little envious of what he *did* have. A wife. Family. I wanted that, wanted to be near that. I just didn't know it."

I blinked at him, startled by the revelation. It had never occurred to me that Nicky had wanted to have a family. I don't know why it surprised me. When I thought about what I'd seen that day in the clearing when I'd looked into his eyes, I realized that I should've known all along that a man with such an amazing capacity to love would make an incredible husband and father. I'd seen a hint of what could be when he'd interacted with his godson. And suddenly I wanted that, too. I wanted that with Nicky.

He pulled the Escalade around to the side of a building where it was less likely to be seen and started to get out when I grabbed his hand. He gave me a quizzical look. "What's doin', doll? You okay?"

I pulled him to me and kissed him. "I love you," I whispered. "I thought I saw everything there was to see about you when I caught a glimpse of your soul, but it was only that—just a glimpse. There is so much more to love than I'd ever imagined."

Nicky's lips claimed mine in a kiss that could've easily led to one seriously hot interlude, but he pulled away with a groan. "We should probably get this over with," he mumbled. "But, just so you know, when I get you home, I'm gonna show you just how many ways I love you."

I had to force down my happiness, bury it deep, as we walked toward the building where the Piggs had set up their on-site office. Calling it a trailer would be a misnomer. It looked more like a three-bedroom ranch on wheels. There was even latticework all around the bottom, hiding the open space beneath the trailer, giving it a very homey touch. The place was huge. Great for them, not so great for us. Too many places to hide weapons. Or henchmen. I didn't like it at all.

And there'd be no kicking in the door, either. The steps leading up to the door were narrow metal pieces of shit that looked like it'd be a miracle if they didn't buckle as we climbed them.

"Well, here we go," Nicky mumbled. "Just stay close to me. I don't trust these fuckers any farther than I can throw 'em."

But before we'd even reached the steps, the door slammed open and a rotund man with slicked-back black hair, a rather porcine nose, and the stub of a cigar between his teeth waddled down the stairs at what apparently was a jog, opening his arms wide.

"Nicky Blue, you motherfucker!" he called, chuckling so hard his belly bounced. "How the hell are ya?"

Nicky looked more than a little mystified when the guy wrapped his thick arms around him in a hug. "I'm good, I'm good," Nicky gasped, stepping out of the guy's hold. "It's been a long time, Orvall."

"Damn right it has!" Orvall snatched his cigar out of his mouth and gestured toward me. "And who is this beautiful young lady you've brought to see us, my friend? If I was twenty years younger and about a hundred pounds lighter, you'd be in trouble, boy. I was a charmer back in the day."

"I'm Trish Muffet," I said, extending a hand.

Orvall gripped it in his plump fist and gave it a firm shake, chuckling again. "Well, I'll be damned—you got yourself a girl from the FMA, Nicky? You got some brass balls, my friend, I'll give you that!" He turned back to their office and motioned for us to follow. "Come on, come on! We're just cookin' up some brats and sauerkraut! Come eat! You two look like you're wastin' away to nothin'."

Bemused by the surprisingly warm welcome, I glanced at Nicky as we followed, but he seemed just as baffled as I was. He obviously hadn't expected it either. "What the hell?" I mouthed.

But he just shrugged. And checked to make sure his gun was still at the small of his back.

When we walked inside, two other men just as rotund as Orvall turned away from the stove and raised their arms, crying out in unison, "Hey! Nicky!"

Not only were the Piggs brothers, they were triplets. Identical triplets.

Nicky nodded hesitantly. "Irwin. Merv."

"Grab a beer!" one of them said, gesturing toward the fridge.

"Ice cold!" said the other.

Nicky eyed them warily, pulling me a little behind him. "I'm grateful for your hospitality," he said, his business grin curling his lips, "but I have to say, boys, it's rather unexpected."

Orvall dropped down into a huge easy chair that still only barely managed to contain his bulk. "Nicky . . ." he drawled, drawing out the word, "we've always been friendly. You've never crossed us. We've never crossed you. No harm in showing a little . . . *cordiality* to a colleague now and then, is there?"

Nicky spread his hands in a conciliatory gesture. "I meant no disrespect."

"Of course you didn't!" Merv chimed in. He wagged his tongs at Nicky. "You're good people. Always showing respect to those who deserve it."

"And even some who don't," Irwin said with a shrug.

"Now, sit down, sit down," Orvall said, waving Nicky and me toward an overstuffed sofa covered in what had to be the gaudiest flower pattern I'd ever seen. "Have some supper and we'll talk business after. Irwin, grab our guests a beer!"

As soon as Nicky and I were seated, Irwin shoved ice cold Heinekens into our hands. I dutifully took a sip while the brothers watched, no doubt forming their opinion of me by how I responded to their generosity. "Mmm," I said, offering Irwin a smile. "Hits the spot."

"She's a good girl, Nicky," Irwin said with a wink. "Any gal not too prissy to drink beer from a bottle is okay with me. Don't understand all them froo-froo drinks. You don't drink none of them, do you, Ms. Muffet?"

I shook my head. "Oh, no! I'm definitely a beer and pretzels kind of girl."

Orvall chuckled and slapped his knee. "Marry this one, Nicky!" he whooped. "Except for liking you, she's a smart kid!"

Nicky actually flushed a little and cast a glance my way before replying, "Trish is definitely a keeper."

As Nicky and Orvall chatted about whether the Blackhawks would make it to the play-offs and the new taxes the FMA had proposed for Tale businesses, I sat quietly, taking it all in. For all the politeness and show of hospitality, there was an undercurrent of tension in the room that had all the men on edge. Nicky's shoulders were visibly bunched, ready to spring at the first sign of a threat. And as all of us gathered around the dinette for an early dinner, I glanced back and forth between them, studying each of them in turn.

Orvall was definitely the dominant brother, the one in charge. And while they all had a genial manner and went out of their way to make Nicky and me feel welcome, there was no mistaking that these men wouldn't hesitate to cut our throats and bury us at the closest city dump if provoked. As soon as the dinner was cleared away, leaving only the lingering odor of sauerkraut in the air, Orvall leaned back in his chair and regarded Nicky with an even gaze, looking down his stubby nose at him.

"So, what brings you to our little corner of suburbia, Nicky?" he asked, getting to the point. "You've never approached us before."

Nicky downed the last swig of his beer and set the bottle aside before leaning his elbows on the table and lacing his fingers together. "I hear you might be doing a construction job for someone. Someone who would prefer to remain out of the public eye. And the sunlight."

Orvall's chuckle was deeper and lacking in mirth this time. "Dracula, Nicky? You asking if we're doing a job for Dracula?"

Nicky pulled back a little, apparently surprised by Orvall's bluntness. "Yeah."

"And what if we are?" Orvall asked. "Why should I tell you?"

Nicky shrugged, regaining his composure. "Professional courtesy. I would consider it a gesture of friendship."

Orvall nodded, scratching the stubble on his chinny-chin-chin. "Here's the thing," he said, talking around the cigar clamped between his teeth. "I hear you're getting out of the business. I hear you've gone soft. So what would it behoove me to be your friend? Especially when you've never once come to me offering friendship before?"

Nicky spread his hands. "You know me, Orvall," he said. "I've never had need of your particular services. But it's not because I think I'm too good to ask for your assistance. It's just that, unlike some of these other incompetent mooks, I clean up my own messes."

Orvall's beady black eyes narrowed at Nicky. "And what about you getting out of the business? That true?"

Nicky shrugged. "Let's just say I'm redefining my objectives."

Merv chuckled, receiving a pointed glare from his brother. He coughed, the laughter dying on his lips.

Orvall jerked his chin. "Not falling in with these Agency assholes, are you?"

"The Agency?" I blurted before I could stop myself. "What do you know about *them*?"

Luckily, Orvall didn't seem to mind me interrupting. "They came around a month or so ago, snooping, asking a shitload of questions. Wanted us to do a job for them, but they didn't say what. I told them they could shove their job up their asses with my compliments. I even offered to help with that. They declined my offer."

"Didn't stop 'em comin' around again, though," Irwin added.

"Brought the Ordinary police with 'em that time," Merv explained. "Slapped a zillion fines on us, some trumped up bullshit about building permits and zoning violations. Somehow they got it in their heads that we were putting in a titty bar just up the road from a school."

"Are you?" I asked, earning a disapproving look from Nicky.

"Forgive her question," he said. "She's not used to working with men of honor."

The brothers gave a terse nod in unison. "No offense taken," Orvall assured him. He then turned to me. "We might be sons of bitches, Ms. Muffet, but we have principles. And some things simply are not done."

I felt my face flushing. "Of course."

"So, why would the Agency be out to cause you problems?" Nicky asked, steering the conversation back to our purpose for coming. "If you said no to the job, why not just hire some Ordinaries to do it? I'm sure they could've found someone willing. If there's one thing I know about Ordinaries, it's money talks."

The triplets grunted and nodded in unison.

"Maybe they did," Orvall suggested, scratching at his chin again.

Nicky was still frowning when we heard the sound of a car pulling up in front of the Piggs' trailer. "Expecting anyone?" he asked, instantly on edge.

Orvall shook his head and heaved himself to his feet. He went to the window and pulled back the edge of the curtains. "Speak of the friggin' devil."

My brows came together and I rushed to the window, peeking out just in time to see Ian Spalding getting out of his car as three other Agency vehicles pulled into the parking lot. "What the hell are they doing here?" I muttered.

"You got a back door?" Nicky asked, grabbing my hand and pulling me away from the window.

Apparently Merv was already thinking the same thing. "This way," he called in a stage whisper from the back of the trailer.

Nicky shoved me ahead of him toward where Merv was motioning for us to get the lead out. Merv lifted a trap in the floor of the trailer, revealing what looked like a tunnel running under the parking lot. Now I understood the need for the latticework under the trailer. It wasn't to make the place look homey; it was to disguise their emergency exit.

"Where does this go?" I asked. But before I got an answer, Merv was handing me down into the darkness. I glanced over my shoulder at Orvall and Irwin in time to see Orvall flipping up the cushions on the sofa and pulling out a pair of UZIs and handing one off to his brother. Apparently they were no longer relying upon a pot of boiling water to take care of the wolves at their door. . . .

I quickly climbed down the metal ladder affixed to the tunnel wall and dropped the last couple of feet to the floor, praying there weren't any rats waiting for me at the bottom. A moment later, Nicky joined me, a flashlight in hand. He flicked it on, then shined it up at Merv. They gave each other a terse nod just as the first *pat pat pat* of rapid gunfire rang out. The trapdoor dropped and I heard hurried footsteps above our heads.

"We shouldn't leave them," I whispered to Nicky.

He looked just as conflicted about leaving as I was, but then he took my hand and began leading me through the tunnel. "They can take care of themselves," he assured me. "Right now, I'm getting you the hell out of here."

We'd only walked for maybe two minutes before the sound of gunfire died down. Nicky came to an abrupt halt and cast a glance over his shoulder. "Shit."

I only had time to get a glimpse of him before he flicked off the flashlight and pulled me into his arms, holding me close as he listened intently. In the distance, we heard the quiet *creak* of the trapdoor opening.

"Go," he hissed in my ear.

We took off down the tunnel, feeling along the walls in the darkness, keeping our footsteps as quiet as possible. The people following us weren't so concerned. Hearing each of them drop down into the tunnel, I picked up the pace, holding tightly to Nicky's hand and hoping like hell he had some idea where we were going.

A loud crack sounded behind us as one of our pursuers opened fire. I crouched down instinctively and felt Nicky's arm going around my shoulders, pulling me in front of him to protect me. We picked up the pace, no longer caring about the Agency assholes hearing our footsteps.

Nicky gave me a nudge to keep going. "Stay low," he whispered. Then I heard him fire off a few rounds behind us. There was a grunt of pain as one of the rounds struck home.

Crouching low along the wall, I ran faster. Relief washed over me as I felt Nicky close behind me. But just when I thought the agents had backed off, they shot at as again, this time in a spray of bullets. Nicky cursed under his breath. I glanced behind me as if I could tell in the darkness whether he'd been hit, and suddenly slammed into a dirt wall, crying out in surprise before I could stop myself.

I felt around frantically, searching for a turn in the tunnel or a ladder, something!

"Up!" Nicky hissed, placing my hands on metal rungs and urging me upward.

More shots rang out, making me climb quicker. I was nearly to the top when pain exploded in my leg. I lost my footing and slid back down the ladder, knocking into Nicky and sending us sprawling on the ground.

"Got her!" I heard one of the agents yell.

Nicky snatched me up from the ground and flung me over his shoulder, then scrambled up the ladder, a deep groan rumbling in his chest. When he threw open the hatch, the late afternoon sunlight assaulted me, and I winced, sucking in the air through my teeth.

"Hang on, doll," Nicky muttered, shrugging me off his shoulders and onto the ground inside one of the buildings that was still under construction. He slammed the trapdoor and glanced around frantically, then grabbed a heavy cinder block and set it on top of the door to slow down the agents.

It was only as Nicky hastily lifted me into his arms that I realized my jeans were soaked with blood and my thigh was raging with pain, threatening to send me careening toward unconsciousness. "Hold on, doll," he murmured as he hurried toward a plastic sheet hanging over a doorway. He ducked under the sheet and rushed toward the doorway across the room, but stumbled, coming down on one knee, clenching his teeth over a sharp cry.

I glanced up at his face, alarmed to see it deathly pale. Then I noticed the blood that was dripping down his arm. "Oh, my God!" I wiggled out of his hold—which wasn't difficult with him weakened from blood loss. Pain punched the breath from my lungs when I hit the ground, but I managed to push up to my knees as Nicky slumped into me. "Oh, no you don't," I grunted, somehow managing to get us both up and moving.

I pulled Nicky's uninjured arm around my shoulders and gritted my teeth as I limped toward the door, dragging him with me. I pulled the door open just a crack and saw the parking lot; the building where we'd parked the Escalade was only a couple hundred feet from where we'd emerged.

"Come on, love," I ground out, glancing around for any agents who might be coming for us. By the time we reached the Escalade, my breath was shredding my lungs, but the pain in my thigh had already started to subside. Not bothering to ponder the faster than usual healing time, I fished the keys out of Nicky's pocket and managed to shove him into the passenger's seat.

I was tearing out of the parking lot, tires squealing, when the Agency bastards emerged from the Piggs' office, firing at us. I flinched with a startled cry when one of their bullets shattered the back window. "Son of a bitch!"

The tires clung desperately to the pavement as I whipped the car out of the parking lot and into the street, fishtailing the rear end when I gunned it. Nicky slammed into the door with a groan. "Hang on, Nicky," I told him, my teeth beginning to chatter from the icy February air blowing in through the shattered window. "I'm taking you to the hospital."

He mumbled something incoherent in response.

"What was that, baby?" I asked, glancing in the rearview mirror to check for a tail.

"Not dying," he said a little louder. "Trust me. I know what that feels like."

I spotted one of the Agency's sedans zipping around the cars behind me, gaining quickly. "Yeah, well, I'm not willing to bet on that, okay?"

I jerked the steering wheel, bounding onto the median and bouncing into the oncoming traffic. Before the Agency could even figure out what had happened, I was racing past them in the opposite direction. But it wasn't going to take them long to come after me. I just couldn't figure out why the hell they *wanted* to. Why were Nicky and I suddenly on their hit list? Had they come at the Pigg brothers to get to Nicky and me, or were we just in the wrong place at the wrong time?

As expected, the Agency's sedan was coming up behind me again. And this time it had a twin.

Shit.

I was in freaking suburbia in an area I didn't know. Outrunning them or losing them was becoming increasingly unlikely. There was no way to call for Gideon without the little mist trick Lavender had taught me. And I'd left my cell phone in my coat pocket, which was back at the Piggs'.

I blew through a red light, drawing the furious honks of several cars, but the congestion managed to at least slow my pursuers for a few valuable seconds. I zigzagged between a cargo van and a sports car, then floored it again, taking the first interstate entrance ramp I saw, not even noting which interstate it happened to be.

As soon as I merged into traffic, I reached over and snatched Nicky's cell phone from the case at his belt and punched in a number before thinking. When I heard the familiar baritone on the other end, my stomach twisted into knots. But pride was going to have to take a number.

"Hi, Al," I said through chattering teeth. "I need your help."

Chapter Twenty-Two

I smoothed Nicky's hair away from his forehead as he slept, then bent and brushed a kiss to his lips. He was so doped up on fairy dust at the moment, he didn't even flinch.

"The doctors say when he'll wake up?" Al asked from where he sat in a wooden chair in the corner of the Tale hospital room.

I shook my head. "Not really. Maybe sometime tonight or tomorrow. His body was weakened by the blood loss and is struggling a little to heal itself."

Even though I'd had no right to ask for his help the day before, Al had immediately sent out several Enforcers to come to our aid. And now with Red safely at home on bed rest, he'd transferred his vigil at the hospital to watching over Nicky and me. I wondered when the last time was that he'd had any sleep.

"Any word on the Pigg brothers?" I asked.

He shook his head. "No blood at the scene except yours and Nicky's and whatever Agency assholes were shot. And I checked with Nate—no calls for a pickup. I'm guessing they're holed up somewhere, waiting things out."

I couldn't help grinning a little. Odds were good the brothers had had more than one escape plan. Slippery bastards.

Al sighed and ran his hand through his hair. "What are you doing with this guy, Trish?" he demanded. "He's going to end up getting you killed."

"If not for Nicky, I'd already be dead." I pegged Al with an angry glare, crossing my arms over my chest. "But you'd know all about that, wouldn't you?"

His brows came together in a frown. "What the hell are you talking about?"

"How long have you been in bed with the Agency?" I demanded. "How long have you just been bending over and taking it?"

"Is that what you think has been going on?" He shook his head and got to his feet with a muttered curse. "Who told you *that*? That *criminal* you're screwing?"

I stormed toward him, jutting my chin up. "That *criminal*," I seethed, jabbing a finger in Nicky's direction, "is the best man I've ever known! I used to rank *you* pretty high on that list, too, Al. But I'm beginning to see that you're nothing more than a bureaucrat out to protect his own ass. What the hell has happened to you?"

Al laughed bitterly. "I gave up everything for the FMA," he reminded me. "My fortune, my wife . . . Do you seriously think after sacrificing all that to protect the Tales, I'd turn my back on all of you *now* just because of pressure from some government agency?"

My huffiness lost a little of its steam. No, I didn't think that. It was incomprehensible to me. But, still . . . "So what's the deal with you and the Agency, then?" I demanded. "What's going on that would make people suspect you're a mole?"

"Who suspects that?" he asked, clearly shocked by the news.

"People who have a lot of power," I told him. "You need to come clean, Al. What the hell is going on?"

He dropped into the chair, looking deflated and exhausted, the gray that peppered his hair suddenly more noticeable. "I'm walking a tightrope here, Trish," he sighed. "I'm not an idiot—I know they're up to something. They've always pressured me, wanting to know more about us, wanting a chance to pick us apart, find out the secrets behind our healing abilities, determine what makes some of us have *talents* that others lack—and how those talents change after coming over."

I shook my head. "We have the same abilities in the Here and Now that we had in Make Believe."

Al gave me a rather apologetic look. "Not all of us."

I eased down into the chair beside him. "What are you talking about?"

"You know as well as I do that some of us have . . . altered . . . since we arrived, based upon how our origin stories are perceived by popular culture," he explained. "Not all of us, obviously, but there are certain Tales who have become something *more*."

I blinked at him. "Do you mean Tales like Vlad Dracula?"

He slumped a little in his chair. "Yeah, I think he's one of them. But there have been others. Most of them are now in the Asylum, undergoing rehabilitation. Over time, the changes they experience . . . it's as if it tears apart their psyches, drives them mad. They become . . . *fractured*. No longer sure who or what they are."

That would certainly fit what I'd witnessed with Dracula.

"So what does this have to do with the Agency?" I asked.

He shook his head. "I don't know. The pressure from them picked up a couple of years ago, right around the time all the bullshit with Sebille Fenwick went down. I was dealing with all that and trying to keep Red from getting herself killed, and I had the Agency breathing down my neck, threatening to impose their oversight and take over the FMA. Then they suddenly backed off. Well, a little. It's just . . . strange now."

"We've got to stop letting them intimidate us," I insisted. "I've never agreed with Sebille Fenwick's or Vlad Dracula's methods, but they had a point, Al."

Al looked at me like I'd just shat monkeys.

"Don't give me that look," I admonished. "Think about it. We aren't just a handful of helpless supernaturals like the Agency is used to dealing with. We're an organized group. We have our own government, our own law enforcement, health system—all of it. We need to stand our ground, Al. If push came to shove, we'd be a formidable force."

Al studied me for a moment, mulling over what I'd said—and probably thinking I was an irredeemable lunatic. But then he took a deep breath and let it out on a long exhale. "The Agency is very well connected. If I push back, it could get ugly."

"It's going to get ugly either way," I told him. "Sebille's network was far reaching. And who the hell knows what Dracula's been up to? And there are others who aren't allied with either one of them who are beginning to wonder if the FMA has outlived its usefulness."

Al shook his head. "That's bullshit. You know that."

"It's time to take a stand, Al," I insisted. "It's time to let the Ordinaries know we're not cowering in fear of them. We deserve to live our lives and be happy in the Here and Now. The Agency is baiting us. They know a fight's coming, and they're trying to draw us into it on *their* terms."

"What makes you say that?" Al asked with a frown.

"There's some connection with Dracula I haven't yet figured out. And they're stealing fairy dust from the Seelies and distributing it to Ordinaries." When he cursed under his breath and ran a hand down his face, I reached over without thinking and put my hand on his knee. "Al, talk to Lavender's father. You don't have to handle all this on your own. He could be a powerful ally if you have to go toe-to-toe with the Agency."

"He'd never see me," Al insisted.

"He remembers your kindness to Lavender after the initial migration. If he offers you his friendship in return, accept it." I chuckled a little and glanced over my shoulder at Nicky, who still lay in a drug-induced sleep. "Trust me, I've learned a thing or two lately about the importance of friendship."

"Even if I did decide to go up against the Agency, they have a tactical advantage." When I gave him a blank look, he explained, "They know where we are, Trish. I have no idea where they're head-quartered, if they have field offices. . . . I've had intelligence officers trying to get a feel for the size of their operation, but they never meet in the same place. Their offices are temporary. They simply don't *exist* anywhere."

I mulled over what he was saying, my brows drawn together in a frown.

After a moment, Al's hand covered mine, jolting me from my thoughts. "Trish, about earlier—"

I gently slipped my fingers from his grasp. "Please don't," I told him gently. "I'm in love with Nicky, Al. This isn't just a fling."

His shoulders sagged a little and the pain in his eyes tore at my heart, but then he gave a slight nod and donned that impassive, contemplative look that I was used to. "Well, he'd better take care of you, or he'll have me to deal with. Believe it or not, I've been known to kick a few asses over the years."

Oh, I believed it.

When he stood, I stood with him and impulsively slipped my arms around his waist, hugging him tightly. "Thanks, Al. For everything. For giving me a chance when I came over. For always being there when I needed a friend."

I felt his ragged breath as his arms came around me and hugged me back. After a moment, he dropped a quick kiss to the top of my head and abruptly released me, then strode to the door. He started to pull it open but paused and turned back to offer me a smile. "Take some time off. Let that leg of yours heal completely. I'll expect to see you back on the job in a couple of weeks."

I frowned at him, not bothering to tell him my leg had miraculously healed within minutes of my injury. "Al—"

"See you at the office." Then he was gone.

For a moment I just stared at the closed door.

"So, I guess you didn't quit after all."

Nicky's voice instantly drew me out of my stupor. Grinning, I sat down on the edge of the bed and smoothed his hair again. "Hey, you. You had me worried there for a while."

He winked at me. "I told you, doll. Unless Nate starts hovering nearby looking all shamefaced and shit, I'm not worried. By the way, you look damned sexy in those scrubs. Might even top the nighty."

"Good thing I get to keep these, then," I said with a saucy grin. I leaned down and kissed him, so glad to feel his warm lips against mine. When I felt him smiling, I pulled back. "What's so funny?"

It was his turn to chuckle. He took my hand and slid it down to the sizable bulge under the sheets. "Want to climb on in here with me, doll?"

"Nicky Blue," I admonished, "you're still healing! Besides, there are people coming in here all the time."

"You're the only one I want coming in here," he said with a wicked grin. When I gave him a disapproving look, he added, "Hey, I nearly died, you know."

"Oh, is that right?" I drawled, looking down my nose at him.

He nodded, donning a comically serious expression. "It was terribly frightening. I think I've been traumatized. I could really use a little comforting."

I couldn't help laughing. "Don't be ridiculous!"

"What's ridiculous is that you'd deny a man a little post-near-death lovin'," he said, lifting the blankets.

"Post-near-death lovin'?" I rolled my eyes. "If you've healed enough for sex, you've healed enough to get the hell out of here. Let's go home and I'll give you all the lovin' you want."

As he sprang up from the bed and shed the hospital gown, reaching for the scrubs the hospital had given him to replace his ruined clothes, I couldn't resist smacking his bare ass. "You're pretty spry for someone who *nearly died. . . .*"

Big mistake.

He quirked an eyebrow at me. "Oh, is that how we're gonna play it?" He went to the door and turned the lock, then came toward me, a wicked look in his eyes as his gaze traveled the length of my body in the baggy teal scrubs I wore. "Spry, was it? Doll, you ain't seen nothin' yet. . . ."

"We need to find the Agency's headquarters," I told Nicky, pulling on my scrubs again.

He was already dressed and looking rather pleased with himself as he sat on the edge of the hospital bed. "I seem to recall hearing Al say that none of his intelligence officers had been able to find the Agency's headquarters."

"True," I said, sauntering toward him and slipping between the V of his thighs to loop my arms around his neck. "But they aren't Nicky Blue."

He gave me a sideways glance but was grinning, no doubt wondering where I was going with this. "Yeah? So?"

I kissed him briefly, then returned his grin. *"I can make anything happen,"* I said, mimicking his accent. Then I shrugged, exaggerating his typical nonchalance. *"I know a guy."*

He laughed and grabbed me around the waist, tackling me onto the bed. "I know a guy?" he repeated, tickling me. "I *know* a guy? I don't sound like that!"

"Stop! Stop!" I squealed, wiggling to get away.

He stopped tickling me to cage me with his body. After peering down at me for a long moment, he gave me a wink. "Know something, doll? I love ya. Love ya like nothin' I ever felt before."

"And . . . ?" I asked archly.

He chuckled. "And what?"

"Was I right? Can you find the Agency's headquarters?"

He shrugged. "Yeah. Sure. At least, I can find out where they've set up shop at the moment. Maybe get us inside."

"Really?" I asked, actually a little surprised. I pushed up to my elbows. "How?"

A slow grin grew on his face, and he shrugged again. "I know a guy."

Chapter Twenty-Three

"No fucking way."

"Get in the car, Nicky," I hissed. "We need a ride home."

"We'll take a cab," he muttered, grabbing my arm and turning me back toward the hospital entrance. "We're not riding in the same car as that asshole."

I pulled him to a stop. "Stop being a man-baby."

He frowned at me. "A *what?*"

"A man-baby," I repeated. "Al insisted that one of the Enforcers take us home in case the Agency tries anything again."

"I'll call Eddie," he said, referring to his former bodyguard. "I trust *him.*"

I turned him around and gave him a look of warning. "You can trust Alex, too. Now, get in the car."

Nicky opened the back door of the FMA sedan for me and helped me inside, then sent a dark look Alex McCain's way as he jerked open the front passenger door, daring McCain to start something with him. He eased inside, still a little stiff from his wounds, then turned his back toward the door, so he could keep an eye on McCain.

"You need directions?" Nicky asked. But before McCain could respond, Nicky sniped, "Oh, *that's* right—you already know how to get to my house, don't you, McCain?"

Alex sent a glance my way, looking a little apologetic—and more than a little nervous. Nicky intimidated him. No surprise there. What *was* surprising was how the guy kept glancing at *me* in the mirror. Why the hell would *I* make him nervous?

We rode in tense silence for the better part of the ride. I kept glancing between McCain and Nicky, wondering if Nicky was ever going to let up on the daggers he was glaring at the Enforcer. Anxious to get the hell out of the car, I was relieved when we finally started to pass landmarks I recognized.

"What's your story, McCain?" Nicky asked, suddenly breaking the silence.

Well, damn. So much for my pending relief.

Alex shifted a little in the driver's seat, adjusting his grip on the wheel. "Don't know," he said with a shrug. "I don't remember anything from before."

McCain was one of the few Tales who came over with no recollection of an origin story. I'd heard rumors of how Al had found him wandering around the streets of Chicago and had taken him under his wing, making sure the Relocation Bureau did right by him, and—when he was ready—giving him a job with the FMA a couple of years ago.

"That's gotta be a bitch," Nicky mused. "Not knowing where you come from, who your people are."

Alex shook his head. "Not really. Since I don't know where I come from, I've got nothing to live up to." He sent a pointed look Nicky's way. "And nothing to live down."

But Nicky was too smooth to rise to the bait. He just donned his mirthless grin. "We all got a past, McCain. And it doesn't matter a damn if you know what it is—eventually, it's gonna catch up." He narrowed his eyes. "So, what are your secrets, you think? What's comin' for you one of these days?"

McCain's gaze darted over to Nicky, then up in the mirror at me. I cocked my head to one side, wondering what the hell was going on with him.

Nicky's grin grew. "But it's not the past that's got you twitching, is it, McCain?" he drawled. "It's the *present* you're worried about."

McCain's gaze darted up to the mirror again but he quickly looked away so he could turn off onto the road leading to Nicky's house. "No idea what you're talking about."

Nicky didn't press the issue, but continued his stare-down. And the minute McCain stopped in front of the house, Nicky threw open the door and got out, helping me from the car and slamming the door. We'd just reached the foot of the steps when he turned and jogged back to the car. McCain rolled down his window, but didn't so much as glance Nicky's way.

"What do you want, Blue?" he sighed.

Nicky leaned in and rested his folded arms on the lowered window. "What do I want? There's a lady present, so I'll save that one for another time. But just know I'm on to you, McCain. I don't know what you got going, but I *do* know when a guy's not being straight with me. I just hope your secrets won't put you in my crosshairs. I don't give a shit who you work for—you get in my way, you put Trish in danger in any way, and I'll take you out. Take you out before you even know it's coming. We understand each other?"

McCain slowly turned his head and met Nicky's gaze. "You don't scare me, Blue," he assured him. "You're just a washed-up thug who hasn't figured that out yet."

Nicky laughed. "Yeah? Well, maybe so. But are you willing to put that to the test?"

"Come on, Nicky," I said, taking his arm and pulling him away from the car. "It's cold out here."

Nicky put his arm around my shoulders and pressed a kiss to my temple. "Sorry, doll." Then he jerked his chin at McCain. "See you around."

McCain shook his head with a scoff, then drove off.

"Wow—are you spoiling for a fight that badly?" I asked as Nicky and I went inside.

"I don't trust him," Nicky muttered.

I slapped my hands on my hips. "No shit. He's hiding something, I'll give you that. But you showed your hand. That's not like you. What's going on?"

Nicky drew me into his arms. "Sometimes you gotta give a peek at your hand now and then, make everyone wonder what *else* you're holding, make 'em sweat a little." When I frowned, he kissed the crease on my forehead. "Now, come on. Let's get outta these scrubs and go track down those Agency assholes."

Nicky had a fleet of cars that would make Jay Leno salivate. Rows of various styles of vehicle—classic and modern—filled the warehouse Nicky called his "garage."

"You actually drive all these?" I asked as I checked out what appeared to be a 1929 Rolls-Royce Phantom II.

He shrugged as he punched a ten-digit code into a keypad that popped open a safe containing several rows of keys hanging on pegs. "Not all. There are a few so rare I don't risk taking them out. But most of them get to stretch their legs now and then." He snatched a set from its hook and shut the door. The safe beeped as its security system engaged.

"We obviously have lived very different lives," I muttered as I followed him to a black Range Rover Evoque.

"Yeah, well, don't say that like it's a bad thing." He opened the door for me, then added with a grin, "Besides, there's a lot gonna change for both of us from here on out."

My stomach tightened, and I almost asked him if that meant he was planning to stick around now instead of taking off again once we'd found Dracula. But the words froze on my lips. It wasn't a conversation I wanted to have right then—if ever.

I was quiet on the drive to meet with Nicky's contact, a fact he didn't miss. At one point, he took my hand and raised it to his lips and gave me a tentative smile. But I wasn't in much of a talking mood. I returned his smile but then turned my attention back to the window and the buildings blurring by as we drove.

I was in love with Nicky. And there was no way I was going to walk away from that. He said he loved me, and I believed him. I just hoped it was enough to keep him here.

I was so distracted by my thoughts, I didn't notice Nicky had parked until he reached over and put a hand on my thigh. "You okay, doll?"

I started a little and nodded, giving him a smile far too quickly to be believable. "Just tired," I said, trying to cover. "Been one hell of a week, you know?"

He cupped my face and smoothed his thumb over my cheek. "It'll be over soon," he promised. "We're close, Trish, I can feel it."

I gave him a determined nod and gladly accepted his brief kiss, clinging to his lips for just a little when a sense of foreboding suddenly squeezed my heart. As we walked down Michigan Avenue with my hand grasped tightly in his, I tried to shake the heaviness that was weighing down on me, trying to figure out what had set it off and coming up with nothing. Every now and then, I'd send a glance his way, studying the planes and edges of his face, his strong profile, committing every line to memory.

I am going to lose him.

The thought struck me so hard I actually doubled over with a gasp, clutching at my stomach as if someone had punched me in the gut.

"Trish?" Nicky said, bending forward so he could peer into my face. "You okay, doll? What's doin'?"

I shook my head, blinking away tears of heartbreak. I was imagining things. Everything would be fine. As soon as Dracula was brought down, we'd figure things out between us and live happily ever after. We deserved it, goddamn it! I swallowed hard, shoving aside my apprehension. "I'm okay," I muttered. "Let's just get this over with."

We walked for a few more blocks, making a couple of turns, but I wasn't paying any attention. The world around me kept going hazy, growing dim, then coming back into focus for a moment before fading again. I shook my head, trying to clear my vision. When Nicky slowed his pace, I squinted at our surroundings, surprised to see we were standing on Wabash Avenue in the middle of Jewelers Row.

My eyes widened when I saw the sign hanging over the store Nicky was heading toward: RUMPELSTILTSKIN'S, TURNING STRAW INTO GOLD SINCE 1956.

"Your guy is a *jeweler*?" I asked.

Nicky chuckled. "That's just his front. You'll see."

The shop was small and cozy, but the glass display cases were filled with a stunning collection of baubles that made my eyes go wide. Even with my decent FMA salary, I couldn't imagine there was anything in the store that fell within my budget. The people who shopped there were the elite of Chicago.

"Well, smack my ass!"

I turned toward the voice and blinked at the Tale behind the counter. He was movie star handsome, his golden brown hair falling in carefully styled, perfectly highlighted waves around his beautiful face. He came out from around the counter, moving with surprising grace. His silk shirt looked custom made, and, considering the way his slacks hugged his athletic build, they most likely were as well. The man's warm blue eyes took us in at a glance and a slow smile curved his lips.

"Hel-*lo,* gorgeous!"

"Um . . . hi," I stammered, glancing at Nicky, a little taken off guard by the enthusiastic compliment.

The man flashed a smooth, swoon-worthy grin. "Well, you *are* an adorable little dish, sweetie," he said, "but I was actually talking to Nicky. How the hell *are* you, you tasty hunk of man?"

Oh. Got it.

My face flooded with warmth at my gaffe.

Nicky just chuckled and shook the man's hand. "I'm hangin' in there, my friend. How's business?"

The man rolled his eyes and sagged, exaggerating each motion. "Oh, honey—I am *so* over Valentine's Day! No one has *any* imagination these days. Hearts and diamonds—how *appallingly* passé!"

"You said it, girlfriend," piped up a tall, slender man whose neon pink silk button-down was a striking contrast to his java skin. He leaned across the counter and gave Nicky a flirty grin. "Well, well, well. If it isn't Little Boy Blue. Did you finally decide to come blow my horn?"

"Stop being such a man-whore," Nicky's friend scolded. "You know Nicky doesn't play that way."

The man sighed dramatically. "A boy can dream."

"Hey, Truman," Nicky chuckled, jerking his chin in greeting. "How's it hangin'?"

"To the left, honey, always to the left," he said with a wink.

"Nicky, are you going to introduce us to your lovely companion?" the man before me prompted.

Nicky's hand pressed the small of my back, sending a little jolt of happiness through me. "Trish Muffet, this is Ulrich Rumpelstiltskin and his partner, Truman. They're friends of mine."

"It's nice to meet you, Mr. Rumpelstiltskin," I said, extending my hand.

"Just call me Rick," he gushed, shaking my hand in both of his. "And I should've known who you were by the ringlets. I've heard all about you, sweetie!"

"Well, *I* haven't," Truman grumped, coming out from behind the counter to shake my hand as well. He tottered a little in his neon pink platform sandals—or it might've been the skin-tight hot pants. Tough call. "Nobody ever tells me anything. And by *nobody,* I mean *Ulrich.* He's such a power-tripping bitch kitty."

"I know one queen who needs to hold the drama," Rick drawled, rolling his eyes. "Don't mind Truman, Trish. He's getting his period. Now, what brings you by?" Rick gave Nicky a sly look. "Are we *ring* shopping?"

Nicky's cheeks went a little red, and he sent a quick glance my way. "No, no. Nothing like that. I, uh, I need a favor."

Rick's blue eyes widened with interest. "Oh, I like the sound of this already." He grabbed my hands in his and said in a stage whisper, "Did you know I've been waiting to do Nicky a favor since he helped clear me of the kidnapping charge?"

"Kidnapping charge?" I echoed.

"Yes! Can you believe it? You try to take *one* baby in Make Believe and suddenly you're the FMA's prime suspect every time a kid goes missing. Puh-lease! As if I would've taken that Lindbergh baby!"

"The Lindbergh baby?" I gaped. "*You* were a suspect in the Lindbergh baby case?"

"Only for a few days," Rick assured me. "I mean, seriously? He was an Ordinary! What would I have done with an *Ordinary* child? Such a sad affair, too. Just heartbreaking. Luckily, Nicky knew it wasn't me and pulled a few strings to get everything cleared up."

"So, what happened in Make Believe?" I asked, familiar with Rumpel—*Rick's* story but knowing, like so many other Tales, stories had a way of being only partially true.

Truman made a whimpering noise and made his way back behind the jewelry counter where Rick joined him, draping his arm around Truman's shoulders and giving him a comforting squeeze. "Just because Truman and I can't have a baby of our own doesn't mean we don't want to be fathers," Rick explained. "So, I made a deal with that stupid girl that I'd make her a queen, but you can see what a little jackass her son turned out to be!"

"She never even paid attention to little James," Truman sighed, shaking his head.

"James?" I said, frowning. "James *Charming*?"

Rick sighed. "One and the same."

"He would've been a hell of a lot better off with us," Truman assured me, patting Rick's hand.

"And he *definitely* would've had better taste in fashion," Rick added, appalled.

"Oh, you know that's right," Truman said, snapping his fingers with a flourish.

"Did you *see* what he was wearing during his trial for fraud?" Rick asked me, clearly horrified. "Oh, honey, it was a pale blue catastrophe. Whoever let him dress himself should be convicted of being an accessory to a *crime.*"

I giggled, and now it was my turn to lean in, anxious to share more gossip with the two imps. "You think that was bad," I whispered, "you should've seen him the night Lavender Seelie accidentally burned down the Charmings' mansion last fall." When they huddled up with me, I broke the news. "Gold lamé bikini briefs with a smoking jacket."

Truman gasped. "Oh, girl, he did *not!*"

I nodded. "And that's not all—"

Nicky cut me off by taking my hand and pulling me to him. "I'll let you gossip all you want later," he said with an amused grin, "but right now I need to chat with Rick about that favor I mentioned."

Rick gave me a wink. "Back to business, I guess," he said, grimacing comically. "Come on up to the office, you two. Truman, mind the store."

"Oh, I mind, trust me," Truman called as we followed Rick to a set of stairs.

"Don't be a bitch, honey," Rick called over his shoulder. "It gives you frown lines."

The second-floor was more an upscale loft apartment than an office and boasted a modern art collection that I guessed was worth millions of dollars. "The jewelry business must be treating you well," Nicky said, his thoughts apparently in synch with my own.

Rick waved his words away. "*Puh-lease!* The jewelry business is a hobby. Who needs money when I can spin straw into gold? Do you have any idea what gold's going for per ounce these days?"

"So that part of your story is true?" I asked. "You can really spin straw into gold?"

Rick shrugged as he eased down onto a plush white sofa. "Straw, leaves, grass . . . take your pick, sweetie." To demonstrate, he picked up a flower in the vase on the glass table beside him and popped off the bud, then ran his fingertips down the stem, creating a delicate white gold chain.

"That's gorgeous!" I told him.

Nicky shook his head in dismay. "Haven't lost your touch, Rick."

"Oh, I'm not finished yet," Rick told him. He then picked up the flower and removed each of the petals, which he twisted and bent, fusing them together in an intricate design. Finally, he created a little loop and slid the pendant down the chain. When he finished, he held it aloft before my eyes. "What do you think?"

To my astonishment, it was an exact replica of Nicky's spider tattoo. My eyes went wide. "How did you . . . ?" My words trailed off. His talent was beyond anything I'd ever seen.

Rick grinned. "A gift for you, sweetie." But instead of giving it to me, he handed it to Nicky. "Care to do the honors?"

Nicky turned to me and fastened the necklace around my throat, his fingers tracing the delicate chain down its path to where the pendant rested at the V of my sweater just above my cleavage. "Beautiful," he murmured, a hungry look coming into his eyes. He took my face in his hands and brushed a tender kiss to my mouth. Then he pressed his forehead to mine, closing his eyes for a moment.

When a polite cough reminded us that we weren't alone, Nicky chuckled. "Sorry," he said, putting his arm around my shoulders and drawing me against him. "I sometimes forget that there's anyone else in the world but this gal right here."

Rick gave us an understanding smile. "Well, I can certainly see that."

Nicky and I sat down on a love seat across from the sofa, our knees touching. His hand rested lightly on my thigh, his thumb smoothing over the denim of my jeans, but even as he did that, he went into business mode.

"I need to know where the Agency is holing up at the moment," he announced, getting right down to it.

Rick scoffed. "Why the hell would you want to find those assholes?"

"You sound like you know the Agency pretty well," I observed.

Rick made a sour face. "Let's just say that peasant girls aspiring to be queens aren't the only ones who find my talents valuable. Whenever the Agency needs a little gold for their coffers, who do you think they call on? And they don't like to take no for an answer."

"Does Al know about this?" I asked, finding it hard to believe the Director of the FMA would allow one of us Tales to be pressed into service that way, forced to use his talent to line the Agency's pocket.

Rick shrugged. "Maybe. Maybe not. I've filed complaints with the FMA over the years, but they never seem to get anywhere. I doubt they've ever crossed Al Addin's desk. I mean, who am I? Just an imp accused of stealing children once upon a time. Who's going to give a shit about me?"

"I do," I told him. "You'd better believe I'm going to make sure Al knows about what's going on."

"So how does it work?" Nicky asked. "When the Agency comes to make you spin gold for them."

"Oh, they take me to wherever they happen to have set up shop here in Chicago, honey," Rick explained. "Of course, I'm blind-folded—or drugged. I told them I prefer the blindfold. Otherwise I wake up with one *hell* of a headache and the gold looks like shit."

Nicky sighed, his disappointment evident. "So there's no way for you to tell us where their office is."

Rick offered us a saucy smile. "Well, I didn't say *that*. Of course, I can find it! I'm an *imp*, honey. I've been pranking them as payback for ages! They've replaced their sprinkler system three times in the last six months because it just *keeps* malfunctioning." He batted his lashes innocently, then sent a conspiratorial wink my way. "But you can't just waltz in the front door looking all hot and alpha male, Nicky. They actually have pretty good security for Ordinaries."

"Just tell me where it is," Nicky told him. "And let *me* worry about how to get in."

Chapter Twenty-Four

As we made our way home along the wooded, winding road that led to Nicky's, my fingers rested lightly on the pendant against my chest as I studied his profile. My heart swelled with such love at that moment, I wasn't even sure I could put it into words. *I love you* felt woefully inadequate. It didn't even come close. His lips curved a little as he drove and he sent a sidelong glance my way.

"What's doin', doll?" he asked. "You've been lookin' at me that way for a while now."

"I can't believe I'm sitting here with you," I confessed. "I can't believe what we've shared over the last few days. I never dared to hope. . . ." I flushed and turned my face toward my window, staring out at the dark woods that lined the streets leading to his house. "I don't want you to go, Nicky."

I heard him heave a sharp sigh. "I can't stay here, Trish," he told me after a moment. "You know that. I need to get outta here, start over somewhere else."

"And nothing could make you stay?" I asked, my voice catching as I turned to face him again. "Nothing at all?"

Not even me?

He shifted a little in his seat. "What if you came with me?"

I frowned. "What, like on vacation?"

He chuckled. "No, not on vacation." He shifted again, clearly uncomfortable. "Like, you know, for good."

My breath caught in my chest and for a moment I could only stare at him, wondering if I could've possibly heard him right. "Are you asking me . . ." I let my words trail off. I swallowed hard and tried again. "What exactly *are* you asking me?"

His grin widened and he turned his attention from the road to peg me with a look so full of love, my heart leaped with joy. Then the headlights behind him framed his head, creating a halo of light that seemed to grow in slow motion. I must've realized in a split second what was happening, but when I screamed Nicky's name, the word took too long to come out, and I saw him whip his head around just as the car rammed into his door.

My stomach lurched as the Range Rover pitched over, slamming into the ground, the impact shattering my window, the shards of glass cutting my arms as I instinctively tried to shield my face. Pain tore through my shoulder as the joint came apart. I screamed, curling into myself as we rolled over again, the SUV careening toward the trees. On the second roll, we slammed into a massive tree trunk, sending a fresh wave of pain crashing over me.

For a moment, I just lay there, shuddering and gasping for breath. I blinked rapidly to clear my vision, only to realize there was blood dripping into my eyes. I managed to lift one of my hands to wipe it away and only then discovered we were lying on our side. I carefully turned my head, hoping to God my neck wasn't broken, and saw Nicky hanging from his seat, the seat belt keeping him from dropping down on top of me. There was a massive gash on his forehead and it was then I realized it wasn't my blood but his that had been dripping into my eyes.

"Nicky?" I called urgently. "Nicky, honey—can you hear me?"

When he didn't respond, I used my good arm to unbuckle my seat belt, but when I tried to push up to get to him, pain in my hip jolted another scream from me, and I collapsed as my vision dimmed and my stomach lurched with nausea.

"Oh, God," I moaned, tears choking my voice. I had to get it together, had to figure some way to get help. My eyes darted around, trying to see anything in the darkness. I could hear men talking, their voices barely above a whisper but still carrying to me on the breeze.

Fear clutched my heart, making my thoughts foggy and frantic. I couldn't think; I couldn't move. My skin began to crawl; the phantoms of spiders that had invaded my nightmares for so many years were suddenly there—thousands of them—crawling all over me, slipping under the edges of my sleeves, creeping into my cleavage, invading my ears, my nose, trying to pry open my lips, waiting for me to scream so they could choke me.

I flailed my good arm, tried to shake one leg, but more spiders came, breeding by the hundreds as I looked on in terror. I pressed my lips together against the scream building in my chest. I felt every single little arachnid leg as it brushed my skin, my scalp. And my brain began to tingle. An itch I couldn't scratch built, sending me careening toward that dark place I'd sworn I'd never go again.

Insanity. Lunacy.

That's what the doctors in Make Believe had called it. I closed my eyes, forcing myself to take several deep breaths and get my shit together. I wasn't going there. I was never going there again. The fear had controlled me once, had pushed me into what Dracula had accurately called a dark prison. And I'd be damned if I was ever going back. Not now. Not when Nicky needed me.

Control the fear, Beatrice. . . .

The words were the same as those my father had uttered when pleading with me to come back to them, but the voice was not his.

I can keep the spiders away. . . . We are one. . . .

My eyes snapped open on a gasp. The spiders had gone. Vanished. Pushed away with strength of will—and something else. Something *more.*

I tried to wet my lips, but my tongue was dry. My throat burned. And a heat began to build within me, starting at the place in my neck where Dracula's fangs had sunk into my flesh in my dream, and fanning out over every inch of me. And suddenly I felt renewed, revitalized.

As the voices came closer, I could hear footsteps crushing the underbrush as the men slowly advanced on the overturned SUV. I could *smell* the pungent odor of their fear. And my vision grew sharper, hyper–focused, as if I was staring into the night with infrared goggles. These weren't *my* enhanced abilities, I realized. It felt different—external. As if something else was working through me.

Time to go.

I shifted, the pain in my hip now just a dull throb, and managed to get to my feet enough to support Nicky. My dislocated shoulder protested, but I could already feel it healing and so ignored the searing pain when I undid Nicky's seat belt and accepted his full weight as he dropped against me.

I glanced around, trying to figure out how the hell to drag both of us out of the SUV. There was no way Nicky's door was going to open. That left the back door or maybe the hatch. My knees shook beneath me as I dragged Nicky into the backseat and tried to open the back door. To my amazement, when I shoved, the door flew open so hard the hinges bent backward, keeping the door from slamming shut on us.

I stuck my head up out of the opening just enough to peer into the darkness. I could see the shadowy figures moving toward us, creeping closer, guns drawn. When I caught the gaze of one of them—Freddy the Ferret, that backstabbing, double-crossing little shit—he stumbled back a couple of feet.

"What the fuck?" he gasped.

I stood now, using the seat back to climb out of the opening and dragging Nicky with me. I had no idea where the unbelievable strength came from, didn't even want to think about it at the moment. I just wanted to get us the hell out of there. Later I could mull over the implications of what was happening to me.

Nicky groaned, his eyes fluttering open as I hefted him up to lean out of the open door and over the side of the car. "You okay, doll?" he mumbled, his words slurred.

I glared out at the slowly advancing agents, a savage protectiveness coming over me. And a hunger like nothing I'd ever known. I licked my lips, anticipating the coppery taste of their blood on my tongue. "Never better."

At that moment, the agents came to an abrupt halt, every single one of them looking at me with shocked, wide eyes. Except Ian Spalding. He was grinning.

"Well, well, well," Ian drawled, strolling forward nonchalantly in spite of the semiautomatic pistol he had trained on my forehead. "That bastard did it."

"What the hell are you talking about?" I demanded, cradling Nicky in my arms as he slipped into unconsciousness again.

"I'll explain it all later," Ian smirked. "But, first, why don't we get you out of here and see what we can do to help your boyfriend?"

As a handful of agents surged forward, I clutched Nicky tighter. "Don't touch him!" I growled. Literally. *Whoa.* "Stay away! You're the ones who *did* this to him, you sons of bitches!"

Ian edged forward, a little less confident now. "Let us help him, Trish," he said, holstering his gun and raising his hands. "Come on— I know you Tales aren't immortal. And he's not looking good. Let us help."

I glanced around, wondering what my chances were of getting through the agents to the road—a road that was rarely traveled. Nate Grimm hadn't showed up, so Nicky wasn't in any imminent danger, but Ian was right—Nicky was advancing swiftly toward Death's door. "Fine," I snapped. "But I swear to God, Ian, you do anything to him, I'll rip your throat out. And I think you know I'm not bullshitting."

Ian inclined his head. "Agreed." He then motioned to his agents. A few of them came forward warily, holstering their weapons before carefully extricating Nicky from my protective grasp. As the men carried Nicky up the hill to their waiting vehicle, Ian came to me and held out his hand.

I glared at him, ignoring his offer of help. Unfortunately, whatever it was that had been sustaining me began to wane. I ground my teeth against the resurgence of pain, not about to let Ian see that I couldn't make good on my threats.

"Stubborn as ever," he drawled as my right leg gave out under me and I stumbled to my knees. I groaned as pain exploded in my hip. Ian grabbed my elbow to help me up, but I jerked away, somehow managing to push up to my feet on my own. Walking, however, was a totally different story. Each step brought a fresh onslaught of agony. Tears streamed down my cheeks, but I didn't bother wiping them away. And when the ground sloped upward toward the road and I couldn't walk any farther, I got down on my hands and knees and dragged myself through the mud and snow until I reached the road.

I have no idea how long it took me to finally hit pavement, but by the time I collapsed beside the road, all the cars—and Nicky—were gone. Only Ian's vehicle and the totaled SUV that had rammed us remained. My stomach plummeted when I realized I was utterly and completely alone.

Shit.

"Where did they take Nicky?" I demanded, panting from the energy spent to get to the road.

"He's safe," Ian said with a shrug, shoving his hands into his pockets. He gave me a smug grin. "For now."

Anger gave me a surge of adrenaline I desperately needed. And I lunged at him, my fingers curled into claws, ready to rip his still beating heart from his chest. But Ian's kick to my ribs landed soundly before I could reach him and knocked me flat on my back.

As I lay there in the snow, gasping, Ian squatted down next to me, his grin having changed from smug to triumphant. "As long as you cooperate, your lover will be safe. But you fuck around with me, and I'll have one of my agents put a bullet in Nicky's brain." He made a gun with his hand and put the tip of his index finger in the center of my forehead. "Right there. A single shot." He put his finger to my temple. "Or maybe there." His grin faded as he jabbed his finger against the center of my chest. "Or maybe one through the heart. That would be rather poetic, don't you think?"

I merely glared at him, waiting to see what happened next.

"What? Nothing to say?" he taunted. When I remained silent, he grabbed my hair in his fist and jerked me into a sitting position. "Well, you'll be talking enough soon. Trust me."

Ian hauled me to my feet, ignoring my cries of protest and pain and doing little more than grunting when each of my punches with my good arm landed. Still grasping my hair, he opened the back door to his car and threw me into the backseat. I instantly flipped over and kicked, my boot nailing him squarely in the chest, but before I could scramble out the other side of the car, he was on top of me, pinning me down on my stomach. One of his hands pressed down on the back of my head, pushing my face into the leather seat. In the next instant I felt a sharp sting in the back of my neck.

Almost instantly my limbs went limp, and no matter how I struggled, my body wouldn't respond. Ian was saying something—gloating triumphantly, no doubt—but the sound echoed strangely and the world began to spin, sending me spiraling into a black abyss.

Chapter Twenty-Five

I was cold. So cold. My fingertips stung with the beginnings of frostbite. I blinked, clearing away the blurry haze from whatever drug Ian had given me to knock me out, and after a moment, the room came into focus. I was lying on the concrete floor of some kind of interrogation room. Chains hung from the ceiling and there was a drain in the center of the room where the floor sloped. I shivered, but I wasn't sure if it was because of the cold or from imagining what horrific acts might necessitate a drain in the floor.

I pushed up to my hands and knees and shook my head with a groan. My hip and shoulder had been popped back into joint, but they still ached from the trauma. I obviously hadn't been there very long.

"Rise and shine, Sleeping Beauty."

I lifted my gaze to where Ian sat in a chair a few feet away, bundled in his coat and gloves, his legs crossed. "Wrong fairytale, you idiot."

His lips twitched with mild amusement. "Sorry about that. You all pretty much look the same to me."

"Where's Nicky?" I demanded. "What the hell have you done to him?"

Ian lifted a shoulder and let it drop. "Nothing. Yet. He's alive."

I narrowed my eyes at him, my hatred and fury bringing much needed warmth to my extremities. "Prove it. I want to see him."

"Of course," Ian said, getting to his feet. "But first, you and I need to have a little chat." He motioned to the chair he'd just vacated. "Would you care to have a seat?"

I shook my head, not trusting his sudden politeness and definitely not wanting to put my back to the two-way mirror hanging on the wall behind the chair or to the heavy steel door. I preferred to have as much as possible in my line of sight.

"No?" He shrugged and resumed his seat, crossing his legs again and clasping his hands in his lap. "So, how did we get to this point, Trish?"

"You're a dick?" I suggested.

He inclined his head, letting the insult roll off. "I must offer you my apologies again. I should've handled things differently. Forgive my . . . enthusiasm."

"Enthusiasm?" I repeated. "You can shove your *enthusiasm* up your ass."

He *tsked* disapprovingly. "Now, now. Let's not get belligerent. I merely want to have a friendly chat."

"Bite me."

"Oh, but someone else already has," Ian drawled. At this he leaned forward, his forearms resting on his knees, his eyes widening with eagerness. "How'd he do it?"

I frowned at him. "How did *who* do *what*?"

"Dracula," he said, his eyes sparkling with excitement.

My stomach dropped at warp speed. "What are you talking about?"

Ian chuckled, shaking his head. "You always were a bad liar, Trish, so don't even try to deny Dracula has been stalking you. We've been aware of it for a while."

No, shit, I thought, remembering the asshole who'd taken photographs of Nicky and me outside Happy Endings.

"So, what if he has?" I replied. "What's it to you?"

"I've got to know how he managed it." A disturbing light came into his eyes, an eagerness that made me seriously uneasy. "How did he bite you?"

My frown deepened. "Uh . . . fangs?" Ian was a dickhead, but he wasn't stupid. What the hell was he getting at?

"Obviously," Ian conceded. "But *how*? How did he *get* to you?"

"I don't know. The same way he gets to everyone." I shook my head, confused. "Why are you asking this? I'm guessing you know as much as I do about Dracula—probably more, knowing you and those other Agency assholes. So, why don't we cut the bullshit, Ian, and get to what you're really after?"

If he had been a Tale, such an opening would've resulted in Ian spilling his guts in a grand soliloquy. Tale villains really just can't help themselves. It's a compulsion. They have to gloat about their plans, hold it over the heroine's head, thereby providing valuable time to come up with a way for said heroine to take them down in an exciting climax. I guess it's true what they say: You can take the Tale out of Make Believe, but you can't take Make Believe out of the Tale. I just hoped Ian was arrogant enough to fall into the same trap.

Ian's lips curved into a grin. "You're right," he said, nodding. "Why screw around? We've known all along that Dracula was attempting to contact Tess Little—"

They did?

"—but it was a bit of a surprise when he switched things up and started contacting you."

"Yeah, it was to me, too," I admitted, not seeing any point in denying what Ian already knew. "How'd you find out?"

Ian's smile grew, reminding me of the grin Nicky often wore when conducting business. But Ian's wasn't nearly so charming—and was twice as deadly. Nicky's smile had a conscience. Ian's . . . well, he'd proven over and over that he had no inner Jiminy Cricket. "It seems starving a vampire has some unintended consequences. Makes them bat-shit crazy, as it turns out." He chuckled at his pun. "We were hoping only to control him, keep him weak enough not to try to escape again. We never expected him to spill his guts in those rants of his."

I stared at Ian, my mind racing. They actually *had* Dracula in custody? All this time we'd been operating under the assumption that Dracula was roaming free, that the vampires Nicky had taken down were somehow his creations meant to exact revenge against the FMA and create the army of undead he needed to claim the power he so desperately sought. God—how wrong we'd been. I swallowed hard, trying to figure out how to play the situation with Ian without letting on that he'd just totally blindsided me. Luckily, for an Ordinary, he was surprisingly forthcoming with the info. *Sweet.*

"So, how long has Dracula been here?" I asked, keeping my voice even to appear unimpressed with his revelations.

Ian shrugged. "Two years? It was right after the thing with Sebille Fenwick. Happened to catch him off-guard when he was feeding on some whore in an alley. Total fluke. Right place, right time, and all that. Lost two agents trying to take him down, but it was worth it."

So, they finally had captured themselves a Tale. . . . And not just any Tale—an extremely powerful Tale with the kinds of abilities they'd been dying to carve up and study for decades. I hated to think what they might've discovered about our kind in the last couple of years. "When did you realize he was trying to contact someone on the outside?"

"Soon after he turned the first person," Ian admitted. "It only took a few weeks to starve him into submission. Unfortunately, he was so ravenous when we finally fed him that he drained dry the first woman we gave him, so we sent in another one. He didn't kill her, but drained her enough that she was near death. And then he gave her his blood before we could stop him."

Holy shit. So he had *been behind the vamps. . . .*

"What happened to her?"

"She was useful. For a while, anyway. But being a one-off, she wasn't as easy to control. We had . . . *issues.* And that bastard the Spider ended up taking her out before we could bring her back in. Did us a favor, really. But the rest of the ones he killed? Well, we didn't appreciate that so much."

"A one-off?" I repeated. "What do you mean by that?"

"They were human—well, Ordinaries, to you," Ian explained, brushing the leg of his trousers as if he was bored out of his mind. "Our attempts to make Dracula turn a Tale were . . . unsuccessful."

I blinked at him in dismay. "How many?" I demanded, my throat tight. "How many Tales have you killed in this twisted little experiment of yours?"

Ian tilted his eyes up to the ceiling, mulling over my question. "Oh, perhaps a dozen? Maybe more." He chuckled. "I really can't say. We had to dump the bodies quickly before Nate Grimm showed up to collect them. But don't worry—for the most part, the Tales we chose were nobodies, nameless characters from literature, generalizations and archetypes from mythology. I doubt their deaths even made the Tale newspaper."

"They were still people, you son of a bitch!" I hurled at him, advancing a few angry steps, my fists balled up at my sides to keep from beating the arrogant indifference off his face.

But if Ian was intimidated, he didn't let on. "We're supposed to be having a civilized conversation, remember?" he smirked. "Don't make me resort to more aggressive methods." When I frowned at him, not understanding, he motioned to the sprinkler system. "Holy water. We've found it works quite well when our vamps get out of hand. I'd hate to have to give you a little demonstration."

I almost laughed at the absurdity of his threat, but then I realized he wasn't joking. He actually thought that *I* was a vampire. That must've been why he was so wary at the crash site and why he kept his distance now. I certainly couldn't explain what had happened after the accident, how I'd been briefly endowed with superhuman strength, but I sure as hell wasn't a vampire. But, hey, if the rep gave me an edge, I'd roll with it.

I glanced at the ceiling, trying to appear worried. "I don't think that will be necessary."

"You always were a bright girl," Ian drawled. "I almost regret the way things turned out between us, Trish."

"Yeah, well," I drawled, "guess you'll just have to live with the disappointment."

"Not for much longer," he assured me. At this he rose from his chair and strolled toward me. "I'm tired of dicking around, Trish," he snapped, walking a slow circle around me, his leisurely pace a direct contradiction to his dangerous tone. "So, let's try this again. How the hell did Dracula turn you from here in his cell? And when? Ordinaries turn within minutes—is it different with the Tales? Your abilities don't seem to be fully functional yet."

"A few days ago," I told him, thinking of the night Amanda had attacked me and of my dream of the attack from Dracula that had left me with actual puncture wounds in my neck. I'd chalked it up to psychosomatic symptoms from the very vivid dream, but as I sat there staring at Ian's eager face, I began to wonder if perhaps there wasn't something to his theory.

Did Dracula have to be present to infect another Tale? Hell, we hadn't thought he could turn anyone at all, but he'd obviously created a shitload of Ordinary vamps for the Agency to play with, so was it really out of the realm of possibility that he'd be able to send out a piece of himself—his soul? his psyche?—to attack me that night? As Lavender had once told me, *"We're fairytales who were magically transported to the mortal world. Call me crazy, but I'm pretty sure anything's possible at this point."*

"Extraordinary," Ian mused, shaking his head as he came to a halt directly in front of me. "Why you? Why did it finally work on *you*? Was it because he did it remotely? Is that the secret?"

It was at that moment a blur of motion behind Ian caught my eye. I glanced toward it, and had to cover a gasp with a cough when I caught sight of the phantom in the mirror.

Amanda.

"Lucky girl, I guess," I muttered, trying to watch her movements without Ian noticing.

She gave me a wicked grin as she strolled the length of the mirror, her fingertips passing along the back of Ian's shoulders. He shuddered a little, feeling her touch as only a shiver down his spine.

With a wink, she transformed herself into a cloud of mist and when it solidified again, where she had been Dracula now stood. I started to cry out, but he held a finger to his lips with a silent giggle as if we were sharing a hilarious joke. And when I blinked, Dracula was gone and Amanda was in his place.

Holy shit!

Suddenly everything began to fall into place. It had never actually been Dracula stalking me, attacking me. It had always been his phantom lover, masquerading as the notorious vampire, drawing me closer, forcing me to track down the man being held captive in the Agency's dungeons. *Christ.* It all made sense now. I forced my eyes back to Ian, trying to focus on what he was saying.

"—under observation for the next few days and see what happens."

"Sorry—what?" I gave myself a mental shake. "Put *who* under observation?"

"You and Dracula," Ian said on a huff as if repeating himself was beyond tedious. "I'd like to see how he reacts to having his favorite plaything right here with him."

My legs finally felt steady enough to push to my feet. "Didn't you just tell me that he'd killed his other 'playthings'?" I asked, giving him the finger quote treatment.

Ian laughed, looking at me like I was a first-class idiot. "Trish, the purpose of my job is to observe and understand supernatural beings in our world so that we can keep them under control—and, more importantly, use their abilities to protect the good citizens of our fine nation. Do you *really* think I give a shit if you live or die if it means figuring out how to safely create our own vampire army? Can you imagine the possibilities?"

I gaped at him in disbelief. Hell, yeah, I could imagine the possibilities. And now their fairy dust thefts made sense, too. They weren't just experimenting on humans to determine the drug's effects; they needed the fairy dust to control the volatile, bloodthirsty creatures they were creating.

"You have no idea what you're screwing with, Ian," I told him. "We spend years rehabilitating our vamps to keep them from losing control. Ours aren't like the ones you've dealt with in the Here and Now."

Ian's omnipresent smirk grew. "Well, we'll soon find out just how different they are, won't we?"

I felt Amanda suddenly appear at my side. "You must get to Vlad," she whispered, her icy breath crystalizing on the edges of my ear. "You are the only one who can help him."

My mind was pinging around like a pinball, rapidly going over my options, trying to figure out just how in the hell I was supposed to help a feral vampire being held captive in a government installation, rescue my lover who was God knew where, and—oh, yeah—somehow manage to avoid getting myself killed in the process.

"I want to see Nicky," I barked at Ian, going with the most important one first. When he looked like he might protest, I growled, "*Right. Fucking. Now.* Or this conversation is over, Ian—holy water sprinklers or not."

With an irritated sigh, Ian motioned toward the two-way mirror behind him. A moment later, the heavy steel door creaked open and Freddy the Ferret appeared in the doorway, his rat face twisted into a grotesque smirk. Then he stepped aside and another familiar face appeared, making my stomach drop so suddenly, I thought I was going to yack right there on the concrete floor. Alex McCain dragged Nicky into the room.

Nicky's hair was matted with blood, but thankfully his head wound had healed. His wrists were bound behind his back with heavy shackles, so he must've recovered enough of his strength to give them a hard time. But he still looked like shit. And based on the smug expression on McCain's face, I had a feeling the Enforcer had played a hand in keeping him that way.

"You fucking prick," I ground out. "You lying, *traitorous* bastard!"

Alex met my gaze briefly, then gave Nicky a hard shove, sending him sprawling onto the concrete.

With a strangled cry, I scrambled over to Nicky on my hands and knees, helping him to his knees and wrapping my arms around his neck, squeezing him tightly.

"It's all right, doll," he murmured into the curve of my neck. "I've got you."

I chuckled in spite of the tears pricking at my eyes. Leave it to Nicky to kneel there, bloody and bruised, shackled so he couldn't fight back, and assure *me* that everything was going to be okay. I took his face in my hands and kissed him hard—twice—before two of Ian's goons grabbed Nicky's arms and jerked him to his feet.

"What the hell are you doing?" I cried. Without thinking, I rushed the first guy and tackled him to the ground so hard, Nicky and the other agent nearly pulled a Jack-and-Jill and came tumbling after.

The next thing I knew, I had three agents trying to pin me down, but there was no way in hell I was going to let them drug me up again. I kicked and swung savagely, my blows landing solidly if the sounds of their juicy curses and groans of pain were any indication.

"Trish!" Nicky's voice cut around my stream of profanity.

My head came up just in time to see Freddy the Ferret swinging a nightstick down toward my head. I brought up my left forearm, blocking his arm, then drove my fist into his solar plexus. As the air shot out of his lungs he gasped and stumbled backward, grasping at his chest.

"Enough!" Ian roared. McCain started for me, but Nicky bum-rushed him, knocking him on his ass. "I said *enough*, goddamn it!"

Ian shook his head in disgust. "My apologies, Trish," he said with a politeness I saw through in a fairytale minute. "My men seem to have experienced a troubling lapse in manners. You're our guest here, after all. Isn't that right, Freddy?"

Freddy just glared at me with murder in his eyes. Yeah, well, I had news for the little bastard—two could play that game. And the look I sent back made it clear he'd better hope no one left him in a room with me or the shit was gonna get *real*. I glanced to where McCain was picking himself up off the ground. And that asshole was next.

"As you see, I've not harmed your lover," Ian said, clasping his hands behind his back. "However, I'm afraid that thanks to this little altercation there might be some hard feelings that could impede our discussions. How regrettable." He sighed theatrically and motioned to his men. "Please escort Mr. Blue out so that Trish and I may continue our conversation."

"No!" I rushed to Nicky, reaching him before any of the agents worked up the courage to get in my way. I grabbed the lapels of Nicky's jacket and ground out through clenched teeth, "I'm not letting them take you away from here."

Nicky shrugged and forced a grin. "Forget about it. I'm sure it's nothin'." He turned his gaze on Ian. "I'll just go hang out in the other room. Right?"

"Of course," Ian said too quickly.

Nicky winked at me. "See? It's all good."

I knew it was bullshit. And Nicky knew it, too. They'd let him live to prove Ian had kept his word. And they'd keep him alive for probably a little while longer, just in case they needed to use him against me. But then all bets were off. We were both living on borrowed time and we knew it.

"I love you, doll," Nicky assured me as McCain and Freddy dragged him toward the door. "Always have. Always will."

My fear choked me, making it impossible to respond. And the ominous thud of the steel door slamming felt like someone had just closed my coffin lid. I needed help if any of us had a chance of getting out of there. And at the moment, the only person I had on my side was the ghost of a dead Ordinary.

I was so screwed. Unless—

"Now, where were we?" Ian asked, assuming that infuriatingly smug nonchalance.

"You were about to take me to Dracula," I reminded him, a plan—albeit a seriously fucked-up plan—beginning to form. "Might as well get on with it."

Amanda's spirit sent me a look of such gratitude and relief, it was a little heartbreaking. Even in the afterlife she still had it bad for the vampire who'd ended her life. Talk about a dysfunctional relationship. . . .

The two agents who had remained in the room—the better to glare daggers at me, from the looks of things—came forward with a pair of wicked-looking iron shackles in hand.

"I'm not going anywhere," I snapped, pulling my hands back before they could slap them on. "Not without Nicky. You don't have to shackle me." When Ian's eyes narrowed at me, I added, "Besides, I need to use the restroom."

The men frowned with such identical scowls it would've been comical had it been in a different context. "Pardon?" Ian asked. "Now?"

"When you gotta go, you gotta go," I insisted.

He sighed and mumbled something indecipherable about women under his breath but gave one of the agents a nod. All three of them escorted me from the room to a door down the hall. The biggest one, whose nose was still bleeding from the earlier smack-down I'd doled out, opened the door and took a quick look inside. I don't know what he expected to find. It's not like I was planning to come out swinging with the plunger. And no matter what the martial arts films would have you believe, I had serious doubts that I could lob the Glade Plug In effectively enough to knock out all three of them. Although they might smell nicer.

"Make it quick," Ian ordered.

I was relieved to see the restroom was little more than a closet with a toilet and sink and—thank God!—a mirror.

"What are you doing?" Amanda hissed, having joined me. "You're wasting time!"

I shook my head, frowning, and held a finger to my lips. "I can't go with you guys listening!" I called out.

"Then run some water or something!" Ian snapped.

Perfect. So far, so good. . . .

I turned on the faucet and prayed the water would actually be hot. Fate was smiling down on me, apparently, as the water was generating steam in seconds. Between Amanda's spirit making the air even colder than normal and the heat of the water, the mirror began to fog up exactly as I'd hoped. I whispered the words Lavender had taught me and sent the call out to the universe, praying like hell it would be heard.

Chapter Twenty-Six

We were underground. Had to be. We'd traveled down several floors in the elevator before finally coming to a stop, and when the doors slid open, we stepped into a hallway made of thick layers of concrete; bare lightbulbs lined the ceiling in evenly spaced intervals. It looked more like a bunker than a prison.

"You've been keeping him down here the entire time?" I asked, glancing toward the doors we passed, wondering who or what was trapped behind them. Angry hisses greeted us as we walked by each of the doors, and I swore I heard dark, sinister laughter beneath the feral susurration.

"Not the entire time," Ian admitted, without volunteering any additional information.

Luckily, I had my ghostly little spy to fill me in. "They kept him in one of the cells upstairs at first," Amanda informed me. "But during one of the starvation periods, he was able to break out of the room and killed two of the agents who had beaten him every day, trying to bring him into submission. The bastards! They had it coming."

Couldn't exactly disagree with her there.

"We'd hoped to have an off-site facility up and running by now," Ian continued. "But we're having issues with our contractors. But then, I imagine you know all about that, don't you?"

"You think you had trouble with the Pigg brothers before . . ." I muttered, letting his imagination fill in the blanks.

A wretched, bloodcurdling scream suddenly split the air, making even Ian start and send a concerned glance toward one of his flunkies.

"Who else are you keeping down here?" I demanded, my skin creeping with unease as the hissing and wailing grew more insistent.

"Just a few of our other guests," Ian said with a shrug that wasn't nearly so nonchalant now.

"It's the women Vlad was forced to turn," Amanda informed me. "They keep them here until they release them 'into the wild,' as they call it. They just turn them loose and hope for the best. They don't give a shit what happens to them—or anyone else!"

Beatrice . . .

My head snapped up at the sound of Vlad's voice.

Amanda apparently heard it, too. "He feels you approaching," she murmured. "He knows you're coming."

My brows came together, and I shook my head, confused. "But I thought—"

"Sorry?" Ian interrupted. "What was that?"

I hadn't realized I'd spoken out loud. "Nothing," I said quickly. "Never mind."

"It *was* his voice you heard," Amanda assured me, apparently understanding where my thoughts were tending. "He had bonded with you through the blood of the woman you bit in the alley. You had taken in his blood, connecting you. But he couldn't really draw you to him without tasting you, so I acted as his physical surrogate."

"Beatrice. . . ." came the eerie hissing from beneath the tightly bolted doors, the many voices slithering toward me in a terrifying chorus. *"Beatrisssss. . . ."*

I shuddered. Apparently, Dracula wasn't the only one who knew I was coming. I heard Ian chuckle and sent an irritated glance his way. "Looks like you have quite the welcoming committee," he drawled, finally coming to a halt in front of one of the doors. He jerked his chin at one of his agents, who produced a pass card. He swiped it through the scanner at the side of the door, and I heard the heavy *thunk* as the bolts on the door slid away.

Ian pulled open the door with more than a little effort and swept his arm. "Shall we?"

"After you," I replied, forcing a polite smile. "Really, I insist."

He pressed his lips into an angry line, his faux cordiality vanishing instantly. Then he grabbed my forearm and shoved me into the dark room.

"Welcome, my dear," came a hoarse voice, reminding me of the sound aged, crumbling parchment made as one turned the pages. The words were followed by a labored wheeze. "I'd stand up, but . . ."

The light from the hallway filled only a small area just inside the door, not providing any illumination within the room. I squinted into the darkness, searching for Dracula, but my vision was inadequate to penetrate the blackness. I felt Ian standing close behind me, could feel his eager trembling as he waited to see what would happen now that I was so close to the infamous vampire.

"Come to me, Beatrice," Dracula rasped. "You are the one I want, the one I need. . . ."

Amanda hovered near me, her fingers an icy vise where she grabbed my arm with nervous anticipation, the chill penetrating my bones. "Oh, God," she breathed, her voice choked with sorrow. "He's even worse."

I edged closer to the voice, my heart pounding so loudly, I knew Dracula could hear it. He would feel each heartbeat like a timpani vibrating in his own blood. I knew this because I could feel the increase in his heartbeat pulsing in mine.

But as I edged closer, went deeper into the darkness, I instinctively knew that the connection we shared was a tenuous one—a phantom of the real, a shadow of what Dracula shared with his other victims, of what he'd shared with Amanda before he had murdered her in a moment of panic upon realizing he'd actually turned an Ordinary.

The image of that moment popped into my head as if I was looking into Vlad's eyes and reading his final thoughts, accepting atonement for his sins. *He was dying.* The starvation, the imprisonment, the beatings and torture had taken their toll, leaving him a desperate, pathetic shell of the man he'd once been. He was clinging to life, clinging to hope that he would be rescued—that the Agency's madness could be put to a stop. And I was the one he wanted to do it. The one he *needed* to do it.

I knew it as surely as I knew we were not alone in the darkness.

Ian sensed it at the same moment and jerked a flashlight from his pocket, flipping it on. "What the fu—"

The startled curse died on his lips as the first vampire lunged forward, her fangs dripping with saliva when she let forth a furious hiss. Ian's flashlight flew from his hand, clattering to the floor and spinning wildly, the eerie strobe effect as it spun revealing easily half a dozen vampires, crouching along the wall, their sunken eyes glowing red with each pass.

Holy shit!

Ian's terrified scream snapped me out of my stupor. I bolted toward where I'd seen Dracula, hoping like hell the vampiresses wouldn't come after me, too. I heard the hurried footsteps of the other agents rushing into the room and their startled cries when their flashlights illuminated the carnage.

I dropped to my knees in front of Dracula and took his face in my hands, turning his gaze up to mine.

"Beatrice," he breathed, attempting a smile that was pathetically weak. "You came to me."

I nodded, tugging frantically at the heavy iron chains that secured him to the wall and floor. "Yep, but your girlfriends are righteously pissed. So now would be a really good time to give me some of that vampire mojo of yours."

His eyes rolled in his head. "Amanda. . . ."

As soon as he said it, I glanced up to where the spirit was standing beside me. In a blur of movement, she rushed toward me. I felt a jolt of energy, a surge of power, as she took control of my body. Ignoring the chaos and cacophony of hissing, slurping, and screams behind me, I grabbed the chains binding Dracula and yanked, pulling first one and then another from the wall, freeing his hands.

I had just taken hold of the chain binding his ankles together when Dracula's arm went around my neck. With a growl, he jerked me off-balance and onto the cold floor. My heart jolted with panic until I saw him lash out, ripping away the throat of one of his own creations.

The vampiress fell back, grasping at her neck as blood spurted through her fingers.

As more agents rushed into the room, shouting and firing at the errant vampiresses, Dracula gathered me into his frail arms and dragged me close to his chest, snarling wildly as some of the agents edged cautiously toward us, their guns trained on us. And I wasn't entirely sure if they'd mind putting a few bullets in me if it meant weakening Dracula enough to subdue him again.

Where the hell was Gideon?

As if on cue, the fairy suddenly appeared before us, his powerful fist nailing the nearest agent with a bone-crushing blow. Then there was a rapid *pop, pop, pop* and corresponding bursts of light. My head snapped toward the sound, tears of joy and relief filling my eyes.

Nicky.

He fired off another couple of rounds, knocking back two of the vampires, then jerked a stake from his weapons belt and sent it flying. There was a loud screech as the stake hit its mark. Nicky spun around just in time to catch Freddy the Ferret taking aim at the center of my chest. Nicky didn't even hesitate. The loud report of his gun made me flinch at the same moment Freddy's head snapped back.

Nicky didn't wait to see Freddy drop before he rushed to me, snatching me from Dracula's hold and gathering me into his arms. "Let's go, doll. There's more of these crazy bitches comin'."

"Wait!" I cried as he tried to drag me toward the door through the path Gideon was plowing with his fists. When Nicky gave me a puzzled look, I hurried back to Dracula, who was far too weak to follow. The vampire's chest heaved as he struggled to breathe, his cheeks growing more sallow and sunken even as I looked at him.

"Go," he said, shaking his head. "Save yourself, Beatrice."

I shook my head. "No, I'm not leaving you here with these assholes."

He brought his hand up to cup my cheek. "Then free me from this dark prison."

I swallowed hard, surprised to find tears blurring my vision. I didn't know him—not really. And what I'd known of him was far from complimentary. But no one deserved to go through what the Agency had done to him, no one deserved to be a pawn in their sick, sadistic games.

"Trish!" Nicky barked. "Let's go!"

"Please," Dracula pleaded, his eyes boring into mine. "Free me."

I glanced over my shoulder at Nicky, who was unloading his Glock into the chest of a statuesque redhead. Gideon had armed Nicky to the teeth just like I'd instructed when I'd asked him to rescue my love and come back for me. I darted forward and snatched one of the stakes from Nicky's belt, then dropped down to my knees.

Dracula closed his eyes and nodded. I lifted the stake, then drove it down, but with a blur of motion, Dracula caught my wrist, and his eyes snapped open. "Tell Red I *am* sorry. For everything." Then his grasp shifted and he yanked my hand forward, driving the stake through the center of his chest.

He gasped as his eyes went wide. I heard Amanda's strangled cry of sorrow and an arctic blast filled the room, forming ice crystals on every surface.

Time to go.

This time when Nicky grabbed my wrist and pulled me to my feet, I limped after him, glancing around to see where the hell Gideon had disappeared to. As we made our way to the hall, a black mist suddenly appeared and took shape.

"What the hell is going on?" Nate demanded over the chorus of hissing and shouts and gunfire as the vampiresses continued to attack their Agency captors. "I got a call for at least two Tale dead—maybe more."

"I'll explain later," Nicky assured him, gripping my hand tighter in his own. "Get the souls and get the hell outta here, Nate."

Nate gave a terse nod, then was gone.

Nicky glanced up and down the hall, trying to figure out which way to go. "Shit."

"This way," I said, tugging his arm. "There's an elevator down this hallway."

My stomach dropped in horror as Nicky half dragged me down the hall and we saw all the doors open wide, the cells' inhabitants gone. Although I still had no freaking clue how the vampiresses had ended up in Dracula's cell before we'd arrived, the open doors certainly explained the number of vampires now running amuck. I hobbled along beside Nicky, my injured leg slowing me down.

We'd just reached the doors to the elevator when a searing pain tore into my shoulder, throwing me back into the wall. I heard Nicky scream my name as he caught me up and fired off a couple of rounds toward my assailant.

Startled and gasping in shock, I turned my head toward where Ian stood with his gun still raised, completely unaffected by the two bullet wounds in his chest. Ian's throat had been torn open and blood stained the entire front of the white shirt that had come untucked from his struggle with his attacker. His lips dripped with blood and his eyes were wild—and glowed red as he lowered his head a little between his shoulders and hissed.

"Fuck me," Nicky breathed. He scooped me up into his arms and rammed the elevator button with his elbow. When the doors slid open, we ducked inside and Nicky punched the button to close the doors. "Hang on, doll. Just hang on."

The doors slid closed at an agonizingly slow rate as we watched in tense silence, but before the doors could meet, Ian appeared before us, fangs bared. Nicky raised his gun and pulled the trigger, but it clicked, the magazine empty. Suddenly, Alex McCain appeared behind Ian, his arm going around the agent's neck.

"Go!" he grunted, dragging Ian from the elevator. "Get outta here!"

Nicky bolted forward and slammed his fist against the button to close the doors. And before they met, I caught a glimpse of McCain getting flung against the wall.

I sighed and let my head rest against Nicky's shoulder as my adrenaline left me. "God, I'm tired of getting shot," I murmured, knowing that unlike last time, I didn't have a vampire and his ghostly girlfriend around to heal me up ahead of schedule.

Nicky dropped back against the wall and kissed the top of my head, but he didn't say a word. He just tossed aside his gun to grab another Glock from its holster and waited. I could feel his tension in his muscles as he held me and I knew what he was thinking. This wasn't over yet. We had no idea what the hell would be waiting for us when those doors opened again.

When the elevator jolted to a halt, I said, "Give me a gun."

Nicky gave me a tight-lipped nod and handed me his Glock as the doors began to slide open. Then he set his jaw and squared his feet, ready to fight to the death if it meant getting me out of there. As if reading my thoughts, he tightened his arms around me and murmured, "At any cost."

My arm came up, aiming the Glock at the opening. At the same instant, a dozen rifles clicked as the men waiting outside chambered a round.

"Hold your fire!"

I nearly sobbed with relief at the sound of a familiar voice. "Oh, God," I moaned, my voice thick with tears. "It's Al."

"We're coming out!" Nicky yelled, carrying me out of the elevator, his steps slow and wary.

As we came out, I glanced around, surprised to see how many FMA Enforcers dressed in SWAT gear filled the hallway. And on their knees lining one wall were easily two dozen Men in Black, their hands handcuffed behind them. I guess Al had taken his stand after all. And he'd had some outside help. As I looked on, Gideon appeared with two more agents, each held in a punishing headlock in the crook of Gideon's powerful arms.

Gideon inclined his head to Nicky and me in a slight bow, then shoved the agents at the Enforcers, who quickly clasped handcuffs on them.

"I need to get her to the hospital," Nicky barked, his steps growing more rapid now that the Enforcers were sure of our identities.

"I'll drive them." I glanced toward the person who'd spoken. Alex McCain. He was bloody, and his clothes were torn, but he was some-how still alive. He jerked his chin at Nicky as he strode toward us. "Looks like you could use a doctor, too."

"No way in hell!" I yelled. "This son of a bitch is a traitor!"

Al and McCain exchanged a look. "I've been working as a double agent, Trish," McCain confessed. "Al needed some eyes and ears in-side. And he knew he could trust me."

I glanced at Al to confirm what McCain had said. "But . . ." I shook my head, growing woozy.

Nicky hefted me up and held me a little closer against him. "How about that ride now?"

But before Nicky could take a step, Gideon muscled his way to-ward us. "I got this."

He wrapped his arms around us, and the next thing I knew, my lungs were gasping for air in the Tale ER. The moment we appeared, a nurse rushed toward us, calling out orders that were just a jumble of words to me. Nicky was saying something to me, murmuring softly, lovingly, as they put me on a gurney, but the words sounded far away, distorted. And then I was drifting, weightless, and my world went dark.

Chapter Twenty-Seven

"Nicky?" I called, my mouth dry.

I felt a slender, cool hand grasp mine. "Nope, sorry, you're stuck with me."

I chuckled a little, still groggy from the fairy dust the doctor had given me, and turned my head, trying to focus on my friend's saucy smile. "Hey, Red."

"About damned time you woke up," she said through her relieved grin. "My ass is killing me from sitting in this chair."

"How long have I been out?" I asked, frowning.

"Three days," she informed me. "You'd been through a helluva lot."

Tell me about it.

"Sorry you've had to wait so long," I told her, pushing up against the pillows so I was sitting.

She shrugged. "I'm just glad it's not me for a change."

"How is everything now?" I asked, glancing toward her belly.

Her hand smoothed lovingly over her basketball-sized bump. "Max is doing great now. No problems at all."

"Max?" I said, grinning.

"Short for Maximus," she explained. "Turns out that was Nate's name . . . you know, *before*. He thought it might be better to change his name when he took on his assignment with the Tales."

"I like the name Max," I told her, nodding. "I think it'll suit your little guy. He's definitely a little warrior."

"Thanks to you," Red said. "Seriously. Thanks, Trish. For everything."

"I'm sorry about Dracula," I told her, meaning it. "If there'd been any other way . . ."

She nodded. "I know."

"He said to tell you he was sorry."

She sighed. "Nate tried to collect his soul, but it was already gone. Looks like he's a ghost now."

I laughed a little at the irony. A ghost. I had no doubt that he'd be well taken care of in the spirit world by the phantom who loved him, who had done everything in her power to rescue him from the darkness that had imprisoned him. I just hoped now that they had each other, they'd leave me the hell alone. "Good to know. And Ian?"

Red grunted. "Talk about poetic justice. That son of a bitch is safely tucked away in the Asylum undergoing rehabilitation for vampirism."

My brows shot up. "The Agency didn't want him?"

"More like he didn't want the Agency," Red explained. "We gave him the option. He thought he'd be better off throwing in his lot with us."

I thought about the experiments the Agency had conducted on Dracula and God knew who else in their quest to understand us. "Wise choice."

Red gave me a wicked grin. "Yeah, well, he might not think so after a few days with his rehabilitation counselor."

I gave her a wary look. "Yeah?"

She nodded, her blue eyes sparkling with mischief. "Gideon requested the assignment specifically. You should've seen Ian's face when Gideon walked in. You'd think someone had walked over his grave."

She probably wasn't far off. For a split second I almost felt sorry for Ian. Almost.

"So, what do you say we get you the hell out of here?" Red said, pushing to her feet and pressing the Call button for the nurse.

"Maybe I should wait for Nicky," I said, a little hesitantly. "When is he coming back?"

Red shrugged and turned away, busying herself with pulling some clothes out of my overnight bag, which someone must've picked up from Nicky's place while I was out. "He said he had some stuff to deal with."

"What kind of stuff?" I breathed, my stomach twisting into knots.

"He didn't say." Red's back was turned—she was hiding something.

I suddenly felt like I needed to hurl. Nicky couldn't possibly still be leaving town, could he? Not after everything we'd been through together. Not after admitting how much he loved me. *Right?*

"When did he leave?" I demanded, peeling the leads from my chest and setting off alarm buttons on the various monitors.

Red cast a frown over her shoulder at the sound. "What the hell are you doing?" she asked as I pulled out the IV with a wince. "Let the nurses take those out."

"No time," I insisted, throwing back the covers and rummaging through one of the supply drawers until I found a piece of gauze and some surgical tape. "I have to stop him. He told me he was leaving town for good once everything was over with Dracula."

"Trish, I—"

"I can't let him go, Red," I interrupted, my heart racing. "I love him. You have to help me find him."

A smile tugged at the corners of her mouth. "I don't need to find him. I already know where he is."

My eyes went wide. "You do?"

She gave me a wry look. "You say that as if tracking people down wasn't my thing. But in this case I don't need to track him down—he's at his house."

My heart was thudding painfully against my breast now. "He is?"

"Yep. Had to go meet with a Realtor."

My stomach plummeted at warp speed. So he *was* leaving town. If I'd needed any better proof than his putting his house up for sale, I didn't know what it would be. I swallowed, but my mouth was too dry for it to do any good. "Take me there."

I barely paused long enough to slam the car door behind me before I raced up the steps to Nicky's front door. "Nicky!" I called, throwing open the door, stumbling over Sasha, who had rushed to greet me. I quickly righted myself and ran into the kitchen, my heart pounding with increasing fear that I had already missed him. "Nicky!"

Not finding him there, I ran to his study, the sitting room, then upstairs to the bedrooms, calling out for him and getting no response. Finally convinced that he wasn't there, I slowly made my way down the stairs, not bothering to wipe away the tears on my cheeks.

Just as I made the bottom step, the front door opened, letting in a blast of cold air. My head snapped up and I gasped when I saw Nicky standing there. With a strangled little sob, I rushed to him, throwing my arms around his neck and hugging him tightly.

"Hello, doll," he murmured against my hair.

As reluctant as I was to leave his embrace, I abruptly released him and put him at arms' length. "You can't go," I told him in a rush. "You just can't. At least, not without me. Not this time."

"Trish—"

I grimaced, waving my hands to stop his words. "No, please— don't interrupt. I need to say this." I took a deep breath and let the words come tumbling out. "You asked me once to come with you and I spent over a hundred years regretting that I told you no. I'm not making that mistake again."

"Trish, just listen—"

"You were trying to tell me something in the car that night of the crash," I interrupted, clutching the lapels of his jacket, "and you didn't get the chance. But I know what you were leading up to."

His brows shot up. "You do?"

I nodded. "And the answer is *yes*. Yes, I'll go with you. I don't care where we go, just as long as we're together."

Nicky's lips curved into a grin. "Yeah?"

I nodded. "I love you, Nicky. And I want to spend the rest of my life loving you."

"Well, thank God for that!" he said, heaving a relieved sigh. "'Cause I was a little worried how you'd react when I gave you this."

He reached inside his pocket and withdrew a tiny blue box with Rumpelstiltskin's logo on the top. My eyes went wide and a thrill of timid joy shot through me. I swallowed hard, not willing to believe it was what I thought it might be and yet daring to hope *just* a little. . . .

I lifted my eyes to his. "Is that . . . ?"

His crooked grin grew as he flipped open the lid of the box to reveal a stunning emerald set in an intricately woven white gold band. "I know it's too soon," he was saying, suddenly a little shy. "And you don't have to answer me right away, but—"

I didn't even let him get out the rest of the words. I took his face in my hands and kissed him over and over until his arms came around me and there was only one kiss. And when Nicky pulled back he was grinning.

"So, even though you had the wrong question, is your answer still yes?" he asked, knowing damned well it was.

But I just laughed, so giddy I couldn't keep my joy from bubbling up, and nodded.

He cursed under his breath and ran a hand through his hair. "I'm actually nervous as hell," he admitted with a chuckle.

Confirming his words, his own fingers trembled a little as he took the ring out of the box and slid it onto my finger. It fit perfectly, as I knew it would. Nicky smoothed his thumb over my hand, then raised it to his lips, a smile tugging at the corner of his mouth. "You know, all those years ago in Make Believe when I was nothin' but a two-bit thug, scraping to get by, I never thought I'd be so lucky to find a woman liked you. And I sure as hell never dared to dream you'd love me, too."

I pulled him into my arms, closing my eyes as he buried his face in my neck, and letting the warmth of his love envelop me. "I have a feeling that from now on, neither of us will be afraid to dream."

Epilogue

I wish I could say that once things were over with Dracula, the concerns about Tale revolutionists ended. And I'd like to tell you that Al's standing up to the Agency ended their efforts to impose their will upon the Tales. But if anything, it added a whole new dimension to our struggles in the Here and Now. Turns out, the adventures for Nicky and me, for Nate and Red, for Lavender and Seth, were far from over.

And there were others—Gideon, Al Addin, Alex McCain, and Tales you've yet to meet—who would end up making all the difference in our struggles to maintain autonomy and to help our kind thrive in our adopted world. The years ahead of us were going to be tough, that was for certain, but—

Well, *that,* my friends, is a story for another day and for another Tale to tell.

But as far as this story goes . . . well, what can I say? Nicky and I stayed in Chicago after all, rebuilding Nicky's business empire to what it once was and continuing to serve our Tale brethren any way we could. And Nicky turned out to be just as loving and devoted a husband and father as I knew he would be. It's been several years now since we joined our hearts, our souls. The home we've created together is filled with love and laughter. And each day I think I couldn't possibly love him more than I do, but then the very next day I discover just how much I'd underestimated the depth of my feelings for the man at my side.

And, so, my friends, I'm happy to report that in true fairytale fashion, we lived—and loved—happily ever after.

Don't miss any of the Transplanted Tales novels.

"Unique and totally off-the-wall, fun, romantic, suspenseful, oh-my-GAWD enjoyable!"
—Kate Douglas

A TRANSPLANTED TALES NOVEL

KATE SERINE

Red

What do you get when you cross an egomaniacal fairy godmother, an arrogant genie, and a couple of wandering plagiarists whose idea of cultural preservation is stealing the stories of unsuspecting villagers and passing them off as their own?

If I were tossing back a few shots of Goose with the guys at Ever Afters, I might chuckle at such an intriguing setup for what has all the promise of a hilarious punch line—except the punch line of this little beauty isn't funny at all. 'Cause what you get, my friend, is a pissing contest of epic proportions.

Imagine two individuals with almost limitless power, one-upping each other in an effort to prove whose story is the most exciting and thereby win top billing in the aforementioned compilation of plagiarized tales. When magic starts flying, you never know how the story's going to end even on a good day, but toss in a couple of giant egos and one very bored socialite cheering them on for her own amusement, and, well, you know disaster's coming.

And, man, did it ever.

Although supporters and detractors of each side still hotly debate which party was actually responsible, the result is irrefutable: Nearly two hundred years ago, a spell gone awry cast the characters from the land of Make Believe into the world of the Here and Now, leaving us to fend for ourselves in an unfamiliar place with unfamiliar realities.

Some of us adjusted and blended in without too much trouble, living among you as perfectly assimilated and productive members of society. Others . . . well, others of us didn't make the transition so easily and still need a hand now and then. And another stubborn few didn't learn a damn thing from the moral of their own stories and have made it their personal mission to exploit and corrupt on this side.

That's where I come in.

When the Fairytale Management Authority, or FMA, has a problem, they call me. I'm an Enforcer—and a damned good one. You might know me by my fairytale moniker of Little Red Riding Hood. But make no mistake, I'm no longer a kid and I ditched the hood when I was twelve—which was long before my little encounter with the wolf, by the way.

Unfortunately, the nickname stuck and followed me into the Here and Now, giving my brethren with more imposing and creative Tale names the mistaken impression they can push me around—that is, until they pop off one too many times and end up meeting the business end of my fist. Then they know I'm not the sweet little gal with the basket of goodies they've read about.

My name is Tess Little. But everyone calls me Red.

THE *Better* TO *See You*

KATE SERINE

The Better to See You

There was no point in trying to summon my magic now—it had deserted me; that was pretty freaking clear. I just hoped like hell my death would be quick.

The creature prowled toward me, its massive bulk a mercifully indistinct silhouette, and I swear I thought I heard it chuckle, the sound sending chills down my spine. Then from behind me came the whisper-soft padding of paws on the underbrush. In the next instant, a great white wolf leaped over me and slammed into the shadow-creature. The two rolled end-over-end in a tangle of claws and teeth, coming to rest with the wolf on top, its lips peeled back in a vicious snarl.

I turned my head to get a better look just in time to see the wolf grab the creature's throat in its teeth. The beast's howl ended abruptly as the wolf gave a powerful shake of its head, tearing out a large section of demon dog's throat.

The wolf flung the chunk of flesh into the underbrush, then cautiously padded toward me, its head down between its shoulders, sizing me up. As it came closer, I realized it wasn't an ordinary timber wolf. This animal was easily twice the size of any wolf I'd ever seen and had a distinctly human intelligence shining in its eyes.

I didn't stand a chance.

It bit through the pine needle rope and shook its head, scattering the needles all over the ground. The rest of the needles instantly fell away and the trees halted their brutal assault.

I raised a bloody, trembling hand, not sure if I'd just exchanged one predator for another. "Please," I managed to gasp between the quick, shallow breaths that were all my punctured lung would now allow. "Please . . ."

In response, a soft shimmering light encased the wolf, and where the beautiful creature had stood, now crouched a man, his ice-green eyes still glowing. As he gently lifted me into his arms, I cried out, pain engulfing me.

"It's all right," he said softly, cradling me against him. "You're safe now."

I looked up into the grim face of my rescuer, now recognizing him. How could I not when I'd seen his face on Wanted posters and in the Tale news so often over the centuries?

As pain and nausea sent me careening toward a dark abyss, his name drifted to me:

Seth Wolf.

ABOUT THE AUTHOR

Kate SeRine (pronounced "serene") faithfully watched weekend monster movie marathons while growing up, each week hoping that maybe *this* time the creature du jour would get the girl. But every week she was disappointed. So when she began writing her own stories, Kate vowed that *her* characters would always have a happily ever after. And, thus, her love for paranormal romance was born.

Kate lives in a smallish, quintessentially Midwestern town with her husband and two sons, who share her love of storytelling. She never tires of creating new worlds to share and is even now working on her next project. Please visit her at www.kateserine.com.

28501077R00162

Made in the USA
San Bernardino, CA
30 December 2015